The Unknown
Epic

The Unknown Epic

Anubhuti Singh

PARTRIDGE

ISBN: Hardcover   978-1-4828-7303-0
            Softcover   978-1-4828-7302-3
            eBook   978-1-4828-7301-6

Print information available on the last page.

To order additional copies of this book, contact
Partridge India
000 800 10062 62
orders.india@partridgepublishing.com

www.partridgepublishing.com/india

Synopsis

Without much knowledge about his life, Airik thinks himself to be a normal 16-year-old boy. All he remembers accurately about his past is the memory of his parents dying right in front of his eyes.

His psychology teacher, Vikram Gandhi, knows more about his life; in fact, he played a major role in his life. He is waiting for the appropriate time to reveal to him everything necessary. Meanwhile, Airik is having weird dreams. To find answers about his parents and childhood, he decides to meet with Mr Gandhi. Before he could get all the answers out of his teacher, he gets teleported to a new dimension called Duvollin, a world of fantasy and magic. He stumbles upon an unknown epic and discovers shocking truths about himself.

Little does he know, everything about his life is a lie and already conceived. Will he accept the fate marked upon him or fall into oblivion like the rest of his sort?

Glossary

Duvollin: A different dimension with mystical living beings, customs, and traditions. The kingdoms in this dimension are as follows:

- Selemara
- Calsenai
- Neadre
- Allekior
- The Forest of Pamretol
- Phoryus
- Delevan
- Belevana

Mertis: The ancient language of Duvollin, which is now seldom used.

Elyrians: The fifteen gods and goddesses of Duvollin.

Elyria: A place created for and by the gods to live.

Belronag: The traditional cloth designed basically to fight.

Prologue
A New World

There is a huge secret kept hidden from humans for a long period of time. The secret is about a different dimension called Duvollin. Even before we came into existence, Duvollin was full of people like us. There were many kingdoms in this dimension. The most beautiful and huge kingdom of Duvollin was Selemara. People used to say that if there is any place beautiful after Elyria, it's Selemara. There were many kingdoms in Duvollin, but there was something very special about this kingdom. People lived in Selemara only because of its ruler, King Phinogar. He was very brave, skilful, good-hearted, and talented with a very striking character; besides, no one could match his endowment in sorcery. He was happily married to Rosatin, a beautiful princess of Delevan. Soon, Queen Rosatin gave birth to a very endearing baby boy. There was happiness all over Selemara; they enthusiastically celebrated the birth of Prince Synoids.

1

Everything was fine in Duvollin until King Phinogar decided to explore the forest of Pamretol. In Mertis, Pamretol means *mystery*. Many people had earlier tried to range over the forest of Pamretol, but none of them ever came back. People believed that the forest had powers of its own, but no one knew what sort of power the forest possessed. King Phinogar was very eager to know about the forest. He reached the forest of Pamretol. Being a sorcerer, he could feel the immense energy field of the forest. He decided to investigate further. He kept walking and walking deep inside the forest.

By dawn of the next day, he reached Selemara. Everyone in Selemara was very happy to know that their king had returned unharmed from the forest.

They were very excited to know about the forest of Pamretol. The king didn't even share a bit of his experience, but this was nothing to worry about. The main problem was that King Phinogar was changing day by day; he was misusing his powers. He acquired more power by absorbing the core life energy of humans in order to gain immortality. This caused humans from whom he had obtained supremacy to go senseless. He was turning evil and insane. Gradually, people started fleeing from Selemara. There was a rumour being spread about the king that the forest had an impact on him. Nothing was like before in Duvollin. Everything had changed since the king had returned from the forest of Pamretol.

The beautiful city of Selemara was now known as the city of dread. The goddess of sorcery, Phelonia, became very infuriated with King Phinogar for squandering the beautiful art of sorcery. She tried to kill him, take his soul away from him, and lock it in the depth of goddess of death Andria's realm. But she couldn't do so as he was too powerful with the energy of infinite humans. If she killed him, the humans from whom he gained power would also die. She was perturbed and went back to Elyria. After lots of thinking with the other fourteen Elyrians, they decided to create anegz, a very dominant pinkish stone. It consisted of some part of power of each and every Elyrian.

She hid the stone in the palace where King Phinogar and his family lived. As the palace made him emotionally unstable, he would literally hit and curse himself. Everyone believed this happened because King Phinogar tried to break free from the curse that was cast upon him.

A different palace was built for King Phinogar's family. A rule was passed that no one will ever step in the palace where King Phinogar resided. If his soul is unleashed from the stone, he will ultimately rise to power and destroy everything and everyone who comes in his way.

PRESENT DAY

'This is the end of the chapter. Any questions?' the English teacher of House of Gods Orphanage, Mrs Georgia Williams, asked us who were blankly gaping at her while I was simply doodling across the margins of my book with my pencil.

'Class! Any questions!' Mrs Williams bellowed at us. I flinched a little at her high-pitched voice. This is the reason we all nicknamed her after a Banshee.

Suddenly the bell rang, and all the students jumped with excitement. It was time for our dearest psychology class. I kept my books aside and walked towards the psychology class with my best friend and room-mate Jason with a small smirk lodged on my lips.

Old Truths

All of us loved our psychology class as well as our psychology teacher, Mr Vikram Gandhi. He was a 37-year-old Indian man with black hair and rich olive skin. He was average sized—what I mean to say is taller than I. He never taught children theoretically. He had his own way of teaching; we loved Mr Gandhi for that. He entered the class with a big smile on his face as if he had just done something extraordinary. The class went very still; they were watching him with suspicion of what was about to happen. Even I did, which was quite surprising as I normally stay with a straight face, but my eyes gave it all. The issue is, whenever he is excited, we all get bored; and I was just curious to know what he has in a brain for us.

'Good morning, class!' he greeted us enthusiastically. Few of us mumbled good mornings, but he seemed least fazed with our lethargy.

'Today, I've got something very interesting for you,' he said and rubbed his palms together. Some of us were blissed out to know this while the others were rattling in their seats with anticipation. Before any sort of disturbances could take place, Mr Gandhi started with his class.

'Students, listen to me very carefully. Today we won't play any games or perform any activity—' The students didn't allow Mr Gandhi to complete his statement because after this announcement there was a rush of oh-nos in the class. I just rolled my eyes at their juvenile attitude.

'Let me complete, dear students. Instead of any fun activity, we will have a discussion on some interesting topics. No more comparative study of animal behaviours,' he spoke with such enthusiasm that it was difficult to argue with him about it.

'What has happened to Mr Gandhi? He is quite awkward today,' the girl with pigtails said and scrunched her face simultaneously.

'Face it, when he is happy, we aren't,' someone responded. I snorted, and the others sniggered.

'Today, we will discuss about emotions,' Mr Gandhi said with a slight grin on his face. 'Now tell me any two powerful negative emotions.' No one stood up to answer these questions; Mr Gandhi ran his sight through the class and found that no one was paying attention or even try to listen a bit of the explanation. This normally never happened in his class. I tried my best to concentrate, but just by thinking about the topic was enough for me to plummet in a deep slumber.

'Students, I know it seems boring, but trust me, it will get interesting. So please I request all of you to concentrate on what I am explaining.' I felt an urge to listen to Mr Gandhi because till now no other teacher had spoken with so much of love and affection with us, considering that we are orphan—thus, neglected children—or that is what some of the staff in here tell us.

'I hope that all of you are trying to focus on the topic. I was talking about the powerful negative emotion that is anger and ego.' Mr Gandhi wrote the two emotions on the blackboard just as he said.

He took a deep breath and started again. 'Today we will be dealing with what these emotions are, how they are caused, what are the effects of these negative emotions, and how we can control them.' No matter how hard we tried, we couldn't focus on Mr Gandhi's lecture. Most of us zoned out. Just then, Jason nudged me.

I groaned and sat up straight in my seat. 'What? Can't you see I'm trying to focus?' I asked him. He chuckled and flicked his peanut-colored hair covering his forehead.

'And I must say you are failing miserably, and as for Gandhi, he is getting boring day by day. It seems like his age is taking a toll on him.' He laughed at his own humourless joke. I emotionlessly stared at him, and this caused his hysterics of glee to die down instantly.

'Is there any problem, Jason?' Mr Gandhi's voice echoed around the class. Jason stood up abruptly as everyone now seemed interested in the scene about to unfold before them. He dragged his fingers through his already-unkempt hair, making it messier, if it was possible.

7

'Perhaps you should answer my question.' Mr Gandhi adjusted his glasses at the bridge of his crooked nose.

'Can you repeat the question?' Jason asked timidly. I heard a few aws at his condition, which was certainly from the girls. Mr Gandhi rolled his eyes.

'Never mind. But make sure you listen while I teach.' Jason nodded hastily. Mr Gandhi motioned him to sit down.

'That was close,' Jason said and sighed in relief as he clutched his chest dramatically. I turned back to the lecture, overlooking my best friend flirting with a random girl sitting behind us.

'This lecture is quite boring,' the girl whined.

'Just look in my eyes. You'll forget everyone and everything around you,' Jason tried to flirt. Keyword: *tried.*

'I find Airik's eyes better. You know, there is a tint of golden and black in his green eyes. I've never seen anything so vibrant like his eyes.' She sighed dreamily. Honestly, their conversation made me sick. I ignored them and focused my gaze on Mr Gandhi.

'For your general knowledge, let me tell you that egoism is the practice of ego. Egoists are the ones who practice ego, and you can also resemble egoism to narcissism. The word *narcissism* has emerged from the name Narcissus. By the way, how many of you know the story of Narcissus?' There was absolute silence in the class except for Jason's comments. He sighed at the students' disinterest in the class.

'Hey, I was the one talking to her, and then she talks about your eyes, 'I find Airik's eyes better.' Jason complained and imitated her voice while sitting next to me.

'So this is how Narcissus's life ended . . .' Everyone in the class heard the bell ring. It was a good sign for us; this was for the first time that we felt our psychology class absolutely boring. Mr Gandhi couldn't continue any longer; fortunately, the psychology class had come to an end.

'We will continue in the next class, students.' Mr Gandhi headed towards the door and then suddenly halted; he turned around to face the class. 'Airik, please meet me in my cabin after lunch.' I knew it was more of a demand than a request.

I got up from his seat and walked towards Mr Gandhi. 'But, sir, Ms Philips has a class after lunch. And you know how grumpy she can get at times,' I muttered the last part so that he couldn't hear.

'Don't worry, I'll have a word with her. She will let you go.' Mr Gandhi gave a reassuring smile and marched away.

Each and every child of House of Jesus Orphanage left their classes and headed towards the cafeteria. It was a massive and beautiful place with lots of tasty meal and information about major dishes of the world. The manager of this place,

Mrs Wendy Quartz, loved eating and cooking food. She was a middle-aged and a little fleshy woman with a coffee-coloured complexion, dark hair, and brown eyes. Ever since she was a child, she wished to open a restaurant of her own. Overall, she is a very friendly lady.

Everyone was sitting with their respective classes. We all were starving and couldn't wait to take a bite of Mrs Quartz's dishes; they were truly mouth-watering and marvellous. She entered the cafeteria with her dishes and gazed the children who were waiting for their meal.

'Good morning, children! I hope I'm not late.' Mrs Quartz's voice echoed down the gigantic cafeteria. We all were very gratified to see Mrs Quartz. She went through each and every group, just like she always did. At last, she reached the last group of class twelfth that was us, practically hungry like wolves.

'Why are all of you so quiet today?' Mrs Quartz asked with scepticism.

'Something is wrong with Mr Gandhi,' two boys said at once.

'The discussion wasn't boring. Only some of you didn't understand the depth of it,' a girl said while scrunching her face, disgusted at their statements. Talk about overreacting.

'I see. Vikram taught you about human psychology,' Mrs Quartz said patiently. Everyone gave an adequate approval.

'Oh god! How long will you keep studying about animal behaviour? You should know something about our kind,' she babbled on.

'But studying animal behaviour is fun and—' Jason tried to make a point.

Mrs Quartz interrupted in between, 'You all are such crybabies. Now we are not into this discussion.' She and the other helpers served meal in our plates and walked away.

Even while eating, the students of class twelfth couldn't stop talking about Mr Gandhi.

'The psychology class was dreary today,' a girl said with her mouth filled with water.

'Grace, it's better if you don't talk about the class. Mr Gandhi always sides with this half-Indian guy just because his roots belong to India.' Ethan motioned towards me with a nasty sneer. I just took a glance at his seething form, and he seemed to be on edge because of it. I was quietly having his lunch. I couldn't wait to meet Mr Gandhi.

Immediately, my best friend as well as my room-mate Jason nudged me. 'Hey, bro, why don't you shut this creep's mouth? He only knows how to blather around the orphanage.' I just smirked at his statement. I stood up to dump my finished plate, and as expected, Jason followed me for a reply.

'Jason, you know very well I don't like to fight with anyone,' I said, maintaining my calm tone. He soon caught up with my long and fast strides, even though he was taller than I.

'Fine! Do whatever you want to. Hey! I forgot to ask you something.' He sank his teeth in his lower lip.

'Carry on.' I already knew what Jason was about to ask.

'Narrate the get-together with Gandhi when you come back.' Jason winked at me. I sighed and exited the cafeteria with Jason towards the orphanage's garden. The afternoon air wasn't pleasant at all, but the beautiful flowers and lush greenery changed my point of view. We plopped on our usual spot, under the huge pine tree.

'I don't understand why the founder of this place invested so much of money in building a huge and luxurious orphanage,' Jason asked and gazed towards the clean sky.

He continued, 'Some of the staff in here want us to be gone. They wish we were never born. Then why did he help us?' His voice grew small with every word he spoke. He was right, though. The way all of us were treated by some people was utterly unfair. Except for some people like Mrs Quartz, Mr Gandhi, and the manager of this place, Mr Abel, everyone seemed to despise the mere existence of us.

I turned my focus towards the leaves of the pine tree and traced each and every pattern of them in my memory. I do this whenever I need to figure out something. Suddenly, the leaves seemed to spin around, and all I could see was a green blur until it cleared out, and I was now standing in an open ground with hot sun leeching my energy away from me. I knitted my eyebrows in confusion. There were many men wearing ancient jumpsuits as if designed to fight. All of them had the same pattern on their clothes. It seemed as if five concentric circles were squashed in between and formed a horizontal eight.

In the midst of all, there was a girl around my age with jet-black hair, pale skin, and steely aquamarine eyes. Even though she was the only female in the group and the youngest among all, she seemed to have the upper hand. I could literally feel the fear radiating from these men towards her.

'We have been seeking persistently, Master. We must try another way. Using portals have created a suspicion around the other world,' one of them spoke with a wavering voice. I could tell he regretted opening his mouth through the way he was trembling with fright.

She directed her intense eyes towards him. 'Don't argue with my reasoning. I know what I am doing. The boy will come around eventually either with or without inclination.' She grinned maliciously. Her eyes locked with mine, and I felt my heart pumping faster than ever.

'Airik? Airik!' someone yelled with such convenience to my ear that I swear my eardrums couldn't take it. I blinked furiously to gain control over my mind, and soon I felt my former surroundings come back.

'Are you all right?' Jason asked with concern burning in his expression.

'Yeah,' I spoke and nodded. He sighed with relief and reminded me for the last time to go and meet our psychology teacher. I was aimlessly walking towards my destination. There was just one enigma lodging my thoughts: what the hell just happened?

I walked through the deserted hallways towards Mr Gandhi's cabin. I soon reached the door and knocked on it thrice.

'Come in, Airik,' Mr Gandhi spoke in a very grim tone. I entered the cabin; I didn't know the reason for this small meeting. He tapped his fingernails on the table, making a trotting sound. I slowly made my way towards the chair positioned in front of him.

'Sit down. Today whatever I'm going to tell you is very important. It's a matter of life and death. Listen carefully and don't speak in between.' Mr Gandhi stood up from his seat and started pacing right to left in his cabin as if trying to contemplate and arrange the words he was about to say. My gaze followed his movements. I couldn't understand this behaviour. What was the thing with life and death anyway?

I walked towards the chair and sat on it. *Squeak.* I immediately stood up as the chair made a peculiar noise. I sat down again with caution.

'It is a vast story. I was an anthropologist before I entered the profession of teaching psychology. I was very happy and satisfied with my job. I was assigned a project to investigate a small village in Himachal, the place your mom was from.

'According to a man's statement, he and his friends were as usual sitting on their common spot where they meet after having their dinner. On that particular day, a blue light appeared, and his friends suddenly disappeared. He was the only lucky one left.

'The next day a group of scientists claiming that their radar had received mystifying signals entered the village. They personally enquired each and every family until they came across the man who saw the incident with his very own eyes. He described the scene in detail to the scientists. The scientists were not sure what this meant. They wanted to keep the information secretive.

'Then, they consulted us, and we teamed up together to solve this mystery. I worked with equipped machines I had never seen before. Then according to a survey, the same incident had taken place in the same village two years ago. We worked day and night to know everything about the disappearance of those men under mysterious circumstances.

'We couldn't find a solution for this big unresolved question. Then, these incidents almost began to take place every month. Whenever these incidents took place, I found some eerie inscriptions with depth of accurate one metre.' He placed a piece of paper in front of me. 'This time, according to my calculations, the same thing will happen here,' Mr Gandhi finished his story and turned his sombre eyes towards me. I took the piece of paper and stuffed in in my pocket.

'Sir, why did you tell me if you had to keep your mission secretive?' I was totally confused.

'I've been scraped out from the project, Airik. They think I'm mentally retarded.' Mr Gandhi's face grew pale.

'Why do you have to tell me all this?' I leaned forward.

'You should know everything when you are allotted a job.' I was out of my senses now. I didn't know what the word *job* actually meant. Even if I need to know this, then why right now?

'What kind of work do I need to do?' I asked cautiously.

'Nothing much. You have to cooperate with me in my work,' he asked more to himself rather than order me about it, like rest of the teachers do when they need help of a student. The only thing is, the work in here is quite different.

'But why me? What have I done?' He raised his eyebrow at my unusual tone.

'I mean, there are lots of students in this orphanage. They always think of me as your favourite student,' I reframed my sentence and persuaded with him.

'They are not wrong. Airik, you are not like other students. You have elevated wit. You know that very well.' Mr Gandhi stared at me for a moment and started again, 'You are unique. The first time I saw you when you were five, I was dazed by your intelligence. It was an unusual intelligence that you possessed at that age.' Mr Gandhi continued, 'You were the one who helped me out during the survey. You knew a lot about those weird incidents, if you remember well.' I tried to gather the bits of my past in his brain. I tried to remember everything about him, but I couldn't.

'Your mom and dad knew me very well. They were so friendly and kind. I still remember your mom, Christina, and your dad, Delphinium, was so surprised when they met me. Your mom was half Indian and half Swedish.' A smile slipped across Mr Gandhi's face as if he just recalled some delightful moments with my parents.

'It's a shame for those who killed them,' he said. My expression turned from calm to fury. I clenched my fists and tightened my jaw. I always admired talking about my life when my parents were alive but not about their death.

'I promised your parents to take care of you, if they die.' I couldn't control longer. My eyes were stinging with tears, but I managed to fight them back.

'Sir, can we get on to the main part?' I was growing restless by every second.

'How are you?' he asked with uncertainty. Of course, he now thought it was a wrong decision to provoke me.

'What?' I asked with a menacing glare that people around me had grown accustomed to. First, Mr Gandhi conversed about my parents, making me sad, and now he leapt unto a very different topic. 'Why the hell did you just—'

'I've just asked a simple question,' Mr Gandhi interrupted me and gazed coldly at me.

It took some time for me to come to a reply, 'I am fine.'

'Have you been dreaming?' Mr Gandhi asked curiously. *What has gotten into him lately? First the boring lecture and now this conversation. Everyone has the capability to dream.*

'Of course, not only I, everyone does.' I scoffed and tried not to laugh.

'No, not this way. It's quite difficult to explain.' Mr Gandhi was trying to say something but decided this wasn't the right time. Unfortunately, I observed his hesitant attitude.

'What are you trying to hide from me?' I stood up from my seat and slapped my palm against the table, pushing my entire weight on it.

'I'll tell you everything when the right time arrives. Till then, have patience.' He stood up and walked towards me. He placed his hands on my shoulders and squeezed them reassuringly and made me sit on the rusty chair again.

'So . . . how was it?' Jason asked pleadingly.

'What do you mean?' I muttered. I knew where this was going, but I wasn't ready to give in—yet.

'You clearly know what I mean, Airik. I'm talking about your meet with Mr Gandhi. It took you so long. We have almost covered up the syllabus,' Jason said without taking his eyes off me. None of us noticed that we had entered our room.

'Speak to me, Airik,' Jason said with a worried expression on his face.

'Nothing much. We were talking about my grades. He says it's dropping down and in a matter of months I won't be able to pass this class, so I need to work harder.' I looked at Jason and was satisfied to see that my reason was convincing him that nothing was wrong. He dropped his bag on his bed and slouched beside it.

'We are having a football match today at orphanage's stadium. Are you coming?' He gazed at me with his puppy-dog face, which is apparently very hard to resist. Luckily, I have grown immune to it. I walked towards my bed and sat on it.

'I don't think so. I've got a bad headache,' I lied and clutched my forehead. I wished to be left alone for some time. Jason immediately stood up and sat beside me.

'C'mon, bro, you'll feel better,' Jason said with concern in his eyes. It made me feel guiltier than I already was. I didn't like hiding things from my best friend who had been with me for almost his entire life.

'I'll get some sleep. Don't worry, I'll be fine by tomorrow.' I gave a fake weary smile and pretended to sleep.

'Fine. Take care. I'll be back soon.' Jason left the room and closed the door noiselessly behind him. As soon as I heard the door close behind him, I jumped on my feet, turned the lights off, and sat on my bed with my back erect and legs folded. My palms were resting on my knees. I wanted answers—no, I needed answers. The incident in the garden and the conversation with Mr Gandhi were forcing me to doubt my mental state. I closed my eyes and concentrated to gather each and every pinch of my past.

First, there was just darkness. Then I saw my first day in this orphanage. I was almost seven. Mr Gandhi was seated by my side in the cab. He had the same dark complexion, brown eyes, and black hair. I saw a massive non-rusted black iron gate in front of him. We got out of the cab and walked towards the sign, which said WELCOME TO HOUSE OF JESUS ORPHANAGE. Mr Gandhi was talking to a middle-aged man. I couldn't make out their conversation. After the conversation ended, we moved towards the gate. I entered the orphanage and was dazed to see such a beautiful place. There were three huge white buildings in front of me and greenery all around. There was a board beside each and every building, which stated the kind of work carried out in it.

The first building was a school for the orphaned children and also an administration centre. The second building was for orphaned girls, and the third building was for orphaned boys. Mr Gandhi moved towards the first building with me following him numbly. The interior of the building was much more beautiful. The floor was of smooth marble, and there were portraits as well information about great people human history.

Mr Gandhi was talking to Mr Abel, the manager of the orphanage. He gave me a sugary smile, and we together headed to the third building. Mr Abel and I marched to the second door to the left of the elevator. He knocked the door. A small boy of my age unbolted the door. He was a bit taller than I, and his peanut coloured-hair was tousled over his cute round face. 'Jason, I've got a new room-mate for you.' Mr Abel pointed towards me. 'Wow! A new roomie.' Jason jumped with excitement.

Everything faded, and then my mother's face flashed in my head. Those brown eyes, dark brown hair, and pale skin overwhelmed me. Then I saw my father—black hair, sun-kissed skin, and green eyes—watching me in a frivolous manner. I rushed towards my dad to greet him when he returned from work. I was trying to run really fast. That's when I realised that I was 6 in this memory. My dad lifted me up with ease. But then, something was wrong. I could see my dad's nerve tense as he lingered his eyes on my mother.

Dad released me and ordered me to go in my room. I pretended to listen to him. I rushed up to my room but crawled back behind the curtain without being caught.

'Christina, they're here,' Dad said with serenity in his voice when I was not in sight. I saw my mother's eyes widen, and there was just one emotion I could decipher—dread—as she gulped slightly. There was a soft knock on the door. Mom and Dad exchanged looks.

'Airik, stay in your room, not until I tell you to get out.' Dad unlatched the door. Suddenly eight tall and dark men came in with equipped weapons. Three of them seized Dad, and other two men held of Mom. The left-out men searched for something.

'Where is he, Delphinium?' a man asked with a smooth tone.

'You'll never get him!' Dad bellowed with anger.

I was listening to everything; I didn't know what to do. I rang up to Mr Gandhi and told him to reach my home as fast as possible. Now I could hear my parents yelling in pain. No one touches my parents and gets away with it. I got out of my room and went out to help them. I could see my parents soaked in blood and the assaulters mocking about their condition. I sprinted towards Mom and Dad. Tears welled up in my eyes, and in no time, they started trickling down my eyes.

'Why did you get out of your room? I told you to stay in until I tell you to get out, didn't I?' Dad scolded me frantically.

'It's him. Master Aiden will be happy,' someone hissed from behind.

'I've found him, Delphinium. But I didn't expect him to be a kid. Anyways, you should've told me he is here. I would've never tried to hurt you or your wife from other world, though Aiden would be quite happy about it.' The man gestured towards my mom, who was moaning with pain.

I felt a rush of anger in me. I got up and walked towards the men, and then all I could see was eight men dropped dead on the floor without a single bruise on their body. I rushed towards my parents, but it was too late. Their bodies lay lifeless on the wooden floor. I was too late. I always am. It's a matter of fact when something like this happens again.

I woke up breathing heavily; I could feel my heart beating faster and louder against my chest. I had been having this dream all over again. Why couldn't I accept the fact that they were never going to return? Though it wasn't entirely my fault, I couldn't stop blaming myself for what happened that night. I can never get answers for these questions because there is no one to answer them.

I sighed and gazed at the clock for a moment. It was almost eight. I got out of my bed to take a cold shower in a futile attempt to wash the thoughts away with water.

I looked at my reflection in the mirror-pale skin, emerald-green eyes with a tad of golden flecks, and glint of black ringlets around the pupils, dark straight hair, and my athletic build. I loved everything about myself except for my height, which was five feet seven inches. I wished I could be a bit taller. Plus my complexion is way too light to be of a human. Another flaw about me was a huge scar running down my bare chest and abdomen. But the only thing that confused me whenever I saw this scar was I don't remember where I got it from. It's obvious that no one hits a kid with a sharp object and leaves him with a permanent scar, so he ends up constantly bawling and whining about it. I just know that I got this after my parents' death because in the rest of the memories, I can't see this scar.

After taking a shower of cold water, I wore my favourite pair of blue jeans, dark-blue T-shirt, and black leather jacket. I was heading towards the garden, where I met Jason dripped with sweat.

'How was your match?' I asked with fake enthusiasm.

'You missed it. Alan won against our team, 4–2. You should've been there. We would've definitely won,' Jason said and placed his palms on his knees and took deep breaths.

'What took so long, Jason? Football matches never last for four hours,' I asked with suspicion.

'We were relaxing in the stadium. The matches left us out of breath. By the way, how are you?' He stood straight and wiped the sweat off his forehead.

'I'm fine. It's dinnertime. We should move towards the cafeteria,' I said, trying not to meet my gaze with Jason.

'Let's go. I'm starving.' He flung his arms around my shoulder to gain support, and we walked together towards sweet-smelling food.

By the time Jason and I entered cafeteria, it was filled with hungry children waiting for the cheerful Mrs Quartz and her helpers to serve food. We choose the seat in the corner and almost at the end of the cafeteria. Soon she entered the cafeteria.

'Good evening, children!' Mrs Quartz echoed. She moved across each table and suggested most of the children to have a proper diet as usual. As soon as she reached our table, her eyes lit up, and she practically started stuffing food in our plates. On top of it, she added a bit of melted butter.

'No, Wendy! Do you have any idea of how many calories this ingredient contains? I have been trying to keep a check on my diet,' Jason whined.

'First of all, it's Mrs Quartz for you, not Wendy,' she said while smiling slightly. Now it's obvious that she likes it when he calls her Wendy. 'And second, you are in a growing stage, so I will see to it that you eat properly,' she stated sternly and walked away.

Jason and I ate our dinner quietly—well, not exactly. He kept on grumbling about the amount of calories stuffed in his plate right now; and surprisingly, we didn't discuss about our day, which we usually do. I wanted to tell him everything that happened with me, but I'm sure he wouldn't believe. He'll probably think that I am pranking on him.

Jason was too tired to speak, and I was too sad and confused to speak. After having our dinner, we moved towards our rooms. My bed was messy with the clothes tossed over my bed. I collected them, and I was about to keep them in my closet when a small piece of paper fell from the pile of clothes. I bent down and picked it up. As I was about to toss it in the dustbin, I halted as my curiosity got the best of me, and I unfolded the paper. My breathing stopped when I saw the drawing carelessly sketched over it. It was the same mark as that of those weird men while I was mentally in a different place. I didn't know what to do. Something was definitely wrong with me. I have been hearing thoughts or voices as I like to put it, and now this mark. I slumped on my bed and rubbed my temples roughly. *A sleep is what I need,* I decided. *The next day I wake up, everything will be just a dream.*

'A dream,' I repeated audibly as Jason eyed me with amusement.

He is surely gone nuts, talking to himself with weird expressions and terms. He snorted and talked to himself, oblivious to the fact that I was unwillingly using my brand-new ability.

'Did you say something?' I asked him innocently. He looked like the actual example of deer caught in headlights.

Did I say that all out aloud? he asked to himself. I shook my head and grabbed a comfortable outfit to call off the night.

I got dressed in my loose green cotton T-shirt and khaki three-fourths. After a few minutes, I could hear Jason snore deeply in his sleep.

There was no sign of sleep in me. I was still thinking about joining Mr Gandhi in his work and the issues going on with me. I needed answers about my life. I should have stayed longer in the cabin.

I got up and took a piece of paper and wrote down everything I was feeling in it. Truth to be told, I am unable to convey my feelings while speaking; but when I write, I pour my every emotion over it and the barriers of my mind let down for a while, and then I know exactly what I need to do.

Almost around eleven, I could feel my eyelids getting heavy. *Hopefully, everything will be fine tomorrow.*

I felt my soul floating up in the air. I felt so light. First, there was nothing around me; the next moment, I saw a uniquely beautiful land. Tall and green trees were dancing against the soft breeze, contrasting the clear midnight-blue sky. I could see purple mosses on trunks of trees. *Purple mosses don't exist, do they?* I asked myself. I moved farther. I could smell the sweet fragrance of flowers. Then I heard a beautiful girlish voice call me.

'Airik, come. You are destined to come.'

I moved towards the voice. It felt oddly familiar. Suddenly everything in my surroundings faded. I was restrained with barbed-iron chains. I struggled to free myself. I heard the same beautiful voice but this time more beautiful and fierce.

'You will come. I know, but you will not join them. I'll see to it.' I could see the peculiar aquamarine eyes staring at me in the darkness.

I woke up flinching and stretching my body after a tragic sleep in my bed. It was an unusual dream I had last night. It was lively and vivid. I could feel my presence over there.

It was six in the morning. The rays of the early morning sun were hitting my room. My eyes dawdled on Jason, who was still snoring in his sleep. I got out of my bed freshen up and prepared myself for the classes. I wore buttoned long-sleeved black T-shirt that hung up till his waist and blue jeans. After having a mouthful of cereal, Jason and I left together for our class.

'How are you this morning?' Jason asked with concern.

'Totally fine,' I replied.

The first three classes went in haze. I couldn't concentrate on any subject. I moved from class to class. The fourth class was psychology; I was yearning to talk with Mr Gandhi. After the psychology class ended, I sprinted towards him.

'Ah! Airik, I didn't hear any answer from you in this class. Is everything okay?' Mr Gandhi asked.

'Everything is fine, sir. I'm planning to pay you a visit after study sessions,' I said, trying to keep my voice under control to not sound suspicious at all.

'Sure. I'll see you in my cabin. We'll have a good talk.' He turned to leave the class.

'This class was incredible,' Ethan said smiling sheepishly.

'That's because you got a chance to answer a couple of times, and most of them were almost right, or should I say Airik wasn't there to correct you?' Ethan gritted his teeth in anger at the girl who taunted him. What was her name? Alice? No, Alicia.

'Did you see that? He is speechless. This is the kind of reply you should give to people like him. Alicia is amazing,' Jason told me. I was busy finishing his lunch.

'We should move towards our class, Jason. We're getting late.' I stood up and headed towards his class.

'Don't call me Jase. I prefer to be called by my name,' Jason said sternly. I wanted to correct him. I called him by his name, not Jase; but then again, I've never heard him talk with such seriousness. I just shrugged off his coldness and walked towards the last class of the day.

I didn't concentrate on maths. I was blankly jotting down all the solutions. After maths came to an end, I enthusiastically walked towards my room with Jason who was whining about his day. I dropped my bag on my soft bed; took the paper, which had questions written on it; and read them in silence. Jason was busy getting ready for another football match.

'Coming for the match?' Jason asked even though he already knew my answer.

'Nope. I've got some homework to do.' I tugged the paper with that mark in my jean pocket without him noticing.

'Doesn't matter. You can complete it after match. We all are missing our star player.' Jason was staring me with hope.

'Don't you think you're making yourself sound like a loser?' I turned towards my bed and plopped down on it.

'What do you mean?' He came and sat beside me.

'Do you think you can't win without me? This is the only field where you can give your best shot. You are the best football player in this orphanage. Just go and set the field on fire.' I tried to add fuel to his dying blaze, which will hopefully work, just like it normally does.

'Thanks a lot, Airik. I know you're making excuses, but your statement has filled me with lots of spirit and energy. I just don't know why this happens. You complete your homework. I'll set the field on fire.' I was relieved that I no longer had to make any more excuses.

'Best of luck, Jason. Win the game,' I said, trying to make Jason more passionate about this match.

'I will,' Jason said proudly. He unbolted the door and moved towards the orphanage's stadium. I snorted. My best friend can be gullible at times.

As soon as Jason left, I hurried towards Mr Gandhi's cabin. I went through the buildings and corridors, and at last, I reached his cabin. I gently knocked on the door.

'Come in, Airik,' Mr Gandhi's voice boomed. I came in and closed the door tenderly behind me. *How does he always know who is the one coming to meet him? There aren't any CCTV cameras in this orphanage.*

'What have you decided?' Mr Gandhi asked me as he twirled the spherical paperweight over the table.

'Sir, I will surely join your work if you give me the answers to some questions.' His gaze immediately left the revolving paperweights and met mine. I could feel the weird tone being emitted from my throat. I have never ever dared to make a deal with a teacher. *Who am I kidding?* No one ever did. Mr Gandhi frowned and nodded sluggishly.

'My first question. Why did your colleagues think that you were out of your senses?' I asked, interlocked my fingers, and placed them on the table in a businesslike manner.

'I came across a conclusion that there is a different world where those people were teleported.' He was staring at me as if he knew something that I didn't. Unfortunately, I couldn't hear his thoughts like I accidentally did yesterday, but my subconscious was telling me not to do so or I'll later regret my decision. Besides, invading someone's personal space doesn't sound like me either. On the other hand, I was stunned; I wanted to laugh but sat there quietly, suppressed my grin, and tried to maintain the tranquillity around me. 'They're not wrong,' I mumbled and covered it up with a cough.

'What did you say?' Mr Gandhi asked with uncertainty.

I cleared my throat. 'Well, um, my next question. Why do you want me to help you in your work?'

Mr Gandhi sighed. 'Airik, you are very knowledgeable than a normal human. You can process everything in your brain within few seconds. Every answer to your question starts from your parents. They had the answers for the incidents in Himachal. It all came from you.' He was increasing his voice by degrees.

'What? I don't remember anything about those disappearances of people,' I said, breathing heavily as if I had just sprinted a mile.

'Calm down, Airik. You could anticipate before these incidents took place.' He placed his hands on my shoulders and tried to calm me.

'You mean future telling?' I asked.

'Sort of.' Mr Gandhi pondered for a minute and then answered, 'When I took you back to your house, your mom and dad were much tensed. They thought that even you disappeared like those people. When they saw you, they were relieved. They told me everything about you.' Mr Gandhi sighed.

'So . . . how did I see the future?' I asked with a sudden gain of interest in me. Who wouldn't? I didn't get to know everything about my childhood whenever I feel like.

'Your mom told me it was normally through dreams. Sometimes you just asked a question, zoned out for a moment, and then you pictured the answer . . . like daydreaming.' I recalled the dream I had last night and the incident in the garden. Do they carry any meaning?

'Okay, I think I got it. My next question. You told me those incidents are related to me. What makes you say so?'

'I told your parents to stay away from Himachal. They did what I told them to do. But those incidents followed you, and anticipating only about these incidents can't be a coincidence.' I gulped at this statement. The question-and-answer session was getting very scary and serious for me.

'Why aren't these disappearing incidents happening around here?' I asked curiously.

'I don't know. But I'm sure I'll answer this question soon enough,' Mr Gandhi answered.

'I remember most of my life before I came here, but I don't remember anticipating those incidents. Why?'

'I don't know. It's your brain. Kids and their imaginations have a strong bond. Maybe you thought it was your imagination and forgot about it,' he reasoned.

'You told me that my parents wanted you to take care of me after they die, remember?' He thought for a moment and then nodded.

'How did they know beforehand about their deaths? It's practically impossible!' I flailed my arms around like a mentally unstable person.

'How can you jump to this conclusion?' Mr Gandhi gushed and got up from his chair, but I could sense his reluctance.

'The night when my parents were murdered, they were already dead before you reached my home. They already knew they would die soon. And what about those eight men? Tell me everything,' I demanded.

'Look, I don't know how you will be able to digest this. There were some people behind your parents. They wanted to use you against the world. Your parents died protecting you. There were still more things they were keeping away about you from me. They felt the need to tell me this. They thought I could be of some help. I don't know about the death of those eight men. Their death was . . . creepy. Not a single bruise on their body. I felt as if they were in deep sleep.' There was silence in the cabin for too long. I was the first one to break it.

'What else do you know about my parents?' I asked with a heavy heart.

'Nothing more. The rest is the same as you know. Your mom was a psychiatrist, and your dad was a surgeon. You won't be having your classes tomorrow. Meet me at six in the morning sharp in the orphanage's garden.'

'Thanks a lot, Mr Gandhi. I'll see you in the morning.' I gave the most innocent smile I could muster up. He hadn't realised that I actually reluctantly peeked in his head, and now I could see an image that he had subconsciously carved in his mind. It was of a frizzy red-headed man with a knife and the same attire I saw those eight men with. I know he won't tell me anything easily, but I'll anyhow find out. Before I could leave, my ability suddenly decided to show up, and I heard something that I never thought of doing.

How can I tell him that he is the sole reason for the death of those eight men?

I couldn't stop thinking about the statement I 'accidentally' heard. It has been disturbing my thoughts since then. How can I kill anyone? Those eight men as a matter of fact. I was hardly six back then. How can I kill eight grown up men without any action?

'How was your match, Jason?' I tried to make a general talk with my best friend to get those thoughts off my mind.

'Real fun, brother. We won, 4–1. Big defeat, isn't it?' Jason said while taking shallow breaths.

'Of course. I always knew you could do very well. By the way, have you completed your homework?'

'I'll do it tomorrow. You know I need your help in it.' Jason crawled back to his bed.

'Tomorrow is a very big day,' I mumbled.

'What? Did you say something? Pardon, I wasn't able to hear.'

'Have a good sleep.' I closed his eyes, and he was soon lost in his deep sleep.

Indeed, tomorrow will be the biggest day of my life, when I'll come to know a lot about my life. But I was gravely mistaken. I would be getting something more than answers.

Discovery

I woke up feeling giddy for the confrontation with my teacher. I looked at the clock hanging on the blue wall of my room. It's four. Still two hours left. I crawled back to my bed and expected my hidden sleep to come back. Fifteen minutes went by, but still, there was no sign of going back to bed in me. I decided there was no use wasting time and energy; I freshened myself, got ready, and completed my homework. There was still half an hour left. I gathered my small belongings, which I always kept with myself: a pen and a notebook.

I went out in the orphanage's garden to take some fresh air. The weather was quite cold. Fog was settling down in the atmosphere, causing difficulty for me to see clearly. I found a seat and sat there with my elbows resting on my knees and my palms resting against my cheeks. I was trying to focus on reading people's mind from a distance. That day my ability seemed uncontrollable. During the small chat with

Mr Gandhi, it popped out of nowhere. I was trying to choose someone who was difficult to read. *I will have to control and enhance my abilities.*

I closed my eyes and narrowed my eyebrows. I entered Mr Gandhi's mind. It was quite easy to invade his brain, but understanding him even through psychological signs and symptoms was difficult. There were many images flashing by. My image lingered in his brain. I saw Mr Gandhi's expression—very difficult to read. 'Anxiety? No Maybe . . . concern,' I said with my voice hardly audible.

'Airik,' a soft voice called out. I flung my eyes open.

'Come, we need you.' The voice was pleading. I followed the voice. My sneakers swished against the sloppy grass beneath my feet.

I caught a glimpse of pure electric blue light and moved towards it. To my amazement, there was someone else waiting for me: Jason.

'What are you doing here, Jason?' I asked with disbelief. A few minutes ago, he was the one peacefully snoring in his sleep.

'Airik, you are the best friend I ever had. Trust me, you are born to do something very important. Good luck,' he spoke with total determination. *Is he pranking? I've never seen him like this.*

'What are you talking about, Jason?' I asked. His words confused me entirely.

'You'll get to know everything. Follow what your brain tells you to do. Don't flow out in emotions. I know my best friend will do very well. You will most probably end up in a different place, but don't lose hope.' Jason kept his hands on my shoulders as if he was motivating me. I glanced at his arms and then at his eyes and tried to uncover the actual emotions dwelling in them, but they were as emotionless as his face. I felt as if someone else was conveying this message through him.

'I hope I'll see you some other day, brother. Remember you used to say that there is a reason behind existence of life and we need to find it before it is too late?' I nodded.

'Here, the reason itself has found you.' Before I could react, Jason stared walking back to the boys' dormitory. I focused on reading Jason. I saw my childhood with Jason. Jason's expression was turning sober. His eyes were wet. I couldn't believe this. Jason never cried. He had always been strong emotionally and physically.

Suddenly a blue light appeared and engulfed me. Through the corner of my eyes, I could see the weather cleared, and it was bright and sunny again.

I opened my eyes and was bewildered to find myself in a muddy place. To my amazement, it was a forest, and it was very familiar. Then it clicked: this was the same place in my dream. Nothing had changed. The purple mosses on the tree trunks were gleaming at night in the moonlight. *Night?*

How is this possible? It was morning a few minutes ago. Am I still sleeping Is this a dream? There were countless questions I had in my mind, but there wasn't anyone who could answer. *Is it necessary for people to talk in riddles with me?* I shook my head and took a deep breath.

'Hello? Is someone there? Can someone hear me?' This time, there wasn't any voice to call me. There was something about this place that gave me shudders. I walked around for quite long until my feet begged me to stop. I took support of the tree and slowly sat down.

As soon as I came in contact with the ground, I felt something hard between the ground and my body. I immediately shot up, and I took a step back and glanced at the object I stepped on. It was a beautiful book. I took the book in my hands. Its hardcover was brown in colour, and its title was *My Life*. The book seemed very old. *Shame for those who can't take care of such a beautiful book,* I sighed.

The weather suddenly turns icy cold. I shoved the book in my bag and hoisted it on my shoulders. I was shivering; I could feel cold prickling my body. My attention turned towards a small and cute creature. It was quite similar to a tiger's cub. It was baby blue coloured and was almost ten inches tall. Its eyes were sparking navy blue. The best part about it was the stone between its eyes. I guess it is sapphire. I moved towards the creature to touch it. Suddenly th creature morphed into a gigantic and vicious tiger with sharp claws, talons, and fangs. But still, the beauty of the creature remained the same. It growled in anger.

'Cool, boy. I wasn't trying to hurt you,' I said, feeling afraid. My legs weren't ready to run. The creature let a slow but vicious crawl as if it was ready to pounce upon me anytime. It wasn't a boy after all.

'Thanks. Why?' I asked in bafflement. He seemed reluctant as he dragged her fingers through his platinum-blonde hair.

'Forget it. The girl who interrupted you was Anedrin. She is the ruler of Selemara, and the other girl is Phileda. She's my sister.' He scratched the back of his head. Did he just say ruler?

'Wait a minute. How can a 12-year-old girl be a ruler? And what is Selemara? I've never heard of a place like this. Is it a minor village?' I babbled on.

'Selemara a minor village? I think the poison has corrupted your mind. It is one of the biggest kingdoms in Duvollin.' He glared at me for considering this place a village. Only if glares could kill, I would be dead by now.

He sighed as if he remembered the situation I was in. 'Palort, I need your help.' I fumbled with the blanket draped around me.

'No, we need your help,' Palort muttered.

'Sorry, I didn't get it.' I detached my eyes away from the silky fabric between my fingertips and gazed towards him.

'Leave it. It's getting dark. I'll come here tomorrow morning again. Tell me everything. I'll help you if I'll be able to.' Palort jogged away.

I observed the room around me. It was normal unlike the creature I was chased by. Thinking about the chase ran a shiver down my spine. I remembered about the book I discovered from the forest. I found my bag lying beside me. The book was perfectly fine in my bag while my other belongings were dripping with water.

I was very tired by now. I decided to get myself some sleep.

History

'**G**et up, Airik Patronus! Your training starts today. Get up.' Palort was constantly shaking me; I was lazily sleeping in my bed. Whatever they used to make this mattress enhanced me in a deep slumber. I didn't have any life-threatening dreams like I usually did. First time in a few months, I had a peaceful sleep.

'What kind of training?' I fluttered my eyes open and asked.

'Just get up.' Palort forced me to get up. I reluctantly got up from the comfortable and alluring bed. He gave me the same costume he was wearing and told me that it was called belronag. He introduced me to my new room. I freshened myself. I saw Palort eagerly waiting for me.

'Come on, Airik Patronus, tell me everything about you,' Palort said excitedly.

'First, answer my questions, I said.

'Fine. Move on.' His excitement died instantly.

'Why did those people try to kill me?' I asked.

'They didn't try to kill you. They tried to knock you down unconscious so that they could erase your memory easily and then use you against the rest of us.' *Wow, he knows how to make me feel better.*

'There was a creature that chased me. It was baby blue in colour. A sapphire was attached between its eyes,' I explained. He halted right there.

'You were chased by a diorel!' Palort said in disbelief. *What is he talking about?*

'I've never seen, one just heard about it. It's found in the forest of Pamretol. The sources say it doesn't leave its prey until it's dead. The greatest hunter ever and you were chased by it. You also escaped the forest. No doubt you are the one.' He smirked, slightly eyeing me from head to toe as if searching for a wound to magically appear.

'Can you please stop talking with me in riddles?' I requested.

'Look, Airik Patronus, you won't understand anything until you know the history of Selemara.' He pursed his pale-pink lips.

'Last question for now. What exactly is . . . this place?' I emphasised on my last two words.

'It is a different world. Very different from where you live. It is a world of fantasy and magic.' He stumbled, pushing me by mistake, and I crashed against a table with a beautiful vase with floral designs. It was about to fall, but I caught it in time. I sighed with relief.

'Come with me, Airik Patronus.' Palort held my hand. *Is he going to punish me for almost getting the vase broken?* We kept walking until we reached a huge room with books. *I guess this is a library.* I forgot about the vase as I ran my sight around. It was the same height as the room I was earlier in and circular in shape. There were rows of cabinets filled with books, and at last, there was a very huge table in middle of the room with uniformly shaped small cut-outs from the trunk of trees, which I presumed did the exact work the chair did.

'What kind of house is this, Palort? It's more than huge,' I spoke while turning in a circle to get a better look.

'It's a palace,' he informed and seemed amused with my reaction to every little thing happening here. Even I was amaze at myself for showing so many emotions, something I've hardly ever done since that uneventful night. This place seemed more homely than the orphanage. Maybe it was the welcoming nature of Palort and the positive aura I felt around him. Or maybe the reason was something else. Whatever the reason was, I felt happy. I closed my eyes and tried to remember every small detail I had seen so far of this palace.

'If you're done with your little meditation, I might as well take you to the history.' Palort cuffed my hands with his death grip again and loosened it only after halting in front of a series of paintings. Each one had a plot of its own.

'What's this?' I asked.

'This, my friend, is the history of Selemara.' He puffed out his chest as if feeling proud about whatever happened in Selemara before, which I had yet to know.

Palort and I moved towards the first painting that depicted a strong and handsome king. He had a beautiful style of dressing. He wore the clothing similar to that of Palort but more royal. 'Selemara was earlier known as Renadium. It was ruled by King Raisez. He was a very good ruler.'

The next painting was of King Raisez stabbed by a masked man. 'His brothers were very jealous of him they always wanted the throne of Renadium. King Raisez was killed in a conspiracy by his brothers. They hired a skilled assassin and murdered King Raisez while he was asleep.'

The next painting depicted a woman grieving over King Raisez's body. I guess she was the queen of Renadium. 'Queen Selemara, the only wife of King Raisez, was in Calsenai. She was in a state of shock after discovering the news of her husband's death.'

The next painting was of four people fighting over a beautiful throne. 'A fight broke out among the four brothers for the throne of Renadium. The eldest one decided that Renadium would be divided into four parts, which would be ruled by them. Other brothers agreed to this. As the days passed, things were getting different among the brothers. They were trying to usurp one another's kingdom through devious means.'

The next painting depicted Queen Selemara standing before the ruined city of Renadium with her army. 'Queen Selemara recovered from her state now. She heard the division of Renadium in four parts. She now understood the planning and plotting of her brothers-in-law. She was an amazing warrior. She decided to take the four kingdoms down one by one.'

The next painting showed one of the brothers pleading for help from the rest of his brothers who were simply ignoring him. 'First, she annexed the smallest kingdom. The ruler of the second kingdom asked help from his brothers for the protection of his kingdom and himself. But they were least interested to help their brother. In this way, Queen Selemara gradually annexed the whole Renadium, and there was happiness all over Renadium for being together again. After Queen Selemara's death, her son changed the name of this kingdom from Renadium to Selemara in her honour.'

We moved towards the next painting. There was a very handsome man on a horse with sword in his hand. The sword was very beautiful. I couldn't stop admiring the beauty of it.

'The greatest ruler of Selemara was King Phinogar. He was the great-grandson of Queen Selemara. He had every good quality in him that anyone can ever imagine. He was one of the greatest sorcerers that ever came into existence.'

We moved towards the next painting: King Phinogar and a woman holding a child beside him. She must've been his wife. Palort continued. 'He was married with Rosatin, a beautiful princess of Delevan. Soon, Queen Rosatin gave birth to a very handsome baby boy, Prince Synoids. His name resembled a bit to Synoidren, the god of bravery. Don't ask any question, Airik. I know you don't know about the Elyrians. I'll tell you about them later,' he said before I could ruin the intriguing tour.

The next painting was of King Phinogar on his horse in front of a dense forest. 'There is a place called the forest of Pamretol. Whoever went there never returned. And as you

Duvollin but couldn't find it. Then, we decided to meet the Elyrians.' He had an evident sparkle in his eyes.

'Elyrians are gods, right?'

'You have a good memory. They live in Elyria. We had to cross the Valley of Death to meet them. The messengers approved the reason for meeting them. We consulted the goddess of creation Palatina, the first Elyrian to come into existence. She is the creator of all other Elyrians. She already knew everything going on in Duvollin. She told us the exact location of the stone. Thankfully, the stone was found, but we feared that the stone could be stolen again. So Palatina allotted a protector. A protector is a human with massive powers. Its job is to protect the stone until his last breath or until the next protector comes.

'Each protector has their own special ability. Like your abilities to see the future through dreams and get to know about people's thoughts and memories.' Palort turned towards me and grinned mischievously. I could tell where this was heading, and I didn't like the indication even one bit.

'You mean I-I—' I couldn't complete the sentence; I didn't have the guts to.

Palort nodded. 'Just as I told you, you are the one,' he said as he smiled more brightly.

I remembered Jason's words: 'You are born to do something very important.' And with those few words, my life was changed forever. I couldn't tell if it's in a good way or a bad way.

Training

'To protect the stone, you need to train first. We will teach you sword fighting, hunting, and sorcery. You will also learn to develop your extraordinary skill. I'm pretty sure you're well trained in archery,' my newfound acquaintance concluded.

'Yeah . . . wait, how did you—' he interrupted me before I could complete.

'Come on, Airik Patronus, I know a lot more things about you than you do,' he grumbled and patted my shoulders roughly as if trying to clean the belronag. I swear I felt a tiny bit of pain where he touched me.

'We all train over there. Come on,' Palort said and pointed towards a large arena. We decided to jog together till there.

'Palort, I still have some questions,' I said while jogging. He nodded, signalling for me to continue.

'Do you know something more about my personal life?'

'A lot. You are an orphan, and you are very close to your friend Jason and your psychology teacher, Vikram Gandhi. Your friend Jason is very easy to control, though.' Palort grinned impishly. It took a while for the words to sink in.

'You mean whatever Jason told me on the day I got teleported here was through you?' Wow, that was the dumbest question I could ever gather up.

'No, Anedrin did that. She is the ruler of Selemara. Though she is only 12, she has got lots of guts in her. And better if you stay away from her. She is quite rude. The funny part about her is that she forgets many important details when she is excited.' He chuckled and shook his head, resulting in his shoulder-length blonde hair to ruffle around.

'What else do you know about me?'

'Everything. My father had been watching over you since he came to know our new protector is not a Duvollinian. He'll tell you whatever you want to know about yourself.' Palort could see a faint smile slip across my face.

'Can I meet your dad?' I asked hopefully.

'You don't have to ask me for that.' Palort smiled gingerly.

'Now keep the questions to yourself. I believe you'll get all the answers to your questions from my father.'

I saw that Selemara was a lot like the world in which I lived except for concrete buildings and pollution. People lived in houses made of wood. The quality of the wood was also very pure and strong than the usual ones back in my place. Transportation was normally through walking. They used relite, a vehicle which was narrow in the front, broad in the middle, and again narrow at the end and had an unusual and smoky bubble around it. They didn't need electricity to run their houses. Sorcery was enough to comfort them.

'Before we start with anything, I want you to meditate.'

'Is it necessary?'

'Of course it is. While meditating, an individual feels calm and maintains serenity around him. Come on, have a seat.' Palort gestured towards the grass beneath. We both sat down.

'Now close your eyes and take deep breaths, and by every breath, you should feel yourself getting relaxed and tensed free. Let your soul feel free and light.' I followed Palort's voice. I was trying to forget everything that happened with me until now. Now everything appeared like a faint dream. Now there was only Palort's voice ringing in my head.

Slowly, Palort's voice was hardly audible. I could feel myself rise from the normal self. I felt free and light just as Palort had told me to do. I suddenly felt myself lifting high up in the air. The sensation of freedom rushed through me. I opened my eyes only to find myself in the sky, staring at Palort and me sitting calmly on the ground. Palort turned his head towards the sky and flashed a big smile on his face.

I opened my eyes with a start. 'What had just happened?' I said, taking shallow breaths. I could feel every bit of tranquillity flow out of me. I was turning back to my normal self. The same Airik who was always curious to know everything going on around him and everything happening to him.

'You are a fast learner, Airik Patronus. You are very good at concentrating. This will help you a lot in sorcery.'

'But how did I rise in the air?'

'While meditating, sometimes people have an outgoing experience from their body. Well, that's possible only if you enter the subconscious part of your mind. Anyways, let's get started. So . . . what do you want to start with?' Palort asked with excitement.

I gazed at the weapons laid in front of him. 'Anything will do.'

'Fine. We start with sword fighting.' Palort took two swords and hurled one towards me. I caught it with my left hand.

'Are you left-handed?' he asked, and I nodded. It is normal for people to ask me about my handedness and stare at it like I had just electroplated gold on it.

'I must say, Airik Patronus, you're born with the biggest advantage.'

'Advantage? You don't have any idea how difficult it is to live in the world being lefty,' I gushed the words out.

'We warriors long to be lefty.' I snorted, earning a cruddy look from Palort.

'There are a very few people in both the dimensions who are left-handed. Their thinking is very different from right-handers like us. Most of the time, it is difficult to understand their next move. The best part of being lefty is you can easily adapt to your surroundings. What else is different about you?'

'My blood group. It's AB negative. Doctors say it is quite rare.'

'What?' he screeched with wide eyes.

'Is there any other advantage in fighting?' I grumbled without interest.

'You are amazing, Airik Patronus! Incredible!' Palort said, getting more excited and happier with every revelation I did about me.

'You are the best protector that ever came here, Airik.' That was the first time he didn't use my surname.

'You took my name for the first time. By the way, what is the AB negative business?'

'AB negatives are less likely to be affected by curses. Almost no chances.' *I think I'll go insane with these indirect and hardly understandable terms.*

'I didn't get what you mean.'

'You never understand what I tell you. Don't worry, you'll get to know everything. We should get started with your training.

'Hold the sword like this.' Palort gripped his left hand on the bottom of the sword while his right hand was steadied on the top.

'This is for beginners. When you'll be comfortable with two hands, I'll teach you how to hold the sword with one hand. Now, follow me.'

Palort twisted the sword slowly between his hands. I did the same.

'Now do the same thing in normal speed,' Palort ordered. I gracefully twisted the sword between my hands.

'You are a fast learner. I like it. Practise the same thing until you do it in this speed.' Palort twisted the sword between his hands so fast and flawlessly that it was difficult for me to make out the moves.

'That was pretty fast, Palort.'

'I want you to be this fast.'

I closed my eyes, took a deep breath, and tightly gripped the sword. I flung my eyes open and twisted the sword carefully between my hands. I performed the move in the same speed two to three times and then accelerated the speed. Gradually, I was twisting the sword so fast between my hands that it became difficult for me to control the sword. The sword slipped from my hands and landed right in front of Palort.

'This is not good, Airik Patronus. Not at all good. Your speed was amazing, but I want you to control the sword. Don't let it slip off your hands. Concentrate.' He picked up the sword and shoved it towards me.

'You need to be comfortable while holding sword. Keep it easy and relaxed. Grip on the sword should be not too tight and not too loose. If it's too tight, it will be difficult for you to fight against your opponent, and if it's too loose, the sword will slip off your hands. You need to gain control over it. Focus.'

The next few hours, Palort spent his time teaching different techniques of sword fighting. And as the hours passed, I learnt to gain control over my sword.

'Enough for now, Airik Patronus. It is lunchtime. We will start with sorcery after lunch. Come with me. I'll lead you to the dining hall.' Palort and I exited the arena after a heavy practice with knives and spears. I was practically dripping in sweat and panting from lack of air in my lungs. I glanced at Palort, and he seemed unfazed with the amount of practice we just went through. There was just sweat trickling through his temples—nothing more. And I thought I was the fittest in the orphanage.

'This is our dining hall. Let's go.' I followed Palort's gaze towards a wooden house. Though the doors were closed,

I could hear the commotion of men whizzing through the walls of this shelter.

Palort opened the doors of the dining hall. I was shocked to see the scene that lay before me. People were not eating; they were hunting down the food.

'They are eating as if they haven't had anything since . . . ages,' I spoke.

'It's normal around here. They practise a lot and cannot stand hunger. Trust me, they'll beat you to death if you disturb them while eating.' Palort grinned mischievously in my direction. I stood there gaping at the people eating food like animals. I'm pretty sure Palort was enjoying my reaction.

'We should hurry, Airik Patronus, or else, there won't be a grain of food left for us.'

'I agree.' Palort and I moved towards the last table of the dining hall. I kept as close to him as possible. The way these people ate was creeping me out.

'Do women also eat like this?'

'Never. They are the best at behaving in a dining hall. You can never see women massacring food in this way.'

Suddenly Palort stood up. He took his plate and moved towards the middle of the dining hall. He banged the plate with the spoon. People stopped eating and turned their gaze towards Palort.

'Attention, my fella mates. Please listen to me. I've got good news for all the people living in Duvollin.' There was a slight murmur in the dining hall.

'Can someone guess what it is?' he asked.

'You are leaving Duvollin?' someone hissed from behind. Everyone started laughing. I didn't find any humour in this joke.

'Was it a joke? I didn't find it humorous.' Palort rolled his eyes towards me.

'Which means it's just good news, not a very good news,' someone murmured.

'Maximus, I heard that,' Palort echoed.

'So . . . the good news is . . . we have got our new protector!' Palort pointed towards me. Everyone turned their eyes towards me. I suddenly started feeling small. I wished I could have the ability to go invisible, but it was in vain. I tried to get away from the surprised gazes of the people.

'All hail for the protector!' someone shrieked. Everyone crossed their right hand over the left side of their chest, bent down on their right knee, and bowed down in respect to honour me. I was slightly taken aback. I didn't know how to respond. So I did what I had to: I turned my gaze towards Palort and gave him a puzzled look.

'That's all, friends. He is not much . . . accustomed to this. He is from the next world.' They got up in one swift moment, and the murmuring started all over again. I was pretty sure that I would be having a great time in Selemara.

'Enough, warriors. It's time to get back to practice.' Everyone headed back towards the arena, leaving the dining hall in a mess. I wonder who will clean it up.

'So . . . how does sorcery work?' I asked excitedly. This skill amazed me.

'It would be quite hard in the beginning. But since you are good at concentrating, it won't be that tough for you. All we need is a tranquil surrounding. Follow me.' Palort and I exited the arena, and to my amazement, we soon entered a dense forest.

'Are we going to practise here?' I asked and looked around the place as the colourful trees surrounded me. Wherever I stepped on a dead leaf, it surged into multiple colours and faded into oblivion. I was enjoying it, and Palort seemed very amused at my childishness.

'Of course. Just like I told you, tranquil surrounding. Tell me, how are you feeling?' That was a good question. *How am I feeling? To be honest, I don't know how to feel. Should I feel proud for being chosen to protect a beautiful stone with an evil soul? Or should I feel scared with such a great responsibility hanging on my shoulders?* Now I knew the exact feeling. I was a lost soul wandering in the eternal darkness, searching for the light.

'I'm feeling confused about everything,' I answered after a long time.

'What does *everything* include?' I just shrugged. I had no idea to the answer of this question. Everything included, well, everything, starting with my life, this new dimension, and, at last, an abrupt obligation.

'You're not sure yet about your feeling. Close your eyes and try to take a look inside you and understand yourself.' I acquired the same sitting position I had in this morning while meditating. Palort was watching me intently.

'Airik, come with us.' I flung my eyes open and searched for the voice that called me.

'Hey, what happened?' Palort asked with concern.

'Was that you?' I asked.

'What are you talking about?'

'Someone called me.'

'Wait a minute. Are you hearing voices like, um, you're destined to come and stuff like that? And the voice is very beautiful and irresistible?'

'Yes, but how do you know all this?'

'Father—see, good sign,' Palort mumbled under his breath. I could catch up with a few words but still couldn't make out the sentence.

'Is everything okay, Palort?'

'Since when did you have those voices entering your head? Did you dream anything creepy in the last few months?' he asked, ignoring my questions.

'Yeah. I've been dreaming about some new land and . . . my past,' I spoke reluctantly.

'And what exactly is your past about?' He pestered a little. Didn't he tell that he knew everything about me?

'I thought you know well about my past.'

'I've been listening about you from my father. He just told me the kind of person you are and your likes and dislikes. Come with me. Right now,' Palort commanded me.

I didn't like this. I was restricted from asking question, and my destination was to guard a stone until I die just because people feared that the king in it might come out again. That was so lame! I decided to sneak in Palort's head to get a rough idea of what was going on with me.

I knitted my eyebrows and focused on Palort. I was amazed that I could perform two tasks at once: following Palort and also reading his mind.

Everything faded, and now I could see young Palort about 12 standing in front of a man with his head dipped down. The man resembled Palort's looks. He must be Palort's father. He had the same handsome features but stronger and fiercer. His inquisitive brown eyes were set on Palort.

'The time is very close, son. It's not easy to be the prime executor. You know that very well,' the man said with dignity in his voice.

'The protectors have turned. We have to wait for the boy patiently until he is ready. They'll search for the boy. That's for sure. But we must be the first ones to find him.'

'But Rimtzal is still on our side.'

'Palort, we need more. Rimtzal is quite old now. Plus, we cannot be totally dependent on him in any manner. He is very experienced, but we need someone young like the boy. His aura is . . . different—very different—from common people like us. It is the light shade of blue. Very close to that of King Phinogar,' he whispered in awe.

'Why can't we get him right away? It's quite easy for you, isn't it?' he questioned.

'Time doesn't work according to us. We work according to time. And it's better if we don't do anything before time. This literally means we are offending our destiny.'

'I didn't get it, Father,' Palort accepted innocently that he wasn't able to understand his father's saying.

Palort's father leant down on his knees and placed his rough and warm hands on his shoulders. 'Look at me, son.'

Palort lifted his eyes upwards and met his father's gaze.

'We are losing on our side. You need to be physically and emotionally strong. We can't do anything except train our soldiers and wait for the boy until the right time arrives. There has to be some reason for a protector not being in our world, right?' Palort's father winked at him.

'Promise me, you'll always stay strong, and yes, most importantly, you will fight for us until your last breath. Do you promise to do these?'

'I promise, Father. I will. I surely will,' Palort reassured him

The Meeting

I stood gawking at the wooden house before my eyes. It was normal looking except for having any windows and trees with colourful leaves. I never imagined a wooden house to be so strong. Palort gently knocked on the door. Someone unbolted the door, and there stood the man with identical features with Palort. Anyone could tell they were related. He had the same typical shoulder-length platinum-blonde hair tugged back from his face, which sprawled around his shoulder blade. His brown orbs sparkling with experience, maturity, and warmth, unlike Palort's, which were normally filled with aggression and passion.

'What a pleasant surprise, Airik! Please do come in. I had been expecting you, but I didn't think it would be so fast.' I smiled wryly at Palort's father.

'Hello, Mr . . . um . . .' I trailed off and scratched the back of his head, not knowing how to address him.

66

'Call me Delver,' he spoke without the smile wavering off his face.

'Nice to meet you, Delver.'

'Why don't you two come in? Does the house smell bad?' He stepped aside for us to enter and tried to joke and failed miserably. I must say the father-and-son duo had something in common besides their looks.

Palort and I entered the wooden house. The interior of the house was unique. It had a pile of different kinds of weapons, which included swords, bows and arrows, spears, knives, daggers, and many more. Besides these weapons, something else caught my eye. There was a breathtaking and magnificent sword kept away from the piles. The hilt of the sword was basically brass coloured. Its pommel and guard were perfectly rounded. The shape of the sword's blade was like flames. Its tip was way too pointed. I know I had seen it before.

I felt as if the sword was calling me. I moved towards the sword to touch it. I shook my head.

What on earth am I thinking? How can a sword call me? Get a grip on yourself, Airik, I scolded myself for being overimaginative. I turned around to see Palort grinning at me. He probably knew about my feelings for the sword right now.

Suddenly, Palort's face turned very cold as if he had just recalled the reason we were here for. His expression matched when I saw him for the first time in the woods, determination and hate distinct in his body language. He walked up to Delver 'Father, I need to tell you something—alone.' Palort eyed me as if pleading me to leave the duo some space. I moved out of the house and sat on the front porch. *What is so important and private that they want me to leave them alone?* I didn't want to invade their privacy, but the last time I took the decision to not read Jason, I ended up here without a clue of the circumstances. So I did exactly what had to be done according to me. I closed my eyes and embraced myself in the conversation of Palort and Delver.

'What is it?' Delver eyed Palort suspiciously.

'It's happening to him.' Delver's eyes grew wide with fear.

'Are you sure?' Palort bluntly nodded.

'The signs are compatible, Father.'

'This is not good. I don't appreciate your work in this, Palort.' Palort's gaze fell down.

'I know what you're capable of. Train him. He has to be trained as fast as he can.'

'Father, he is able to gain control over himself. I don't think he'll be influenced by them.'

'We need to be sure, Palort. You have to work hard on him. I expect more out of you.'

'I will do my best, Father.'

'Good. You can go now.' Palort obediently exited his house. I quickly opened my eyes and grabbed to nearest object to make it less obvious that I was eavesdropping.

'Airik, what are you doing?' he asked me as I played with a blue leaf fallen on the ground.

'I am just trying to examine the leaf. It is very different from the leaves back at home,' I lied.

'It's okay. Let's get started with your practice.'

The day was very hectic for me. I never thought my life would be turned upside down in this way. I knew there would be problems in my life, but something of this kind? I never imagined.

I learnt the basics of sorcery; it was all about concentrating and connecting to our inner self. That was very easy for me. My skills were also depended on the same mechanism.

I entered my temporary room exhausted and cleaned myself after the massive workout. My food was already in my room, waiting for me. I ate just like the men in the dining hall.

More questions struck my mind. *Is the orphanage searching me? Will I ever go back in my own world and my own normal life?*

I dropped the delicious delicacy and rubbed my temples. In simple words, my life was totally destroyed. All I had to do was aimlessly protect a stone, which was not at all needed. That didn't make any sense.

I reached out for my small belongings. That was when I remembered about the book. The book was still there in my bag. I ran my fingers through the hardcover of the book. How can a novel be found in the forest of Pamretol? Palort said no one normally visited the forest. *Then whose book is it?*

Probably years ago, someone must've ventured in the forest and dropped this book by mistake, I answered my own question. I was somehow satisfied with my answer.

I opened the book. I felt something twitch inside me. Something in me wanted to go through the book. I flipped the index displaying the content of the book. I stopped on the first chapter.

The Book

CHAPTER 1

*T*oday *is the best day of my life. I'll be turning 15. At last, Airis will turn 15. Father told me he'll get me a relite of my own!* I got out of my bed excitedly and charged towards the undersized cupboard beside my bed. I took out my favourite purple-coloured belronag to dress up. I quickly freshened myself and got ready to go to school.

Usually, I walked to my school; but today as it was my birthday, Father decided to take me to school with his relite. I reached my school pretty fast. Father gave me a quick goodbye hug as he was going with his comrades in Allekior.

I took a deep breath. I don't like going to school. It's not that I miss my family at the school. The thing is, no one likes me there. Probably they don't like my decision of choosing the Warriors group. I've never confessed it to anyone, not except my sister Ikaria. My sister Ikaria says they are jealous of my smartness, intelligence, and the way teachers always trust me with a task.

Our school is divided into two parts. The first part is known as the Warriors. In this part, the school teaches us the techniques of fighting and the way to lay out battle strategies.

The second part is very boring. It is known as the Necessities. In this part, they teach us many things like cooking, sewing, handicraft, and boring stuff like that. Sometimes I feel weird being in a group with boys.

I forced myself to walk with my feeble legs in the school. My first class was archery. I took my allotted bow and arrow and took my place before the target: a circulating board. We had never done anything with a circulating board. It was probably going to be the toughest class ever. Our archery teacher entered the room.

'Line up!' he ordered. We were not allowed to take our teacher's name at any cost. It was considered as objecting the teacher. We did just as our teacher said.

Right then, all the students jostled in to stand first in the line. I move away from their way and waited up for them to form a proper line and stand at last.

'This is a circulating board. You have to come one by one and target right on the lion's open mouth in the corner of the board, moving along with it. You will be given only two chances. Understood?' he echoed.

'Yes,' we all replied.

Everyone came one by one and tried their best to hit the lion. But no one could hit it. Now it was my turn. I've always been good at archery, but this task was quite tough.

'Shoot it, Airis,' someone said from behind. I left the arrow. It just missed the lion. I had one more chance in my hand. I concentrated hard on the lion. I took each and every detail of the movement. I left the arrow.

'Yesss!' I jumped with happiness. I was the only one who hit the lion.

'That was good, child.' My teacher patted my back awkwardly.

'All right, students, I've got some work to do. You can do anything you wish, but remember, don't get out of the room until you are ordered to move in the dining hall.' The kids scampered to their groups, leaving me alone. I sat and waited for the class to finish. Those minutes seemed like ages to me. At last, it was time for moving in the dining hall. One thing was for sure: I'll be the best target for everyone in the food fight.

CHAPTER 2

We quietly moved towards the dining hall. Thankfully, one of the teachers was already there. This meant no food fight. I could feel my soul dancing inside. The last food fight we had was very wild. I wasn't affected by it, though. I grinned at the memory when I had hit a sophisticated girl with the cake in anger.

Everyone sat on their places with their groups. I sat in the corner, waiting for Octavian. He was my only friend in this school and was a year older than me. We had known each other since we were toddlers. His father worked as a chief protector of Aegera and expected Octavian to do the same. Octavian came running towards me and hugged me. 'Happy birthday, Airis. Look, I've got a new bow for you.' He handed me the bow deliberately.

'Wow. It's beautiful.' I ran my fingers through the beautifully carved structure on the bow. I felt as if water were flowing through my fingers.

'Where did you get it from?' I asked without taking my eyes from the bow.

'I've carved it myself.' I stood with my mouth open.

'Are you playing a prank on me?'

'I took my mother's help.'

'Oh. That explains.' Octavian's mother was very interested in carving. She learnt it from her grandfather.

'What are you going to do after school?' Octavian asked me with mouthful of cake.

'I'll go in the woods. Would you like to join me?' I asked.

'What is the relation of you and the forest? You always talk about those woods,' he asked.

'I like it in there. No one disturbs me. I'm left by myself to explore everything I need to.'

'You know, sometimes you sound a lot more than your age.' Octavian was staring me with his severe grey eyes.

'So . . . would you like to join me?' I spoke while squirming under his gaze.

'I'd love to, Airis. But I'm busy. I'll join you after completing my work. We all will have fun.'

'We all in the sense including your friends?' I asked.

'Of course! Who else do you expect?' He raised his eyebrows teasingly.

'Well, um, no one.' I didn't know what to say.

'Octave!' someone squealed from behind. It surely has to be her: Cora. She was the only one in this school who calls him Octave. She was in the Necessities group. She would start her melody, and Octavian would be attentively listening to her.

'Octave, I need your help. Can you come after school to help me?' Cora said, twirling her blonde strands of hair between her fingers.

'Sure, why not?' Octavian said with a sweet smile on his face, revealing his deep dimple. Didn't he say he had work to do?

Sometimes he behaves like a wimp in front of Cora. I don't get this. Why does this girl have an influence on people? What does she do to them?

'I thought you had to do some work.' I snorted.

'Yeah. I'll join you after finishing my work with Cora. And I'll celebrate with you after I'm done with Cora,' Octavian said without taking his eyes off Cora. I rolled my eyes.

'I wouldn't mind even if you didn't come,' I muttered. I think Octavian heard me but didn't pay much heed to it. He was busy smiling at Cora.

I walked out of there and attended the rest of the classes left. I was waiting for the school to finish so that I could go and stay in the woods—alone.

CHAPTER 3

I hurried to my house and quickly dressed in comfortable clothes. Ikaria was out with her friends. I exited my house and marched towards the woods. I took a deep breath after entering the forest. The smell of sweet pine and beautiful flowers energized me. Now I wasn't walking. I was running with happiness towards my forest house. Elyrians know why I always feel rush of many emotions at once when I am in this beautiful forest.

I halted in front of my small forest house. I checked the wooden walls of the house. They were strong. I still remember Father gifted me this small forest house on my last birthday. No one knows about it yet. Not even Ikaria, Mother, and Octavian. I stepped in the house with relief. I cleaned the house and went out to venture in the forest. I stopped beside a massive tree.

I remembered the tree-climbing lesson Father gave me when I was very young. I sighed at that memory. Those days had been so pleasant. I felt a sudden urge to climb the tree. Probably, I needed to know whether still I could climb it.

'Wrong logic,' someone whispered from behind. I turned to see who it was. Surprisingly, it was Ikaria. She, as usual, looked stunning. Her sparkling blue eyes were staring at me curiously.

'What is it?' I asked her and leaned against the tree.

'You know, sister, I didn't wish you. So I thought probably I should come and meet you personally. Happy birthday,' Ikaria said casually. I tried to look infuriated. *I'm her only sister. She knows she hasn't wished me yet. I am supposed to be angry.* Her expressions softened.

'Are you mad at me?' Ikaria asked innocently. Part of me was angry because she wasn't the first one to wish me. But my 17-year-old sister was so innocent and kind that I couldn't stay mad at her for too long. But I displayed that I was still angry. I like to see her when she is apologising.

'I'm sorry, Airis. I swear it won't happen again.' I couldn't control myself any longer and burst into a fit of giggles.

'You're turning into a good little actress,' Ikaria said with her arms folded in a defensive attitude.

'I have a right to play a prank on my sister, right?' I asked between my shallow breaths.

'Come on, Mother and the rest are waiting for you.'

'I'll be back in a minute,' I said apologetically.

'Fine. We'll wait for you.' I could see my sister fade away in the woods. I took a deep breath of the evening air and gazed at the orange evening sky overhead. According to me, sky is the definition of eternity. It doesn't have a start or an end. I wish happiness and our lives would be like the sky: beautiful and eternal. Unfortunately, wishing doesn't help. I let out a breath and tore my gaze away from the sky, leaving the support of the tree; I stood on my feet and brushed the mud away from my clothing.

Suddenly, I could feel hotness burn my neck. Something was wrong. I glanced nervously around me. I could feel uneasiness creep over me. I heard faint growls. The growls were familiar. It was so much like . . . klerites. My eyes widened. Those yellow-eyed, purple-tongued, and overweight monsters were in my city, the place where I live. I had never seen a real one in my life. People say they are vicious. Elyrians forbid the existence of those foul creatures around Aegera.

The growls were coming closer to me. I had to do something to stop them, or Aegera would be in ruins. The only way to kill them was by changing the weather to freezing cold. *I'm not a trained sorceress to do so. I don't even know whether I have a sorceress in me.*

All of a sudden, a thought occurred to me: *What if there is sorcery in me? No, that should not happen.* The thought of being a sorceress sent a chill down my spine. Society never accepted people like me to be a sorceress. They always wanted royals and high-class officials to be sorceress. The rest are considered unlucky to have a great art like sorcery in them.

Before I could get away from my unnecessary thoughts, a klerite was already standing with hungry yellow eyes glaring right at me. It was not at all like the monster that people described.

It was over four feet tall with blue translucent body. He was square teethed, his eyes were yellow, and I could not see his pupil. Probably he didn't have any pupil, and he was overweight. I still didn't know about his purple tongue. Unexpectedly, I wasn't afraid. I felt a sudden surge of power in me.

The weather around me changed to cold. The cold was getting colder by every minute, I could tell. The man eater fell down on his knees and suffered until he was dead. Somehow, I wasn't affected by the cold. The energy in me was draining. I turned to my normal self. I fell down fainting right at the spot.

'Airis!' I could hear Ikaria call me. She rushed beside me and caught me.

'See, I told you it's happening because of her.' I could hear someone accuse me.

'You shouldn't have done that, Airis,' Ikaria said with regret.

CHAPTER 4

I woke up flinching in my bed. I had a very bad headache. I felt as if someone was hammering down my head. I took off the quilt from my body. When I tried to stand up, I felt my legs getting weak. I couldn't remain balanced for long, and I faltered down. Someone's strong arms caught me.

'You are not well. You need to take care of yourself.' I looked up to see Octavian in front of me.

'What h-happened to me? Why am I so weak?' I stuttered.

'What happened last evening, Airis? Tell me everything.' Octavian made me sit down on my bed and handed me a glass of water.

I took a sip of water and placed the glass back on the table. 'The klerites were coming. I don't know. It just happened. It's not my fault,' I said with lots of confusion.

'Here, I think you need more water.' He forcefully handed me the glass and made me the drink the whole glass of water.

'Now take a deep breath and tell me everything in detail with patience.' He rubbed my back in attempt to calm me.

I let out a deep breath. 'After Ikaria left me, I heard some growls. It was of the klerites. I was afraid at first, but I don't know how but I could feel myself getting stronger. I was standing in front of the klerite, but I wasn't scared. The weather suddenly changed to freezing cold, and I fainted.'

'Okay. You need to have something. When did you last eat?'

'I had breakfast in the morning and then—'

'So you hardly ate anything yesterday.' I nodded with my head bowed down. Octavian pursed his lips.

'Airis, are you up yet?' Ikaria came with a plate of food in her hand.

'How are you feeling right now?' Ikaria sat beside me and placed her hand on my cheeks with concern.

'I'm fine, Ikaria. Did I do something wrong?' I asked Ikaria.

Octavian and Ikaria exchanged looks. 'Everything is fine. You need to have some food. Come on.' Ikaria offered me her hand. I got out of my bed with Ikaria and Octavian helping me out to walk without a fall. I had a mouthful of fruits while Ikaria and Octavian watched me with concern.

'Where's Mother?' I asked Ikaria.

'She's out of town in her mother's place,' Ikaria said without blinking.

'Can one of you tell me what's wrong with me? Your stares are very . . . unsettling.'

'Did you ever feel the way you did last evening in front of those creatures?' Octavian asked. I shook my head.

'Airis, there is a sorceress in you,' Octavian whispered. It was clear enough for me to hear. My breathing was ragged. It should have never happened.

'Will they do the same they did to Melancus?' I asked timidly.

'No, sister. I won't let them.' Ikaria hugged me.

CHAPTER 5

'The Supreme Authority is here,' Octavian informed.

'We'll be there in a minute,' Ikaria replied.

No, my birthday cannot end up like this. I should not be punished for saving lives of many humans. I will not end up like Melancus. We entered the hall where the Supreme Authority was seated. Ikaria and Octavian never left my side.

There was hardly anyone in the hall except for the five members of the Supreme Authority and three of us. I looked around myself. The golden pillars of the hall smelt of sandalwood. Probably, they applied the scent more often. The hall was full of abstracts of King Aseptus and his family.

My thoughts drifted to King Aseptus. He should've been here. He is the best at decision making. Except for the last he made for Melancus.

Melancus was one of the students from our school. He was very nice compared to others. He was never rude to anyone.

When there was an attack from the neighbouring kingdom, he unexpectedly managed to kill many of them. In spite of the existing law that normal subjects of the kingdom weren't allowed to practise the art of sorcery, we appreciated him and his skills. Thus, we anyhow bent the rules for him.

By every passing day, Melancus was changing. He was considering himself superior than the rest of us. He gradually began to threaten people. King Aseptus wasn't happy with Melancus. King Aseptus banished him from the city. Since then, it was made official that any normal human with sorcery will stay away from the city, and this would most probably never change. King Aseptus didn't want any threat to hover around his kingdom He wished to keep his kingdom safe and sound from any unexpected dangers.

'Airis, you are accused of performing sorcery. What do you have to say about it?' a dark-haired middle-aged man asked me, taking me away from the thoughts of Melancus. I was not in any mood to answer any questions. I was already pretty shaken up.

'She saved the lives of many people,' Octavian said in my favour.

'Melancus did the same. How can we be sure that she doesn't change into the same human as Melancus again?' the man with white greasy hair asked.

'She is my sister. I've known her for my entire life. She'll never do anything threatening,' Ikaria said with fury in her voice and tried to keep it under control.

The same man leaned on the table. 'We all knew Melancus. He was also very kind. At least, I never expected him to be threatening,' he said with his fingers crossed.

People were arguing from both sides. I was the only one quietly sitting in the hall. I couldn't control any longer.

'Enough!' I shouted. There was silence all around me. All of them were staring keenly as if they were absorbing each and every word I just said.

'Just let the Supreme Authority do whatever they want to, Ikaria. They'll always at last stamp their decision on us,' my voice reverberated across the hall.

I turned my gaze towards the Supreme Authority. 'Throw up your decision. I'm not interested to live around filthy people like you. I'll better live alone,' the words poured out of my mouth.

Everyone stood up and gazed at me with their mouths open. That was obvious. None of them ever saw me like this. I couldn't help it. My fifteenth birthday ruined, those klerites, sorcery, and now this decision making. Everything made me angrier.

I guess I overreacted. I had spoken too much for sure. But I wasn't wrong. Why do they have to call a meeting if it was already decided?

'I'll pack my stuff. And for your first question, which I didn't get to answer, how would you feel when you help many people at once and they are dying to see you in pain? I'm feeling the same way right now.' I stood up to walk out of the room. I saw that white greasy-haired man smirk at me.

'Wipe that smirk off your face, or I'll do it myself. And trust me, it is painful.' His smirk dropped instantly. I snorted.

Ikaria placed her hand on my shoulder. 'I think you've surprised us a lot lately,' she whispered.

'I never saw you this hot-headed,' Octavian said.

'Do you have any problem with that?' I asked, being rude than ever.

'I appreciate it. I would like to see you like this more often.' Octavian chuckled.

'Let's go. This place stinks,' I said it pretty loud so it was audible to the Supreme Authority also.

Those people gave me a blank stare. Three of us walked out of the hall. I felt courage fill up in me. Now nothing mattered at all. *They want me to leave? I'll make them regret their decision.*

CHAPTER 6

'Why did you heat up in there?' Ikaria yanked me by my arms and made me face her.

'Then what exactly did you mean? Can you elaborate your feelings?'

Ikaria placed her hands on my interlocked hands. 'Look, Airis, I know many problems have suddenly pounced upon you. You're very young to handle these. Don't lose your temper. Have control and faith in the Elyrians. I know they'll never let anything happen to you.' I couldn't control any longer; hugging her tightly, I broke out in a sob.

'Everything will be fine. I'll never let anything happen to you.' She gave me words of reassurance and stroked my hair. I felt as if I were a small child and I'd done something wrong. Being my elder sister, she's giving me the words of comfort that I needed. I gave a faint laugh at that thought. She is the best sister anyone can ever have. She always managed to get a smile on my face even on the harsh times. I thank the Elyrians for the greatest sister they have given to me.

There was a soft knock on the door to ruin our beautiful moment. Someone peeped in. It was Octavian.

'Sorry to disturb you, sisters. I have to go. Mother is waiting for me. See you tomorrow.' Just as he was about to leave, Ikaria stopped him.

'Octavian, wait.' Ikaria eyed him suspiciously.

'What is it?' He entered in and hung his head low. Something was definitely wrong.

'Tell me the truth,' she demanded.

'You caught me.' He sighed and ran his fingers through his unruly dark hair.

'You know very well it's not easy to win when you compete with me,' Ikaria said proudly.

'Okay. I'm going with Cora. She is standing on the front porch of your house.' Octavian blushed. I had never seen him blush.

'You should invite her in,' I said teasingly.

'She is afraid.' He tried to keep his voice low. My tight smile fell down. People had already started showing resentment towards me.

'In that case, you should probably go, Octavian,' I said in a very small voice. Ikaria stroked my black thick hair. He didn't say a word and left. A tear slipped from my eye. He was my best friend, and I thought he would stay with me until I will leave this kingdom and complete the duration of my banishment. He left me for a girl who always hated me for no reason. He had said once that our friendship will last forever. I guess the definition of our forever was too short. Ikaria noticed my gloomy face and pulled me up with her.

We headed towards the kitchen, and Ikaria started preparing the dinner. I just sat across her as she cooked and stared at her movements.

'Have you ever tried after the incident?' Ikaria asked curiously as she stirred the warm water in the pot.

I clearly understood her indication. 'I never got a chance to do so, and I don't think I would like to try it, knowing it would get me into trouble.' I shrugged.

'Try it now. Airis, I don't care what society thinks about people like us performing sorcery, but I know in my heart that it is a talent that you have deep in yourself. Don't hold it back, sister. Use it for your own good and also for others. Let this society regret their decision of banishing you, in case they ever do. Just remember one thing: the more pain you feel, the stronger you become.'

'Thanks. Your speeches are very motivating,' I muttered with lack of concern.

'It wasn't a speech. I was trying to make you happy about being a sorceress.' Ikaria scowled at my laid-back attitude.

What can I say? When circumstances change, the person can't help but mould themselves according to it.

CHAPTER 7

'Show me everything you can do with your new talent,' Ikaria said with excitement. I sighed and slumped down on the dry grass out of exhaustion. It is me we are talking about, and she is the one getting happier about it.

'I haven't explored yet,' I reminded my overexcited sister.

'Then explore now. Come on, I can't wait to see my sister do something a normal human can't. Do anything you want to. Think of the deepest desire within you and work on it,' she said with her arms folded.

'The deepest desire within my heart right now is to take this talent off me,' I droned in my sassy and sarcastic tone. Ikaria stomped her foot in frustration and rubbed her temples roughly while muttering something incoherent, 'Airis, don't do this. You should be happy to have a talent like this. No one except for few people have it. You are unique. I don't like to see you like this.' She hushed all of a sudden.

Before I could say anything else, she continued, 'You are very powerful, Airis. You changed the weather, and thankfully, you just fainted. There is no damage to any of your body part. The last person who did this is dead.' I gulped. She was right. *What if I develop my ability in such a way that people respect me? I am able to change the weather without killing myself. I can surely do much better than that. Why am I trying to fit in the crowd where I don't belong? Unfortunately, I don't have answer for these questions. The worst issue about questions is that only you can have a way towards answers. They are just like every other leaf that falls off a tree and gets trampled.*

'The Supreme Authority will be sending their orders by tomorrow, and you know very well they never leave the ones they target, and now you are their target. I'm sure they'll banish you from the city for what you did today. It was very humiliating for them,' Ikaria spoke and detached me from my thoughts. I don't know what's wrong with them. I just spoke the truth, which they already knew well.

'Truth is always hard to digest, sister. The world doesn't permit us to be straightforward. Being straightforward means you are rude.' She pointed out the unfair invisible rule accidentally made by us.

If that is the way they think, I can't help it. But I'll never change myself just because the world wants to see a change in me. Society knows how to suffocate someone. Why should I care about the world if the world doesn't care about me?

'Stop thinking so much about this conversation we just had. All I know is King Aseptus will be returning tomorrow. He'll handle everything. He is a good decision maker. And Melancus deserved to live alone. He was turning into an animal.' I huffed. People only know to criticise.

'Animals can be controlled, Ikaria. They can be controlled with love. Only if any one of you would have the courage to oppose. He would have surely understood the point you made a few minutes ago,' I answered back.

'But you did stand up for him, and I assure you, King Aseptus still remembers you.'

'All I did was stand for someone who deserved to live happily. We don't even know how he is. Poor boy, who knows if he is alive or . . .' my voice trailed off. The last time I met Melancus, he was very guilty. I could see sorcery was controlling him.

The power for him was far too beyond to handle. It was eating him up from the inside.

'What is it?' Ikaria asked.

'I'm feeling sleepy. I'll hit the bed.'

'Okay. I'll see you tomorrow. Goodnight. Sweet dreams.' I snorted. The last two words were hardly applicable for me.

CHAPTER 8

I really miss Melancus. He was just like me: quiet, mysterious, and the easiest target. Something surely went wrong in him. I could clearly see at the day of decision, he was guilty but something in him was trying to suppress it. He must be around 18 right now. Only if I knew where he was, I could have brought him back and changed the mind-sets of people like us being sorcerers.

After this distressing thought, I drifted in a deep sleep.

I took a look at my surroundings, but all I could see was endless darkness. My eyes stopped on a dark figure that chuckled at me.

'Airis, join me. The world hates us just because we have done something good to them,' he said with serenity.

'Who are you? And what do you mean by joining you?' I asked and tried to reach out for him, but he vanished into mist.

I felt warm breath fanning against my neck. In an instant, I turned around only to see the mysterious boy standing a few feet in front of me. I still couldn't make out his facial features. 'Your sister is right. You are very naïve. We are more powerful than the rest. Elyrians want us to rule the tiny humans.' The corner of his pale-pink lips lifted a little, and it took a while for me to understand that he was smirking. *It's just a dream*, I reminded myself again and again.

'You are the biggest fool I've ever seen in my life.' I frowned at his statement. 'Don't you see, your sister is jealous of you being a sorceress.'

'No, she isn't. If she would be jealous, she would be motivating me to kill myself. Instead, she wants me to explore more about the new skill I possess. And yes, she is very happy for me,' I replied rudely.

'I'm going for now, Airis. Think about my proposal, and then you will know.'

What does he mean by I'll know? What will I know? Before I could ask him any more questions, he faded into a grey mist.

I woke up and saw Ikaria sitting beside my bed. Her expression was unreadable as if she were in a dreamlike condition where the person is conscious but is unable to identify the right and wrong.

Then the realisation dawned upon me. The decision is today, and I'll most probably be banished. Even the thought of getting banished sent chill down my spine. *Where will I go? How will I support myself?*

I hurried out of my bed and freshened myself. While I was having my breakfast, there was a sharp knock on the door. I held my breath. *Please, not the Supreme Authority. At least not right now.*

Ikaria opened the door. I took a peek to make sure it wasn't the Supreme Authority. To my relief, it was Octavian. Last night's incident came crashing back. I diverted my gaze from him and concentrated on the breakfast before me.

'Did they send their decision?' Octavian asked with concern. As if he actually cares.

'No. Not yet,' Ikaria replied.

'They should be sending the decision by now,' Octavian said with confusion. *So now he is waiting for me to leave.*

'They will not care much about this issue. After all, Airis is still a child,' Octavian said with a tone of reassurance. This phrase boiled my blood.

'Melancus was 15 when they banished him. He wasn't younger or older,' I spoke with narrowing my eyes at no one in particular.

'But he was a boy, and you are a girl. So probably, they'll reduce your punishment.' I stood up in anger.

'What kind of punishment is this? I haven't done anything wrong! They'll punish me because I spat their truth on their faces,' I said with my voice rising.

'Airis, what's wrong? I've never seen you like this. You were so quiet, gentle, and calm. What happened to you?' Octavian tried to grab my flailing arms to comfort me.

'When your life takes a nasty turnaround, you can't stay sane for long. And remember one thing: the quiet, gentle, and calm Airis is long gone.' I left Ikaria and Octavian and headed right towards my room. I suddenly started feeling that I should listen to the boy in my dreams.

CHAPTER 9

I locked the door behind me and tried not to cry. I took deep breathes and fought back my tears. There's one thing I couldn't understand. Why was I even crying?

I could hear muffled steps towards me. It had to be Ikaria. I turned my gaze. It wasn't Ikaria. It was Octavian.

He smiled at me with sympathy. 'I'm sorry. I didn't mean to say you were wrong.' He sat beside me. I didn't say anything and tried to calm my messy mind.

'I'm sorry,' he said abruptly. I knew he meant it, because he had never apologized before. I smiled at him, indicating that I was no longer angry.

When I stood up to move out of my room, Octavian pulled me down and made me sit. 'Did you actually mean that you'll change?' he asked pleadingly. He didn't want me to change.

'Cora is here, Octavian. Maybe you should go.' I tried to avoid the question as much as possible.

'I'll talk to her later on. I'm not finished with you. What's wrong? Tell me, Airis. I need to know everything,' he said with his voice changing to dominant.

Within a few seconds, I could see Cora in my room. She came in my room, eyeing me suspiciously. No. *Hatred* would be the most appropriate word. She sat beside Octavian. He turned his head towards Cora.

Now he'll be leaving. I was thankful to Cora for the first time.

'Wait for me with Ikaria. I'll be back soon.' She wore a fake smile at Octavian. When he fixed his gaze back at me, Cora frowned.

When Cora left the room, Octavian started again. 'So . . . tell me everything,' he said being bossy than ever.

'Does it really matter? We all know the decision of the Supreme Authority. They'll make my life miserable. Better for you and my family to stay away.' I stood up and headed to leave my room.

'I'm sure there is something going on in you. I'll come to know soon, Airis,' he hollered behind me.

I was walking with my head bursting with thousands of thoughts. The contents of the dream always replayed in my head. My thoughts seemed like the untamed raging sea. I was confused without any clue to plan out my future. My instincts said that I would have to wait and watch, but my mind said otherwise.

CHAPTER 10

The Supreme Authority was seated in my house. When I entered the main room, everyone sitting there wore a serious face at me. The man who last smirked at me was seated at the far end of the room; I guess he was still scared of me. I looked at King Aseptus. He was the only one smiling at me. I forced a smile on my face.

Sometimes I feel bad for King Aseptus. He had everything with him: power, money, success, skills, and such a huge kingdom. The only thing he was left out with was an heir. He was almost of my father's age, probably a year or two younger. Fifteen years ago, King Aseptus's wife, Queen Astrea, gave birth to a dead baby girl.

Unfortunately, I was born on the same day as the princess. Since then, some people have considered me unlucky for this kingdom, but many people don't pay much heed to it.

'Let's start with the meeting,' the man said who last smirked at me.

He continued. 'Sir, this girl is not good for our kingdom. She is a sorceress. She'll cause destruction. She also threatened me the last time we had a meeting.' I narrowed my eyes at him. He was getting uneasy under my stare. On the other hand, King Aseptus seemed amused.

'She had seen too much at such a young age. She was just . . . not in control,' she defended.

'We have to end the meeting at the point that she meets the same fate as Melancus.' King Aseptus was attentively listening to all the arguments.

'I don't think Airis would ever make trouble for us,' King Aseptus said. He was in my favour. The thought made me want to jump around, but I decided against it.

'Melancus was also a very good child. He never did anything wrong before he came to know he was a sorcerer. How can we know? She might be the biggest threat for our kingdom in the coming future.'

'I know her very well. She always rethinks the situation and only then takes any step. She is a good decision maker,' King Aseptus said.

'Melancus exhibited the same qualities. Who says he wasn't a good decision maker? We appreciated his each and every quality, but what has he done in return? Threatened the subjects of this kingdom. People are now afraid of her. She can't stay in the kingdom. We can't keep a cat and mouse together in the same place when we want the mouse alive.'

King Aseptus was in a deep thought. That man too gave a very common example.

'I need each and every family in the ballroom. Right now.' King Aseptus gave importance to the last two words.

Everyone scampered away from my house except for King Aseptus. Now, there were only four people in my house.

King Aseptus walked right up to me. 'Please sit all of you.'

We all sat quietly in the chairs. No one spoke a word. The silence was making me uncomfortable. I felt as if I were being prepared for a war and be leaving to sacrifice myself. As usual, I was the first one to break the silence.

'Are you all hungry? Should I get something for us to eat?' I stood up and walked up to the kitchen.

Ikaria rolled her eyes at me. 'The decision has not yet come, and you think we all will be hungry? I'm waiting for the decision, and I want them to let you stay in here.'

'Ikaria, don't let your anger boil up. If the decision will be that of banishing me from the kingdom, then why do we need to wait for it?'

'Why do you think the decision will be of banishing you from the kingdom?' King Aseptus asked. He somehow sounded hurt and betrayed. I think the other two also noticed because they had a confused look across their faces.

I walked back to my seat between King Aseptus and Ikaria. 'That's understandable. Some of the people in this kingdom think that I'm unlucky for this kingdom. No one used to believe them. But after this incident, they will surely never want me to step in this kingdom.'

'Who says you're unlucky? We never lost any battle since you were born. Just because my daughter and you were born on the same day and my daughter turned out to be dead doesn't mean you're unlucky for the kingdom.'

He placed his hand on my head. 'I see you as my daughter. My daughter would've been of your age if she would be alive.' I turned my gaze to his face.

His eyes were wet, but he never let the tears spill down his black eyes. This was the first time I had been so close to King Aseptus.

His olive-coloured skin reminded me of a pony that Father had given me for a week to take care. It belonged to the royalties. My father was assigned to train him in a war horse. I named him Swifty. We had become very good friends. I wonder how he might be doing.

'Sir, how is Swifty?'

'The horse!' He laughed. His laughter echoed in the room. I was longing to hear this kind of laugh.

He continued, 'He is doing very well.' I felt as if I were talking to my father. My thoughts shifted to my father. How will he react when he comes to know about all this?

'You should come sometime to meet him. He is as swift as air. I must say you chose the perfect name for him,' King Aseptus said, diverting me from my thoughts.

'Sorry to say, but that would be nearly impossible. I'll be leaving this kingdom by tomorrow or so. I think.'

'Airis, why do you have so much of self-revulsion in you?'

'You are mistaken. I am not the one who hates me. People in this kingdom don't like me.' All of a sudden, I found my pale palms interesting.

'How will they like you until they know you? I've seen you. You always stay reserved with yourself. Or, should I say, occupied with thoughts.'

'Sir, I have a simple rule in my life. Don't let anyone enter in your life who is selfish, hypocrite, and pathetic. Whenever I look around the school, everyone is filled with these negative emotions. So I can't help but stay reserved with myself.'

'Well, um, I think we should go,' Ikaria said in between.

'Not so early. They'll be gathering the subjects, and it will take a lot of time to accomplish the task. Till then, we can talk about Airis and her capabilities.' Did I hear something wrong? Are my ears stuffed? Did King Aseptus actually say that?

'I thought sorcery is only allowed to the ones who are royalties or warriors.' It is not that I don't want this newfound ability if people accept me the way I am. I am just . . . curious.

'Everyone who has sorcery can use it only if they utilise it for the benefit of people and not for themselves. Melancus was using it for himself. He was changing or the correct term would be sorcery was changing him.' His tone somehow turned darker, and so did our room. I cleared my throat for King Aseptus to come out of his trance and stop affecting my house.

'Anyways, show me what you can do with sorcery. I'm eager to see.' King Aseptus was acting like Ikaria. He was using the same thought Ikaria had while she wished to see my capabilities.

I could see in the corner of my eye that Ikaria was giggling with excitement.

'I don't know how to use it.'

'Not an issue. Come with me.' King Aseptus took my hand, and to my amazement, we were heading towards the woods. Ikaria and Octavian were following behind me. We walked until we came to the waterfall. That was a long way.

'Now do as I say,' King Aseptus ordered. I simply nodded.

'Sit down and take deep breaths. Forget everything that happened with you in the last few days. Try to gather the power you have right now, and do anything you want to.' I followed the voice of King Aseptus.

After closing my eyes, I saw the incident where I met the klerites. I saw myself, the brave Airis, who wasn't afraid of a man-eating monster. Then, I saw myself changing the weather. The klerites were dead, and Ikaria and Octavian were by my side.

I knew what I needed to do. All of a sudden, I felt coolness around me. I opened my eyes to see water hovering around me like a transparent shield protecting me from the outer world. King Aseptus was smiling at me, and Ikaria was literally jumping with excitement. Octavian was gaping at me. With the gesture of my hand, the water hovering around me went into its right place.

Ikaria rushed towards me and hugged me tightly. 'You are special, Airis.'

'Sister, you're choking me,' I mumbled in her ear. She retrieved her slender hands and giggled.

'How did you feel, Airis?' King Aseptus asked.

'Divine.'

'Now I think we should go in the ballroom.'

My heart started pounding again. The decision was pending.

CHAPTER 11

We entered the ballroom with King Aseptus. All eyes were staring at me as if I had just killed tons of humans. I wished these eyes could disappear. King Aseptus led me to the middle of the room.

'Good morning, my dear people of Aegera. I'm sure you all know about Airis.' The silence broke out in murmurings.

'For those who don't know Airis, let me tell you she killed klerites with the help of sorcery. How many of you think she should stay?' Only a few held their hands up.

'What about the others? You don't want her to stay?' Everyone bowed their heads down.

'It seems you don't want to express your thoughts verbally. There is a box right there.' King Aseptus pointed towards the far end of the room.

'I'll arrange some papers there. Each one of you has to come and express your thoughts in that paper. Decision will be declared by tomorrow.'

Everyone obeyed King Aseptus's orders and moved towards the corner.

'Airis, you can go now. Ikaria and Octavian, you should also vote.' Ikaria and Octavian nodded.

'Go right in the house,' Ikaria ordered.

'I'll do as you say,' I said and left the ballroom.

CHAPTER 12

I had been sitting in my house for an hour, which seemed like ages. Does it really take so much of time to write on a piece of paper?

I wondered what the decision will be. The only possibility my mind told me was banish. Thinking so many things, I drifted into sleep.

'Wake up, Airis,' I heard a solemn voice.

'Let me sleep.'

'You've been in bed for too long. Get up.' Ikaria held me and helped me to get out of my sleep.

'It's still morning?'

'You've been in bed for one day. I thought you were unconscious.'

'Then why didn't you wake me?'

'I tried a lot. I slapped you almost ten times. I also made you drink water with lemon and salt. But still, you didn't wake up. Then I called a healer.'

I jumped on my feet. 'Slapping is okay, but how could you make me drink lemon water and salt? The last few days had been worse than nightmares and the decision—Ikaria, what's the decision?' Ikaria didn't say a word. I could see her beautiful eyes were swollen. I already got the message, but I wanted to hear from her.

'Please, say something,' I pleaded.

'No, she won't, but I will.' The Supreme Authority was standing behind Ikaria.

'I'm sorry, sister. I tried a lot. But no one listened.' Ikaria hugged me tightly and broke in a sob. I didn't know how to feel. Should I feel sad for leaving my family? Should I feel depressed for living all by myself? To be honest, I could only feel numbness taking over my senses.

'It's okay. Eventually, everything will be fine. Nothing bad will happen to us until we turn out to be impure from our heart.' I tried to comfort Ikaria.

I felt weird because Ikaria never cried. I had never seen my sister cry this bad. I stroked her hair tenderly. It was normally the other way around. I used to cry, and she used to comfort me. But the situation was totally different. Everything had been changing since my birthday.

Someone from the Supreme Authority cleared his throat. 'If you sisters are done with your spectacle, can we proceed? We all have a lot of work to do,' the greasy-haired man hummed.

'What did you just say?' I sounded threatening even with a bird's nest over my head and very sleepy eyes.

'Well . . . I . . . um . . . meant take your time, as much as you want. We will be waiting for you,' he fumbled with his words.

'There's no need to wait. I'm not a kid. I can find a place by myself. I don't need anyone to escort me out of this kingdom.'

'I think we should go.' The Supreme Authority rushed out of my house.

'Airis, you have been my best friend before being my sister. People don't know what you're capable of. When they'll know you, they'll regret their decision.' I ignored her words because every time I heard them, it gave me false hope, which I didn't want to dwell on.

'I'll go and pack my stuff,' I said formally.

I went in my room and took everything that I needed: clothes, books, and the last gift that Ikaria gave me, which was a necklace. I'm not a girly girl or interested in accessories. Ikaria told me about the specialty of any necklace. I still remember her words: 'When the beads of this necklace are together, they are useful for someone. But when the beads are scattered, they are not of any use. The same and simple rule should be followed by humans. The beads are the humans living in the world. They are not useful individually, but when they come together, they evolve by helping one another. The most important part of the necklace is this string. It's the only thing that holds it together. It is only unity that will hold us together. Sometimes people forget about the string that exists between them. Sometimes you yourself have to act like a string.'

I smiled at that memory. Ikaria was the only one who taught me moral values with such ease. The years had passed so rapidly I never had the chance to look back.

CHAPTER 13

I left Ikaria behind. Thankfully, Mother was not yet home. She would be broken if she came to know about this mess. She will come to know about it anyway, and I wish that she won't take it too hard upon herself.

I knew the place where I had to stay. My small forest house that Father gifted me. It was perfect except for the cleaning aspects.

I soon reached my temporary house. I cleaned it thoroughly. Now I needed some basic necessities for my house. There were three wooden chairs and a table. I needed a bed to sleep. I surely won't be going back to that kingdom at any cost. I decided to make a bed for myself.

I ventured out in the forest and got some wood for my bed. I evenly got the wood cut into a rectangle, tied some twigs at the end, and made sure that it was strong for a permanent bed.

I made containers out of wood and leaves. After all, I had to stay here for quite long. After settling everything in my house, I decided to stay beside the waterfall till the nightfall.

Soon I reached the waterfall. I sat beside the lake. It was so beautiful and serene in here. I gazed at my reflection in the water; I hadn't realised I did not see my reflection for many days. Last I saw my reflection, I was quite healthy. But today, I was so skinny and bony. My skin was pale and dry. My aquamarine eyes were trying to bulge out of their sockets. There were huge dark circles around my eyes. My ebony hair was straight and neat without a single curl. It had to happen. I haven't eaten properly since many days.

CHAPTER 14

I woke up and found myself beside the waterfall. *Oh god, I've ditched many meals.* I was hungry like a wolf now. I desperately needed something to eat, or I would die in hunger.

I ran up to my new house and expected some food to be there. I had stored it yesterday. I checked in the cupboards, and thankfully, I found some of the fruits that I had stored yesterday.

I ate contently. There was a knock on the door. No one knew the place where I live. Who can it be? This time, the knock was harder. I gulped and unlatched the door. To my surprise, it was King Aseptus.

'Do you mind me having a small talk with you?' He gazed right into my eyes. His coal-black eyes seemed to be penetrating deep into my soul as if trying to reach out for each and every secret.

'Yeah, sure. Please do come in.' I gestured him in my house. The wooden floor made a scraping sound whenever he walked.

'You've got a nice place to stay,' he said, looking around my house.

'Thank you,' I said.

'Why don't you come in Aegera?'

'I was banished yesterday from Aegera. How can you expect me to come?'

'We didn't banish you from Aegera. You can come anytime in Aegera if you want to. But you can't meet your family. That's it.'

'These details were not specified by the Supreme Authority,' I said with my arms folded.

'Probably, they forgot to tell you.' I opened my mouth to protest, but there was no sense in arguing with a king who was blinded by trust.

'Why did you decide to meet me?' I asked, trying not to be rude.

'I want you to join the school.' *Is everything a joke to this kingdom? The subjects kick me out, and the king invites me to visit again.*

'No one will accept me. The moment they see me, their first move will be to kill me.'

'No, they won't. You are the most powerful sorceress I have ever met. You changed the weather without being affected. Trust me, I have a problem doing so. You did that without training. Just imagine what you will do when you'll be trained. I'm here for you, Airis. I want you to train yourself.' It took me a while to understand his intentions.

'No, you're not here for me,' I boomed.

'What?'

'Yes. You are here just because you need another soldier in your army. I don't think anyone can ever think good for a stranger.'

'No, you're getting it all wrong, Airis. I've told you once and I'll tell you again. You're like a daughter to me. I want you to move ahead in your life. Think about it. I'll come tomorrow. I hope you'll decide till then.' King Aseptus left my house.

Even if King Aseptus was here for his selfishness—maybe he wasn't—the point is that he was right. *If I can do something big unaffected and without being trained, then I'm capable of reaching the sky. I should resume with my life. I should not be affected because of a stupid decision.*

The day passed in haze. There was nothing I could do. I wasn't permitted to meet anyone, not even my family. The only thing I was waiting was for the next day.

CHAPTER 15

I woke up early in the morning. My new independent life had already begun. Nothing can be so disastrous than living alone. There was a knock on my door. I knew who it would be. I unbolted the door. Just as expected.

'I hope you've made a right decision.'

'I'm ready to go to school.' King Aseptus's face lit up.

'Great! I'll drop you with my relite.' He gestured towards his relite.

I thought its design would be different. But it was the same compared to the other relites.

'Expected it to be different?' King Aseptus asked.

'Yes. I thought you are a king, so you will be having a different one from the rest,' I said.

'This is what people expect out of me. I'm not so arrogant and self-obsessed.' But whatever he did with Melancus was something that a self-obsessed king would do. He seemed to read my thoughts because what he said next didn't surprise me even a bit.

King Aseptus let out a deep breath. 'Melancus was changing, Airis. He was not under control. He needed to be taught a lesson.' I snorted. *A lesson? Then why am I being given a privilege to come and go as I please? That is certainly not banishment.*

'Do you think he can't make a living with the help of sorcery? He was fit and fine to keep himself on his track. I don't understand how banishing someone can help you. You are indirectly making that person hate not only you but also others.'

'He has understood the facts now. He has returned a few days ago and was found guilty.'

I couldn't help but regard my suspicions about it. He just returned and acted as if everything was normal?

'Where are you lost?' He waved his palms in front of my eyes.

'He is fooling you. He cannot be guilty,' I said seriously.

King Aseptus broke out in a laugh. 'Why are you laughing? It's nothing to laugh about. I'm serious.'

'You must have imagined, Airis. He has been with me for every second since he has returned.'

'Probably, he did something with sorcery.'

'No, he hasn't. I've got a mirror to watch him. It tells me everything about his actions. It's all your imagination. I think you should have probably reached your school by now. Climb fast.'

King Aseptus drove silently through the woods. None of us spoke a word. I was already feeling very foolish. We soon reached the school.

'Let's go,' he said while getting off the relite.

'You're coming with me?' I asked.

'Yes. Any problem with that?'

'It's not normal to have a king walk beside you at school. Not until you're a princess.'

'You are more than a princess, Airis.' King Aseptus smiled at me.

CHAPTER 16

We walked in the school and moved towards the dining hall. When King Aseptus pushed the doors open, everyone was seated in there. They were staring me as if they were having the biggest nightmare of their life. Who knows, maybe I was.

'Good morning, young students of Aegera,' King Aseptus echoed.

'Good morning, King Aseptus,' everyone replied. I looked around and saw Octavian. He didn't regard me and stared ahead at the superior middle-aged man standing beside me. I furrowed my eyebrows. What's wrong with him?

'I'm here for one of our talented students of Aegera, Airis. I think you all know her.' Everyone gazed towards the floor.

Good. They all were ashamed for casting me out of the city. They all knew what I was capable of.

'I want Airis to join the school again. She should carry on with her abilities and skills. I would also like to appreciate her for joining the school on her will after all these . . . unfortunate incidents.' King Aseptus began to applaud, and then he was joined by the rest after a few seconds. I'm completely sure that everyone in Aegera except for some of the students was happy with this decision.

'I'll leave now. Hope you all have a grand welcome for Airis.' He smiled at me again and left the dining hall.

My heart started pounding again. *These students are going to make my life miserable. That is for sure.*

'Welcome back, Airis,' Octavian said nonchalantly. I didn't reply. I couldn't understand the reason for him being so rude towards me.

He was followed by Cora. 'Welcome back, Airis!' She faked her surprise and hugged me. 'I hope you can survive the school,' she whispered in my ear so it was hardly audible to Octavian. She knew if Octavian heard her, he would surely say something that would get them on disliking each other, which either of them didn't want to happen.

But she was right. I had to survive the school without using sorcery. This might be an impossible task for me.

CHAPTER 17

It was sword fighting now. I quickly grabbed a sword from the heap and took my position. Sir soon entered the arena.

'Everyone, sit on the right of that tree.' He pointed to the far end of the arena. We jogged and took up our positions.

'I'll call you in pairs. Then you have to show me everything that you have learnt in the previous classes with a quick summary. Understood?'

'Yes,' we all replied.

He called out the pairs one by one. They all followed the words that our teacher had taught us. At last, everyone was done except for me and a boy I hardly knew.

'You come here.' He pointed towards the boy.

He numbly walked up to the arena. 'You'll show them with me.'

This is not fair! I was the only one left now. He did it purposely. 'Sir, but I'll be left then. I think we both can do it together,' I said in protest.

'How dare you argue with your teacher? And I don't think you need to learn sword fighting. You can live by sorcery,' he taunted.

Everyone giggled. I shot my head in the direction of the other students. The giggling died eventually.

'Popping out eyes doesn't help, Airis,' the sword fighter barked at me. Great! This was the only thing left. I have to survive through the school.

People have forced me to think: did I do wrong by killing those creatures that were here to harm them? The only answer my soul told me was I shouldn't have helped them.

CHAPTER 18

The next few days were the same. Each and every teacher taunted me for performing sorcery, which was wrong according to them. The students, as usual, jeered at me, and Octavian hardly ever had a decent talk with me. I gradually began to feel that I should leave this school and live in isolation.

While I was processing these thoughts in my mind, I didn't realise that someone had hurled water on me. It was Cora.

I was not at all surprised with this behaviour. I shot my eyes towards her, only to see Octavian standing beside her. He just had his emotionless mask on and stared at me.

'Stop glaring at Octavian. Talk to me,' she said in a bossy manner. She was a year older than me, but this didn't mean she could bark orders around and I would listen to it.

'I'm not interested to talk with you.' I tried to walk past her, but she blocked my way.

'Why? Afraid that Octave wouldn't help you?' she said and made a face, which made me laugh.

'Cora, you look so funny,' I snapped back at her.

'Don't talk about her like that again.' Octavian stood between me and Cora. Now I understood most of the things. Cora must have stuffed Octavian's ears against me, and now he was mad at me.

'Now who is taking help, Cora? You or me?' I smirked at Cora.

'Did you see that, Octave, the way she talks with me?' Cora said, leaning on Octavian. His grey eyes were now close to black. The hatred he saw me with was enough for me to burst into tears.

'Airis, you should be ashamed of yourself. Everyone is taunting you, and you're still standing here with pride. You should hide in your whatsoever house you are living in right now.' His words stung my heart like it was being ripped into pieces, but I didn't show any emotion. I wouldn't give them the satisfaction of knowing that they mattered.

Instead of being sad, I was angry. I clenched my teeth and walked past Octavian while bumping purposely past his shoulders and slapped Cora hard on her face so that the print of my four fingers was visible on her olive-coloured cheeks.

'Cora!' My *former best friend* paced towards her and helped her to stand up.

'I always wanted to do this.' I smirked at Cora. His vision was clouded with hate as he stomped towards me and clutched my arms, which would surely bruise in a matter of seconds considering the death grip he had on me.

'What's wrong with you, Airis? How can you hit someone so badly? I get it. You are jealous of Cora. You can't stand any beautiful girl in front of you,' Octavian muttered rudely and pushed me behind. *I stumbled, but I didn't fell.*

'I know what I feel about her. I'm not interested to tell you anything that I feel. You don't matter anymore,' I said with gritted teeth.

I left the dining hall soaked with water. I was obstructed by the teachers. 'You know, Octavian is right. You are not eligible to live with us. We are also not interested to teach you anything about these subjects. You are here just because King Aseptus wants to see you here, or else, we would have kicked you out of here the first time you entered the school after that incident,' the one who taught sword fighting said.

'Really? As if I'm interested to learn what you are teaching me right now. All you do is make me sit in your class. What do you think? I can't learn anything without you? I can do a lot of things that you can't. I challenge you. I'll learn everything I feel is important. Meet me after six months. Then you will know.' I laughed on his face.

I turned towards the dining hall where everyone was glaring at me. 'And one more thing for all of you to remember. You all would be dead if I didn't kill those creatures. Such a reward to save lives.' I gave a dim smile and walked away.

CHAPTER 19

Nothing was in its place. I didn't know what to do next. Everything was so quick that there was no time left for me to think over my life.

I sat down beside the tree that was at the exit of the school. I clutched my forehead and sat there with my dark thoughts. A firm hand grabbed my shoulder. I turned around to see who it was. My eyes met the familiar blue ones.

'What are you doing here? Don't you know you're not supposed to meet me until I'm banished from the kingdom?' I asked Ikaria, afraid that someone might see us together.

'I'm here to help you, Airis. I'll always be there for you whenever you need me. What happened?'

'I had a huge fight with Octavian. I don't think we will remain friends after this fight. Everything has been seized away from me since the society came to know about me,' I said while staring at my fingers.

'Don't let anything crawl over your path. They are jealous of you, Airis. You have something that is not easy to possess. Make sorcery your power. Practise so hard that people start respecting your skills instead of cursing them. Meet me anytime you need me.' Ikaria took my hands in hers and gave it a gentle squeeze. We sat in comfortable silence until I decided to break it.

'Are Mother and Father back yet?' I asked. She shook her head and gave me a look that said that they will come back soon and they will eventually face the truth.

'Take care of them, Ikaria. I will return in this kingdom only when I earn respect and direct my skills in the right direction,' I reassured her.

CHAPTER 20

Today was very exhausting. Everything was incompatible. But why did Octavian turn up? What did that girl stuff in his ears? Even if she did, this didn't mean he will listen and follow everything like a kid.

Now the reason also didn't matter. He said the worst thing that anyone could ever say to me.

'Airis, you should be ashamed of yourself.' *I already am, because I befriended someone like you.* 'Everyone is taunting you and you are still standing here with pride.' *This isn't pride, it is self-respect. People taunted me just because I am different and they are all the same. They know it very well.* 'You should hide in your whatsoever house you are living in right now.' *I don't have to hide, because people hide when they are scared, vulnerable and simply broken. I might be scared and vulnerable, but I am not broken.*—those words were running in my head like reminders.

This was not the correct time to make myself mentally ill. There were other things that needed to be taken care of.

There was a sharp knock on the door. I knew who it would be. I unclasped the door. As expected. King Aseptus.

'Can I take a few minutes of yours?' King Aseptus asked sincerely.

'Why not?' I invited him in my not-so-perfect house. He comfortably sat on one of the chairs. I sat beside him.

'I've heard that you've left your school.'

I rolled my eyes at him. 'I didn't leave the school. They made me leave the school. The main point is they don't want to teach me anything. Then why should I waste my time over there? Better if I stay by myself and do something productive.' King Aseptus was attentively listening to me. He cupped his chin with his hands.

'I can talk to them for you. I'll recruit the best teacher for you. Will you come back then?' he asked hopefully.

'What's wrong with the people of Aegera? First, I'm banished from the kingdom, and then you come and motivate me to join my school again, but those people don't want me in that kingdom again. Then why should I bother to go back?' I yelled on top of my voice.

'First of all, let me clarify that you are not banished. You are not permitted in the kingdom only for six months. You can come for the basic necessities like food only if you need. After six months, you can return to your home,' King Aseptus echoed down the small dining area.

'No one told me about that,' I mumbled.

'Probably, they didn't remember to tell you.'

'No. They didn't want me to know. Why can't you understand your employees clearly?' I asked. I could see uneasiness creep over King Aseptus.

What am I doing? He is the only one after Ikaria who supports me. Why am I trying to put him down? I am such a fool. I decided to change the topic.

'Are you here to get me back to the school?' I asked like a small kid who was afraid to go there.

125

'No. Not anymore. I was here to take you back, but the way they behave with you is not right. If you have decided to stay here, I'll not force you. I came to know about the challenge.' I flushed at the incident. It was not at all like me.

'Here. You'll need this.' King Aseptus handed me a big, fat, heavy, and beautiful book. It was totally plain navy blue covered in velvet. I ran my fingers through its glossy structure. The feel of it beneath my fingers was . . . different.

'What is this?' I asked without taking my eyes off the book.

'When I came to know about your challenge, I thought you'll need this book. It's not easy to learn everything by yourself. You need someone to guide you in the right path. You'll learn everything you want to right from this book. It includes every art of war. I'm sure it will help you a lot.' I wanted to hug this man tightly. He helped me without me asking for it. He is a great king.

'Can you do me a favour?' I asked, but my voice was muffled against his rock-hard chest.

'Yes. Please ask.'

'Don't let anyone come in here. Not even Father when he returns,' I requested.

'As you wish. I'll go for now. I'll come anytime if you need my help.' Surprisingly, he hugged me.

He mumbled something incoherent and instantly backed away. 'I'm sorry I got a bit emotional.' He dashed for the door, leaving me behind with confusion.

What happened with him? Why was he terrified?

The most important question was, why did he care so much about me?

There were so many unanswered questions. I wish Ikaria was here.

CHAPTER 21

Three months already passed by. I'd never been to Aegera in these months. Surprisingly, no one came to meet me. Not even Father. A part of me was hurt while the other part was relieved to not see the state in which Father might be. Probably, King Aseptus found a way to keep everyone away from the place where I live.

Many things had changed in these months. I knew how to control sorcery without letting it control me. I could command over any object I wished to. But still, it left me drowsy and exhausted. I was also capable of walking on water or in the air. Fire also least affected me.

The book that King Aseptus gave me was of huge help. I can say I was turning into a small warrior. *Ikaria would be very happy to see me like this. I wonder what their life is now. How they are feeling without me.*

Only three more months. After that, I will return and show everyone that I am not evil.

I practised sword fighting in the mornings, archery in the afternoons, and sorcery in the evenings.

It was almost evening. I took the book and walked towards the waterfall. It was time to get started with the practice.

I started right away with flying in the air. But this time, my aim was to fly close to the clouds. I closed my eyes and focused on getting myself lighter.

Gradually, I started rising in the air; and by few seconds, I was above the tallest tree in the forest. I could see Aegera. It seemed very beautiful from this view. The tiny buildings were sparkling in the evening, and there was hardly anyone seen outside their houses at this time. I closed my eyes and focused on the kingdom and tried to find out what they were doing. I could see that King Aseptus was with my father, sitting solemnly beside my mother and father. Surprisingly, my father was trying to comfort him.

'There is not much time left. She will come soon,' my father said. I didn't understand who *she* was that they were talking about.

'I know. But I have no idea what she'll turn into. You have taken care of her for so long. Thank you. And yes, get ready. We have to go for some work in Allekior,' King Aseptus said and exited my house.

My thoughts shifted to Ikaria. *Where is she? Is she all right?* I needed to find out.

I could see Octavian's house now. His house was tightly packed with people. There was Ikaria, my beautiful sister, in a green-sleeved gown. Octavian was standing beside her. Was he trying to stuff her ears against me?

'Why does she bother you?' Octavian asked. I clearly knew they both were talking about me.

'What do you mean? She is my sister,' Ikaria growled at him.

'But she is wrong. You should be enjoying yourself and—'

'Octave!' Cora stood beside Octavian and eyed my sister suspiciously.

'Why aren't you enjoying the party? It is the biggest success that you have ever achieved. You are promoted as the chief protector of Aegera. Come on.' Cora grabbed Octavian's hand and took him towards the treasure of food, leaving my sister behind.

This was enough. *They don't behave properly with Ikaria because she is my sister! That is ridiculous.*

Now it was time to touch the sky. I twirled in the air towards the sky and flew like a speeding wind. The air was working against me. I spread my hands and tried to absorb the cool air around me. Wow, this was so amazing. I doubt I'll ever get tired of flying in the sky.

I had not realised that I had almost crossed the boundary of the forest. I turned back to return to my house, but something caught the corner of my eye. There was a group of black figures moving towards Aegera. I concentrated hard. I could see a group of ten people covered in black from head to toe. They seemed like warriors to me. They were sitting in a circle.

'Ready to attack?' one of them asked.

'Yes,' all of them roared at once though it seemed a bit forced.

My eyes widened with realisation. *How can I be so stupid? They are the Pimarvs from Allekior.* Every time, they all were reincarnated after their deaths to take care of Duvollin, but their leader had turned greedy evidently, and now the rest of them had to follow what he said. Allekior and Aegera had been in a state of war since centuries. Now, the king of Allekior was taking advantage of King Aseptus being busy with people like me. I had to inform him before it's too late.

I flew on the top of my speed to Aegera. As soon as the palace came into view, I pushed harder; and as soon as my feet came in contact with the land, I sprinted towards the entrance only to be halted by a couple of glowering soldiers.

'What is it?' one of them asked.

I took a huge gulp of air and answered, 'The Pimarvs from Allekior are coming towards Aegera.' I panted.

'Do you think we will believe you?' one of them said. I wanted to come back with a sassy remark, but I didn't have time to deal with them.

'You have to. I'm serious. They are coming here.'

'There is no reason for us to believe you. Go back to your house, kid.'

'If you are not going to believe me, then I'll talk to King Aseptus himself.'

'He is not in the palace right now. He is out with some soldiers, including your and your friend's fathers.'

I didn't wait. I headed right towards Octavian's house. Now he was the only skilled warrior in the school who would be capable of handling at least one of them. I ran right into his house without knocking.

Everyone was staring at me with their mouths open. I saw Ikaria. She was delighted to see me. I smiled at her intently. She smiled back.

'What are you doing in my house?' Octavian asked.

'Yes. What are you doing here?' Cora asked the same question in her irritatingly high-pitched voice.

'I am not here to talk to you, grumpy swine.' I rolled my eyes at Cora.

'How dare you talk with her like that?' Octavian bellowed.

'I'm here to warn all of you that the Pimarvs are coming right towards Aegera. Octavian, you are the only one who can handle them. Please come with me,' I pleaded.

'Don't listen to her, Octave. She is trying to call you in her death trap.' She laughed.

'Do you believe me?' I asked Octavian.

'No, I don't. Nor will I ever do,' he said through his gritted teeth.

'Then get ready to die.' I felt like crying. But this wasn't the right time to weep. There were a lot of things that needed to be taken care of. I flew back to the forest. I was left all by myself. One thing was for sure: either they will die, or I'll meet with the same fate. It's not that those ten warriors were very skilled. They were just crammed with abilities they can't handle.

I closed my eyes and prepared myself to face the Pimarvs. There was no weakness that I ever heard about the Pimarvs. It indeed must be difficult to handle them. *Should I try to create barriers? No. I'm not yet good at it. Probably, it won't even affect them.*

While I was thinking of a way to kill the Pimarvs, there was a soft rustling behind the bushes. *They are here.*

Two men jumped out of the bushes. 'What do you think? Should we start with her?' one of them said.

Don't know why, but I laughed. One of them cocked his head to right side and asked, 'What is there to laugh, girl?'

'You don't know who I am. Better if you don't mess with me,' I said calmly. I was shocked to see the serenity in my tone. A few seconds ago, I was afraid of these people, and now I was laughing and talking with them. Exceptional.

'Come on, pal, let's show her what we are.' They took their swords out slowly from their sheaths. The sharp blades were meant for me. Both of them charged together at me. I smiled wickedly at them. I effortlessly escaped their assault. I could see their eyes wide with amazement.

'Wrong blow,' I said loudly.

I took out the small pins from my sleeves. I hurled it at them. It perfectly pierced their arms. They were groaning in pain. This was the first time I was feeling amazing in the last three months.

Suddenly, those two men made an irritating sound, something like a housefly flapping its wings. There were more rustling sounds behind the bushes, and now all the Pimarvs were standing in front of me.

This was the correct time to use sorcery. Before I could do anything, one of them launched two big knives in my direction from behind. I could see that at the corner of my eye. It was easy to dodge them. I ducked down, but they somehow managed to pierce the back of my shoulder. I fell down to the ground in pain. My eyes widened with horror.

Blood was dripping like waterfall from my back. I felt as if a thousand pieces of glass were embedded in my back.

'This will be a lesson for kids like you to know our power. The knife I attacked you with is not normal. It eventually changes into small pieces of glass and multiplies. And also it never misses its target.'

I wished to kill them. But the pain and the wound were restraining me to do so.

'Why don't you get up and fight? Don't you have guts to at least stand in front of us?'

This was enough. Despite the pain, I stood on my feet and turned my gaze towards the man who was speaking to me.

'Yes, this is the spirit! Cheer for this girl, pals.' He tried to make fun of me.

I cocked my head to one side, and then the weather turned windy.

'Airis, stop it!' I heard a voice from a distance. The weather was back to normal.

I turned around to see who it was. Octavian and Cora together on a horse. I would've considered them both a perfect couple if they weren't so frustrating to handle.

'Cora, wait here,' Octavian ordered Cora. He ran towards me. 'Why do you always change the weather?'

'That's none of your business. Get back to your house with your grumpy, pig-like girlfriend,' I said rudely.

'I'll deal with you later on. First, these men should be thrown out.' He took his sword out from the sheath.

'Got your mates with you. We are scared.' They all laughed aloud.

'You guys don't even know about jokes.' I smirked at them.

One of them gestured towards us, and one of them jumped on Octavian, and the rest were staring me.

'What? Do I look funny?' I asked.

Now the rest were coming towards me. I took a step back, and then the weather was turning windy again. They ignored the wind. I turned the weather stormy now: heavy rain, high-speed wind, and lightning. I motioned every drop of water that had fallen until now. They worked on my gestures. Lucky me! I forcefully motioned the water towards them. My aim was to make them stay in water until they suffocate.

'Airis! That is enough! You'll kill them,' Octavian rumbled behind me.

I didn't listen to him. I concentrated hard on giving them pain. I had to return what they had given me. Octavian shook me, breaking my concentration, causing the water to fall; and then all of them were free.

'You will pay for what you have done, kid,' one of them said while coughing.

'As if I am afraid of you,' I said through my gnashed teeth.

They all took their belongings and moved away back to Allekior.

CHAPTER 22

'Cora!' Octavian cried.

I turned around to see what happened to her. She was lying on the ground. She must be unconscious, scared of what she had seen right now.

I jogged towards her. 'What have you done to her?' Octavian sounded terrified.

'What do you mean? She is scared,' I replied nonchalantly, not caring about his so-called future wife.

'That's all because of you,' he snapped back.

'First, let her drop back to consciousness,' I said rudely. People always know how to accuse me. He shouldn't have brought her here in the first place.

Octavian lifted her in his arms. 'Do you know a shelter nearby?' he asked me.

'Follow me,' I said. I took him in my forest house. This would be probably the first and the last time I am helping people like them. The ones who are not grateful instead full of hate when I help them. I didn't even know why I am doing this.

'Here.' I motioned towards my small bed. He carefully lay her down.

'Got a nice place to stay.' He suddenly thought of being gentle with me.

'Whatever.' I was not interested to talk with him. I still didn't forget his words that stabbed my emotions. I walked out of my house and stood at the front porch. Octavian followed me. Couldn't he pick the hint?

'Why did you walk out?' Octavian frowned at me.

'I thought you both need some privacy,' I said without looking at him.

'You are still mad at me,' Octavian beamed.

'Does it really matter?' I asked.

'No,' Octavian said, trying to keep his voice as cold and distant as possible, but he failed miserably.

'Don't you want to know the reason?' he asked.

'Not interested. Take your girl when she'll be fine, and don't dare to come this way again in your entire life left to live,' I said lamely.

He grabbed my elbows and made me stand in position. 'What is it?' I hissed.

'Look at you. You have changed so much,' he said apologetically.

'That is none of your concern, and you don't have to apologise for that.' I rolled my eyes at him.

'Airis, look at you. You are changing. The last time I saw you, you were so thin and fragile. But now, your skin, your eyes—they look so beautiful.'

He raised his hands towards my hair. I leaned back towards the wall. 'Ouch!' I cried. I forgot about the shards of glass sticking behind my back.

'What happened?' he asked.

'I—'

'Octave!' Cora cut me off. I was thankful to Cora for the second time. She came and grabbed Octavian's hand and then took him in my room and closed the door.

I sat there with my eyes closed for a few minutes. I was trying to get the small pieces of glasses from my back with the help of sorcery. But it was of no use. I was not able to concentrate because of the pain.

Cora opened the door. I turned back to see Octavian staring at me with hatred again.

'Octavian, I need your help,' I requested.

'And you think he will help you? That is impossible. You can do whatever you want to.' Cora made a face again. I laughed.

'Don't you dare laugh again,' Octavian scolded me. As if I was scared of him.

'We are here to tell you that it's in the middle of the night, so we will be staying at your house to spend this night. You can manage in your dining hall.' Cora smiled at me. *They think they can get away with that?* I marched up to her and looked her straight in the eye, ignoring the excruciating pain in my back.

'This is my house, and you better listen to me, or I won't regret slitting your throat open. Is it clear?' She seemed unfazed about my recent threat and whined like a little child to Octavian.

'Airis, you—' Octavian was about to start tampering me about how I shouldn't try to harm his beloved Cora, but I didn't let him.

'Don't you dare tell me the dos and don'ts! You have lost that 'privilege' a long time ago.' I took a deep breath to control the faint wrenching in my heart. 'I am sorry for using such words on you. I owe you both an apology. No matter how rude anyone is, I shouldn't change my personality and act like a total stranger.' I didn't believe myself for the impending message I was about to convey. 'Since you have already been familiarised with my house, feel free to choose any room you want to. Since you can't go back and you need special offers, I'm letting you stay in my room,' I said in a sickeningly sweet tone. They were too stunned to say anything, so they just sauntered away in my house. I always had doubts on my mental state and now they were confirmed.

I sighed and sat on the front porch. *What have I done to lead a life like this?*

I sat on the front porch and tried to remove the pieces of glass with my hand. In a few minutes, a heap of pieces of glass coloured with my blood were present beside me.

I was not strong enough to walk back to the house by myself. I decided to spend the night beside the front porch.

'Airis, wake up.' I opened my eyes. Octavian and Cora were sitting by my side. They were looking at me apologetically.

Well, only Octavian was, but Cora just played along. She wouldn't even care if I die.

'Both of you, I don't like this stare.' I rolled my eyes at them.

'Why didn't you tell us?' Octavian frowned. I raised my brows questioningly. The least they can do was talk to the point.

'Your back and it's bleeding profusely.' He gently dabbed my wound with a warm wet cloth, resulting me hissing in pain.

'Relax. The cloth is dipped in the lake of healing plant,' he assured me.

'Leave,' I managed to say through my gritted teeth.

'We can help you now. We are not going to leave you until this bruise is sore.' *Why is he being so kind towards me? This lad needs to get his thoughts and priorities straight.*

'Even I tried to help, and what did it result in? I was partly banished from the kingdom.' I let out a humourless laugh.

'It's funny how helping can be considered as an act of threat,' I concluded. He didn't say anything for a while. What was even there to say?

'Can I talk to you for a minute?' Octavian asked with hope. I just nodded. He looked at Cora with pleading ogles. She squinted her eyes as if trying to understand the nonverbal gesture he wanted to convey. Cora huffed and left us alone.

'I just want to explain my behaviour towards you.' He suddenly seemed interested in his palms.

'Look, Airis, I love Cora, and she doesn't like you at all. I just want to make her happy. Our friendship seemed to disturb her a lot. So I had to do it for her. I was wondering. Maybe we could get back like we were before those incidents. But in front of Cora, we must stay aloof,' he stated. I slapped him. He held his cheek in shock. I was also surprised at my own actions, but that's not exactly my mistake. He provoked me.

'You think that low of our friendship? I hate the fact that you were once my best friend,' I seethed.

'Try to understand, Airis! I want us to be friends again. I don't want to lose you or Cora. You both are very important for me... You know you can't ignore me. You'll come back eventually, and after all, you are quite vulnerable at this stage,' he reasoned.

'You are an abominable hypocrite. And what makes you think I'll come crawling back to you? I may be vulnerable, but I have dignity that is missing in Cora. I don't want to see you ever again.' I stomped and tried to walk away, but he caught my arms and made me face him.

'What happened to the naïve Airis I used to know?' he asked.

'She grew up,' I answered without an afterthought. He let go of my arms and stood there awkwardly.

CHAPTER 23

Soon I reached my house. Yesterday, there were a lot of things that happened. All I want to know is about the girl my father and King Aseptus were talking about.

Probably, they were talking about an animal. Who knows? But the way they were talking, it sounded like they referred to me.

There was a knock on the door. It had to be King Aseptus. He was the only one who frequently visited me.

I opened the door. Men covered in black were standing in front of me.

'Who are you?' It was just a normal question that turned out to be ruder than I expected it to be.

'We met yesterday. Thirteen of us had a great time together,' one of them said. His voice sounded familiar. He reached down for his sword, and before I could comprehend, it was shoved in my gut. I cried out in pain.

'Didn't I tell you that you'll pay for what you have done?' He twisted the sword in my stomach. The pain was unbearable. I felt as if someone was trying to rip me into two pieces. He pulled the sword out of me. I fell to the ground.

'That boy said she is very strong. I proved him wrong.' He chuckled.

'Who?' I asked with great difficulty.

'Melancus.' He smirked and walked away.

I lay there motionless without speaking a word. Blood was dripping from my body. I was waiting for someone to come and help me out of this situation. My death was near. Gradually, I floated into unconsciousness.

CHAPTER 24

The thoughts of Pimarvs didn't leave my mind. The scene where those two men tried to kill me drifted in my brain. Everything was vivid and clear. When I woke up, I could hear people calling for help. I rushed to Aegera. I saw everyone dead in front of me. I sprinted towards my house. But it's too late. Ikaria, Mother, and Father were lying dead on the floor.

'No!' I yelled. I was sweaty all over and was panting badly. I looked around myself. I was not in my house or my father's house. This place was probably of royalties. The room was very huge, undoubtedly equivalent to five times of my bedroom. Its floor was of silky marble. The curtains in front of me were of velvet.

Suddenly, a thought struck me: *Am I in Allekior? They'll kill me if I stay any longer.*

I tried to get up, but my stomach was paining. I anyhow stood up and charged towards the door. I noiselessly closed it behind me.

'You are awake?' I heard a familiar voice.

'Ikaria?' I stood, gaping at the beautiful brunette.

'You can't move like this. Come on. Get back to bed.' She grabbed me by my elbow and shoulder.

'Am I in Aegera?' I asked.

Ikaria began to laugh. 'Of course you are in Aegera.'

'Why didn't I die?'

'King Aseptus found you soaked in blood. He got you here for medical attention.'

'I have to get back to my house.'

'No, the period for banishment is completed.'

'Wait a minute. I have been unconscious for three months?' My eyes widened in horror. 'How is it possible?' I said under my breath.

'The sword damaged some internal organ of your body. It took time to heal.'

'So . . . what do I do next?'

'Airis! You are back to normal. It's pleasant to see you . . . alive.' King Aseptus entered the room and sat beside me.

'Thank you for saving my life.'

'Don't mention it. You should start with your practice again. Come on. There is someone dying to meet you.' King Aseptus grinned at me.

Who can it be? Father, Mother, Octavian, or someone new?

'Yes. He is right here.' King Aseptus gestured towards a boy in the garden. His back was turned towards me, so I couldn't see his face. He was tall, muscular, and his hair was ebony black.

'Go.' King Aseptus pushed me a little so that I stopped taking his support and walk by myself. I walked up to that boy.

Singh

'Hi. I'm Airis.' The boy turned to face me. My breathing hitched. His green eyes held me in place as the corner of his mouth turned up, forming a beautiful smile. He knew how to charm girls.

Melancus. He is back.

'Airis, I had been waiting for you.' I took two wobbly steps backwards.

'Are you okay? Have I scared you?' he almost whispered.

'No. I am surprised to see you after such a long period of time.'

'What are you two sorcerers talking about?' King Aseptus interrupted us.

'Nothing much, King Aseptus. I think I'll go.' He now faced me, and my heart skipped a beat.

'Nice to meet you, Airis. I hope to meet you some other day.' He gave a big innocent smile.

'He is so well mannered and gentle. The girl who will marry him will be very lucky,' King Aseptus said while looking at my direction.

CHAPTER 25

After taking permission from King Aseptus, Ikaria and I headed towards our house. We remained quiet for most of our walk. We both would glance at each other once in a while and smile as if nothing ever happened. It was the comfortable silence when endless blabbering doesn't explain anything and silence is the only explanation for everything.

'How have you been?' Ikaria asked finally.

'I don't know,' I answered honestly after a while. She sighed, and the realisation dawned upon me that she just wanted to make a conversation.

'How much had Aegera changed in three months?' I asked.

'You have no idea. People hardly glance our way, and talking with us seems like an act of bravery,' she kept on complaining as if there was no tomorrow.

We soon reached our destination. I sighed in relief as my sister's rambling halted abruptly. Mother and Father were sitting and discussing.

'Father,' I said slowly. Mother and Father turned their eyes towards me. They were relieved and happy and engulfed me in a warm hug.

'Airis, we have desperately been waiting for you,' my mother murmured against my hair.

'So have I.' I felt a rush of emotions in me. I was so relieved to see them.

They released me. 'Welcome back, Airis.' Father caressed my cheeks.

CHAPTER 26

For the next one week, Mother, Father, and Ikaria forced me to narrate every incident that happened to me in the forest.

I told them everything except for the fight that I had with Octavian. When I told them about the encounter with the Pimarvs, they were curiously asking me what I did. How did I defeat them?

I also illustrated to them everything that I had learnt so far in sorcery. Ikaria was very happy to see my developed skills. Gradually, everything was back to normal. We never talked about the banishment again.

The only thing that Father was concerned about me was that I never wished to go to the school again. I told him the reason several times, but he didn't seem to listen. At last, Father won, and I lost. I reached the school and started with my classes. The first one was archery. I was the first one to enter the arena. I sat in the corner so that people didn't notice me.

'Good morning, children!' The teacher came in with a fresh attitude. He didn't seem to notice me.

'Get in the line. I will teach you how to aim only with the help of hearing.' Everyone scampered without spotting me. I didn't join the line. There was meaning of standing in the line, knowing that sir would not let me practise in here. I stood away from them in the corner of the room, busy in my own thoughts.

'Excuse me!' someone said behind me. 'Do we especially have to invite you in the line?'

I turned around to show myself. Sir was holding the arrow in my direction. He left it unknowingly I could tell. I halted it in the halfway. Everyone widened their eyes and stared at me as if they had just seen a ghost. I dropped the arrow with the motion of my hand.

'Sorry,' I muttered. They didn't say anything. They stood the same way for a few minutes.

'Can you say something?' I asked.

'Beautiful,' one of them said.

'Huh? What are you talking about?' I asked.

'Children, get back to practise. Would you like to join us, Airis?' sir invited me in the group.

'Thank you for asking, sir, but I have my own stuff to work out with.' I tried to sound gentle and calm. Sir nodded in my direction. The actual problem was I already learnt these things in the forest with the help of that book.

'All right, kids, we will continue tomorrow. Stay like good children in the dining hall. No games with food,' he warned.

Our batch was the first one to enter the dining hall. I sat in the far corner of the hall. Soon, everyone entered the dining hall. They all were staring me. I grabbed some fruits from the treasure of food.

I caught Octavian's gaze on me. He waved at me. I waved him back. Holding grudges towards someone when he was trying to be diplomatic was kind of . . . wrong. Cora was sitting beside him. She too was gaping at me.

Is it something about my face? Have I done something wrong? I wanted to crawl under the table. I felt so embarrassed. Soon I was finished with my fruits, I decided to leave this school for some time. The best way to make myself feel good was to visit the waterfall. I flew the whole way till there.

Soon I reached the waterfall. It was so beautiful and serene in here. I gazed at my reflection in the water. Last I saw my reflection, I was skinny and bony. But today, I was so fresh and healthy. My skin was pale and smooth. My aquamarine eyes were glistening in the reflection. There was no sign of dark circles around my eyes, which once made me feel like a ghost. My ebony hair was now slightly wavy at the end.

I wonder, *Is this because of my old diet I've been back to? Or the reason is something else.*

CHAPTER 27

I had no idea about how long I had been sitting in here. I decided to fly back to school. I entered the dining hall. It was completely deserted. I had sword fighting now. I hurried towards the arena. It was also vacant. I sprinted towards the archery room. No one was there. *Where have they gone?*

'Is someone there?' I echoed. Uneasiness was crawling over me. I ran back towards the arena. I grabbed two swords.

I checked everywhere in the school. No one was there. I decided to check the backyard of the school.

My feet were rustling against the dry grass. I entered the backyard. There, I could see all of them. Students were sitting and watching me hopefully. The teachers were tied up against the tree trunks. Octavian was barbed with iron chains. He was struggling to free himself.

What is going on in here?

I tilted my head and concentrated on the chains. Soon, Octavian was free. He was rubbing his wrists. I moved on towards the teachers. They were also free now.

Octavian rushed to my side. 'What have you done, Airis?' he asked.

'What do you mean?'

'There was a troop of soldiers from Allekior searching for you.'

'Why? What have I done?' I panicked.

'How will I know?' He shrugged.

'What do I do now?'

'Get out of this place as fast as possible. We will take care of them.'

I turned around to get out of the school. There was already a troop standing in front of me.

'Nice to meet you, Airis,' one of them spat. He moved towards me. I was not at all scared. This was quite normal for me. Fretting over the situation and then handling it as if it was nothing.

'May I know who you are?' I said calmly. I could see Octavian raise his right eyebrow in my direction. He too must be surprised to see the way I was talking with the soldier.

'I am the chief general from Allekior. Anyways, it doesn't matter who I am.' I gave a dim laugh. *First, he introduces himself and then says that it doesn't matter.*

'Why do you need to meet me?'

'You are so naïve.' He smirked at me. 'I am here to offer you to join Allekior.' I could see that the weather was turning a bit windy. Sometimes I was not under control. Octavian shook his head in disapproval.

The weather was stormy now. I tried my best to control the weather, but I wasn't successful. Weather was like the definition of my mood.

'Airis! Enough!' I could hear Octavian behind me. I tried that only the troop was affected by the weather, not the others.

I turned around to see if it worked. I was surprised to see a barrier behind me. I was surely not the one who did that. I looked around me to see who it was. Melancus.

What is he doing here? Who told him?

He walked up to me. 'Are you okay?' he asked with concern.

'Yes.' I was held by his captivating green eyes. *Are all sorcerers very good-looking?*

'Are you listening to me?' He shook me by my shoulders. I nodded.

'Airis.' Octavian came to my side.

'Who is he?' He frowned at Melancus.

'He is Melancus,' I said without looking at Octavian.

'I think you both need to be left alone,' Octavian said and walked away.

'So . . . um . . . I'll see you some other day.' I foolishly smiled at him.

He walked out of the backyard.

We all were seated in the dining hall. I could say by looking at all of them that they were stunned.

'Airis!' I heard someone call me.

'Are you okay? I thought they might have hurt you. If something bad happened to you, then what will I do?' King Aseptus said in alarm.

'Nothing will ever happen to me. They were normal soldiers, and you look so terrified as if they just tried to kill your daughter.' I bit my tongue. I can be very stupid at times. *Learn to control your tongue,* I scolded myself.

'I've told you many times. You are like a daughter to me.' He stroked my hair.

'Thanks,' I said.

'For what?' he asked.

'Everything that you ever did for me.'

'You don't have to be thankful for that. I was just helping. I will be with school's Security Council. Tell me whenever you have to go.' I nodded.

When King Aseptus went in the corner to take his seat among the soldiers, my sword-fighting teacher came and stood in front of me.

'What is wrong with you?' he roared at me.

'But what have I done?'

'How dare you argue with your teacher?' he said with arrogance.

'You are not my teacher anymore. You all have lost the respect that I once had for all of you,' I almost whispered.

He raised his hands to slap me, but it stopped in the midair. King Aseptus was standing by my side.

He was so fast! I didn't even notice him.

'Don't you dare talk to her like that again! She is my daughter. Do you get that? Anyone who will ever behave with her in that way will be severely punished,' King Aseptus echoed in the dining hall.

CHAPTER 28

After a hectic day, we all returned to our houses unharmed. My family was concerned for me. I tried to tell them nothing will ever happen to me, only if they listen. Father and Ikaria understood my point, but Mother didn't want to listen. At last, she announced that she will talk to King Aseptus about my safety.

I was sitting in my bedroom and thinking about King Aseptus. *The way he reacted today was as if I was actually his daughter. But he already told me that I am like a daughter to him as far as I remember. He has been visiting me for months now. He must be emotionally attached to me. Probably, I make him remember of his daughter. I can't tell. His expression changes rapidly whenever he spots me.*

'Not able to sleep?' Ikaria sat beside me.

'No. The day was extraordinary,' I replied.

'There is something else troubling you. What is it?' She jumped right to the point.

'Today, my sword-fighting teacher was about to slap me. But King Aseptus didn't let him do so. He announced in front of everyone that anyone who tries to treat me that way will be severely punished.' I hid the other part.

'What else?' She caught me.

'He considers me as his daughter. He said that in front of everyone.' Ikaria gasped.

'He actually did that?' she stuttered and blinked her eyes several times.

'Yes. I don't know why he did that.'

'Your teacher was about to slap you. King Aseptus tried to help you. Don't overthink.' She stood up to leave the room.

When she was out of the room, she popped her head in. 'I'll see you tomorrow, Airis. Goodnight. Don't overthink.'

It didn't matter whatever she said. There had to be some reason.

CHAPTER 29

I woke up early in the morning. The rays of sunlight were hitting the floor of my room and motivating me to get up. I walked into the kitchen and grabbed anything that could satisfy my hunger. It has been days since I had proper food made by my mother.

I ventured out of the house. It was still dusk. I could see the pinkish-coral sky above me. I sat on the front porch, wondering about the talk that I had with Ikaria. Everything had been rapid and sudden in my life.

'Airis.' I felt a firm hand on my shoulder. It was Mother. Her blue eyes were wet.

'What is it, Mother? Why are you crying?' I asked her.

'Come in. We all have to talk.' I frowned.

'It is very important. King Aseptus will be arriving shortly. Come on.' I followed her in the house. Father was anxious. He was pacing up and down the main room. Ikaria was sitting with her fingers crossed.

What is going on in my house?

'What's wrong?'

'You'll know everything, Airis. We will tell you. You had to experience too much at a very young age. You were not the one. I am sorry.' My father fell down on his knees and buried his face in his hands. Mother rushed to support Father. I had never seen him like this since the last few days.

'Can someone tell me what happened?' I was panting badly because of the confusion. *What do they need to tell me?*

There was a knock on the door. King Aseptus was standing happily on the door. His excitement faded when he saw the state of my father. He entered my house and gently placed his hands on Father's shoulders. 'I'm sorry, Ranik. I never had the intention of doing so. I have myself been waiting for her. She has to return now. It was for her own good.'

'I know, sir. You don't have to apologise.' Father controlled himself and stood up to meet King Aseptus's gaze.

'We will have the gathering today evening. Please come and tell her everything.' He looked with sympathy at me. I am sure he was trying to fight back his tears. King Aseptus left our house.

'You are the biological daughter of King Aseptus,' Mother admitted. Those were the only words to let my good morning turn into a bad one. I stood with my mouth open. I felt as if someone had control over me and didn't let me say anything. I had lots of things filled in me right now.

'I knew it!' Ikaria said beside me. I turned my eyes towards her. If she knew, why didn't she tell me? Why didn't anyone tell me?

'Say something, Airis.' Ikaria stood beside me for my support.

'Why? When? How?' I said with my voice hardly audible.

'Aegera and Allekior had been enemies since centuries. It was obvious that the child of King Aseptus will also have sorcery in his or her blood. When you were born, there was an attack from Allekior. They were here to get hold of you. He was afraid that they would kill you or maybe use you against Aegera. He decided to change you and the daughter that my wife gave birth to. She was born dead.' Father sighed.

He continued, 'We exchanged children without anyone knowing about it.'

'I see. That's why Airis looks a lot like Queen Astrea,' Ikaria added.

'I look a lot like Queen Astrea, but this doesn't mean I am their daughter.'

'Do you remember Swifty?' Father asked me all of a sudden.

'Yes.' I frowned.

'Why do you think I'll give her to an 8-year-old girl?'

'Because you wanted me to take care of her.'

'You are really very naïve. I wanted you to bond with her, to know how to control a horse.'

'But . . . why me? Why always my life takes turns like these?'

'Everything has a bad side and also a good side. Aegera needs their princess back.' He patted my head.

CHAPTER 30

The day passed in a haze. I wished that the time would have stopped wherever it was. I didn't want to go with my biological parents. I wanted to be with my foster parents, the ones who had always been with me, supported me when the society didn't accept me. I was lost in my thoughts. But my actual parents were right in their place. Slowly, tears started flooding down my cheeks. I never got the reason for crying.

'Airis! Are you ready?' Mother asked me from the main room. I wiped my crocodile tears and grabbed the gown that had been sent from the royalties.

'I'll be there in a minute,' I yelled back.

I didn't get a proper look at the dress in the morning. I changed and gazed at the reflection of the gown in the mirror. It was magnificent. It was overall a purple satin gown. The sleeves were very different from the normal ones. On the right side, there was a clustered net sleeve; and on the left side, there were strong heavy purple gemstones, guarded by small pieces of diamonds. There was a loose chain of small diamonds hanging around my waist. The cloth below the waistline was completely straight. There was a slit in the right side of the gown starting an inch above my knee.

'Airis, are you done?' Ikaria popped her hair in my room.

'Yes,' I replied.

'Wow! You look beautiful,' Ikaria beamed, checking me from head to toe.

'But there is one problem.' She frowned at me.

'What?' I said while taking a look myself in the mirror.

'You didn't make your hair,' she said and placed her hands on her hips.

'This is okay, Ikaria,' I said, touching my hair. I braided my hair without leaving any hair out of the braid.

'Come. Sit here. I'll do your hair.' She grabbed me by my elbow and made me sit on my bed.

'Now don't move,' she ordered.

After a few minutes of redoing my hair, she was done with my hair. 'This is what the princess of Aegera needs. See yourself.' She stepped out of my way.

I couldn't take my eyes off myself. I never felt so beautiful. She made my hair into a bun, leaving a group of strands of hair in the front, which came into fluffy and soft curls. I turned around and hugged her tightly.

'I love you, sister, and I'll really miss you.'

'I'm not going anywhere. We all will be in Aegera. You can visit us anytime you want to, and you are choking me right now. Let's go. We should reach there as soon as possible. I can't wait to see everyone's face when they come to know about you.' She giggled.

CHAPTER 31

We reached the ballroom within time. There was no one in there except for the royalties and a troop of soldiers.

'Welcome, Airis. We have been waiting for years for this day,' King Aseptus echoed in the hall.

'Astrea is longing to meet you. She never saw you since you were . . . exchanged.' There was a deadly silence in the room. I broke the silence.

'Can I meet Queen Astrea?'

'Call me Mother now.' I heard a bold voice behind King Aseptus. I saw a woman in about her late 30s. She was a lot like me: her eyes, hair, skin—almost everything. She smiled heartily at me. She began to walk towards me. She had a very elegant walk. I never saw anyone walk so beautifully.

'I'm so happy to meet you, Airis. I had just heard about you from your father, but I never got to meet you. I have been waiting for you like . . . eternity.' She hugged me. I could feel her heart pounding rapidly. All of a sudden, I realised how difficult it must be to live without knowing their only daughter is alive. She released me.

'I think you ladies need a room,' King Aseptus said.

'Yes, we do.' Queen Astrea motioned towards a room upstairs the ballroom.

She moved towards my mother. 'Thank you for everything you have done for Airis. I owe you my life.'

'It was my duty to take care of her. I wasn't the only one who took care of her. Ikaria has the biggest right on Airis. She taught her everything that took. She always motivated her to use sorcery.' Queen Astrea turned her eyes towards Ikaria.

'You have got such lovely eyes, dear,' Queen Astrea said to Ikaria, who was now blushing.

'Tell me, what do you need? You have done so much for my daughter.'

'I want permission.'

'Permission?' Queen Astrea sounded puzzled.

'Permission for meeting Airis.'

'You don't have to ask for that. You can meet her whenever you want to. After all, you are the ones who supported her all the time she needed me.' There was silence again in the room.

'The guests are here,' King Aseptus said behind the closed door of the room.

'Let's join the party.' Queen Astrea almost jumped with excitement. I also stood up with her to move out of the room. 'No, Airis. You have to stay here,' she told me to sit down.

'Ikaria, you wait with her for a few minutes. I'll tell you when to come.' Ikaria nodded. She turned towards me and smirked when she noticed how anxious I was.

'Nervous?' Ikaria asked me.

'A lot,' I answered.

'You don't have to be nervous. Trust me, the guests will be nervous when they'll see you. Cool down.' I obeyed Ikaria like a good sister. Nevertheless, she was right. The ones who discarded me off should be nervous.

'Ladies, gentlemen, and children of Aegera, I, King Aseptus, have called a gathering for one of the young talented students. Airis, who was recently ordered to stay away from Aegera just because you all were not comfortable, is among us all. I hereby declare that, henceforth, no one will ever accuse her of anything. No more discussions will be held on these subjects. Sorcerers will live with harmony in the place they want to live in. I invite the young, beautiful, and talented girl Airis.'

Ikaria and I exchanged looks. It was show time. I could hear applause for me. I gathered my strength and stood up. I was relieved that Ikaria was by my side. We both started walking. We both climbed down the stairs. Everyone was gawking in our direction. Had the hairstyle been damaged?

I turned my eyes towards Ikaria. She shook her head, denoting that there was nothing wrong with me. King Aseptus rushed to my side.

'I would like all of you to tell your views verbally about Airis living in our kingdom.'

The Supreme Authority was the first one to speak about me. 'I would just say Airis is not capable of living with humans. She threatened me.'

'My sister didn't threaten you. She just expressed her views. That is not called threatening.'

'You should know the difference between expressing views and threatening someone. When you come to know, teach it to your sister.' I was about to say something in my defence, but King Aseptus didn't let me.

'Stop, both of you,' he hollered. 'Now, Jerkin, tell me, if instead of Airis I would be the one to speak those words to you, then how would you take it as?'

'A warning,' he replied without thinking.

'Exactly! You have to think the same way about her.'

'But why should I? She is a mere bad luck for our kingdom.'

'No, she is not!' King Aseptus raised his voice. Everyone stood silent. 'She is my daughter, the one that Astrea gave birth to. I had exchanged her to protect her from Allekior,' he declared it publicly.

'I don't think I need to give any further explanations. Please enjoy the party now.'

CHAPTER 32

Queen Astrea took us out of the ballroom and then to the backyard. *Why does a backyard attract people so much?* It was decorated with flowers, leaves, and candles. There were other students talking among themselves in groups. Queen Astrea left us by ourselves in the backyard. Ikaria was fine but was very anxious. I felt something bad was about to happen.

'Here comes our centre of attraction,' someone said from behind. Everyone erupted into laughter. They didn't hear the announcement. They had played many pranks on me. Did it really make a difference if I play one? But first, I will eat something. I was very hungry.

I walked towards the treasure of foods. Everything was present there—everything that I loved. I felt a hand on my shoulder.

'Why did you walk away? Why didn't you tell them who you really are?' Ikaria asked.

'Just wait and watch.' I took a sip of cup. Whatever it was, it tasted delicious. The tangy flavour of this drink was whirling in my mouth.

In the corner of my eye, I could see Cora with a glass of water. As expected, she hurled the water on me. I halted it with the motion of my hand. I didn't let even a drop of water touch me. Cora was standing shocked. Her plan had miserably failed. Instead of throwing it back at her, I gently placed it in the glass she was holding. She dropped the glass on her feet.

'Octave!' she cried. Octavian rushed to her side.

'Look what she has done to me.' His eyes turned towards me and widened instantly as they scanned me from head to toe.

'Wow, Airis, you look beautiful,' he complimented.

'Thank you,' I replied.

'Why are you complimenting her? Scold her. Shake her. Get some sense in her,' she ordered. Annoyance sparked in his face as soon as she told him what to do.

'I am not your servant, Cora. I'll do what I want to,' he snapped back.

Cora stomped her foot in anger.

'I guess they don't know about you yet. Someone ought to tell them.' He winked at me.

How did he know? He was not present in the ballroom. 'I told him,' Ikaria whispered.

'My dear friend, there is an announcement. Please pay attention.' Everyone stopped gossiping and fixed their gaze towards Octavian.

Cora rushed to his side. 'What happened?' Octavian asked under his breath.

'You are going to announce that we are getting married, right? Then, I had to come.'

'You are unbelievable, Cora. There is another announcement that I have to make.' Cora frowned at Octavian.

'Our Airis is none other than the princess of Aegera!' he thundered. Everyone began to gossip among themselves.

'What is it, friends? You can express your thoughts.' Octavian gazed at me.

'Why didn't you tell me that you are about to get married?' I elbowed him.

'Nothing was right between us. I thought it didn't matter if you didn't know.' He kept his voice small.

I had to say something that will cheer him up. 'Are you inviting me to your wedding? Or you think it doesn't matter?' I asked mockingly.

'Provocation is not my style.' He giggled.

'Are you two done with your gossip? People are waiting for answers,' Ikaria interrupted us.

'I don't think they have asked any questions yet.' Octavian opened his smart mouth.

'I have been doing the answering job. You didn't hear the questions.' Ikaria folded her arms and gave him a your-smart-mouth-doesn't-always-work look.

'I give up.' Octavian held his hands out.

'I think we should answer the questions,' I said while looking at Cora. She was burning with rage.

'I have a question,' Cora said beside Octavian.

'I would be a better princess than her,' Cora said. That technically wasn't a question.

'What makes you say so?' Ikaria asked.

'A princess has to be sophisticated. I don't think Airis can ever play that side.' Cora couldn't keep the sarcasm off her tone.

'A princess also has to be strong, which you are not and—' I held Ikaria's hands.

'I think she got it,' I mumbled under my breath.

'Anything you people have to say?' Octavian said aloud. There was no reply from the audience.

'Let's get started with the party!' Octavian and Cora rushed towards their group, leaving me and Ikaria alone. We both cornered ourselves in the backyard and talked about our days together. I remember when I was three, Ikaria used to read me bedtime stories regardless if she understood one. She always enjoyed being my elder sister.

'Can I join you, ladies?' I heard a gentle voice asking me. I was happy to see Melancus again.

'Please do. We will be privileged,' Ikaria said. He soon started conversing with my sister while I was just listening and admiring his thoughts.

What is wrong with me? Why don't words come out in front of him?

'Airis! Are you listening?' Melancus asked me.

'Huh?'

'Airis, are you okay?' Melancus shook me by my elbows.

I blinked several times. 'Yes. I am fine.' I could see Ikaria giggling.

'You sisters are quite affectionate about each other.' Ikaria and I exchanged looks. People normally didn't compliment us on our sibling bond. He just hit the right point.

'How was your banishment?' he asked me all of a sudden. I felt my hands clenched. I didn't want to talk about it.

'Tell me.' It sounded more like an order than a request.

'Not interested to share it with anyone,' I muttered. I walked out of the ballroom and flew right towards the waterfall. I sat there quiet and motionless for too long. I was totally blank; there was nothing I could focus on. *My life is so abnormal; nothing is in its right place. How do I change it? Right now, talking to Ikaria would be the best solution. It always is.*

I rushed back towards the ballroom's backyard. Something wasn't right. I shrugged off the feeling and searched for Ikaria. I spotted my sister standing all by herself and enjoying the delicious delicacies.

I beamed and walked towards her. Ikaria's gaze shifted to mine, and she smiled at me. All of a sudden, her expression drastically changed as she had a horrified look on her face.

I frowned and turned around, only to see an arrow heading in my direction. I caught a sight of a few soldiers and grasped the arrow before it could hurt me and threw it in the route of the soldiers. It took down two, and I smirked evilly at them. Now everyone was extremely quiet. The soldiers were cautiously moving towards me. An injudicious one had the guts to come running towards me with a sword. He flailed it towards me as I ducked in time and punched him right at his gut. It was strong enough for him to crumble down in pain. He cursed a few words while doubling over the floor. I bent down and glared at him straight in the eye.

'Maybe you should think before taking action. Plus, you should know not to mess with me.' I smirked cockily and stood up. Just then, I felt something sharp strike the back of my neck. My vision turned blurry. I felt like someone had just made me run a mile after abstaining of food for a few days.

'Airis!' someone yelled. It sounded like my family. I tried to get back to my senses and keep my eyes open, but I failed miserably. I stumbled over my own feet and lost balance. Someone caught me in time. All I could remember before passing out was mesmerizing green eyes.

CHAPTER 33

I opened my eyes in a completely different room. That's when I realise that my arms were chained and I was completely helpless. The incidents that took place last night returned to me. My eyes roamed across the room. There was utter darkness. That's when my eyes fell upon a human figure sitting right in front of me. He must be the one who got me here. Meanwhile, my eyes adjusted to the darkness.

'You're awake?' my captor asked.

'What does it look like?' I retorted back.

'Quiet aggressive, just like I've heard,' he commented and leaned towards me.

'Shut up before I rip your head into pieces. My hands are chained, not my skills. I can kill in the worst ways with just my stare,' I threatened. He gave out his sinister laugh. I was confused. I just warned him, and he was cackling like a maniac.

'Do you think I'm a fool, little princess?' He laughed again. I wanted to say yes, but I kept quiet.

'This is the Infesten Tower of Allekior. Does this ring a bell?' He got up and left the room.

I was legitimately feeble. There was no hope of me getting out of here without someone's help or if I was not restrained like this. This tower was coated with infesten, hence, the name Infesten Tower. This term means no sorcery. If I tried to do anything, it would harm me in return. I gave up struggling and tried to remain motionless. I wish Melancus was here to get me out of here. He was just so perfect in every single way. I let out an audible sigh. Just thinking about him got my hopes high.

The creaking of door got me back in reality. My captor walked in with a tray.

'You haven't eaten anything for a long time.' He sat in front of me.

'Here.' He shoved the tray in front of me and lounged back in his seat. Even though he couldn't figure out my expressions in the dark, I raised my eyebrows questioningly at him. I huffed in annoyance at his stupidity.

'How do you expect me to eat when my arms are chained?' I asked and rattled the iron chains like a kid. He stood up from his chair and released my hands. I rubbed my wrists with my icy-cold fingers.

I dragged the tray towards me and glanced at my captor. He stared at me as if I were a prize. I took in a deep breath and charged at him. I pushed him off his chair and punched him straight at his jaw, knocking him down in the process. I ran out of the dark room, trying to find a way out. I found a staircase and climbed down. There was a metallic door right in front of me. I ran towards it. Before I could reach there, a litror screeched and stood right in my way. I took back a few steps as the creature lowered its head, resulting in its horns aiming in my way.

The litror charged at me. I ran towards it and took a huge leap in the air and stepped on its bulky head. I landed safely behind it and opened the door and closed it behind me. I leaned against the door frame and slid down against it towards the ground. I sighed with relief. This was one of the strangest days of my life. I stretched my aching legs and let out a stifled yawn. My energy was reducing, and my body was getting sore. No matter how hard I tried, I couldn't get up without support, let alone walk.

'Airis?' I heard a familiar voice ask. I snapped my head up only to meet with Melancus's green ones. He walked towards me and helped me up on my feet. I noticed a huge army behind him.

'How did you find me?' I asked.

'This is the only place as far as I know in Duvollin to keep sorcerers. Are you all right?' he asked with his deep husky voice. I blushed a little regarding the proximity we were in.

'Yeah, I'm fine. I'm sorry you have to see me like this. I mean, I look like a ragged torn-up creature,' I rambled on, which I usually do when I'm nervous.

'You look adorable, Airis.' He flashed his famous heart-melting smile. He drew imaginary circles against my lower back to get me calmed down.

'You are simply gorgeous. I like the way you are, and no one is as beautiful as you,' he commented. I am sure my face must be turning beet red like a tomato.

'Th-thanks,' I stuttered. We stood and stared into each other's orbs for what seemed like eternity. I was the one to tear my gaze off and reduce the intensity in the atmosphere. I cleared my throat.

'Let's go.' He took hold of my hand and gave it a gentle squeeze. I liked the way his palm fitted into mine. I felt as if it was just made for each other. This moment felt seamless.

CHAPTER 34

Melancus and I teleported back in Aegera, leaving the soldiers behind. 'Your father must be worried by now,' he said more to himself. He tightened his grip on my hand and entered the palace. The familiar scent of sandalwood hit my nose. I licked my lips.

'Airis!' King Aseptus ran towards me. He embraced me as if there was no tomorrow and muttered something incoherent. He turned towards Melancus and patted his back.

'She wouldn't have reached here safely without you, my boy. Probe for any assistance.'

'I need a job, King Aseptus, but people are still scared of me.' He broke his eye contact and sighed with despair.

He continued, 'But I assure you I have changed.' King Aseptus thought for a while.

'Come with me, Melancus.' He turned towards me. 'Rest for a while. The news will reach to you shortly. They will lead you to your room.' He motioned towards the young ladies behind me and ruffled my already-unkempt hair. I simply nodded and followed the maidens.

I ended up in a huge chamber with beautiful and blue velvety carpets. There was an unconditionally huge bed that had space for at least five people. The walls were full of pictures of my ancestors. I felt like these walls were telling me the history of my family. There was a corner of the room where every type of weapon was kept. I walked towards it and skimmed my fingertips across each one, but they couldn't be compared to the gift Octavian gave me. I felt the corner of my lips lifting up at the moments I spent with my best friend.

'This will be your new room, princess,' one of the maidens pulled me out of my enchanted state and notified me.

'Thanks. I want to be alone for some time.' I gave a tight smile to them, and they soon sauntered away. I picked out an emerald-coloured dress with sleeves reaching till my wrists.

I cleansed the dirt I acquired from the Infesten Tower and decided to meet King Aseptus. I braided my hair and left my chamber.

After searching around for a long time, I dashed into King Aseptus himself.

'I was looking for you everywhere,' he stated. Melancus was standing beside him.

'I have news for you, Airis,' he beamed excitedly. I knitted my brows.

'Melancus will be your trainer from now on,' he stated. Melancus smirked at me. That was just the beginning when my feeling as well as my skills intensified. That was all because of one boy: Melancus.

It has been almost seven months since Melancus was announced as my trainer. Even though I didn't need one, King Aseptus insisted for my security. I was getting accustomed to the kind of living where I didn't have to do anything except bark orders at people. To be honest, this life is very difficult to lead. It's all about how you portray yourself in front of the subjects. You have to make them like you. It's like having a burden on your shoulders. I wish I could get back to my normal life. Just like people say, veracity is far from fancies.

Today is my sixteenth birthday and also the day when I'll be crowned as the successor of the throne. Everyone will be present to witness this great event. My maidens had completed my makeover. I almost felt like a doll being dressed up by little girls. Queen Astrea made me wear a silver ballgown with sequin work along the sides of the dress. My straight hair was now curled perfectly in a braid-like formation. Just then, King Aseptus entered my chamber.

'I wish to talk to Airis—alone .' Every maiden scurried away.

'It's time.' He smiled encouragingly at me. I walked towards him and intervened my fingers with his.

'With responsibility comes maturity and great power. You have both. I know this is the most logical decision I have ever made.' He kissed my forehead.

'This is the day everyone will remember,' I breathed.

CHAPTER 35

I stood with King Aseptus behind the curtains of the throne room. Melancus was standing in front of the audience as the soldiers were trying to get the commotion in control.

'Attention, everyone!' he yelled on top of his lungs. The chitchat stopped at once as they focused their gaze on him.

'Today is a very great day for us. Our beloved king Aseptus will crown our gorgeous princess Airis as the future heir of the throne! Let's show the colours of Aegera!' Melancus hollered. The crowd cheered and hooted for me.

I linked my arms with King Aseptus. He smiled at me as we walked down the carpet with dignity. We halted right in front of the crown. This is the moment.

'This is the obligation you have to carry for your entire life. Make your decisions wisely,' he said and lifted the beautiful tiara in his hands as if it were the most delicate object in the whole world.

'You have made me proud,' he whispered. He placed it on my head and the crowd burst into roars. I glanced at Melancus. He winked at me. I remained emotionless as I stared ahead at the crowd. Still, I could feel the colour rising to my cheeks.

'All hail for Princess Airis!' someone yelled. The voice belonged to Octavian. Everyone bowed down at once.

I cleared my throat. Everyone understood my indication and went back to their initial position. 'Please enjoy the celebration.' I gave them a tight smile.

After a few minutes, Melancus interrupted all of us yet again. 'I'm sorry to interrupt your talks. I think it is time for a small dance. So, everyone, search your partners because the night is still young,' he stated smugly as if he was up to something.

Everyone sauntered away to seek out their partners. The music started, and the couples began to dance around and enjoy their time. I noticed Octavian and Cora dancing together. He gave me a small smile, which I gladly returned while Cora, well, she was being Cora.

Someone cleared their throat behind me. I turned around to find Melancus staring right through my soul. I suddenly became self-conscious and dragged my slender fingers through my thick hair. I heard a deep chuckle coming through him.

'You look absolutely fine, Airis. There is nothing to be anxious,' he stated.

He cleared his throat again. 'Can I . . . no . . . yes,' he muttered something unintelligible as if he was having an inner battle with himself. At last, he looked at me.

'May I have a dance with you?' He held out his hand to me. I gladly took it. He kissed the back of my hand, making my cheeks turn slightly crimson. He halted right before the open area where the blackish-blue night sky was visible. We inched closer until our bodies interspersed with each other. His hands gently rested on my waist as my hands found a way to the back of his neck. We swayed to the beautiful music as I stared at the beautiful features, trying to memorise every part of his face.

The way his black hair ruffled against the cool breeze, the way my skin tingled with anticipation through the contact we were in, and the way his green eyes held so much of emotion that it was difficult to decipher any.

His hands slowly left my waist and travelled above and cupped my neck. His other hand tugged the strands of hair behind my ear and caressed my cheek. I gasped at the contact with his cold skin.

'Beautiful,' he whispered, but it was loud enough for me to hear. His hypnotising voice sent chills down my spine. The hand of my cheek left and went back on my waist. Our faces inched closer. I closed my eyes and puckered my lips. I could feel his body heat radiating.

'That was an amazing night!' someone's voice hollered down the throne room as the music ended. I opened my eyes and pushed Melancus away. I breathed heavily as the realisation dawned on me as to what was about to happen.

'It was a pleasure dancing with you,' I breathed out and turned around to walk away.

Before I could leave him, he caught my wrists. 'Airis, can I ask you something?' I winced a little at his strong grip. I turned around, and he let go of my wrists immediately.

'It's kind of . . . private.' He scratched the back of his neck. I scrunched my nose in confusion. *What does he want to talk about? Maybe he doesn't want to train me anymore after the little incident that was about to happen today or—*

I was pulled out of my own thinking world when he took hold of my wrist and guided me out of the throne room. I rubbed my fingers gently down my arm as the cold wind embraced my bare skin. I turned to face him.

'So?' I cocked my eyebrow at him.

'Well . . . I . . . it's harder than I thought it to be,' he muttered to himself and fiddled with his fingers. We stood there quietly as I impatiently tapped my foot. Melancus kept on muttering inaudible statements to himself. I was losing my patience as the time passed.

'Look, Melancus, get your words straight. We can talk about this later. I can wait.' I turned around to walk away. He caught my wrists yet again and pulled me towards him. My palms rested on his muscular chest, and his hands automatically encircled my waist.

'Just listen to me.' His green eyes were now unconditionally dark. I gulped. I've never seen him like this.

'I just don't know how to say it. I'm just not sentimental like other guys, so I'll ask you to the point. I love you. Will you marry me?' he asked with a slight smirk on his face. I widened my eyes.

'But King Aseptus and Queen Astrea—' He interrupted before I could finish.

'I've already asked them. They too want this to work. Now it's all up to you. I don't like to repeat myself, but I'm doing this only for you. Will you marry me?' he asked again. I looked deep into his green eyes. There was only one emotion visible in them: fear of being rejected and fraught. A grin broke out on my face.

'I'd love to,' I whispered. He laughed and twirled me around.

'This is the best day of my life.' He stated between his melodious laughs.

I felt uneasy all of a sudden. Something is not right. 'Stop.' I said. He noticed my bewildered expression and planted me down on my feet.

'Are you all right?' He held my face in his large hands. His gay face was now full of concern.

'Just peachy.' I faked a smile. He didn't seem convinced.

'I think we should join the event before your father sends his soldiers to find us.' I giggled.

I still don't believe this happened. I agreed to marry Melancus. Never in my life had I imagined that he'll love someone like me.

CHAPTER 36

We rushed back to join everyone in the throne room. I had not seen Ikaria in a while. I wondered where she was. Meanwhile, King Aseptus seemed distant today. I found him talking to Melancus at last. They both seemed worried. The colour left my face. Plus, I was already pale.

'I thought everything was under control, but it isn't,' King Aseptus blurted out.

'What are you talking about?' I asked. Melancus stared at him as if telling him to admit to me about everything going on in here.

King Aseptus cleared his throat. 'A troop was trying to attack us during dusk. I sent some of my men to gain control of the situation. I thought it worked out, but it didn't. They are now too close for our liking, and their numbers have also increased.' He sighed.

'Where are they now?' I asked.

'They are in this palace,' Melancus confessed.

'Our men are hunting them down. I guess we can handle it,' my father tried to convince me.

'You guess?' I snorted loudly. 'I want everyone out of here. No one is supposed to get hurt,' I demanded. King Aseptus and Melancus were quite flabbergasted with my sudden outburst and scurried away to fulfil my wish.

They returned after a few minutes, claiming that everyone was out of here now and those filthy people were caught and put up in the dungeons. I went back to my room and changed back in my comfortable robes. There was a sullen knock on the door. I jumped out of my bed and unbolted the door. I saw the familiar blue-eyed and brown-haired girl with a giddy attitude.

'Ikaria? What are you doing here at this hour? It's not safe,' I scolded her. She laughed and entered my room.

'Can't I visit my baby sister?' She pouted a little. I chuckled at her childishness.

'So . . . what do you want to talk about?' I asked and propped myself on my bed and patted the spot beside me. She sat beside me comfortably.

Her giddy expression suddenly changed. I couldn't muster out what she was thinking. I felt negative aura inflicting from her. *She wouldn't do anything to me. I'm her sister.* I shook my head at those silly and petty thoughts and reached for water at the far end of the table beside my bed. I poured some water in my cup and gulped it down. I placed the cup back on its place and took a deep breath. I have had an uneasy feeling since my crowning.

I turned around only to feel something sharp penetrating my stomach. I gasped as I looked at my assaulter: Ikaria. I staggered backwards and pulled the knife out of my gut. Ikaria stabbed me. My own sister attacked me.

'W-why?' It was the only word I could think of as the pain surged through my body and tears threatened to spill.

'I shouldn't say, but I'm jealous of you. You got everything I should ever get. First, my parents give you more attention than me. Th-they love you more than me. You are not even their real daughter,' she sneered at me. I could tell just by looking at her that she didn't wish to inflict pain upon me, but still, she did.

'Don't you remember the time we used to play together and care about each other so much? Did you just forget the time we spent together? Where is the old Ikaria I used to know?' I asked.

'The old Ikaria you used to know was a silly, stupid girl, but now I've grown up. You took Mel away from me.' By this time, tears were rolling down her cheeks and mine too.

'Mel?' I asked.

'Melancus, you ignorant fool. I'm talking about Melancus. We used to love each other so much.' A ghostly smile played on her lips. *She is lying, isn't she?* She was the one who told me that Melancus was a bad influence.

'But he left me-for you. He promised me he would break your heart, make you feel worthless. He broke his promise.' Her smile now completely vanished as she took menacing steps towards me.

'I don't believe you,' I implied.

'Well then, I think you should talk to Mel. He'll come soon,' she stated nonchalantly. On a cue, Melancus strolled in. His eyes widened with concern when they landed upon me. He broke into a sprint and cradled me in his arms, ignoring the presence of my envious sister.

'Who?' he asked me. I turned my eyes from Melancus to Ikaria. He followed my gaze, and as soon as they landed upon Ikaria, his lips were set into a thin line. He picked me up without breaking his eye contact with her. He laid me on the bed and turned towards her. He walked towards her, and to my utter shock, his pursed lips broke into a genuine smile as he snogged with my sister. When they broke apart gasping for breath, they sent a small smirk own towards me.

'What will the little princess do when everyone in the palace has been killed?' Melancus slowly walked towards me, and it took a little while for the message to sink down.

'You killed my parents,' I croaked out. He sat on my bed and tugged my messy black hair behind my ear.

'You see, I had to get back at this kingdom for what they did to me. I had to play with your little fragile heart for my love, Ikaria,' he spoke as if he had no choice. Instead of feeling broken and worthless, I was filled with anger. He played with me and also killed my parents. I didn't realise that fire was making its way around my palms.

'If I were you, Airis, I wouldn't do that regarding since we are covered with infesten,' Melancus mocked. My glare at him strengthened, and he immediately left my side and slipped his arms around my sister's waist.

'You are a smutty, obnoxious prick to the entire Duvollin,' I cursed at them.

'Looks like helplessness is affecting your mind, sister. So sad that you couldn't do anything with us,' she moped. I smirked sinisterly at them as I healed my wounds with sorcery. If they can be bad, I can be worse. I slightly cocked my head to the right side and let a small smile appear on my lips as the area around me was in flames. I was the only one here unaffected by flames. They both tried to find a way out, but I wouldn't let them go—yet.

'We were just playing a prank on you, Airis. You just took it seriously!' Ikaria yelled frantically as the flames were erupting with hunger to engulf them.

'Of course, Ikaria, since you stabbed me with a knife. Who thinks of a prank like that? It's truly amazing,' I muttered with dry sarcasm.

'You love me, Airis, don't you?' Melancus asked with hope glimmering in his eyes. This made me angrier. How could he? The yellowish-orange flames were now emitting blue. I felt powerful. I felt divine. The cries and yells of people were audible in my ears, but this didn't stop me. It served them right. Ikaria and Melancus were stupid enough to play with my feelings. The rest of them were also like those two traitors.

'Stop, Airis, you are killing the ones you are supposed to protect,' a serene voice called out.

I searched for the voice everywhere, but I couldn't find the source. 'Who might you be?' I asked with a tone of arrogance.

'I'm Palatina, the goddess of creation,' she seethed. Seems like she's infuriated with me.

'Don't you see? You're hurting everyone, even the ones you love and—' I snorted loudly on purpose to interrupt her.

'Yeah right—love. There is no such emotion because people have already set my thought in motion. That rhymed.' I chuckled wryly and gained my former posture.

'Humans are pathetic. They don't know the right way to live. I will teach them. Also, they need to learn a lesson. I'll show them greatness.' I gritted my teeth in anger.

'This is wrong, Airis. I agree they've inflicted too much of harm upon you. But mark my words: there will be no difference between you and the rest of them while you are literally trying to kill them. Greatness lies in forgiving.' Her voice was now nothing but empathic. This drew me on the edge. I don't like when people pity me. Even if they are a race of immortal beings.

'Just stop! Don't mess with my head here,' I yelled because I was angry. Angry at the fact that she was right. I wouldn't be different from the people who have tried to betray me. But I still loathed everyone. Her sweet talking wouldn't change my mind.

The race of humans will learn the right way to live, either willingly or forcefully.

'No, Airis! You shouldn't do this.' Palatina panicked.

'Too bad, I've already decided. You are an Elyrian. Shouldn't you be killing me by now?' I mocked her.

'I'm sorry, Airis, but I have to do this. I cannot kill you—for now. You are immortal concerning the control you possess over your skill and power, but remember you are forced to stay here—forever .'

'Your barriers won't hold me long, Palatina. You know I will return. I know someday I will. And that day will be the last day of freedom. I vow.' With my small oath, I was caged for a while. But that wouldn't be long, contemplating that I'm immortal and I have quite some time to try to be free. That sometime might persist. After all, I have forever, don't I?

What Is Aegera?

I was sleeping peacefully until someone jolted me awake. 'Wake up, Airik. You need to be active.' Palort was surely trying to wake me for the practice.

'Good morning, Palort.' I yawned.

'Nothing is good about this morning. Meet me in the library after your morning routine,' Palort grumbled. I was confused. His mood swings were difficult to understand.

I quickly ate my breakfast and made a dash for the library. There were two girls and Palort, deep in conversation. They were seated on a round table, and their proximity made me curious about their discussion. What is so important and confidential?

'We don't have time. He is a good sorcerer. We will manage,' one of the girls said.

'Forget about that—' Palort spotted me. 'Airik, we have been expecting you.' Palort gestured me to join the table.

I gently walked towards the table and sat between Palort and a chocolate-haired girl, probably Anedrin. Another girl was sitting next to him, his sister.

'Let me introduce.' Palort jumped.

'She is Princess Anedrin, and she is my sister Phileda.' I just nodded.

'As I was saying, there is not much time left. Something is wrong with Allekior.' I remembered the kingdom Allekior from the book I read last night. My intuition was telling me that I should tell Palort about the book.

He continued, 'I suspect that they have a base where forbidden businesses are being carried out. This kingdom anyways has the reputation of being illegal in every way possible.' Palort moved towards the massive cupboard at the far end of the library and took out a small box and returned to the table.

He opened the box and took out a small piece of paper. He exposed it to the three people sitting around the circular. I recognised it as the map of Duvollin. There were eight kingdoms. I analysed the map and then realised that there were only seven kingdoms, the eight one being the forest of Pamretol.

'According to this map, the base is right here.' He pointed at the far end of Allekior almost near the forest of Pamretol. As

I started going through the places on the map, I was a little shocked to not see Aegera anywhere.

'Where is Aegera?' I asked all of a sudden.

'Aegera?' Palort sounded puzzled.

'There is nothing as Aegera in Duvollin,' Anedrin spoke for the first time. Her voice was like every other child in their early teens I have met so far, but the manner she spoke was strangely composed.

'How is it possible? The book I read last night specified Aegera as a nemesis of Allekior.'

'Which book?'

'I found a book in the forest.'

'Where is it?'

'In the room I am living in.' The rest of them exchanged looks and dashed out of the room. I followed them. They were running towards my room.

'Get the book,' Palort ordered me. I searched for the book, but I couldn't find it anywhere. They were looking at me expectantly. Anedrin had an 'is he crazy' look while the twins stared at me with questioning gazes.

'It was right here. I . . .' I trailed off, not knowing what to say. It was obvious that they won't believe me. I slumped on my bed, clutched my forehead, and took a deep breath. *It has to be here,* I reassured myself.

'What did you read in the book?' Palort asked as he walked towards me and sat beside me.

And that is how I told them everything. They were listening intently until the end.

'What does this mean?' Palort asked.

'There is no kingdom as Aegera. I think this boy is hallucinating,' Anedrin answered. I might have a strong imagination, but this doesn't mean I'll hallucinate about something so vividly.

'We can't put a finger on it. After all, we are not sure,' Palort argued.

'I think we should meet Rimtzal,' Phileda said in between.

'What can he do? He is just an isolated old man,' Palort mumbled. His comment seemed to concern Anedrin as she gave him a death glare.

'He is our only hope,' Anedrin reminded sternly.

'Airik, Rimtzal was a protector once,' he told me and kept me included in the talk.

The Secrets

'Come on, Airik. We have to hurry up,' Palort said. Palort, Anedrin, Phileda, and I were heading towards the outskirts of Selemara. That is where we will find Rimtzal. We all had been walking on foot, which seemed like eternity. On the other hand, the three Selemarians were rather enjoying the walk. Not even a bead of sweat had formed yet while I was seating as if I had just been chased by a nasty dog suffering from rabies.

'How long will it take to reach his cave?' Phileda asked.

'We are almost there. Not more than a few minutes,' Palort replied. That was the only reply I heard since Phileda asked him the same question at least a dozen times.

Anything in Duvollin never failed to amaze me. People always walked barefoot without the fear of getting their soles muddy. When I asked this question to Palort, I felt as if I had just requested him to behead someone. At last, he answered my question, 'Being inadequate is better than being a sophisticated sovereign.' I didn't understand his simple statement back then, but now I do.

'We have reached,' Palort stated nervously.

'What is this Rimtzal like?' I asked as I noticed his hesitant approach towards the cave.

'I have never met him. He normally doesn't expect visitors.' Palort scrunched his nose.

'Why?' I asked.

'I don't think you would like to see infinite bones decorated all around.' Palort glanced at my shocked expression and chuckled. I gulped. *Is he serious? If it's true, then that's quiet inhuman. How can someone even live with animal bones around him?*

'Let's meet Rimtzal,' Anedrin interrupted my thoughts. Everyone was anxious except me because I was terrified.

'Seek me only if you essentially need guidance. If you are here to dissipate the knowledge, you will meet the same fate as the others who have earlier tried to squander,' an ancient voice thundered.

'What are we waiting for? Let's go,' Anedrin said. I didn't want to meet this Rimtzal guy. The description that Palort gave was awful.

'How old is he?' I asked out of the blue.

'Hundred seventy three,' Palort said casually. *Is it normal for people in here to live this long? Or the reason is because he is a protector?*

We all entered the small mouth of the cave. But it was big enough for all of us to squeeze in.

'I can't see a damn thing,' I mumbled under my breath. Actually, I was getting suffocated in here. I never revealed it to anyone I am claustrophobic.

I once told my only vulnerability to Jason. He made me hide in my cupboard and locked it. He told me to hold on for a minute, but I was struggling too much to free myself. He let go of me at last. When I asked him the reason for his senseless action, he said that he wanted to see the reaction of a claustrophobic person when gets out of a small area. I couldn't stay mad at my only friend for long.

I never thought about the orphanage in these two days. *Have they even realised that I am missing? Is Mr Gandhi happy that his prediction is true? Or is he mourning over his loss that I didn't help him? Did someone genuinely care about me at all?*

'What now? He is not here. Where is he?' Phileda asked, detaching me away from my thoughts.

'He is here. I am sure he is right here,' Anedrin said sternly. *Why does she need to be bossy?*

My fear was gripping me from inside. I know I was panicking, but I was trying my best to hide it. Except for my ragged breathing, no one can tell that I am claustrophobic. The darkness was gnawing me away from inside. I didn't know for how long I will be able to cope with this small space.

I wished there was light around me. Even a flicker of fire would be fine with me.

According to my wish, there was a flicker of light in some distance. Gradually, the whole cave lit up with candles by themselves. I felt as if someone had left me on a dating spot. I hadn't realised in the darkness that the cave was quite huge from the inside, and like Palort said, there were bones not lying but decorated in a fashion as if to warn everyone to stay away from this place or their bones will be the next to be used for a cave's interior.

There was a man sitting in the centre of the cave. He was neatly dressed in a dark-grey belronag. He was in his late 20s. His eyes were coal black like his hair. His skin was tanned. Overall, he was very handsome. Any girl would fall at his feet. He surely cannot be the 173-year-old Rimtzal.

'I am Rimtzal. Seek me only if you need.' He kept his gaze fixed on me.

I looked at him from head to toe. He certainly didn't look like a 173. I didn't expect him to look so . . . handsome.

'Then what did you expect out of me?' He smirked and seemed amused. I didn't even realise that I spoke my thoughts aloud.

'I thought you would be hunchbacked with long white hair and beard standing with the support of a wooden stick. But you are so young and handsome. It doesn't seem like you are about to cross two centuries,' I gushed out.

'Thank you for your compliments, Airik. But I think you should concentrate hard on acquiring the perpetual sword. I believe that you can do it,' he said in his bold voice.

'What is the sword you are talking about?'

'The perpetual sword. They didn't tell you about it?' He referred to the three companions with me.

'No problem. I will tell you everything you need to know. I would like to be alone with Airik. You all may leave now.' The rest of them left without protesting.

'Please have a seat.' He gestured a small log of wood, which came twirling in the air towards me. I sat on it.

'Would you like to have something?' he asked me.

'Thank you for asking. But I am all right.' His expressionless face was now unconditionally sober.

'Did I upset you?' I asked.

'No. Not at all. Whatever I am going to tell you right now is serious, so I was just trying to adjust the surroundings according to it.' Well, that's awkward. The surrounding seemed gloomy enough to me.

Rimtzal rubbed his palms and started. 'Let us start with the beginning. In the universe, even before anything was created, there was an eternal soul wandering in the universe alone without knowing anything about her past. All she cared was about her present and future.

'One day, she discovered that she could do anything she wanted to. She could create and destroy anything. She didn't like to live aimlessly. She wanted to do something new, something creative. Then she decided to make a new world for herself where she could live happily without wandering from place to place. She named herself Palatina and crowned herself as the goddess of creation.

'But the beautiful Duvollin and Elyria didn't satisfy her. So she made creatures like litrors, klerites, clerows, diorels, and many more to accompany her. But all the creatures used to set out in the dawn for exploring Duvollin and return in dusk in Elyria. Palatina was fed up with this behaviour. She created those creatures to accompany her, but they were busy with themselves. She created a fireball, which chased each and every creature out of Elyria.

'This fireball is none other than Phelonia, the goddess of sorcery. Palatina was very happy to have someone like her to accompany her. Meanwhile, in Duvollin, the creatures were getting weak because there was nothing to eat. Palatina and Phelonia together showed their kindness by making the barren land of Duvollin green with fruitful trees. Everything went fine in Duvollin and Elyria.

'One day, Phelonia dropped her sapphire ring in Duvollin by mistake. A fight broke out among the creatures. They were fighting over a piece of sapphire that fell down from Elyria. The fight was hurting every creature. Palatina and Phelonia tried to stop it, but there was no one who paid attention. They both unsuccessfully returned to Elyria. After lots of discussions, they both decided to create more of their type to stop the destruction. They created thirteen more Elyrians.

'With the fifteen Elyrians together, they stopped the fighting. But they were uncertain that this fight could start again. At last, they came to a conclusion to create creatures with capacity of processing knowledge much faster than the rest, the one who could oversee them, and then they made creatures that resembled their physical appearance a lot to the Elyrians. These creatures were termed as humans.

Each Elyrian created a group of ten humans. That made 150 humans for the beginning. You can come to know which human belongs to which god by their surnames,' he concluded.

'Really? I thought people in here don't have surnames.'

'They do have. But telling their names along with their surnames is considered as an act of arrogance in Duvollin.' *Act of arrogance? In that case, everyone on earth is arrogant.*

'Why?' Rimtzal scowled. *I should not have asked this question.*

'When you say your name with surname, you are revealing that which god created your ancestors. If you say that you are one of the Palatina's creations, people will surely think that you are boasting around about yourself. To stop this, we don't reveal our surnames, not until necessary. Any more questions?' I nodded.

'How do you manage to stay so young?' I asked in awe.

'It's easy. Eat healthy, practise every day and follow your good routine, and take care of yourself in every way possible. You will age very slowly.' I felt as if he was lying. There are many people who follow a fixed routine. Still, they don't have such a long-lasting life. They eventually die. I shook those thoughts away and concentrated on the talk.

'What happened next?' I asked.

'Humans forced Elyrians to swear that they will never interfere, only suggest to them. They can interfere only if it is very necessary. Humans were not taming. They were ruling the creatures. Gradually, they began to divide Duvollin

201

in kingdoms. They were multiplying in numbers. According to their vow, Elyrians could not intervene in their affairs. With the increasing time, humans were developing themselves in every way possible.

'Then one day, this girl Airis you read about in the book, infuriated with people around her, decides to teach humanity how to live. This meant she would cause destruction, not like the ones who started Buddhism and Jainism. In this case, Gods had to stop the girl for Duvollin to exist. But this girl is so powerful that she can lure anyone in Duvollin. She is the reason why beautiful Aegera is now a dense forest and is known as Pamretol.'

This is it? That girl is simply sitting in Duvollin for these many years, probably for decades or maybe centuries. No one knows about it? That is so absurd!

'Why don't people know about it?' I asked.

'Elyrians don't want them to know.'

'What do you mean by *them*? We are also humans. But we know almost everything about Pamretol.' I scoffed.

'We know everything because we need to know everything. If we don't know what we are dealing with, we can't fight with uncertainty. It is our job to keep King Phinogar in the stone. Besides, gods don't want people to panic that their end is confined in a forest. They should live with freedom.'

'Why do protectors exist? The so-called Elyrians can take anyone down. After all, they are gods.'

'Gods have lots of work to do rather than taking down immortal evils. When Airis was trapped in Aegera, the

Elyrians were sure that her powers would never work outside the shield they have created. But eventually, the shield was wearing off. The gods have no idea of how this happened. Probably, she found a way to diminish the shield. The gods are since then trying to get back the power of the shield, which will surely take many years. The way she controlled King Phinogar terrified the gods, and then the stone went missing. So they introduced protectors to take care that King Phinogar is not unleashed until Airis controls him.'

'Have you ever been there?'

'No. I never tried to. I was never like other protectors who would risk their existence to gain fame.'

'I heard that the protectors were siding with our enemies. Is that because they ventured out in Pamretol?'

'Yes. The truth is they were forced to venture out in Pamretol whereas some of the protectors were willing to go there.'

'How were they forced to go there?'

'They heard someone calling out their names, showing them everything that they desired.' I shuddered at the thought by being lured that way.

'How didn't you get trapped? Everyone has desires.'

'Everything comes from here.' He pointed towards his brain. 'If you have control over here, no one can ever lure you into anything. It all starts from whatever you crave for. They don't change you, but they just add fuel to your negative feelings,' he explained.

'Can they lure me?' I asked.

'Of course they can. You are a child with raging hormones and numerous desires. You also don't have good control over yourself. They can easily lure you. You need to learn.'

'Do they fulfil our desires?'

'Yes.' I felt a strange rush of joy in me. *What am I doing? I should not be doing this. Whatever they do, they cannot return me my parents back. Can they?* I shook my head.

'They can,' Rimtzal answered.

'Did you just—' he interrupted me.

'You are not the only one with abilities, Airik. You should control yourself. They can return you your parents, but it would be of no use when that girl would be destroying the world.' Rimtzal raised his voice.

He was right. After King Phinogar, there was probably no one who could match him. But still, he was being controlled by her. He almost destroyed Duvollin. Everything must be in a very bad condition that the Elyrians themselves had to come down and stop him from doing so.

'What about the sword you were talking about?' I tried to change the topic.

'The perpetual sword, the one you saw at Palort's house. It belonged to King Phinogar. It is a very special sword. When King Phinogar was alive, there was a very skilled craftsman. He used to make different kinds of swords, bows, spears, and many other weapons. He was fed up of making so many weapons he imagined a weapon that could turn into any weapon that the owner wished. He started with his work. The result was a very beautiful sword. But he couldn't come up with any idea of how that sword could turn into any other weapon only by its owner's wish. He decided to let it be that way it was. The sword turned out to be very useful. The metal balls attached to its pommel have the capability to increase and decrease their density when a person touches it. If the person is not able to lift the sword, this means that the density of the balls is high and he is not worth it. If the density is low, then the person is capable of handling the sword.

'And I am looking forward for you to be the one to handle the sword. It has more special features that you can ever imagine. Back to the story, the craftsman was satisfied with his new creation and decided to present it before King Phinogar. He was capable of handling the sword, so the craftsman gave it to King Phinogar and warned him that he won't be able to use the sword if he changes.'

'You mean changing from a gentle and calm person to a totally opposite one?' Rimtzal nodded.

'How does the sword judge?'

'It mainly judges on the basis of your soul. If it is pure, you can lift it but cannot use it until you are skilled in that art.'

'Were you able to lift it?'

'Yes. And I used it once. But it was quite heavy than a normal sword, so I decided to leave it.' He shook his head as if he recalled a very bad memory with the sword.

'Any questions?'

'Why do you have bones decorated around your cave?'

'It is a secret that I am going to tell you. They are animal bones. I need some protein. I hunt and eat. Besides, these bones help me to keep people away from here.' He winked.

'That is unusual,' I said.

'Anything else you want to ask?'

'Should I tell them everything?'

'Are you extorting me?' That is when I realised how my question sounded.

'No. I mean they will ask questions about the meeting. How will I answer them?'

'Use your brain and make up anything that is suitable and convincing. Your comrades are so impatient,' he snapped.

'Come in.' He returned to his grave tone.

'Sorry to disturb both of you.'

'No, it is fine. We both are through with our little talk.'

'So can we seek what we need to know?'

'Drawbacks of getting a human from the other world,' I answered spontaneously. I looked at Rimtzal. He was smiling at me. He was looking at me as if I saved him from doing a sin. Lying was a sin, but lying for someone's benefit cannot be a sin.

'So we are done for now. I guess,' Palort murmured.

'Yes. We should ride back to the palace. It won't be very uncomfortable. I have sent the horses back and replaced them with relites,' Anedrin said.

'Thank you for giving your precious time to us,' Anedrin said to Rimtzal.

'No offence. You can come whenever you really need my advice,' Rimtzal replied.

'We will go now. Thank you.' We were moving back towards the place where we came from. I was excited about relites. I had seen them a couple of times, but I really didn't know the way it worked. I was looking forward to ride it.

Suddenly, I felt something creep over me.

Don't trust anyone, Airik Patronus, not even the ones very close to you. The path of a protector is full of dangers and betrayal. And most importantly, keep your life a bit secretive, even from Delver, and be safe. Be conscious. Being naïve is just a way to get through the wicked world. I am looking forward to see you some other day and I hope you remember my words, Rimtzal boomed in my head.

Attack

We stormed out of the cave. It was close to noon. I could see four relites in front of me. I took the blue relite, Palort took the green one, Phileda took the crimson, and Anedrin chose the purple one. I never got to see a relite in these three days properly. The two-feet-tall vehicle was circled by a six-feet-long blue glow. Palort motioned me to enter the glow. I obeyed him and entered the glow. They sat on the fluffy 20-centimetre-wide black seat. I held the blue handle, and it automatically started and lifted me in the air. I think one foot above the ground. Then with the speed of light, the relite took off towards the palace. I could see blue smoke behind my trail. Within seconds, we reached the palace.

'That was . . . different,' I spoke. The twins smiled, but the arrogant young teenager remained laid-back. *Why is she so emotionless? What can cause a 12-year-old girl to possess such a level of indecorousness?* I shook my head, steered clear of the thoughts, and walked towards my new room with Palort.

'Rest for a while and get ready. I will familiarise you with this place,' Palort informed. I knew the fact that it wasn't a request but an order.

I just lay on my bed and replayed the conversation I had with Rimtzal. He masked his emotions in front of everyone, but when we were alone, he was a little more like himself. Honestly, I have no idea about his original personality, but when we were together, he was different and he seemed more at ease. Sometimes I could feel that he was lying to me, especially when I asked him about the secret for his youth. *Why are people so difficult to understand?* I groaned in frustration at the same time when Palort barged in with a banana smile on his face. I collected my emotions and counted from one to ten. Every time, this method calmed my anger. I stood up and brushed my belronag.

'Ready to go?' he asked.

'As ready as I will ever be.'

We were walking on foot, and I couldn't understand the reason for travelling on foot when we had relites. So far, we had just exited the palace and not spoken a word since then. The whole way, he would open his mouth to say something but close it again, probably trying to pick the right words. That's when I realise that he was not shy but antisocial, just like me. I smiled as I was grateful to know that there was something that was common in both the worlds.

'Where are we going?' I asked after deciding to break the awkward silence building around us. He seemed more than happy to answer me.

'You know it is just what friends do. Get to know each other and make their relationship stronger than it already was.' He grinned coyly and played with the strand of his shoulder-length blonde hair. *This is something I have seen only girls do when they feel shy or nervous. It seems like Selemara believe in equality.* All of a sudden, I dashed into something firm and fell down. I rubbed my forehead and stood up. Palort was laughing his heads off.

'I apologise for my clumsiness,' a babyish voice pleaded. My eyes widened when they fell upon a teenager, probably a few inches taller than me. He was no more than 14, but his height was intimidating. I swear my neck ached a little by looking upwards at his innocent face. *Is he sort of a giant?*

'Don't apologise, Verdin. He is, after all, our new generous protector,' Palort bragged proudly.

'Don't you think he is too young to guard it? He looks like a 15—'

'Sixteen,' I interrupted and then corrected him. He seemed amused.

'The point is that you seem quite young to protect it. The rest of the protectors were at least 21 when they were given the job,' he completed.

'He might seem young, but he is very mature and understanding,' Palort defended me.

Verdin just ignored his remark. 'What are you both here for?' he asked.

'You see, Airik Patronus is from the other world. He knows nothing about—' Verdin didn't let him complete.

'The prophecy wasn't gibbering. He is actually the one?' he asked with astonishment.

And that is how a few minutes passed. He asked me several questions about the place where I live until his friends pulled him off to play. Palort and I sat beside a nearby tree silently, just consuming the beautiful view in front of us. Children were playing with those peculiar crystal-like leaves, which would transform into sparkles and then into nothingness in a few seconds, women chattering away about how lazy their husbands are and how much their children cause trouble, and men returning from their exhausting day. It was as normal as I used to watch back in the orphanage. It is funny how the normal human tendencies remain the same wherever we go, no matter how different the place, customs, and traditions are. No matter how many similarities I come across, I don't belong here. I am supposed to live in the place where I was born. This just doesn't feel right.

'Why am I here, Palort? Why am I chosen?' I asked without turning my gaze towards him. I heard a deep sigh coming from him.

'Elyrians chose you because they know you are better than all those people out there. There is always a motive behind every action.' He smiled tightly at me, and I gladly returned it.

'Why is Anedrin so . . .' I trailed off, not knowing the right word to use.

'Distant? Egoistical? Mature? Emotionless?' he offered many phrases, and I had to agree that every term he used described Anedrin perfectly.

He let out a bitter laugh. 'She has been through a lot. I am not at all shocked at the way she acts. I know she is a child, but circumstances sometimes compel you to change, and you have no other option than to bow your head down before destiny.' He pulled his left knee towards his chest and rested his elbow on it.

'What had happened?' I asked cautiously after witnessing his outburst. He turned his head towards me and looked at me right in the eye.

'That's not my place to tell you. I am sure that Anedrin will confess it all to you someday. After all, you look a lot like . . . him.' His eyes watered a little, but they were gone as soon as they arrived. Who was he talking about? Whoever he was, my intuition said that he won't tell me and there was no use of asking him about it.

'I think we should go back. It's close to nightfall.' His voice cracked in the end, but he soon regained his composure. He needed someone right now. I awkwardly hugged him, and his arms soon wrapped around me. His grip literally squeezed the life out of me. His silent tears rolled down his cheeks and landed on my shoulders. After a few seconds, he pulled back and wiped off his tears and took a deep breath.

'I am sorry. I just lost control. I'll make sure it won't happen again.' With that, he was back with his old self.

The walk back to the palace wasn't as awkward as it was in the morning. We were joking around, and I now knew most of the things about Selemara. The ruler is the most eligible person in the royal family. They make the main decisions for their kingdom. Then comes the Supreme Authority. They can make decisions in the absence of the ruler and guide them when necessary. After that, we have a chief executor who makes sure that the army is properly trained and everything runs smoothly in the kingdom. It sounds very easy to handle, but it isn't.

We soon reached the palace. Phileda and Anedrin were chatting with straight faces, of course.

'I missed my favourite girls!' Palort exclaimed dramatically and rushed towards them. He hugged both of them but twirled his twin around. For once, Anedrin had a smile on her face—a genuine one. It suited her; she should wear it more often. On cue, her eyes met mine, and her smile instantly dropped. I was the first one to break the eye contact. *What makes her hate me so much?*

I sighed and walked away from them. *Why don't I belong anywhere? Even in the orphanage, kids thought of me as a freak. I was always jealous of Jason. He got everything he ever wanted, he was treated far better than me, he could easily make friends, and I had always been the egoistical and know-it-all friend of Jason. The only thing common between us was the absence of our parents.* I groaned in frustration. *What kind of friend am I? When did I stoop so low?*

'Why do you think so?' a sweet voice asked from behind. I turned around to see Anedrin staring at me with sympathy.

'What do you mean?' I asked in a fake firm voice.

'You just said everything aloud. And I have ears, so I couldn't help but listen,' she reasoned and rested against the trunk of the tree.

'There is nothing to say,' I mumbled.

'Maybe you should cry a little more often and let your anguish out. When you keep everything sealed in your memory, you worry too much, and this results in early death.' *Damn, this girl, she is very persuasive.* And I also knew for the fact that she wasn't sugar-coating me into telling her everything. She sat down on the sloppy grass and patted the spot beside her. I reluctantly walked and took the place she motioned.

'Have you ever felt worthless? Like you don't belong somewhere?' I asked her.

'Trust me, I do. Every single moment of my life,' she spoke nonchalantly.

'Why are you so . . . emotionless?' I asked without a second thought. She laughed for what seemed like eternity to me.

'What can I say? I've had a very rough life, and that is what makes me regret my existence, but I'll show my destiny that this is my life, and it has to work the way I want it to.' My brows arched upwards. *This girl is . . . different. She sure as hell has a very unique perspective.*

Suddenly, there was a rumbling noise from the ground as if an earthquake was taking place. But I was sure it was not a mere earthquake.

'Flowdge!' Anedrin screamed and stood up. I followed her deed.

'Wait a minute. I have heard it somewhere,' I knew and I am sure I knew this flowdge thing. I heard of it before. The twins came running towards us.

'We have to get out of here!' Anedrin ordered.

'Why?' I asked.

'I don't think you will love to be rolled to death!' she roared.

'I would have created a portal, but I don't have enough energy right now after training the soldiers in sorcery,' she gushed.

'In that case, we have only one option,' Phileda said. Three of them turned to look towards me.

'Don't look at me that way. I have never breached a portal,' I said and took a step back.

'We are not talking about breaching. We want to pass through it,' Anedrin huffed in annoyance.

'But I have never opened any portal.'

'It is easy. Just think where you want to go and work on it.'

Where would I want to go? The first place in my mind was Paris. I thought about Eiffel Tower. I waited for a few minutes—nothing. I was in the same place with my three companions fighting with a flowdge. It was not surprising that the three of them were jumping at one creature to kill it. It was over ten feet slender stick made of stone. There was no face that I could see, only three eyes in a line. Its eye was beady black and way too protruding. I was gaping at the creature. I had never seen anything like it. All of a sudden, it fell to the ground with a loud thump and rolled towards Phileda. She effortlessly jumped above the flowdge and landed behind it.

'How much time do you need?' Anedrin thundered.

'I am not able to do it,' I replied.

'Think of a place you know very well,' Anedrin suggested.

There was only one place that I knew very well: the orphanage. I focused on the orphanage's clothing shop, the only place that will be deserted right now. I could feel air sweeping me. I opened my eyes to see the circular portal trying to pull me in.

'Yes! I did it!' My holler was enough for the three of them to stop fighting and rush towards the portal. They sprinted in my direction and pulled me with them, leaving the creepy creature behind.

Lie Detector

'A little warning before jumping please!' I said in pain. I landed on my back. The pain erupted was hideous. Palort held out his hand to help me get up.

'Thanks,' I mumbled.

'Where are we?' Anedrin asked.

'Orphanage,' I answered.

'This is where you teleport us after thinking a lot?' Anedrin asked sarcastically.

'You said to teleport to a place I knew very well,' I replied, keeping the bitterness off my voice.

'I am sorry, Airik. I—' I interrupted Anedrin before she could finish.

'You don't have to be sorry.' This is what I don't like. I just don't like to be pitied by anyone. Whenever someone visits our orphanage, they shed their empty tears and show false sympathy towards us. Why can't anyone face the reality? We are nothing to be pitied about.

'No one should see you in these clothes. I think you all should change. Follow me.' Palort, Phileda, and Anedrin were following me in the orphanage's clothing shop.

I searched for three denims that would fit my new friends. Thankfully, I found their size in time. Now it was time for some T-shirts. I got a cool one for Palort, but I knew nothing about what girls liked to wear. I told them to choose one top for themselves from the girls' section. When we were done with the shopping, I told them to change in the trial room. I myself too changed back into my denim and T-shirt that I last wore when I was forced to teleport unwillingly in Duvollin. I came out of the trial room. They all took a few minutes to figure out to wear the clothes I gave them.

'Are you done?' I tried to keep my voice low. No answer. Probably, they were still trying to figure out a way to wear it. I heard the lock behind one of the trial rooms open.

'Is this the way I need to wear it?' Palort asked. The plain black T-shirt and denim suited him. He looked really handsome.

'You look amazing, Palort,' I complimented.

'Thank you.' He ran his fingers through his unkempt blonde hair.

'Is this okay?' I heard another question. Anedrin stepped out of the room.

'I am stuck!' I heard Phileda yell.

'Hold on, sister! I am coming.' We all rushed towards the trial room in which Phileda was stuck.

'You are not able to unlock the door?' I asked.

'Yes!' I could hear fear in her voice.

'Don't panic, Phileda. Can you see a small rectangular-shaped thing on the door?' There was no answer from the inside.

'Yes! There is a structure you are talking about! I can see it.'

'Twist it gently,' I ordered. Phileda twisted the doorknob and leaped out of the room and caught Palort in embrace.

'You were so scared, and you still are,' Palort mumbled.

'No, I wasn't,' Phileda said against her brother's shoulders.

'Come on now, siblings, we have to move before someone thinks there is a burglary going on in here,' I stated. Phileda loosened her grip on Palort. That's when an important thought struck me.

'Wait a minute. I have a doubt,' I said.

'What is it?' Anedrin asked.

'I have been in Duvollin for three days. Did they come to know that I am missing?'

'Of course they did notice,' Anedrin said casually. My jaw dropped. *What will I do now? I have to make up a story so that they believe me. If not, I am in trouble.*

'Listen to me carefully. None of you will speak a word. Let me do the talking. Understood?' The three of them nodded.

We all walked out of the clothing shop and moved towards the first building.

We were waiting in the first building for someone to show up. We had been sitting in here for too long and chatting about random issues. It was almost seven. I don't remember having such a lengthy talk even with Jason.

'Oh my god! Airik, where were you?' someone squealed. Mrs Quartz along with her colleagues was standing in the hallway. I gulped.

'I think I'll keep that story for another day,' I said humbly. Her eyes soon fell upon my three companions.

'Who are they?' she asked. Her gaze was filled with curiosity until they landed on Palort and turned into bafflement. It was obvious that she was confused with his different hairstyle.

'A long story, Mrs Quartz.' I sighed.

Every employee gathered and sat to interrogate me about my sudden disappearance and my three new friends with me.

'Four to five days ago, I decided to run away from the orphanage,' I started with my false story.

'Why did you suddenly decide to run away from the orphanage? Don't you like it in here?' one of the employees asked.

'No. I love this place. Half of my early childhood has been spent right here. But I thought I am 16, now and I'll be turning 17 soon, so I should know how to earn a living by myself,' I lied.

'Why did you suddenly thought that?'

'No, this was going on in my mind for many days. I just didn't get it into action.'

'What about them?'

'I found them during my journey. Three of them are orphans like me.' Anedrin glared at me.

'This kind of behaviour will not be tolerated, Airik,' Mr Abel warned.

'I am sorry, Mr Abel. I'll never do this again,' I apologised.

'All right then. Let's get started with the day. Airik, please tell them how the orphanage works,' Mr Abel ordered.

'Sure, sir,' I said sincerely.

'May I know your names and ages?' Mr Abel continued to talk while other employees left us alone.

'I am Anedrin, and I am 12,' Anedrin answered swiftly.

'Anedrin? That is an unusual name,' Mr Abel muttered.

'Actually, she is Infinity. We call her Anedrin. He is Paul, and she is Darcy.' I jumped before anyone doubted over us.

'I think it should have been the other way around. You should call her Infinity if her name was Anedrin. Anyways, Paul and Darcy look like siblings. How old are you two?'

'Yes, we both are twins. We are 16,' Palort said as if it was a heavy curse that made his life worse than hell.

'Who is older?' Mr Abel asked with interest.

'Unfortunately, she is older.' Palort sighed.

I always thought that Palort was older than Phileda. I didn't know so much about my companions even though I was the one who stayed longer with them rather than Mr Abel. I don't know how people manage to do this. The way he conversed was so friendly and gentle.

When Mr Abel left us alone, I had to face the wrath of a 12-year-old girl. 'The names you have picked are not at all suitable. I am Infinity, he is Paul, and she is Darcy! On top of that, you state us as orphans like you?' Realisation struck her at how rude she had been until now. She massaged her temples and spoke profanities under her breath.

'I am sorry for being so rude,' she apologised.

'Don't be. You were angry, and you just spilled out your thoughts. It's totally fine. It happens with everyone.' There was heavy silence between us.

Whatever she said was true. I was a measly orphan unlike them, and no one can change the fact. But now there were many problems that I needed a solution. All I was worried about was Jason and, of course, Mr Gandhi.

It was time to have breakfast. We entered the cafeteria. Thankfully, there weren't many kids in the orphanage who knew me very well except for my football teammates and opponents and, of course, my roommate, Jason. But each and every kid was staring intently at me. I had no idea how I will get away from the infinite pair of eyes gazing at me. Amazing! I had grown famous in three days by being secretively teleported into another dimension.

These kids were only staring; I had no idea what Jason will do. I told my companions to sit with me at the corner of cafeteria, and I grabbed some apples and grapes for them. Before I could start with my breakfast, I heard a loud smack at my table.

'Where have you been on earth? And when were you planning to return?' Jason asked, infuriated. His dirty-blonde hair was damp with sweat.

'I was about to tell you, but I didn't get a chance,' I lied again.

'Really? There is nothing you ever tell me. I am the one who shares everything, not you.' His face was dangerously close to mine, and I felt intimidated at him for the first time.

'I have always shared everything with you. There is nothing I ever hid and will ever hide from you.' *Except about my parents and the destiny that has been marked on me.* His gaze left mine and eyed each one of them.

'Who are they?' Jason asked and took a seat beside me.

'I found them during my expedition.' Jason arched his eyebrow.

'All right, during my run away,' I mumbled.

'What did you say? I didn't hear. Can you repeat?' He pretended. Is he serious? I just returned, and he was back with his cocky attitude.

'Stop it, Jase, or I'll—'

'Don't call me Jase.' His expression suddenly turned grim. 'And yes, I have been searching for this spark, Airik. Welcome home.' He hugged me. I still had a problem in understanding his mood swings.

'I want to know the truth. I know you are hiding something. You will eventually have to spit out the truth.' He loosened his embrace and flashed a nothing-can-be-hidden-from-me smile.

Decision

It was time to tell the Duvollinians about the orphanage. I chose the most comforting place—garden—for this small get-together. Anedrin was already there, waiting for me. I sat beside her.

'Where are they?' I asked.

'Devouring the breakfast,' Anedrin answered.

'I gave them a lot of fruits to eat. Doesn't it satisfy them?'

'It did satisfy them, but they say that the other thing that was being served is very delicious. What is it called?'

'Toast with peanut butter,' I answered. Sometimes a different breakfast can turn mouth-watering.

'Are we late?' Palort and Phileda came along hand in hand.

'How was it?' I asked.

'You have got so much of amazing dishes!' Palort exclaimed.

'You both should not overeat. It is not good for your health,' Anedrin scolded.

'Couldn't help it.' Palort chuckled.

'Airik, you were about to tell us something about your orphanage,' Phileda said. Thank god, someone noticed I was present there.

'I just wanted to tell you about the orphanage we will live in until we return to Selemara,' I informed them. 'You all will be given rooms to stay. It won't be as big as your palace's rooms. We have school from eight to four in which we will be given lunch. After that, we have to proceed towards our rooms and then come back to the cafeteria to have dinner at eight. We all will be in different classes. Anedrin, you will be in a different class and far away from us, so please try to mingle in the class or stay quiet. Palort and Phileda, you both will be in the same class and close to me. If possible, talk less or don't talk at all. If someone asks about your parents, tell them they died in a car accident. If they try to dig up further in your personal life, say that you don't want to talk about it. Clear?' They nodded.

'What is *cafeteria*?' Palort asked.

'You have your dining hall. We have our cafeteria,' I answered.

'Do we have classes now?' Phileda asked.

'Not today. It is Sunday,' I replied.

'Does it really matter? Work shouldn't stop no matter which day it is.' She scowled. I couldn't argue on that with her.

'Can you show us around this place? I have never seen any orphanage like this,' Anedrin said.

'There is a stadium, free clothes shop, cafeteria, garden, and resting rooms for everyone. You have already seen the garden, cafeteria, and clothes shop. Ms Hobbs will guide you girls to your rooms, and Palort will stay with us. I'll show you the rest of this place.' We all headed towards the stadium.

When we entered the stadium, I hadn't realised that I had not been in here for a long time. Jason was playing wild on the ground.

'This is our stadium,' I said, taking a huge breath through my nostrils and exhaling through my mouth.

'Isn't that the boy who smacked our table today's morning?' Phileda asked, almost snarling.

'Yes. He is my best friend and also my roommate. Thankfully, we are in the same grade. We have been together since we were 7.'

'Kitty! Where are you?' I heard someone.

'Grace?' I was surprised to see her in the stadium. She was a new orphan, almost 5. We had our birthdays on the same day. She was a very quiet and humble girl, which was missing in each and every girl of his orphanage. She never came in the stadium, afraid that a ball might hit her. I always told her that it was an invalid fear. No one in here will hurt her. But she doesn't listen.

'Airik! Where were you?' she complained. I knelt down on my knees to face her.

'I was away, doing some work,' I lied.

'Why didn't you tell anyone?' she almost whispered.

'I forgot.' I pursed my lips.

'Don't do that again. You have no idea how much tensed we all were. We all care for you. Please don't ever leave without telling anyone,' she requested. Her ice-blue eyes were wet. She had been crying.

'Why were you crying, Grace?' I asked.

'I had a kitty to keep for myself, but Jason took it away from me.' She began to cry again.

'Don't worry, I'll talk with Jason. He'll give it back,' I assured her.

'Please get it for me. She is very small and white in colour. I really miss her,' she admitted adorably.

'I'll get your kitty. Come with me,' I ordered. She nodded, wiping away her tears. Jason loved to play pranks on almost everyone except me. But he should not try to do anything with kids.

'Jason, what have you done with Grace's kitten?' I asked.

'I had it for my dinner last night,' he answered playfully.

'Airik, he ate my kitty!' She gasped and started crying again. *Why are children so gullible?*

'Tell me, Jason. The girl is crying in here for her kitty,' I raised my voice.

'All right, cool down. Don't make a fuss out of it.' He took off his shirt and dropped it on the grass beneath him, revealing his perfect muscular body. He gulped most of the water in the bottle and then emptied the bottle by pouring the rest of the water on himself. I could hear gasps and stares of many girls for Jason.

'Don't you know, Jason, it is bad to undress in public? Everyone is staring right at you,' she reminded.

'Really, kid? I don't mind the stares,' he said.

'Just give me my kitty back,' Grace said.

'It is in my room in my cupboard. Go and take it. I can't leave my match in between,' he said.

'What? You confined my kitty?' Grace sounded infuriated.

'That is not confiding. It is called safekeeping.' Grace scowled.

'Stop it, you two,' I halted their argument. They didn't get along very well. I don't understand why people hate kids. They are so cute and innocent. I forget all my worries whenever I see them.

'Let's go get your kitty.' Grace held my two fingers with her small and soft hands.

'Here. Take your kitty and take care of her. Don't let Jason touch it.' The kitten scratched me, but I managed to suppress my cry. Blood had begun seeping from my cut.

'Thanks, Airik. How do you know it's a he or a she?'

'You mentioned her as a girl, remember?'

'Did I? I have a weak memory.' She giggled. I pulled her soft and rosy cheeks.

I always thought that if I had a sister, she should be like Grace.

Confessions

I dropped Grace back to her room and rushed towards the stadium where the Selemarians were waiting for me. I could see them watching the match.

'Sorry. I left you guys.'

'You are very friendly with children,' Phileda commented.

'Thanks.' I ran my fingers through my hair. People normally suggested me to talk more with teenagers rather than small kids; she was the first human ever who commented in a good way.

'Do you play?' Palort asked.

'What?'

'This game. It looks intriguing,' Palort said, keeping his hand on his chiselled face.

'I used to play, but I think there are many more things that need more attention. Do you have any idea of when we will be returning to Selemara?' I asked to all of them.

'When any one of us will regain our normal strength,' Anedrin said. We were absolutely normal right now.

'We both look fit and fine.'

'I am talking about the internal strength that is required for performing sorcery.' She smirked.

'I didn't understand anything.' It was true. Everything bounced above my head.

'Inner strength means the power our soul holds. We use the power of our soul for sorcery. It weakens us. We need time to recover this strength.'

'How much time does our inner strength need to recover?'

'Depends on what kind of power we have used. It might take a day, a week, or a month to heal the inner strength.'

'Airik! Did you see the match? We won again,' Jason interrupted us. Did he hear our conversation? I hope not.

'Let's go and have some food. I am starving, and it is close to eight,' Jason said.

'There is an hour remaining for eight,' I reminded him.

'Does it really matter? We will go and sit there. Till then, you can introduce me to your new friends. By the way, I am Jason.' He hugged each one of them. Palort didn't mind, but the girls felt repulsed from his sweaty hugs.

We exited the stadium and marched towards the cafeteria. Throughout the way, Jason kept on asking me questions about the experience I had during my 'run away', which was not at all a run away. I was forced to leave the orphanage. *I wonder what Mr Gandhi is doing.* He must have received the signals when the portal appeared. *Why hasn't he talked about it yet?* I had just seen him during the interrogation held in the morning. He didn't say me anything or ask any questions about my disappearance.

'Airik, are you listening?' Jason snapped in front of my eyes.

'Where were you dreaming? I have been talking about the last three days spontaneously only to discover that you are in your own world.'

'I was thinking about how many assignments must be given in these days,' I replied.

'Not many. So far, we have done mind-sets of people in different cultures and their body gestures in psychology. In English, we have to read a novel that Ms Philips gave us. I don't remember its name. Buddy, I forgot to tell you about Ms Philips! She had been absent in this school just after you ran away. I have heard that her legs are broken after she had a long drive with her fiancé.'

'You mean her future husband fractured her legs?'

'I think so. Teachers said it is because of an accident, but I am sure it is a lie.'

'We can't say it is surely because of him.'

'It is surely him. I have seen him smoking, and he is alcoholic.'

'What connection does smoking have with this?'

'Ms Philips hates smokers and alcoholics. She came to know about it and threatened to leave him. But her fiancé must be so obsessed with her that he almost killed her.'

'That's really bad,' Phileda chimed in.

'Come again?' Jason said.

'Palo—I mean Paul lost one of his collection kits. He is very close to them.'

'I thought you were listening to our conversation,' Jason said.

'Excuse me! Our parents didn't teach us to snoop in conversation,' Anedrin said with fury.

'Hey! I didn't mean that. Calm down. Wait a minute. I thought you were orphans.' We are screwed.

'I meant when my parents were alive,' Anedrin said with her eyes pointing towards the ground.

'When did they pass away?' Jason kept his voice low.

'When she was 10,' I answered before Anedrin would smack Jason down.

'That must be really painful,' Jason said. Anedrin was pretty close in losing her patience.

'Let me introduce,' I jumped in.

'She is Infinity, she is Darcy, and he is Paul.'

'You all must be really special,' Jason said.

'Why?' Palort asked.

'He easily doesn't make friends.' There was pin-drop silence.

'Let's hurry in the cafeteria. We will be late.' I motioned all of them to walk.

We reached the cafeteria and chose the table at the far end of the room beside a window—our usual spot.

'Now that it is just you, me, and your friends, can you tell me what is going on?' Jason interlocked his fingers in a businesslike manner. He will surely make me throw up everything.

'What do you mean?' I blinked several times.

'You have been talking about sorcery and some place called Duvollin. As far as I know, there is no place called Duvollin, at least not on earth. Fine if there is any place called Duvollin, but what is the work of sorcery? I don't think these things exist.'

What can I say? How did he make this all out?

'Have you been overhearing our conversation?'

'What do I do then? The only good friend that I had is hiding everything from me. You never tell me anything.' He had no idea about how much I wanted to tell him everything. Hiding things from him made me guilty.

'You will never believe me, Jason. All I tried is to keep you away from my life, which is in a mess right now.'

'Then tell me. I might be able to help you.' He held my hands tightly. I gulped.

'No, you can't. Anyone cannot help me. You won't even believe me.' He loosened his grip on my hand.

'Is it that bad? Try me.'

'Fine. Did I ever tell you my parents were murdered and somehow I was responsible for their deaths and, yes, I watched them die?' I didn't realise that I was almost leaning over my roommate. Jason gulped. I sat back on my seat and tried to relax myself.

'One day, some men showed up at my house and killed my parents and then died on the spot. After my parents' death, Mr Gandhi got me here, and since then, I have been in this orphanage. A few days ago, Mr Gandhi told me a lot about himself and my family that I didn't know. I was also getting some weird dreams, and then I got teleported in another dimension called Duvollin. There I came to know that I am not a normal human. I am destined to protect a stone that has the soul of a very powerful and once-lively king. If I fail to do my job, the world is in danger,' I gushed. He threw his head back and laughed.

'Are you serious?' he managed to speak between his laughs.

'See? I told you, you won't believe me.' I kept a straight face. His laughter died down instantly.

'No, I mean, well, yes, it is unbelievable. I don't know what to say.' Jason was staring at me as if I had just looted a bank.

'Good evening, children.' Mrs Quartz was standing beside our table. How long had she been here? Did she hear our conversation?

'Don't you youngsters think that you came here way too early? It is still 20 minutes to eight. I like your enthusiasm. Other children hardly eat.' Mrs Quartz sighed.

'Don't sit like this. Eat something. I'll get hot chocolate for you.' Before we could say anything, Mrs Quartz hurried towards the counter and strolled back with six hot chocolates.

'Here.' Mrs Quartz gave each of us a hot chocolate. Palort was inquisitively eyeing the sweet dish, and so was Phileda. Anedrin, as usual, had masked up her emotions.

'I'll go and check the dinner. I tried an Afghan dish. I hope you'll like it.'

'We always like everything you cook, Wendy. Bring it on. We are ready to hunt down the food,' Jason said mockingly. Mrs Quartz laughed, so we all were forced to join the laughter. After the laughing ceremony ended, we all sat and drank the hot chocolate without disturbing one another. There was only a clatter of dishes and Mrs Quartz's cursing. Soon, other children came along, and we ate our dinner grimly.

Fate

As soon as we finished our dinner, we ran into Mr Abel. 'I have been trying to find you. I want you to know that there are no rooms free right now, so Paul has to adjust with someone.'

'Paul can live with us,' Jason jumped in.

'Perfect. Ms Hobbs will be coming and escorting the girls to their rooms.' Now that Jason knew everything, I didn't have to pretend. It was a relief. Ms Hobbs came soon and as decided escorted the girls to their room.

'Where is our room?' Palort asked.

'The last building,' Jason answered.

'What are we waiting for? Let's go,' Palort said. His excitement will not last for long. The room had to be untidy. I wasn't there for three days. Jason surely would have morphed the room into a dustbin. I will have to clean up the room again. We entered our room. I switched on the lights to see most of the things in place. I eyed Jason suspiciously.

'I came to know you came. I tried a bit of clean-up. I hope you like it.' Jason scratched his head.

'You tried. That's really nice. I hope you will do better next time.' I appreciated his work.

'You will again run away?' he asked playfully.

'Haven't got any option, buddy,' I replied. I never thought about this. *Why am I being paranoid?*

'Palort, will I ever return from Duvollin?' I asked.

'Not until the next protector comes.'

'And how long does it take?' Palort didn't answer me. He stood there, quietly staring at the ground.

'Answer me,' I demanded.

'Normally it is . . . 10 to 20 years.' The whole world fell below me.

Ten to 20 years—these were the only phrases that destroyed my future. I had so many plans for my life. I always wanted to do nuclear engineering and become a nuclear physicist. Everything was out of my reach now

'Are you okay?' Jason asked me.

'I need some sleep,' I mumbled and changed into my comfortable clothes. That was another thing: I was not at all sleepy. *If the Airis girl shows up again, I'll kill her and end everything that has ruined my life.*

'Why are you sleeping, Airik? This is not the time to sleep. Get yourself into action,' I heard a sweet voice. I jumped out of bed and grabbed my pillow.

'Where are you? Show yourself.' I barged through the room.

'I know your intentions, Airik. I am here only to tell you that you can have the job of a nuclear physicist and also your parents. That is possible only if you join me. We sorcerers are born to rule. Why do you think gods will give us powers almost equivalent to them?'

'Nothing buys me. You cannot bring back the dead ones!' I echoed.

'I can do anything I want to. Resurrecting the dead is quite hard, but I can do it. Now listen to me.'

'No, I won't! Are you afraid of me?'

'Me afraid of you? That'll never happen.' I could feel the arrogance in her tone.

'Then why don't you show yourself? Where are you hiding?'

'I am not hiding!' she bellowed, which pealed in my ears.

'I am a prisoner in Aegera! Soon, the shield will become weak, and then everyone will know the wrath of Airis!' she hissed.

'If you are not with us, this means you are against us. And I can't leave my enemies alive,' she threatened.

'But I can't kill you while I am away. I would like to see your face when you die. I know that day will come soon,' she whispered.

'I will be the reason for the death of the strongest protector. Trust me, Airik, it will be very slow and very painful. Your slow death starts now. If I say trust me, then do trust me.' She laughed wickedly.

Was this a dream? I wish it was a dream, but it wasn't a mere dream. It was my fate that she announced. The slow painful death that I will experience in my future and it had already begun.

I woke up early with my head throbbing as if someone had just hammered it down. Palort and Jason were still asleep. It was three in the morning. I groaned. I remembered last night and thought about its consequences.

How has she planned my death? Hold me as a prisoner for my entire life? She said it would be painful. 'Your slow death starts from now.' What does it mean? Has she bewitched me? Not a good choice. Another option will be chocking me slowly to death. But she said it has already started. I haven't experienced any pain or difficulty since the encounter except for my little headache. Did she plan on some sort of cancer? Or was she trying to paralyse me? I grumbled for the second time since morning. I clutched my forehead in distress. *She has left me with multiple options. Or is it possible there are no options at all? She was trying to scare me.* I whacked the table hard, erupting daggers of pains in my hand.

'Who is it?' Palort woke up and held an axe in his hands. *When did he manage to bring his huge weapon in the orphanage unnoticed?*

'It's nothing. I was . . . frustrated. That's it.' I tried to calm him.

'Wake me up if you think something is not right. It would be my pleasure to stick by your orders,' he said sincerely.

Was he serious? Until now he was the one barking orders and I was the one following it numbly. He returned back to his bed and started snoring deeply again. I sank back in my chair.

'Get up! Why are you sleeping here?' Palort shook me awake. I opened my eyes and yawned. Jason was standing by his side.

'Had a bad dream . . . or maybe not,' I said. Palort went totally pale.

'What do you mean? You can't differentiate between dream and reality?' Jason said in amusement.

'I don't know. I mean I felt it was a dream, but it wasn't or the other way around.' I shrugged.

'What was it about?' He stroked his chin.

'Airis came and—' Jason interrupted me.

'Wait a minute. Who is Airis?' he asked mockingly.

'She is a forever 16-year-old sorceress who is planning to destroy the whole world,' I snapped back.

I continued, 'She offered me to join her once again, and I refused. So she is planning to give me a 'slow and painful death', which has already begun.'

'Is the sorceress beautiful?' Jason asked. *Why does he care about her?*

'Yes. But why did you ask?'

'Then you are lucky that she is messing up with you, buddy.' He erupted in ribbing laugher. Palort and I didn't join him. I folded my arms across my chest and kept my gaze fixed on Jason until he stopped laughing.

'Poor lad. Can't differentiate between dream and reality.' I 'accidentally' overheard Palort's thoughts.

'I was trying to make you guys laugh,' he said apologetically.

'That was a nice try, but we don't need to laugh. My life will end at any moment,' I said rudely.

'It is possible that she was just trying to scare you,' Jason said.

'No. I am sure she actually meant those words.'

'Are you experiencing any pain?' Palort asked with concern.

'No. I had a minor headache in the morning, but now it's fine,' I said.

'Are you sure?' Palort asked me. I nodded.

'If you both are done with your talking, let me tell you it is a Monday morning. It is a working day. You both better hurry up,' Jason suggested.

'Let's go.' I sighed. I loved to attend the classes, but now it's the least of my interest. We all left towards the cafeteria together. Phileda and Anedrin were already waiting for us.

'What's for breakfast, Darcy?' Palort asked.

'They call it pasta.' She concentrated on the last word.

'How is it?' he asked excitedly.

'Don't know. I have been waiting for you,' she said genuinely.

'Did you get your classes?' I asked Anedrin.

'Yes. They say it's seventh grade.'

'What about Phileda?'

'Senior or something like that,' she answered.

Good. Phileda and Palort will be with me. All I am concerned about is Anedrin. I hope she doesn't raise the curiosity of students around her.

Invitation

Jason and I sat together on the second last bench on Jason's persistence whereas Phileda and Palort sat on the last bench. I hate being one of the last benchers.

Each period passed by, and every teacher warned me not to run away like that. I felt shouting on top of my voice that I didn't run away. Everyone asked questions about Phileda and Palort's life. I answered only first few questions and then told them to mind their own business and poking in someone's personal life doesn't help. I hardly paid attention to anything going on in the class. All I cared about was the kind of death Airis planned for me or her next step towards Selemara.

Suddenly I thought about the stone of Phinogar. No one was there to guard it. *What if she tries to—no, this should not happen.* I shook those untenable thoughts away. I jiggled my head. Just then, I felt a firm hand on my shoulders. I looked up to see Mr Gandhi gazing at me with concern.

'Any problem, son?' he asked.

'No. I'm fine,' I replied. Wait a minute. Did he just call me son?

'Let's get started with today's topic. Criminal psychology.' Mr Gandhi smiled. I didn't listen even to the half of the lecture. I didn't notice Mr Gandhi giving us work to do and then creeping his way towards me.

'Airik, I would like you to meet me in your maths class. I hope you know about Ms Philips's condition. I very well know you didn't run away. Plus, I have to know about your new friends you have got with you. I would advise you to come soon. I've discovered many things during my research during the last three days that you need to explain,' Mr Gandhi whispered. It sounded strangled as if someone was making him say so, but he didn't have even a speck of desire.

Why do I need to explain something that was in his research? What will I do in there? My instincts were telling me to hide the truth from him or something will surely go wrong.

The Pretender

Mr Gandhi focused his attention on me with a broad grin. His eyes never budged, and he didn't smile. I kept my glare on my book but couldn't help and check on with this creepy teacher. Soon the indication of the end of the class rang in my ears. I let out a breath of relief. It was lunchtime and better chance to meet Anedrin and know about her day. I hope she didn't create any suspicion or someone found her intriguing.

When we took our seats in the cafeteria, Jason elbowed me. 'What did Mr Gandhi say? You know, after the whisper he did, you were pretty shaken up.' Others were heartily eating their lunch while Phileda and Palort snuggled up closer in the conversation.

'There is a huge problem.' I sighed.

'What is it?' Palort mumbled.

'Mr Gandhi wants me to meet him after lunch and explain to him something about his research and he—'

'Why can't he figure it out himself? Your being an inked-brain gargantuan genius doesn't mean that he can force you into helping him anytime,' Jason cut me off with his stupid logic.

'It is nothing like that. He suspects that my run away is not a 100 per cent truth. I am sure that he has received signals and wants me to splutter out the truth. I have a very bad feeling that he shouldn't come to know about any of this.'

'What's the big deal? Make up anything that totally suits the situation. Why would he care?'

'There is something on earth called body language. He is very well knowledgeable in psychology. He will catch me easily if I lie, and now don't suggest me to fake the body language!' I halted Jason from saying anything that would only make me annoyed.

'Why do you need to fake your body language?' someone asked. Everyone turned towards four of us, particularly me. Realization struck me that our hushed whispers were loud enough for some students to hear.

'Nothing much, pals. We were just . . . talking about people who fake their body language flawlessly. It's so difficult,' Jason gushed the words out without a second thought. But the reason did work.

Jason is a friend that anyone would long for. I agree that he doesn't apply brains in the right direction, but sometimes he is very helpful. I am glad I have a friend like Jason. He is always there with me when I need him. He gives me space whenever I need it.

'Yeah, whatever,' Ethan said.

I had no idea what's wrong with Ethan. I tried to peek in his head a couple of times, but the only thing I saw and felt was pang of jealousy in him. He was jealous of Jason's good looks and charm and my witty brains and smart mouth. Well, that's what I heard him call me in his head.

'Ignore him and give me a solution,' I whispered.

'I don't think you need any help. You are Airik Patronus. You can figure it out yourself,' Jason tried, motivating me.

'I can if I had time. There is no time.' I grunted.

Someone grabbed my shoulders from behind. I turned around to see Anedrin panting badly and way too anxious. 'What is it?' Palort asked with concern.

'Vibes,' Anedrin said.

'What does it mean?' I asked.

'There is a man who has very mixed emotions concerning you, I suppose,' Anedrin said.

'Where and who?' Phileda rushed to Anedrin's side.

'I think he is a staff of this place. I've seen him many times observing Airik,' Anedrin said and ran her gaze around the cafeteria as if she was trying to find that man and then pointed towards someone facing his back towards us and talking to Mrs Quartz.

'It's him,' she said with certainty. Five of us snuggled closer and were trying to see who it was. When he was done conversing with Mrs Quartz, he turned around. We took our seats swiftly with Jason stumbling and regaining his balance, but still, we kept our gaze on him. Now he was effusively facing us. My heart stopped beating right there. Mr Gandhi was the man.

'Are you sure?' I asked.

'Yes. It's him. He wants something from you. The vibes are very strong,' Anedrin told me. I gulped.

It was practically impossible. He had always helped me; in fact, he was the one who got me away from the horrific place of ten humans dead around me. He supported me throughout and kept me away from trouble. My intuition told me that it's not him. It cannot be him.

I had to know. I needed to know. The best way was to enter his brain. I narrowed my eyes and glued my gaze on him. I could feel myself in his head now, and then blades of pain erupted in my head. I groaned and fell on my knees. I rubbed my temples roughly.

'What happened?' Jason held me firmly by my shoulder. Everyone gathered around me.

'A small headache. Nothing to worry about,' I said with great difficulty. Everyone cleared out and took their seats except for my four friends.

'What did you see?' Jason asked.

'He blocked me from reading him,' I said.

'How?' Jason asked.

'I have no idea,' I said.

'Then it's not your teacher. It has to be someone else,' Palort said.

'You mean that guy stole his identity?' I asked.

'It's not only him. They do this in group,' Phileda said.

'How do you know, sister?' Palort asked.

'Well . . . I was . . . I was once with a group who called themselves as Infinite Identity.' Phileda bit her lip and let out her breath she was holding. 'They stole identities for a good cause.' She concentrated more on the words *good cause*.

'You never told me about that.' Palort scowled.

'What's the next step?' Phileda asked, ignoring Palort.

'We are returning to Selemara by tomorrow. We can't take any more chances. Airik, you have to avoid that man. I'll be regaining my strength by tomorrow at max. Till then, you should be alert,' Anedrin said.

'I can't avoid him. He told me to meet him after lunch,' I explained the whole situation to her.

'Make any excuse, but don't meet him alone,' Anedrin warned. I nodded and reassured her.

Bitter Truth

After lunch, I excused myself for my headache and paid a visit to the infirmary. I pretended to have a very bad one, so the nurse ordered me to go back to my room and rest until I would be fine. I obediently rushed to my room gingerly and closed the door behind me. *Such a relief. There is no man with a stole identity, no Duvollin, and no job.*

I wriggled in my bed made myself comfortable and let out a breath. The Airis girl didn't attempt to kill me like she threatened. So it was nothing more than a figure of speech. There was an odd itching sensation in my body. My eyes were getting heavy, so I couldn't help but sleep. I just hoped that no crazy dream would be tossed over, but it was in vain.

I was sitting on a cold marble floor. I tried to move only to see that I was tied to a metallic pole. I heard sharp and loud cries of a girl beaten by a whip. I tried to free myself only to be entangled tightly. The cries and pleas of the girl died the rest of the days remaining, but yes, the level of insanity increases with every passing month. Or you'll turn super smart. But still, it's fine.' She tried to comfort me. It's good she tried, but it really didn't work. I was horrified. *Is this the way she comforts? This didn't work for me. She is nothing but a crazy girl in her early teens. I need someone like Palort or Rimtzal to explain to me and assure me.* I shook my head in distress.

'Are you sure your cuts are not in pain?' she asked.

'Of course, I am sure. I know what I feel. You don't have to remind me by asking again and again,' I snapped. I apologised and trained my eyes over my room's floor, which was covered with splashed of blood, which was mine.

'How did you get infected by this poison? You always need a medium,' she mumbled to herself. I tried to rack my brain for anything that could help me. That's when it clicked: Grace's cat!

'You don't have to say anything. I'll get rid of it,' Anedrin said before I could utter even a single word.

I quickly cleaned up the drains of blood, which was all mine. Anedrin informed that five of us will be meeting at six in the evening to discuss the further plans.

I felt very weird as I wasn't feeling pain anywhere. The blood rushing down my biceps was tickling me. The sensation was altogether weird. I cleared the wound and used a bandage to cover it. There was nothing I could do for the bruises, though. The place where I had bruises and cuts were only tickling and itching. *Really? Can anything get creepy than this?* I smirked and put back my T-shirt. The idea of becoming insane or ending up dead sent shivers down my spine. My smirk was instantly wiped away by the thoughts of it. *I hope they remove the venom in time.* I was exhausted and now needed some time to refresh myself. Seriously, having indescribable and abrupt scars is not something that happens every day.

'Holy sh—cow, Airik! I heard about your bruises,' Jason said right after bursting into the room and lobbing the bag on the bed.

'I'm fine. It's not in pain. Hang on. Who told you?'

'Anedrin. I met her coming back to my room. She explained everything to me and the twins. Dude, she was talking about some king of venom in your body and if not treated soon, you'll end up a zombie, dead, or super smart. I mean, that's crazy and hilarious. I mean, is it even possible that venom gives you three outcomes? I think they are scaring you.' He laughed. He finds my condition hilarious. I have a great friend. 'Anyways, she also has a small get-together today at six in the cafeteria,' he informed again.

'I know. She already specified. And yes, it is not a zombie. It is something . . . different,' I said.

'I would like to have a look at your wound and bruises.' Jason pursed his lips in a grim line.

'Forget 'bout that. I'm not interested to show off my wounds.'
I pulled the sheets on myself.

'Where is Palort?' I tried to change the topic, and I think I
accomplished my mission. Jason chuckled. 'What's so funny?'

'He is doing homework,' Jason whispered.

Yep, Jason wasn't wrong. He was sincerely completing the
work given. Amazing. His perfectly shaped brows were
knitted together in deep thoughts. He sank back in his chair
and closed his eyes as if trying to remember something
sweet and memorable, and then he smiled. He quickly
opened his eyes and merrily carried on with the work. Jason
and I exchanged looks.

'What was the smile about?' Jason asked. I shook my head
and shrugged.

'Why don't you read him, buddy?' Jason suggested.

I smiled, and my smile widened by every passing second. I
should've tried this before.

'I'll try to read Mr Gandhi's mind,' I snapped.

'But why? It's of no use. He has blocked you before,' Jason
said.

'I'm not talking about the identity thief. I am talking about
the actual Mr Gandhi. Now don't distract me,' I said.

I relaxed and let every inch of tension dissipate in me. *The
real Vikram Gandhi,* I reminded myself. The darkness behind
my eyes was accompanied by painful moans of someone. I
searched in the darkness for the person. The room suddenly

lit up with lights. I could see Mr Gandhi barbed with iron chains. There was no blood, but I knew he was in pain and agony. A man around his early 40s was sitting on his chair and sipping coffee.

'Want some?' He motioned at the coffee and chuckled like a 5-year-old boy.

'Get to the point, Aiden,' Mr Gandhi groaned. I've heard the name Aiden before. Aiden pursed his lips in a grim line.

'Tell me something 'bout your student,' he boomed and scratched his frizzy red hair.

'Why do you think I'll help you now? I never told the truth to him about his parents' death, and now you want me to spat everything about him? Not so easy, Aiden. What do I get in return?' Mr Gandhi turned had a businesslike tone. I appreciate his nerve. Knowing that he was the vulnerable one, he still managed to get on with his profit.

The question is, who was Mr Gandhi talking about? The way he spoke, I felt as if he was talking about me. I shook the thoughts away and concentrated on the conversation.

'You are not a fool, Bert. I am the chairman of multiple companies. I can fetch you tons of cash in a minute. Oh, I forgot to tell you. I know what you plan to do with the little boy.' He gave out his wicked laugh.

'Why does it bother you? He doesn't remember his hometown well. What use can he make to you?' Mr Gandhi continued to talk in his business tone.

'He killed the best ones. I won't leave him.' He gritted his teeth. They were surely not talking about me. I had never killed a mosquito in the 16 years of my life.

'He didn't do it purposely. It was just a mistake, and trust me, he didn't realise that he killed them. Plus, he was a kid then, and any kid will react the same way he did those years ago,' Mr Gandhi defended.

'Yeah right. I will kill you right now, and then I won't even know I murdered you. Or maybe I'll kill you accidentally. Something like we will hang out in my apartment's terrace and then I'll push you by mistake. Another option is drawing a knife through your gut unknowingly. How do you like it?' Aiden said sarcastically. 'It is just not possible to know that you just killed eight men!' He yelled.

Eight men . . .

'He didn't know the reach of his power. Well, he still doesn't know. I bet he watched his parents die. This must've triggered adrenaline in him, and he killed your men in anger.'

What is he talking about?

'I don't care, Bert. I want him right here. Those eight men were more than friends to me. The boy will regret for what he has done.' He clenched his palm into a fist and hit Mr Gandhi with all the strength he had.

I fluttered my eyes open. Jason and Palort were staring intently at me. More like waiting for me to tell them everything.

'I . . . um . . . actually, I saw . . . nothing,' I lied. *I'll tell them later on after I confront the actual Vikram Gandhi.* It's high time to let them know about every chapter of my life. And I can't forget the suggestion—no, the warning—Rimtzal gave me. Probably, I was imagining everything I just saw. Yes, it is possible. I was keen on finding him, so I made up something in my subconscious and made my normal self perceive it.

'Impossible. You have been sitting in the same posture for the last 40 minutes,' Jason boomed.

'I saw . . . a forest?' It came out as more of a question than a statement.

'You're saying that you were imagining a forest for this long?' Jason said with his nose flaring with every word he spoke. It took a lot of control to not laugh at him.

'Look, Jason, I tried, but Mr Gandhi seems out of reach. I have no idea about his location,' I explained them.

'It is almost six. Let's go,' Palort said. I sighed and was thanking Palort within myself for saving me from detective Jason's questions.

Why did the red headed man addressed him as Bert?

'There is a very bad news,' Anedrin said with clenched teeth.

'Does someone know about us?' Phileda asked.

'The way everything works in Duvollin is a lot different from here. Elyrians exist. They talk to us when we really need them. After all, they have created us, so their job is to look after us,' Palort explained. I choked on my own spit.

'So when do we get to meet the Elyrians?' I asked.

'Do you have a quiet place where we could sneak in and no one disturbs us?' Anedrin asked.

'Our room. Plus, you don't have to sneak in.' Jason chuckled.

Five of us headed towards my room. Phileda closed it behind us noiselessly. I searched for the switches and turned on the lights.

'Everyone, sit down on the ground, relax, and wait for the gods to show up,' Anedrin ordered.

'You think they'll come?' Jason asked to no one in particular.

'Of course. It has already happened before. Why won't it happen now?' Phileda answered.

'What? It did happen? You saw gods?' Jason asked in amazement like a 3-year-old kid.

'Now it's our time to meet them.' Anedrin winked.

'How does it work?' Jason asked. I narrowed my eyes at his sudden interest in the topic. *Why does he believe them?* I elbowed Jason to shut him up. Jason gave a little fake whimper. Was it too hard?

A few minutes passed by in silence . There was no sign of the so-called Elyrians. I also doubted their existence. I drifted my eyes towards the wall clock. Thirty minutes had already passed by.

'I don't think they'll come,' I said and stood up to leave the room.

'Sit down, Airik. They are on their way,' Anedrin said with the unruffled tingle in her voice that was missing for all these days. Neither did I sit nor leave the room. I would like to see for how long their patience lasted.

I could only hear the ticking of clock and my gentle heartbeat. No one spoke a word. I turned my eyes towards the clock every now and then.

'Thank you for giving us your precious time, Goddess Phelonia,' Anedrin spoke, facing towards the wall. I couldn't see anyone.

I walked up to Anedrin. 'Who are you talking to?' I whispered.

Palort tugged me, forcing me to sit. 'Don't disturb her. Sit here and listen,' Palort whispered back.

'We need your guidance. Our protector needs his energy, but the torment nights prevent him to do so, and on the other side, he has litror venom running in his veins. Please help us. Duvollin needs the protector,' Anedrin pleaded.

A few minutes passed by. No one except Anedrin kept blabbing. Her face lit up when she thanked the invisible Elyrian for her 'guidance'.

Anedrin turned to face us. I could tell she was very happy. Her blue eyes were shimmering in excitement. 'I got to know the solution!' She let out a cry of victory and hugged Phileda.

'Solution for which problem?' I asked.

'Both. For the venom to be discarded from your body, we need to get some kind of plant and food items. Then we will inject it in your body.' *What does she mean by some kind of plant?*

She continued, 'For the second one, like you said, there is another way to please the gods, but I didn't get the meaning.' She sighed.

'Wh-what do you mean yo-you didn't get the me-meaning?' I stuttered.

'It was like a riddle, and she said to figure it out myself.'

'What is it?' I asked, desperate to know.

'Wait, I don't . . . remember.' She chewed her lips. I tried to control the flaring temper in me. How could she not remember?

'How can you forget?' The rest of the words I wanted to say remained in my throat.

'Well, I got really excited, and I just . . . forgot to tell.' She shrugged as if she couldn't help it. I'd never heard of anyone forget anything so important just because of excitement. I groaned when I remembered the day Palort told me the same thing.

I puffed out my cheeks. 'How will the draining affect my body?' I asked. All of a sudden, Anedrin gasped.

'What's wrong?' I asked.

'I'm sorry, Airik. I forgot to tell you more about the working of the litror venom.' She glanced apologetically at me and started pacing in my room. *I hope whatever she is about to tell is not much deadlier.*

'If your energy is drained, the venom will work faster.' She gulped.

'H-how fast?' I stuttered for the second time in my whole lifetime.

'Depends on how much your energy has drained.' She halted again.

'Please complete the truth, Anedrin. I want to know,' I pleaded.

Tears trickled down her cheeks, but her face remained emotionless. *Is it so bad? I don't want to feel it.* Phileda and Palort were standing with their heads lowered down. Jason and I were, as usual, confused of what was going on.

'Someone, answer me!' I groaned in frustration.

'If you drain your energy, your endurance decreases. Thus, the venom spreads really very quick . . . almost within eight to nine hours,' Phileda answered.

'How?' I tried to say, but no sound came out.

'Either speak or stop your lip movements,' Jason said.

'But its works within three months. Even if the energy gets drained, how can three months get reduced to nine hours?' I asked in my hoarse voice.

'Don't worry, Airik. You might turn into the smart one, like I said, maybe die. If you turn into the insane one, we'll cage you and stop you from killing anyone. Have hope,' Anedrin tried to comfort me again.

'Anedrin, I don't believe I'm saying this. You shouldn't comfort anyone—ever,' I retorted.

Anedrin smirked and wiped her tears. 'Really nice that you're expressing yourself. I thought you were a lost kingdom that we would never know about,' Anedrin said. I scratched my temples.

'Actually, you know a lot about me than I do.' I sapped in my bed, ignoring the worried glances at me. I tossed in my bed, searching for an indication of comfort, which I'll surely never get with the question reverberating in my head.

What will I turn into in a few hours?

Whatever it is, I shouldn't barge about it every time.

I glanced at my wall clock. Seven thirty. 'It's close to dinnertime. I guess we should get going.' I jumped out of my bed and exited the room. I expected the rest to do the same, but they stood there, stunned.

'Hey. Why are you guys standing there? Don't want to have dinner?' I played casual.

'How can you be so composed after knowing that you might turn into a monster or die in a few hours?' Palort asked.

I laughed like a lunatic. 'When I was 3, my maternal grandma died because of cancer. She always had a strict diet. Still, she suffered from that disease. In her funeral, I asked why

Grandma couldn't stay with us anymore. No one came up with a convincing explanation. All they could say was that she is dead. I didn't know back then the meaning of death. At last, my mom said that everyone takes birth because they are assigned a certain task to do. When the task is completed, they go back from the place they have originated. In the same way, Grandma completed her task, and now it was her time to return. There is nothing we can do to stop them. If it is written in your fate, it will happen unless you change your path.' A smile crept across each and everyone's face.

'I love the way you bring smiles to our faces, buddy.' Jason squeezed me.

'Don't you think you're getting quite emotional?' I asked.

'Speak low. What will girls think about me?' he jeered. We all laughed feebly.

We ate our dinner, and everyone except me exchanged a few worried gazes among one another. I felt a sensation of being watched. The hairs at the back of my neck stood up. I rolled my eyes for being paranoid.

'What's wrong?' Jason asked.

'Nothing. I just felt we are being watched. But I think I am being paranoid.' I grinned.

'No, Airik. We are being watched.' Jason motioned behind me. Five of us turned behind to see the duplicate Vikram Gandhi wear a frown and watch us from a distance.

'I'll go and deal with him.' Phileda snickered.

'Wait! What are you up to?' I asked. The Selemarians just smirked, and Phileda walked towards the identity thief. The wide frown on his face disappeared as Phileda approached him. He was calm now.

Recovery

'She shouldn't go there,' I whispered to Jason.

'I feel the same way. But both of them seem confident about her. Let's see what she has got,' Jason said without taking his eyes off Phileda.

Meanwhile, Phileda was talking to the thief. His eyes were wide with fear as she spoke a word. Her beautiful features were creased with confusion as she returned to our table. The thief followed her and sat next to me.

'What have you done to him?' Jason asked.

'He is a little . . . dead,' Phileda answered.

'What do you mean by a little dead? Either it's totally dead or not dead at all,' Jason argued.

271

'We'll start the debate later on. Ask him anything you want to.' Phileda darted her eyes between me and the thief.

'Not until you tell me what you've done with him,' I demanded.

'Nothing much. He is a little dead, like I said. Apart from that, I think he is fine.' She took a look at the man beside me.

I groaned. 'What does little dead mean? Is he some kind of zombie?' I asked.

'No. A little livelier than that creature,' Phileda gave us a hint.

'Vampire?' Jason chimed in. Phileda shook her head.

'Stop your riddles, and tell me what he is!' I hissed.

'He was an infected one, just like you,' Phileda whispered.

'You mean he had that venom in him?' I asked. Phileda nodded.

'Which one was he? Smart one or the insane one?' Jason asked.

'He was neither. I've never heard of a case like this.' Anedrin and Palort, who were busy with their dinner, turned to face the man sitting beside me.

'The most important thing is he still has the venom in his body. Still, he is not affected,' Phileda confessed. Palort's and Anedrin's jaws dropped down.

'Before giving any more surprises, tell me what you've done to him,' I said firmly.

'I hypnotised him.' Phileda played with the curly blonde locks of her hair.

'That's nice. I'm happy you guys did something that didn't include sorcery.' Three of them stopped munching and narrowed their eyes in my direction.

'I think I should control my mouth more often,' I muttered.

'You better do,' Anedrin scolded.

She is so bossy. Being ticked off by a 12-year-old in front of my best friend doesn't sound good to me.

'How did you aid yourself?' Phileda began with her interrogation.

'Grind and mix dandelion, aloe, and castor oil plants in equal amounts and insert it in his nerves,' he answered the question, which wasn't asked at all.

'Hold on. Castor oil is the most poisonous plant in the world. How can it cure me?' I asked.

'Son, castor oil might be one of the most poisonous substances but not more poisonous than litror venom. It reduces the effect. But yes, you need to take it every day. I'll never want you to die.'

'Which means you're still not cured?' I asked, ignoring the last sentence he said.

'No. I cannot be cured until I get the antidote. I can stop the effect for the rest of my life but never get the venom out of my body. It pains a lot, but now I am used to it.' He sighed.

'How bad does it pain?' I asked.

'The first few pain attacks are very unbearable, but gradually, you get used to it.'

'I frantically want the antidote,' I mumbled. I didn't want to end up like him regretting my whole life.

'Don't worry. You are different. Probably, it won't have the worsening effect on you,' he guaranteed.

'How did you get infected?' Phileda asked.

'I was the commander of Calsenai. We were returning to Calsenai from Bunatil. My comrades and I were attacked by the soldiers with litror venom and turned. When we reached Calsenai, King Calcaneal came to know about the venom and ordered our public execution. One of my friends and I ran out of there and saved my life, but my other friends were killed. I hadn't realised that I was now near the border between Calsenai and Allekior. All of a sudden, a portal appeared in front of me, and we got teleported here.' The man smiled as if he remembered someone very memorable.

'There I met the most beautiful woman in the world.' He was about to start the story of his love life.

'She—aah!' the man groaned in pain.

Can anything get better than this? Probably, he was about to tell me something important concerning my life. That girl didn't leave him. I rushed to his side. No one seemed to notice the poor man wriggling in pain except us five?

'Are you all right?' I asked him.

'Don't worry, I won't die right now. They are calling me back. Kill the spirit and bring peace.' He gagged.

'You were talking about the woman you loved. Is she anyhow connected to me?' I asked.

'Son, I am very happy to meet you again after so many years. I'm sorry all these years. You had to live like an orphan. The lady I am talking about—' His eyes fluttered and appeared as if they closed for eternity, and he disappeared into a grey mist. I left his side.

'What was his name?' I asked to no one in particular.

'Whose name?' Anedrin asked.

'What do you mean, Anedrin? The man who told us more about the litror venom,' I reminded.

'Who is Anedrin? And what is litror venom?' she asked.

'What? You are Anedrin, and I was infected by litror venom, remember?' These guys were driving me nuts.

'I think you need to visit infirmary. I'm Infinity. You got me, Paul, and Darcy here.' This had to be a prank.

'All right, guys, you got me, but I'm not getting further in this. It's enough.' I held my hands up in mock surrender

'Infirmary is not enough. You should be in psych ward, Patronus.' Palort rolled his eyes.

'What do you mean? Don't you remember anything?' I whispered.

Jason placed his hands on my shoulders. 'Look, Airik, I know you fell from the tree and hurt your head. But—'

'Stop it! I didn't hurt my head, and yes, I don't remember climbing any tree.' I squinted at all of them.

'In case you have some junk filled in your head, let me remind you. You had a very bad headache today, and then you decided to climb the tree in the garden for no reason. You fell down from a good height and slashed your arm with something sharp. Remember anything?' Palort said. *Something is really very wrong. They really don't remember anything.*

'Have you seen Mr Gandhi?' I asked.

'Nope. He is on a leave. But why did you ask? We all were informed a few days back,' detective Jason came back in mood.

'I think I hit my head pretty hard.' I pretended to believe them and scratched my left temple.

'Then I guess you don't remember that Ms Philips is back,' Jason informed.

'When?' I asked.

'Today,' Jason answered.

What happened with me? Why do they have different memories? I am sure everything happened. I don't have such a strong imagination. I need to find out. If they don't remember anything within time, I'll turn into something very smart or insane or . . . dead.

It was close to nine, but still, my friends and I sat in the garden and talked about the day. I didn't speak much and just nodded only if necessary. My mind was already on the torment nights. I had no idea of how the draining works and when it will work. The issue is that all of them had a different memory than mine.

'Why aren't you saying anything?' Jason asked.

'I have an amazing story,' I lied on my back and placed my hands behind my head. Probably, this would work.

'Carry on,' the twins said at once.

'There was a great king. He was very powerful and kind-hearted. There was a mysterious forest that was never visited by anyone. The one who ventured out in the forest never returned. The king decided to visit the forest, and he did like he said. Fortunately, he did return, but he was turning evil. And then, he was destroying humanity. The destruction led to the gods to be angry, and then they themselves had to come down to stop him. They trapped him, and it is said

277

that if he is unleashed, then the days of humanity are over,' I completed.

'I feel as if I have heard of this story,' Anedrin mumbled.

'You do?' I asked excitedly. Anedrin shot her eyes in my direction.

'I mean you do?' I asked gentler this time. They still had some bits of memory then.

'Something is happening,' Anedrin said between ragged breaths. I stood up and hurried in her direction.

'I'm feeling as if someone is taking my life away from me.' Anedrin fidgeted in agony.

'So are we. But it is not so strong.' Palort held Phileda by her shoulders.

Is this called a draining? If it is, then why isn't it happening to me? Jason and I look perfectly fine. Palort and Phileda seemed to be controlling themselves, but as for Anedrin, she was worse. *Anedrin specified that it has to do something with the skill. Does this mean I am not at all skilful?*

What if something happens to them and I couldn't be able to save them? No, I don't want to experience this again. I'll take them to Duvollin. I'll confront someone knowledgeable like Rimtzal. I'll do anything to save them. I created a portal back to Delver's house. I felt enervated after creating the portal. My other friends were gawking at me. I struggled against the portal, which was sucking me.

'Come on!' I signalled them towards the portal.

'What's this?' Palort asked. He was supporting Anedrin and Phileda at the same time.

'It's a portal back to your house,' I answered.

'My house?' he asked with an expression of confusion on his chiselled features.

'Never mind. Come closer,' I ordered. We huddled together and got sucked by the portal. We fell in front of Delver. He looked at us as if he was expecting us.

'Did you experience the night?' he asked with concern.

'No,' I answered. He seemed very confused.

'Who is he?' Palort asked. Delver looked at me with confusion.

Someone messed up with his memories, I telepathically talked to Delver.

Is it the same with the others? he asked me.

Yes. We need to aid Anedrin. She looks exhausted.

You were the one who initiated the portal? He looked startled.

Yes, I answered.

You need to be aided. Don't worry about others. They'll heal soon.

'Get them in,' He said out aloud.

'Why? We don't even know this man. Airik, if you are playing a prank on me, let me tell you I'm not paying it off. Did you add something in my drink? Hey, guys, you got me. Come out now.' He looked around himself to find others.

I never thought my son would behave like this. If he had his memories, I would have whipped him in front of Selemara. Delver shook his head in condemnation. I chuckled.

'Paul, wait. He looks a lot like you.' Jason checked Delver.

'Come in, Paul. I'll explain everything. You all need to rest, especially Infinity,' I tried to convince them.

'Fine. But only for Infinity,' he said. *I'm okay with anything. I just want you to get your memories back.* I huffed. We all huddled in Delver's house. He gave us retlen to drink. It tasted amazing. It was not too sweet or less sweet— absolutely perfect. Probably, they add some drugs in it. Who knows?

'What's this?' Jason asked.

'Whatever it is, it makes me puke,' Palort jeered. They both high-fived.

I'm sorry, Delver. I gave him an apologetic glance.

Don't worry. I know about the sorcery performed on them. I'll eradicate it.

How do you know to communicate telepathically? I asked.

Sorcery. Communicating this way is natural for you but not for me.

Why? I grabbed the cup and started sipping retlen.

It is related to your parents, he answered.

I completely forgot. I needed to talk to you about my past. I want to know more.

Curious as ever. But unfortunately, I can't tell you much about your past. My job was to keep an eye on you, not your parents. But I do think they are alive. I choked on my cup.

'What's wrong? You both seem to have a conversation exchanging between your eyes.' Palort eyed me suspiciously. I chose not to answer and began to sip my cup again. *My parents are alive! This would be one of the happiest days in my life.*

I think they are alive, Airik. I'm not sure. Delver reminded.

'You owe us an explanation, Patronus.' Palort went dead serious now.

'Not required,' Delver said and mumbled something inaudible. He shook their heads as if they were feeling dizzy.

'Did you give them their memories?' I asked.

'Yes. Their memories will come back within a few minutes. The drink I gave all of you had a little bit of antidote in it. You see, it can restore the lost memories. I'll give you the antidote,' he informed. 'Now that you had just breached a portal, the venom must've started working its effects on you. Come with me before you turn,' he warned and took off without a word. *There is no need to tell me again.* I rushed behind Delver. It led me to an isolated room, which I think had not been cleaned in centuries. Everything was covered in filth. This room really needed to be cleaned. Delver moved towards the corner of the room. I followed him.

'Show me your nerves,' he ordered. I still couldn't see what he was holding.

'What are you holding?' I asked. He turned around to face me, and my eyes widened. It was like a tranquiliser gun.

'What are you planning to do with this?' I asked.

'This is not exactly an antidote, Airik. According to some people, this is not good, but for me, it works better than that.' He patted the device in his hand.

'Unlike the antidote, the sweeper separates the venom from your body instead of killing it,' he answered.

'What are its effects?' I asked and soon regretted to ask this question.

'Don't worry about its consequences. The only effect important is the venom out of your body.' He gently placed the gun on my popping nerves, and then, he shot. I fell on my knees, and the world around me exploded in bits. My vision went blurry. I felt every ounce of life being sucked away from me. And then, I blacked out.

'His eyes flickered!' I heard a familiar excited girlish voice. I tried to open my eyes only to struggle against my heavy eyelids. At last, with every grain of energy, I managed to open my eyes to see the anxious stares at me. Everyone was present, except Anedrin.

'What? Have I turned?' I asked.

'No. You look . . . different.' Jason mouthed. I scowled.

'I mean . . . you look pure.' *Pure? What does he mean by* pure?

'You flesh, your eyes, your hair—they are so different from what they were.' He modified his statement, but still, I didn't understand its meaning. I arched my eyebrow.

'He means to say your flesh, your eyes, your hair, and everything have changed in a good way.' Delver covered up for Jason. I got up from my bed and asked for a mirror. Palort smirked as if he knew I would do that. He held me by my elbows and guided me towards a seven-foot-long mirror. My pupils instantly enlarged in amazement. My face was quite different. It was more charming than usual. But I couldn't put a finger on the alteration.

'When and why did this happen?' I asked in amazement at the freshness that was absent throughout these 16 years.

'It has simultaneously been happening, but you have been unconscious for a week. And it happened because you performed sorcery,' Delver tried to explain.

I've already heard this theory before. I better not risk telling them about anything. But why was I unconscious for a week?

'After the venom was removed from your body, the draining took place. You are very powerful. The draining almost killed you,' Delver conveyed.

'Why is Jason still here? I mean, he is supposed to be back in the orphanage. I don't want to drag him in my messy life.'

'He can't go anywhere. He has the blood of Pimarvs running in his veins. Even he needs to be trained,' Phileda notified. My breathing hitched. In some part of my heart, I was happy that my best friend could stay with me, but some part of me didn't wanted his life to be messed up like mine. He deserves a lot better.

Before anyone could say anything else, I caught Jason's arm and exited Delver's house. I didn't know where I was taking him. All I knew was that I need to talk to him, tell him to stay out of this mess. It is possible that Airis would control and use him against me, and I could never let that happen. I was half dragging him with me. At last, he yanked his arm away.

'I know we need to talk. But this isn't the way, you know.' Jason rubbed his biceps and folded his arms against his chest.

'You shouldn't be here. This place is not safe for you. Go back,' I implied.

'You are not my guardian, Airik. I'll do anything I want to. Besides, being in that place galls me up. I feel damn useless over there. I know you care for me, but I would rather die than to leave this place. At last, I've got a reason to live. I can't grieve over my family who abandoned me.' Jason sighed. He kicked the pebble that was beside him. He stuffed his hands in his jean pocket and tried to look casual. But he failed.

He never told me about his parents. I never asked him. I was already way too mentally messed up and infuriated for I saw my parents die. He had been in the orphanage since he was 3. Still, he remembers them. It must be so anguishing for him. I had read him several times, but I never saw his parents. All I saw was football matches that he played and watched.

'Do you mind if I . . .' my voice trailed off.

'Go ahead. Conversing about them will make me cry. I hate to cry. Moreover, I don't want to talk about them.' I huffed and closed my eyes.

My brain raced with numerous thoughts. I pushed them aside and concentrated on Jason's past. The darkness was eradicated by a very beautiful girl, around 6, holding a 3-year-old kid. It must be Jason. I knew she was weeping before.

'Where are we going, Jane?' Jason asked innocently.

'It is a place where happiness dwells . . . unlike our house,' she said with a heavy heart.

'No, Jane. There is happiness in there, but we can't be a part of it,' Jason said with maturity.

'So what is this place called?' Jason tried to cheer up Jane.

'You'll see that yourself in a few minutes, Jase.' Jane wore fake happiness on his face. Jason clapped his hands in excitement. After a few minutes, they reached the orphanage.

'Go ahead. Explore this place,' Jane whispered. Jason stood on his feet and let go of Jane's strong grip on him.

'Come with me, Jane,' Jason asked playfully. Jane said nothing. I felt as if I could stare right through her woeful soul. She must've faced too much. She stared at Jason until he finally made it through the orphanage's gate. She gave a sigh of relief and left the place.

Meanwhile, Jason trudged into the stadium unnoticed. He blissfully walked around the orphanage until he bumped against someone big and strong. I remembered him. Dave. He was the one who helped me a lot during the first few days in the orphanage. He often visited us when he had time. He once used to live in the orphanage. After he turned 18, he left the orphanage and now is a CEO of a company. He often visits us.

'Whoa! Hold on, kid. You should be in your class right now,' he said. He seemed quite friendly. He picked up Jason and took him towards the first building. Jason didn't struggle. He was happy with wherever Dave was taking him. They approached the first building. He then consulted Ms Wellington, the caretaker of all the kids, who was responsible for each and every child below 5. She frankly answered that she had never seen Jason. Dave asked again, but the only answer he got was no.

'Jane must be waiting for me. I have to go,' Jason informed.

'Who's Jane?' Dave asked.

'Jane is my sister. She got me here, telling that this is a place where I'll stay happy and she is waiting outside for me.'

'No, kid. Whoever got you here is gone forever,' Dave said with pity.

'No! She will not leave me. She is waiting for me outside. You can see for yourself.' Jason struggled, and at last, Dave let him stand on his feet. Jason took hold of the two fingers of Dave and guided him out of the orphanage. Jason called out for his sister only to have no response in return. He shouted until he felt a hand wrap around him to take him to his new abode of happiness.

I flickered my eyes several times to digest what I just saw. I could feel a lump form in my throat. I never thought he had so much gloominess behind his exciting brown eyes. Now I know why he didn't like to be called Jase. Jane was the only one who had the right to call him Jase.

'Where is your sister?' I asked.

'She left me there, and then she was killed in an accident.' Jason exhaled a heavy breath.

'What exactly happened?'

'You couldn't see?' he asked in return.

'No. You were still in a dilemma and resistant for me to know your past,' I lied. The thing was I wasn't ready to see more. I never am and I'll never be strong enough to deal with painful pasts. Like mine or Jason's.

'My mum died after two years of my birth,' Jason began with his former life.

'My dad married another divorced lady. She had two sons. They were in a boarding school. At first, she really liked us and we loved her. We thought of her as our own mother. Then, one day her two sons came by. Her behaviour towards us suddenly changed. She treated us like we were lepers.' Jason clenched his jaw and shook his head.

'Dad never gave a damn about the way she was treating us. Her kids always troubled us. We were slaves in our own house. No one cared about us. Then one day, Jane took me for a stroll. It was supposed to be a stroll, but she dropped me in the orphanage, and then she was gone,' Jason completed with his story.

'She should've stayed with me in the orphanage. I was just three years younger than her. Why did she leave? She would've been alive,' Jason confessed. I placed my hand on Jason's shoulders and squeezed them.

'Let's get back before they send a search party for us,' Jason said without trying to know the answer. I agreed. We both strolled back to the Selemarians waiting for us.

'Sorry. It took quite long,' I apologised.

'We understand,' Delver retorted.

'Tell me more about the Pimarvs,' I said.

'At the beginning, Pimarvs were mere humans like us. When Duvollin was being divided into kingdoms, ten humans opposed the idea of it. They did everything to stop the partition of their motherland. The chosen leaders brutally killed them in front of everyone. Their death was so grave that people loathe those leaders even now. The actual story begins now. The Elyrians were not at all happy with the death of those people. It was not their time to die. Goddess Phelonia resurrected ten of them, those ten humans known as Pimarvs. Besides, their skill in any form of art and their teamwork are the only things that bind them together. Elyrians appointed them as the travellers of Duvollin. They travelled in Duvollin and stopped every illegal activity hazardous for humans. Allekior was once a very rich kingdom. They bribed the leader of Pimarvs to join Allekior. The leader's feelings were lusty for money. He joined the kingdom and made the others to do the same. For a few years, Pimarvs were evil. Everyone feared them. After a few decades, they came to know everything about their leader's planning and plotting. They left Allekior, making nine of them. The leader stayed behind. Since then, we have nine Pimarvs. They are very much-skilled fighters. The one who takes them down is known to be a great warrior, and until now, no one has done it. Those nine humans are always resurrected and brought back to Duvollin. Jason is one of them. He has to stay,' Delver completed.

'Oh.' It was all I could say.

'Even Jason will be trained with you, Airik Patronus,' Palort informed.

'I don't want to be trained,' I protested. Before Palort could say anything else, there was an eerie noise ringing from everywhere.

'What's that?' I yelled. No one seemed to listen. Jason and I were standing with our hands on our ears while others were having a silent conversation among themselves. Three of them nodded at each other and took off running. Jason and I exchanged looks and followed them. They were running towards the palace.

'Wait!' I ordered. *Ordered? I am the one who is being ordered around. Why would they listen to me?* I shook my head and looked up. Surprisingly, all of them were standing in front of me, panting heavily.

'What was that sound about?' I asked.

'That means some important people like us need to gather in that palace and get informed,' Phileda said.

'Informed?'

'You can see it for yourself. You are one of us now.'

'We have to hurry. There is a lot to announce and also to know,' Delver said and took off running towards the palace. We all had to follow him. We could've used the relite; we would've reached faster rather than on foot.

No. Not when we have a gathering. The people you are about to meet loathe our technological machines, someone echoed in my head. It must be Delver.

'Who are they?' I asked.

'Supreme Authority. They are the most powerful people in any kingdom after the king or queen. They are very old compared to me and quite young compared to Rimtzal,' Delver tittered.

We soon reached the palace. 'Wow!' Jason said in esteem.

'Where are they?' I asked out aloud, ignoring Jason's mumblings about the palace.

'Library,' Delver answered. We walked till the library only to find five old people with white hair and too-pale skin to be human sitting comfortably with identical books in their hands.

'Excuse me,' I said. When they didn't reply, I asked them again. No one seemed to care about them.

'Are they deaf?' I muttered. I sighed and tried one more time. They ignored me. *This is enough. No one ignores me, especially when I am one of the most important humans in the world right now.* I started marching towards them, and then I dashed against something strong and rough.

'Ouch!' I clutched my head and fell on my knees. 'What was that about?' I felt a pair of hands on my shoulders. 'You shouldn't have done that. They have a barrier around this library,' Palort said.

'How long do we need to wait?' I asked.

'We have no idea,' Delver answered for all. I rested against the barrier for god knows how long. Jason and I talked for a while about the orphanage to cheer ourselves up from the former conversation and revelations we shared. The barrier suddenly wore off, and I stumbled. *Do people have problem with warning me?* I brushed my shirt and headed towards the chair between Jason and Palort.

'We don't appreciate latecomers. And protectors are supposed to be prompt in every way.' A man with a long white beard said with narrow blue piercing eyes fixated on me.

Delver cleared his throat. 'Let's discuss the issues,' Delver suggested.

'Do you have any idea of what's going on in Allekior? The Pimarvs have not yet been assembled. You have to act on this, Delver, or it will lead in mass destruction of Selemara,' the same man warned.

'What's wrong?' Delver asked.

'They are assembling against this boy.' His shaky fingers were pointed towards me.

'What? Why? What have I done?' I freaked.

'You have not yet been lured by the creature dwelling in the forest of Pamretol.'

'So?'

'So they think you are taking the place of King Phinogar,' the man admitted.

'No. I'm perfectly normal, and no one can control me!' I snapped.

'We know that. But those people don't. According to the prophecy, you'll do something destructive for Duvollin if not stopped,' he retorted.

'That is impossible,' I mumbled under my breath.

'We'll know when the time comes, child.' The man sighed, and then the Supreme Authority vanished.

Distant Memory

'You guys never told me about the prophecy.' It sounded more like a statement than a question.

'We thought you won't be able to train properly after knowing the truth,' Delver disclosed to me.

'But now I know, and it surely is not affecting my training, and it has made me more determined to prove to them I'll never turn my back against my own people. I would have preferred to listen to the truth from you folks.'

'You know everything now. There is nothing to barge about. We should plan our next move.' Jason stepped between the conversations.

'Pimarv has got a point,' Anedrin said.

'Plan out and tell me your moves or let me suggest something,' I said.

'What do you suggest?' Delver asked.

'I suggest boarding on a journey towards Allekior,' I said out aloud.

'What did you just say?' Anedrin asked.

'There is no way I'm going to repeat that, and it was crystal clear for all of you to hear. Either come with me or I'll go—alone,' I announced.

'You are not alone, Airik Patronus. We are coming, and so is my sister and of, course, your friend Jason.' Palort stepped in front with pride. He was followed by Phileda and Jason. Anedrin stayed behind with her arms folded. She was staring at me intently.

'Are you not coming?' I extended my hand towards her. I needed someone to taunt me throughout the journey so that I would remain focused and serious. Anedrin suited the best.

'Trust me. This is a very stupid choice that you have made right now. You'll regret it,' Anedrin warned.

'We don't give a damn about your opinions. You are a mere kid. Either join us or just shut up,' Jason gushed. Anedrin narrowed her eyes at him. Jason rapidly backed up and grabbed my hand. I think no one told him about Anedrin's actual identity.

'Don't ever mess with her. Even though she is 12, she gets the crap out of you,' I admitted. I truly meant those words.

Her simple stare was enough to kill anyone. Whenever she stared, I seriously felt like she'd kill me.

'I'll join you only on one condition.' She smirked. Condition? Her smirk was enough to tell me her condition was not in my favour.

'Before you start with your journey,' she continued, 'you need to defeat me in a combat where each and every skill counts. Be ready. We'll meet in the arena tomorrow at dawn,' she defied.

'I knew it!' Palort said while we left the library. He knew it? 'I knew she'll eventually do something really very smart. She just challenged you, Airik Patronus! Do you have any idea of how stubborn she is? She doesn't want you to visit Allekior, and she will try her best to stop you,' Palort warned and stomped his feet. I gulped. *If Palort is so serious about it, then it is an issue.*

'Anyways, don't be nervous and keep your eyes open in every direction. Anedrin is very skilful, and check out for her traps. They are very promising. You get in one of them, you are already defeated,' Palort huffed.

'I think I'll take rest before the combat,' I suggested and carried on to implement it. I still remember the way to the room that was allotted to me a few days ago in my first visit to Duvollin. Jason was there silently sitting in the room.

'Thinking about Jane?' I asked.

'Did you just read me?' he asked another question in return.

'I don't have to read you to know what you are thinking. We've been staying together for quite long. I know you very well.' I walked and took a seat beside Jason.

'I'm happy we will be staying in the same room until I get trained and go where I belong. You'll get away with your job of protecting the anegz, and then I'll start touring around to get things right in Duvollin. Everything will be changed. I'll have a reason to live.' Jason smiled for the first time since we came in Duvollin. There was a heavy silence hanging between us. I didn't know what to say. My thoughts swirled with endless possibilities of finding my parents. *Where are they? How will they identify me?* Jason cleared his throat.

I took a deep breath and tried to compose myself. I opened my eyes to see Jason scrutinising me.

'Why are you checking me out?' I asked.

'Be careful the way you talk. You should know that your statement carries many meanings,' Jason sneered.

'Only if you could apply your brain in the right direction, you would've been on the seventh sky,' I admitted.

'I don't think there's any need to change me. Girls like the way I am. The day I turn into a nerd, I'm sure girls will hardly notice me. But you are an exception among the nerds. Girls pour their soul over you. I've heard a bunch of girls gossiping about you. They even had a fight over you. The best part was when a small girl came over and announced a catfight. The 4-year-old girl understood the situation!' Jason burst out into a fit of giggles.

'Don't you think this incident is quite outdated now? I've been hearing it through you since we were in seventh grade.' I kept a straight face.

'I can't help it. No girl ever fought for me. To be precise, girls never fight over boys. It is vice versa. There is something about you that gets girls off their rails as if you are some kind of trophy,' Jason stated.

'Stop it, man, or I'll heave. Your statements are making me puke.'

'I'm serious, Airik. I'm not taunting or trying to just mortify you.'

'Can we change the topic?' I asked and stretched myself.

'Tell me something about your parents,' he asked hesitantly.

I could feel a lump form in my throat. There weren't tears dwelling in my eyes. I sobbed when I get nightmares from the day of their death, but now that had ended too. I closed my eyes and remembered the happy times when there was just me, my dad, and my mom; and then I spoke, 'My dad hardly had time for us. You see, he was a surgeon, but whenever he was done with his work, he savoured each and every free time with us. My mom, being a psychiatrist, always taught me about psychological terms like *anger*, *ego*, *jealousy*, *fear*, *love*—and the list seems endless. I never understood her words back then, but I do understand them now. Her words mean a lot to me. Once, my mother was teaching me the term *fear*. My father never appreciated my mother for telling me stories that made me understand the meaning of life more than I really need to. He used to say, 'For Elyrian's sake, stop it, Christina. He is a small boy. Trust me, even Goddess Phelonia doesn't strive so hard to decide the right human for protecting the anegz, and I didn't face such difficulty when I faced Allekior. You are being very harsh on him. Let him be—' 'My eyes widened with realisation. He mentioned Elyrians! He knew about Duvollin, and so did my mom.

The memories of the identity thief came flashing back in my head. He was about to tell me something related to my life. Why did he disappear? Why was he in such pain?

'Did he really mention them?' Jason asked with his mouth slightly open.

'I, uh, I didn't remember this memory. I just don't know. Probably, it was just my imagination.' Deep in my heart, I felt it wasn't a sheer imagination but reality.

Jason grabbed my hand. 'Come on,' he said.

'Where to?' I asked.

'What do you mean? Obviously, I'm talking about our friends. They need to know.'

'Forget about it. It was just a memory. Not so important,' I said though I actually didn't mean it. Rimtzal's words were still in my head, and I did not intend to defy him.

'It is important, Airik! Not for you. But for me, it is important!' he yelled.

'How do you get concerned in this?' I asked, rising to my full height, though I was quite shorter than Jason.

'I don't believe you are actually saying this, Airik. I am a Pimarv. I have all damn right to interfere in every matter that is related to Duvollin.' Jason tried to make himself sound diaphanous.

'They already must know about everything that happened in my life. It is of no use,' I covered up.

'I don't care. I feel they need to know. If not you, I'll tell them.' Jason shoved his finger against my chest. 'I never expected this from you, Airik.' He turned around and began to walk towards the door.

'Jason, stop,' I said in a hushed a tone.

'Stop, Jason.' My voice came out firmer than before. Jason turned around and faced me. I locked his gaze with mine.

'I'm sorry I need to do this.' I made him forget the former conversation we had.

Being a protector didn't turn out to be a good job after all. I had to play with my best friend's memory. Now that I had a memory about my parents that somehow they were related to Duvollin especially Allekior, my decision of moving on a journey was more compact. But for that, I need to win the combat. And I will do anything for the sake of my parents.

The Combat

I woke up early in the morning before dawn to get prepared for the combat. Palort constantly kept repeating Anedrin's traps. I ought to see Jason only for once and make sure he was all right.

'Have you seen Jason?' I asked Palort.

'He is in the arena,' Palort replied.

'Thanks, buddy.' I patted Palort's biceps. I never realised they were so strong.

'Don't forget about Anedrin's traps!' Palort hollered.

'I won't!' I replied.

I ran as fast as my legs could carry me. There, I could see Jason, having a friendly contest with a blonde guy. I know his name: Maximus. Yes, Maximus. He had a deep ugly scar running across his right cheek. He spotted me.

'All hail for the protector!' he shrieked. Everyone except Jason bowed down to honour me. Jason had no clue of what was going on. He looked at me in confusion.

'I think we should get back to our practice,' I suggested. Everyone went back to their initial position and dispersed to their practising areas.

'How are you this morning?' I asked and tried to be casual.

'Fine. And you?' he asked me.

'I'm doing well. Just a bit tensed about the combat.' I rubbed my palms. He seemed totally fine to me.

'You need to win, Airik. Everything depends of this combat. Plus, everyone will be watching,' Jason notified.

'Is it something like Hunger Games?' I asked.

'I don't think so. You don't have to kill one another to win,' he replied.

'I didn't mean that, silly. I'm talking about the arena. Is it an illusion?' I asked.

'I don't know about that,' he retorted.

'Anything else you know about this combat?' I asked

'It is supposed to start within 90 minutes.' He snickered.

'Improve your sense of humour,' I said.

At last, the time for the combat arrived. Basically, there were no rules. The one who gives up will lose. The fight will be held in an open arena with most of the warriors of Selemara watching us. There was no way in which I'll ever get in that kid's trap. I'll hardly let her build it. But one thing was for sure: she was much more skilled and agile than me. I needed to figure out something. I had been in their restrooms, which they called serene chamber, for quite long.

'Are you sure you want to do this?' Palort asked.

'Stop asking me the same question again and again. I'm pretty sure I want this impractical combat to happen.'

'We can sit and talk. She is very determined to win this combat. Probably, we can prove to her in some other way. I can cancel this fight right away,' Palort declared.

'There is no need.' I tried to keep the anxiety off myself.

'Ladies and gentlemen! Hold your breath!' I could hear the announcement taking place. *Wait a minute. Ladies?*

'Is the whole Selemara here?' I asked.

'Yes. Why do you ask?'

'I thought it would be just the warriors.'

'It was actually decided that it would be confidential, but Anedrin insisted it to be publicly done for the whole Selemara should know that the protector has arrived.' His eyes were saying sorry to me.

'It's about time! To see our young protector!' Maximus announced. I could hear exciting shouts of people meant for me.

'Let's go, Airik Patronus. Show them you are not at all like the former protectors.' Palort patted my shoulders and smirked as if he knew something I didn't. I took two swords and exited the serene chamber.

'All hail for the protector!' someone squealed. Everyone bowed down in respect. I didn't like this at all. I sighed. They were going to do it whether I admired it or not. They sat down after a few seconds. I was quite close to the place where the audience was seated.

'He is so cute!' I heard someone say. I glanced in the direction from where the statement came. I could see a group of girls ogling me. I gave a short nervous smile and put back my grim face. Maximus was barking a few sentences about the fight, the arena, and the participants. I wished Jason was here.

'Nervous?' I felt a hand on my shoulders. I sighed with relief—my best friend Jason.

'Jason. I'm much more nervous because of those girls to my left.' Jason twisted his neck.

'I can see why,' he grumbled.

'Why wouldn't they? I've been standing beside you for the last ten minutes,' he said. *Seriously? Why is he so self-obsessed?*

'Yeah right,' I muttered.

'Thereby, let the battle begin!' Maximus shrieked. Everyone in the stadium bawled. Anedrin was soon standing by my side.

'Ready, protector?' she asked. I could see a huge bow and a bunch of arrows with her.

'Don't be so arrogant. Probably, I'll defeat you,' I said.

'In your dreams!' she snapped back.

'I always strive to get my dreams true,' I retorted.

She sighed. 'Let's see if you've actually got your skills huge like your smart mouth and witty brains.'

Delver came and wished us luck. 'I'll always watch your backs,' he reassured.

With a distance of 50 metres between us, the battle began. I gripped tightly at the swords. Anedrin charged two arrows at me at blinding speed. I dodged them and hardly realised that there was a dagger effusively running in my direction. Before I could react, it slightly passed my right forearm, giving rise to a small cut. Still, I kept my gaze steady on her moves. She tried to keep her distance from me. I got that. *Long-distance fight is all she wants as if I'll give her one.* I smirked and teleported right behind her. Poor girl didn't had time to react. It took me a fraction of a second to realise she caught me in her trap. She swung her legs and hit me hard at my abdomen. I backed away. It wasn't so hard that I'll fall and cry with pain. I rubbed my abdomen.

She took out her sword from its sheath and took tender steps towards me. At once, she flung her sword at me. I blocked it. All of a sudden, she jabbed her hand at my fresh wound she abruptly caused. I yelped with pain. This distraction was enough for her to attack me again. The spot she chose were my temples. Her knuckles soon met my temples. I was unable to block her hands. It felt like being smashed between two rocks. *Where the hell did she get these moves from?* I dropped to my knees, clutching my head and rubbing it harshly.

'Forget about travelling Allekior, protector. I won't let you win,' she said through her gnashed teeth.

'Get up, Airik! You have to! For the sake of your family!' I could hear Jason motivating me to get up. Even if he didn't motivate, I would have resumed the fight. He was working like a reminder for me, though.

For my parents, I told myself. Something suddenly happened that I couldn't realise. The ground shook, and a murmur broke out among everyone. Anedrin had her eyes wide with shock. And within a few seconds, the clear weather turned stormy. My vision turned blurry, and I fainted on the spot.

It was very dark. I was very afraid, but I didn't show it. I was walking through the woods. I didn't know where to go. My friends had already disappeared, leaving me behind. All right, I know I was the one to blame, but I couldn't help it. When they talked about hiking, I got overexcited. Plus, Infinity was already gone. I needed something to pass my time. Who cares for a 5-year-old kid like me? I kept walking, and at last, I saw a camp. I sighed with relief and walked towards it. Probably, those people could help me. I marched towards my destination. A man with hairs on his face came running towards me. There was a specific word for the hair that grows on a man's face: *beard*. Yes, the bearded man came running towards me.

'Stop! You are not allowed in this area,' he said between scruffy breaths.

'I need some help, anonymous. Can you help me?' I asked with the most innocent smile I could ever have.

'First of all, I have a name. It is Rajan.' It was weird that he spelt each and every letter of his name, and every time he said a letter, his nose splayed. He was simply wasting his time by spelling out his name.

'And second, no, I can't help you. I have a job to be done rather than helping 5-year-olds.' Mean man.

I said nothing and turned around and began walking towards the woods. I was not in the mood of arguing with anyone. I had already devised a plan for myself. All I did was peek in his head and gather information about this place.

I hid behind a huge tree and watched as Rajan reverted to his position. I walked around the camp with the dense forest hiding me from Rajan or anyone like him. There, I found the spot that would get me help. Just like the image in his head, there was no one. A perfect place to sneak in. I gingerly climbed the three-feet wall and tried to be as noiseless as possible. I didn't bother to check on my surroundings. All I needed to do was find a white camp with telephone. But the problem lay when most of the camps would be white and telephone would be available in only one. I entered a random camp.

'Guys! Intruder!' someone yelled. I was pretty sure they were referring to me. I ran where my little and chubby legs took me until I bumped into someone.

'Sorry, anonymous,' I muttered.

'Anonymous? Now people of this era don't speak that way,' he said in amazement.

'What are you doing here, Mr—' he trailed off.

'Patronus. Airik Patronus.' I extended my hands towards him. He shook it. 'Vikram Gandhi,' he introduced himself. I'm sure he was amused. I didn't need to read him for that. People normally tend to get creeped out around me when they meet me for the first time. I have no idea why.

'So, Airik Patronus, may I know about your presence in this camp?' he asked.

'I need some help, Mr Gandhi. Only if you are willing to help me. Because the man I met with the beard—Rajan, right? Rajan wasn't kind enough to help me,' I said.

'I can and will help you, but before that, what are you doing in the middle of the night in a place like this?' he asked and folded his arms across his chest.

'Hiking,' I answered. He raised his left brow. Oh, he didn't believe me.

'My friends decided to go hiking in the woods. They refused to take me, for they considered me very small. So I followed them and lost their track. And then, I ended up in this place,' I explained. Mr Gandhi nodded in understanding.

'I understand. But don't you think you shouldn't be roaming in this place alone without anyone's consent? Do you have any idea what is going on in your town?' he asked me.

'If you are talking about the mayor, I know what's going on in his life. In fact, I know everything going on in each and everyone's life. I can also tell you about you that you don't know,' I said with pride. This is a rare talent I had. My parents told me to keep this talent secret. Don't know why. Mr Gandhi laughed.

'So tell me, um, why is this camp in here?' he asked. That was a very silly question. Everyone knows about it, but I won't say it aloud. He might feel humiliated and then refuse to help me. After all, my skills were not yet so developed that I can converse with my parents from this huge distance.

'People are disappearing and being teleported to another dimension. I already warned everyone, but no one believes me,' I complained like a 5-year-old I already was.

'Really? Have you seen your so-called another dimension?' Mr Gandhi created air quotes for *another dimension*. This was enough. People don't believe me, but they don't throw scrutinising statements on my face.

'You were born in 1987 in New York to Geet and Bharat Gandhi. Your mother was a gymnast and died giving birth to you. You were brought up by your father, who used to teach anthropology. He then married your aunt for she could take care of you. You adore Audrey Hepburn, Sylvester Stallone, and Einstein. You always had a crush on Pallavi, a classmate, until you saw her being swept off by your best friend, and since then, you are being an introvert. Your favourite colour is black, and you always stay confused between what is more important: money or satisfaction. You are an anthropologist. You're here to investigate the disappearing cases of people under mysterious circumstances. Am I right, Mr Vikram Gandhi?' I finished. He was speechless.

'How did you find out so much about me?' he asked.

'That is a question complicated to answer.' I scratched my head. *Should I tell this man everything? He seems pretty stable to me. Still, I can't take risks. I've already told him too much. Mom won't be happy with the little act I've done today.* Vikram Gandhi was still staring at me curiously as if he'll right away scoop me up and operate me in the laboratory. I cleared my throat. He blinked several times and cursed under his breath. Suddenly, he did something I never expected anyone to do. He smirked. I frowned. I don't think anyone will ever manage to keep a smile after listening half of their life through my statements.

'You need to rest, Airik. I'll get you to your home,' he assured me. I merrily slept in his bed, dreaming of fairies and mystical creatures that I had never seen before.

The Decision

I woke up after having a merry dream of the first encounter with Mr Gandhi. I never thought that the memory was still intact in my brain. I had a very bad headache from the combat yesterday. My breakfast was right beside me. I ate heartily and stretched myself. After hitting the shower, I went straight to the library. I found everyone in there.

'You are awake?' Jason asked.

'What do you think?' Anedrin grumbled.

'Did I win the combat?' I asked desperately.

'That is exactly what we are trying to decide. We have been in a dilemma since you blacked out,' Jason informed.

'What happened in the combat?' I asked.

'You mean the act you pulled out? You changed the weather unknowingly,' Anedrin answered. I frowned.

'I didn't change the weather. It is not in my hands. It depends on the ro—' Anedrin interrupted me before I could complete.

'This is Duvollin, Airik, not your orphanage. Things don't work the way they do in your place. Everything is different!' she snapped.

'It is technically impossible!' I argued.

'Everything that happened within the past few weeks with you was technically possible?' Jason asked.

'No, but—' the arrogant girl interrupted me again.

'Exactly, Airik. No one is blaming you here for what happened. You didn't hurt anyone but yourself,' Anedrin said. I took a deep breath and let it out. I cannot argue with her. It is damn difficult to win, especially when the odds are not in my favour.

'Stop it, all of you!' Delver stood between me and Anedrin. 'Why do you folks always need to fight like kids?' he scolded. 'Oh, I meant very small kids,' He reframed his statement.

'It's not me, Delver. It's always our new regal protector Airik Patronus,' she hissed.

'Fight is never one sided, Anedrin. I understand you want to protect him and keep him alive. We all wish to do the same, but this doesn't mean you'll fight with him. He is not a kid. I know after everything you've gone through, you don't want him to end up like Fein.' Delver explained Anedrin. *Fein? Who the hell is Fein?* I opened my mouth to speak, but

Delver gestured me to stop. Probably, he understood my query. Anedrin remained motionless for a few moments. Was it because of the Fein guy? I could tell she was trying to restrain her tears. I knew what to do now.

I concentrated hard on Anedrin. First, there was just darkness. Then I could see a younger version of Anedrin, probably 8 or 9. She wasn't grim like the present but cheerful and bubbly. Beside her, I could see another boy, almost 12; and he looked a lot like me: green eyes with glint of black pale skin, black hair, and lean but more masculine.

'Fein! I got it!' Anedrin exclaimed in her babyish voice. Fein clapped for Anedrin. 'Very good, Anedrin. We need more lilies. Come on.' He held out his hand for Anedrin to take. His expression suddenly changed. He sensed something wrong.

'Faster, Anedrin,' he commanded. The 8-year-old girl was struggling between the rocks. At last, she came out of the lake and the bed of rocks. Fein grabbed her hands and ran as fast as he could. Anedrin had to jump to keep up with him. She never objected. They seemed lost in the greenery around them. At last he found a cave—a very deep cave.

'Hide here and don't come out until I tell you to do so,' Fein ordered.

Anedrin sat there very long and fell asleep right there. The next day, she waited until noon when there was no sign of Fein. She exited the cave and went in search of him. She searched him everywhere possible, but she couldn't find him. At last, she returned to Selemara.

'Anedrin!' A lady came running towards her and hugged her. 'Where were you?' she asked, exasperated. The lady looked a lot like Anedrin. Blue piercing eyes, tanned skin, and brown hair. The rest of his family members were relieved to know she returned safe, but all they wanted to know was about Fein.

'I lost him,' Anedrin muttered and broke in a sob.

'Stop crying, Anedrin. Everything will be fine. Just tell us where Fein is.' Another boy who looked like Fein tried to comfort Anedrin.

'We were collecting lilies for Delver. Then something went wrong. We ran and ran. Then he saw a cave and told me to hide there until he comes and gets me out of there. I sat there for many hours, and then I fell in sleep there. The next day, I searched him, but he was nowhere to be found.' Anedrin coughed.

'Did you eat something?' the boy with Fein's features asked Anedrin. She shook her head briskly.

'Come with me.' Anedrin followed the boy. Darkness came again.

After the memory I saw about Anedrin and Fein, the way I think about her had totally changed. I never dared to ask about Fein the same way no one asked me about my parents. The day passed in a blur. There was no sign of decision that was about to be taken. I was resting in my room after a very heavy workout with Palort and Jason. The thought about my parents never left my head. The only thought that remained was that somewhere they were alive and I'll get every answer about them from Allekior. I'll convince Anedrin to go to Allekior with me.

'Hi, protector.' Jason came and slumped on the cushiony chair beside me.

'Have they decided yet?' I asked.

'If you are talking about the travelling part, they are still in a dilemma, and if you are talking about the combat, Anedrin has agreed her defeat,' Jason notified.

'She actually did that?' I asked in wonder. *What if he is trying to pull a prank on me?*

'I'm serious, Airik. Only if that weather-changing art wouldn't have happened, we would already be leaving for Allekior by now.' Jason huffed.

'Who is Fein?' It was all that came out of my mouth.

'Anedrin's cousin. People think he was kidnapped by Allekior because they suspected him to be the new protector, which he wasn't. Since the kidnapping incident, no one has seen him. People think he is dead,' Jason told. It makes sense that Fein looks like me.

'Who told you about this?' I asked.

'Maximus,' Jason answered.

'You mean the blonde guy with an ugly scar on his face?' I asked. Jason nodded and smirked. I can't help it. I'm really bad at remembering names.

'So what do you plan to do now?' Jason asked lazily.

My eyes brightened with excitement. 'I think I know what I'm about to do right now.'

'Where the hell are you taking me, Airik?' Jason grudged from behind.

'I already told you,' I yelled over the speeding wind and dancing trees.

'You said just one word: Rimtzal. That doesn't explain anything,' he complained.

'Rimtzal is not a word, silly. It's a name of a prior protector,' I explained.

'Your mistake. You didn't mind to spare me the details,' he nagged. We continued our journey with Jason disturbing me with his silly questions.

At last, we reached Rimtzal's cave. 'Seek me only if you essentially need guidance. If you are here to dissipate the knowledge, you will meet the same fate as the others who have earlier tried to squander,' he roared. Jason grabbed my arm.

'What was that about? I doubt we should meet this guy.' He turned his head in every direction to find the owner of the ancient voice.

'Come on.' I rolled my eyes. We squeezed into the cave. 'I thought you were claustrophobic,' Jason said.

'I still am. Nothing has changed,' I admitted.

'Everything has changed, Airik, between you and me.' There was silence after Jason's last statement. Everything had actually changed between us, I keeping things from him and Jason doing the same. Thankfully, the cave lit up with candles, and the same feeling of the dating spot aroused again. I chuckled.

'What's this?' Jason asked while pointing towards the bones.

'Interior,' the word rolled off my tongue as if it was normal to have interior like this. Jason narrowed his gaze at me. I turned towards the centre of the cave where Rimtzal's lips were turned in a tight smile. Maybe he was supressing his smile to keep himself from destroying the image of being dangerous.

'I think this is the second time we are meeting, Airik Patronus.' His voice came out husky.

'Yes. Actually, I, uh, we need your guidance.' I pulled Jason with me who was busy admiring the 173-year-old man.

'Were you the protector before Airik came?' Jason asked.

'I was a protector a hundred and fifty-five years back. Why do you ask, and who are you?' Jason's eyes widened.

'Hundred and fifty-five! You look as if you've just crossed 20!' Jason gushed the same way I did when I saw Rimtzal for the first time. His stern expression melted, and his face softened. He likes the ones who compliment him.

Rimtzal cleared his throat and chose the gentle way to speak. 'You didn't tell me who you are, boy.'

'I'm Jason,' He replied.

'Jason? Haven't you got any surname?' he asked.

'I used to . . . have one,' he said heavily.

'By your looks, you look like one of the Pimarvs to me,' Rimtzal said.

'He is one of them,' I said.

'So . . . why do you need my help?' Rimtzal came to the point.

'We wanted to know about Fein,' I said. For a fraction of a second, I saw a gleam of fury in his eyes. Something was really wrong. I felt as if I should peek in his head, but I couldn't risk it. He could surely understand it. I had to leave it for another day.

'Where is Fein's family?' I began with my questions.

'They left in search of him around five years ago and haven't returned since then,' he answered. I guess he was being honest.

'How do Elyrians choose a protector?' I jumped on a different topic. Jason shot me a confused stare.

'They look all over Duvollin to find the physically and mentally strong human. When they find him, they bless him with the powers of a protector,' he answered.

In my case, it was different. Technically, I don't belong to Duvollin. But the spirit in Pamretol is growing stronger, or maybe the shield is growing weak and everything in her is the same.

'Is Fein alive?' I asked.

'I think he is alive. He can be used as bait for the downfall of Selemara. I don't think they'll kill him so soon,' he replied thoughtfully.

What about the memories I watch in my dreams? I asked him telepathically so that Jason won't listen.

The drink Delver gave you contained the antidote, and somehow it managed to trigger the memories back, which were wiped from your brain, he answered.

'It was nice meeting you, Rimtzal. We should get going,' I said curtly. Rimtzal smiled at us.

Long-Lost Friend

Jason and I didn't talk the whole way from Rimtzal's place. When we reached the palace, Palort, Delver, and Phileda were already leaving.

'Why are you going so soon? Anedrin needs you,' I said.

'She'll be fine, Airik Patronus,' Palort said.

'How can you be sure? The way her expression changed after mentioning Fein was distressful. I am pretty sure people blame her for Fein's disappearance,' I spat. No one said anything.

'You should talk to her, Airik. You remind her of Fein. She'll feel better,' Delver admitted and took off on his relite with Palort and Phileda following closely behind.

Jason and I sat quietly in our chamber for a few minutes. 'Why don't you talk to her?' Jason broke the silence.

'And what exactly will I say? You know very well I'm really bad at starting conversations,' I said.

'Gain her trust and talk to her,' he suggested.

'How can I gain her trust in a matter of minutes?' I wrinkled my nose.

'In this case, go talk about any topic that comes in your mind.' He pushed me out of the chamber and closed the door behind me before I could protest.

'These doors will be remained closed until you don't talk to her.' He gave me the details after closing the door. There was no other option rather than talking to Anedrin. I searched the whole palace for her, and at last, I found her in the palace's garden.

'Hi,' I walked up to her and said casually.

'Get out of here, protector. I'm not in the mood to taunt you,' she said. Wow, I feel at ease.

'Nor am I in the mood to be mocked,' I muttered.

'What are you here for?' she asked.

'I'm here to share my sorrow with someone who can understand me,' I said.

'What about Jason? Is he unable to understand you?' she asked innocently.

'No, it's nothing like that. Actually, I feel you and I have a lot in common,' I said timidly. I doubt she even heard me.

'What is your favourite colour?' she asked.

'Mixture of purple and blue. It tells me of the light inside the darker side,' I replied honestly. 'What about you?' I asked.

'Green. It reminds me of Fein's eyes.' For a moment, I could see the child who wanted to break free in her.

'Why haven't I seen your parents around? Where are they?' I asked curiously.

'There was a bloodbath after Fein's disappearance. His parents attacked us, killing my father. My mother fled. I have no idea where she is. Probably, she is not in this world anymore. After that, at the age of 9, I took over the throne with Delver directing me to keep people happy,' she confessed.

'Why do you taunt me?' I faked a whimper. She laughed heartily. I swear this was the first time I heard her laugh, and trust me, it reminded me of someone indistinctly familiar.

'What happened?' Anedrin shook me.

'You remind me of someone really familiar, but the problem is I don't remember her.' I kept it short and simple.

'Can I ask you something?' she requested hesitantly.

'Go ahead,' I said briskly.

'Who is Infinity?' she asked.

I was in my house alone sitting by a window. My friends passed by without noticing me. Mom and Dad were as usual on their work, leaving their 4-year-old child that is me alone. Practically, I was not alone; the lady who was babysitting me was over the phone, talking to her boyfriend. Don't ask me how I figured it out. It was quite obvious to understand. She was hyperexcited, throwing some romantic, stupid, and idiotic line like 'My love is unlimited', 'I love you more than the stars in this world', and all those inefficient sentences. *Love is a feeling. Why the hell is she comparing it to stars? How can stars be related to love? People need to be practical in life.*

I walked to my room in boredom to find something interesting. Plus, I wanted to get away from the love lines she had been quoting for her boyfriend. Even after closing the door of my bedroom, I can hear her getting sentimental over her phone. I'm pretty sure she didn't know about the word *privacy.*

'Airik, come here. I need your help,' I heard Infinity call me.

'How did you get here? My balcony is on the second floor,' I said in muffled voice so that the romantic babysitter couldn't listen.

'The pipe, silly.' She hit the back of my head lightly with her soft hands.

'The pipe? Do you have any idea of how dangerous it is?' I scolded her.

'I'm here to meet you, and you are scolding me like my mom.' She scoffed and folded her arms.

'I was just worried, Infinity, that's all. I'm sorry.' I held my hands to my ears.

She burst out in a fit of giggles. 'How can I be mad at my best friend?' She caught my hands and forced them down.

My friend Infinity was the most adorable person I'd ever met. She was four just like me, and we had been together since we were toddlers. I personally like brunettes like her. She had the turquoise eyes, and I thought they were the prettiest eyes I'd ever seen. Her warm ivory skin always glistened against the sun. She looked like an angel from heaven.

'Come back to our world, Airik. I've been talking about my day. Did you listen?' She shook me.

'You were talking about your day?' I could feel heat creep over me. Not in front of Infinity.

'Airik, are you blushing?' she asked. She caught me.

'No. You are not able to see properly in the dark. There is no reason for me to blush. What were you about to say?' I changed the topic.

'I'm going, Airik.' *Is she playing a prank on me?* Infinity kept a grim face. She wasn't kidding.

'Where to?' I asked.

'Mom and Dad are not telling me. They say it is a very beautiful place, and I'll love it.' I pursed my lips.

'Probably, they are taking you to Paris,' I suggested.

'That's exactly what I said. They denied.' She sat on my bed and took off her shoes. I did the same.

'I'll miss you, Infinity,' I said.

'I know. I have something more to tell you,' she said as if it was the secret she had been keeping from everyone.

'Something is happening to me, Airik, something really different.' She paused for a second to consider whatever she was about to tell.

'A few days ago, I talked to a squirrel.' I burst out laughing.

'Airik! I'm sharing my secret with you, and you are laughing at me? I never told anyone about your secret, and I didn't laugh when you told me about it.' She got infuriated and got up to leave my room.

'Hey! Stop.' I caught her by her wrist and forced her to sit beside me. 'I'm sorry.' This was the second time I was apologising to the same girl.

'Let me complete my story first. Then I'll think of forgiving you,' she said. Sometimes girls are very difficult to understand.

'A squirrel was under my bed. I reached ahead to take it, but she seemed very frightened of me. I told her that I won't hurt her. Then I heard a voice saying, 'That is what people say to lure me in their trap. After that, they don't care about me.' I looked everywhere to find the source of this statement, and then I realised it was the squirrel herself who said it. Then we became friends.' She smiled.

'You still don't believe me?' She looked at me tentatively through her turquoise eyes.

'Of course I believe you, Infinity,' I replied honestly.

'There is more I need to tell you.' She blinked several times.

'I've heard your dad and my dad talking about Elyrians. Do you know what it is?' she asked.

'No,' I replied.

'Why don't you read their minds?' she asked.

'I'm not so skilled, Infinity. I can only communicate,' I reminded her.

We sat there the whole evening, scrutinising the babysitter's conversation. When it was time for dinner, Infinity left my room and climbed down the pipe, leaving me with the 'busy' babysitter alone.

Embark On A Journey

The next day I woke up early in the morning and told Jason everything about the dream I had last night. He said it was just my imagination, which I believe is not at all right.

'There is a meeting in the library. I hope you won't be late. And stop thinking about Infinity,' Jason informed and left the room. Infinity—now I know why the name seemed so familiar. She was my childhood best friend. How did I manage to block her for so long? The truth is my subconscious knows each and every answer to my question. I sighed and headed for arena.

'Do you have any idea what just happened? You will go berserk with happiness!' Palort exclaimed excitedly.

'Let me guess. Anedrin will not taunt me anymore,' I said with least interest.

'You're close. Fine, let me tell you. She is coming to Allekior with us. Isn't that amazing?' Palort was almost jumping with excitement.

'Of course it's amazing!' Phileda came from behind much happier than her twin.

'I think we shouldn't disrupt our practice. Get on sword fighting with Jason,' he instructed.

The whole day I couldn't think about anything but Infinity. Each and every memory about her came crashing back in my brain. So many questions but no answers.

'Airik, something is really not right with you,' Jason said. 'We have been in the dining hall for over an hour, and you haven't eaten anything properly.' He clenched his jaw.

'I'm not in the mood to talk.' I got up from my chair and exited the crowd gathering in the dining hall. Jason was following me.

'Wait!' he yelled. I turned behind and faced him.

'Infinity is just a girl. Get her off your mind and concentrate on the problems that are on the brink to erupt. Why are you behaving like this? Don't tell me you are sorry for yourself that she left you,' Jason spat.

'For me, she is not just a girl. She was the first close friend I ever made, and she didn't leave me. I'll never be sorry for that.' I directly headed towards the library. I didn't feel like practising.

Jason was right in some places. There were actual problems that I particularly needed to face. But the drawback is that

was those years ago. I want you to be like a peacock feather, which means I want you to be happy for eternity. Keep it with you. I won't be with you for long. I have to join the Pimarvs. I hope this feather will remind you of me.' We both experienced a manly hug.

'Why don't you tell me something about your old friend Infinity? She seemed really cute to me in the library.' Jason asked and blinked away the tears that were about to trail down his cheek.

'Not only cute, Jason, she is the most beautiful girl I've ever met. Now I know why I was never interested in any other girl,' It rolled off my tongue as if it was there in my mind since the start. I could see he corners of Jason's mouth twitch. I'm flushing red again.

'Apart from being happy, you are blushing quite too much lately,' he commented.

'Look, I didn't mean that. You are getting it all wrong. She is just a friend, and that is what she will always be.' My subconscious was asking me, *Do you actually mean what you said?*

I shook my head. 'I think we should go to sleep.' I took the cover and hit the bed. All I know was I'll have a restless night.

The whole night went really boring. I didn't get sleep. 'Airik,' Jason grumbled. *I'm not the only one who talks while sleeping.*

'Airik,' he repeated my name.

'What's wrong?' I asked.

'Do you think Phileda is interested in me?' He flipped on his stomach. I never thought he would ever ask me about girls.

'I don't know. Probably, you should ask her or maybe Palort.' I never thought we could ever converse like this.

'Man, have you seen Palort's biceps? I cannot handle him. He'll kill me, and then he would keep my corpse as a decoration on his bedroom's wall.' I imagined Palort carrying Jason's body and hanging it to the wall. I chuckled at that thought.

'I never thought you would ever like girls like Phileda. Don't you think she is really strong considering that she is a 16-year-old girl?' I tried to carry on the conversation. Only if I had something to record this moment and show it to him the next morning. *Well, I do have my brain.*

'Phileda is different from other girls. She is self-respecting, not like the girls who can do anything if they have decided they want it,' he muttered something and flipped on his back again.

'Goodnight, Jason,' I said. He nodded.

Fortunately, I somehow managed to sleep through the night. When I got up, it was still dark. I tried to wake Jason.

'Get up. We have to go.' I shook him. He mumbled something I couldn't understand and covered the pillow over his head. I shook him several times. He didn't seem to wake up. I took a bucket full of water and kept it beside Jason's face.

'I'm asking you again, Jason. Are you going to wake up?' I said it loud and clear. He didn't respond. I asked again. I got him up by his collar and dipped his head in the bucket. He shoved me and gasped for air.

'I'm sorry, Palort! Don't kill me,' Jason begged.

'It's me, Airik, not Palort.' A smile tugged my lips when I remembered about the previous conversation we had.

'Why would Palort kill you?' I continued, secretly mocking him, and trust me, I loved each and every second of it.

'I . . . um . . . don't know. I think I'll better get ready.' Jason stormed out of the room. I fell on my bed and laughed till tears dropped from my eyes. I never laughed so much in my whole life until I regained a memory about Infinity. I quickly showered and had my breakfast.

A few minutes later, Jason returned. 'I see. You look really excited.' He patted my shoulder.

'What did you dream about? When I tried to wake you, you began to beg for life from Palort.' I asked with a naïve expression on my face. He seemed quite tensed.

'If you want to talk to me or you need my help, feel free to tell me anything you want to. Your secret is safe with me.' I brushed my hand on his damp hair.

'Airik, I, uh, I feel something about Phileda. And this 'something' is really different of what I felt about the rest of the girls I ever dated. It is not a simple attraction. It is something else.' He gulped.

'Here, have a glass of water. Do you think this 'something' is love?' I asked him tentatively. I tried not to push him hard on the topic. He remained silent for a few minutes.

'I don't know,' He replied.

'Are you ready?' Palort came in with a cheerful attitude. Jason jumped when he heard him.

'Hey, hi, Palort. I mean good morning,' Jason jumbled up whatever he was about to say.

'Is something wrong? You look quite jumpy. By the way, you are a very funny boy.' He punched Jason's back. Jason said a silent 'Ouch!' I'd already seen how powerful he was in my near-death experience.

'When are we leaving?' I cleared my throat.

'Right now. Here.' He handed each one of us a dagger. 'This might be useful,' he whispered. The three of us together headed our way to the library. Phileda and Anedrin were already waiting for us. Each of them had a bag full of silver coins. Anedrin handed me and Jason two bags. 'In case we get separated.'

'Phileda will always be by your side, Jason. Palort and I will be with Airik.' Jason was flushing a bit. I looked at him once, and when he caught my eyes on him, he gave a mischievous smile. Something was on his mind. I didn't apply my skill on knowing what it was. Phileda too was trying to supress a smile.

'What are we waiting for? Let's go,' I said.

'Restless. Aren't you, protector?' Jason mouthed and bumped his shoulders against mine.

'I think you are the one dying to go on this journey, Jason,' I teased. He didn't say anything except for grumbling compliments on Phileda. Soon we got our relites. Jason was gaping at it. 'What are you waiting for? Go ahead. This is the transport we will be using to travel.' I urged him to take a look at his relite. He moved towards the five relites. He chose the black one, but he tried to stay away from the cloud of glow.

'Get in.' Phileda pushed him in. He looked around himself and smiled broadly. We all got in our respective relites and initiated our travel to Calsenai.

Infinity

Calsenai was a three-hour tour from Selemara. I hate travelling, but I'll do anything to meet Infinity. There were two reasons for it. First of all, her dad will be of huge help and my first clue to the tracks of my parents, and second, I would really like to meet her again.

Jason was the one thoroughly enjoying the journey. Almost after an hour, we had our first stop in Selemara's Travelling Chalet, a quite infamous lodge in the outskirts of Selemara. The manager didn't seem to recognise Anedrin. All he cared about was the silver coins. He charged three ostentatious silver coins for five of us as we were here to have food and refresh ourselves.

Jason and I clung together and made our way through the gathering crowd. The three Duvollinians were ordering something for us.

'You seem very happy, Jason. What's the matter?' I interlaced my hands in a businesslike manner.

'Why do you ask? You can read my mind,' he retorted.

'It's not about reading you, Jason. I want us to be the friends we were before we came in Duvollin. Nothing is like before between us.' I sighed. I guess I just overreacted on his meagre statement.

'I didn't mean that, Airik. We still have the same bond we had in the orphanage. In fact, our friendship is getting stronger day by day. Positively, people need to have secrets.' He gripped my clenched hands, which were digging in the flesh of my palm. I didn't notice that Phileda was standing by our side and listening to our conversation.

She cleared her throat. 'I bought breakfast for both of you. Here.' She quickly passed us two plates with a dish with a very delicious aroma and took another chair between both of us.

Palort and Anedrin joined us a few minutes later. We quietly ate our breakfast. Soon it was time to go. We took our stuff and mounted on our relites.

We travelled in silence for a long time until the sun was leeching our energy away from us. Jason was busy telling her about our life in the orphanage, and Phileda was intently listening to him. He somehow managed to engage her in a talk. Palort was sharpening his axe, and Anedrin was simply throwing pebbles in the pond.

Everyone was busy except me. I took a look around myself; I could see only tall unearthly green trees with colourful mosses. Then something caught my eye. There was something transparent on the grass. It looked like a huge pure colourless puddle. I was walking towards it.

'Stop!' someone yelled behind me. I spun around to see Anedrin running towards me. 'Stay away from it,' she warned.

'What's that thing?' I asked out of curiosity.

'I'll tell you later on. Right now, we need to get out of here before it wakes up.' She grabbed my hand, and we walked towards the place where Jason and Phileda were talking like lovebirds and Palort was sharpening his axe.

'There is a change of plan,' she said sternly. The twins and Jason stood up at once and walk towards us.

'I just spotted an adorv. We must get out of here,' she informed. *What the hell does she mean by Adorv?* Phileda looked afraid, but Palort remained emotionless. Everyone took off with their respective relites. After spotting civilisation, we halted.

'Now will you tell me what the hurry was about? And what is an adorv?' I asked.

'The transparent creature you saw over there was an adorv. Thankfully, it wasn't in its conscious state. The moment it comes in contact with a living creature, it takes over its mind and body and controls it,' she explained.

'That sounds really awful.' Jason scowled.

'It always is. We have reached Calsenai. Now all we need to do is find your girlfriend.' She turned towards me.

'She is not my girlfriend,' I stated sternly.

'Then why do you blush every time I mention her?' She was such an observant.

'I give up. There's no use arguing with you.' I held up my hands in mock surrender. She smirked and gestured us towards a shelter.

'Where is she?' I sounded quite desperate.

'You are so damn eager to know about her whereabouts,' Jason teased.

'How romantic!' Phileda exaggerated the situation. I puffed out my cheeks. They won't shut themselves up that's for sure. Anedrin was already trying to get away from my interrogation.

'Hey! Wait up!' I caught up with her.

'What?' she screeched, totally irritated with my interruption.

'Where is Infinity?' I asked.

'You really want to know?' she asked grimly. I nodded. She pointed towards a wooden house. I took off without another word.

I ran as far as my legs could carry me. I was really close to meeting my childhood friend. When I reached there, the door was open. I didn't mind knocking the door. When I entered, all I could see was a group of old ladies around late 60s sipping a cup of tea, I assume. Apart from them, a very young lady in her early 20s I presume was eyeing me sceptically.

'Why are you here, young man? And why didn't you knock on the door before coming in?' one of them asked. This cannot be Infinity's house.

'I'm sorry. There was . . . confusion. I'm really sorry. I won't bother you ladies any longer.' I ran away from the group with flushing red with embarrassment. When I reached my 'buddies', they all were trying to eat away the laugh that was struggling to erupt from them.

'Did you get to meet your girlfriend?' Anedrin asked with sarcasm.

'That's not at all funny. Those ladies in their late 60s were having a great time together, and I interrupted them, assuming that was Infinity's house.' I sighed.

'You should've listened the details I was about to spare to you.' She was right in some places.

It was my mistake. I should've listened to her whole statement. Jason coughed behind me. The day I'll tell Palort about his crush, he'll literally solicit for a peaceful life. He understood my indication and shook his head.

'Where is Infinity?' I asked her gently this time.

'Aren't you desperate to know?' She twirled her brown strand of hair between her fingers.

'Why wouldn't he? Come on, Anedrin, it's obvious. He talks her name whenever he is asleep. He blushes when we talk her name, and I swear as far as I know him, he'll never blush in millennia. All I know is the girl is about to change his life. She has the capacity to make you do something that is impossible. That's what true love is all about.' He dreamily blinked his lashes.

Where the hell did true love come from?

I stood up. 'Look, I don't care what you guys think. Just tell me where she is,' I snapped.

'She is in Calsenai,' Jason and Anedrin said at once and high-fived. I left the lodge and mounted on my relite.

'I am going on a ride,' I yelled and took off. The afternoon hot breeze was beating against my pale skin. Everything in Calsenai felt amazing. I walked for a while and decided to return when something caught my eye. A small girl, around 10, was staring at me. Something was really familiar about her.

I frowned. Probably, she was staring at someone else. I looked behind me and both the ways. There was no one except me in her way. I concentrated hard on her brain.

Fein was being dragged by a troop of soldiers. The girl was slyly watching everything. I came back in the present and blinked several times. *How does she remember something that happened so many years ago?* I walked towards her, but she ran away from me.

I followed her noiselessly. She entered a house and closed it. After waiting for a few seconds, I approached the door and knocked it. *Wait a minute. What will I say to the one who opens the door? Hi, I'm Airik Patronus. I'm the new protector of anegz. I'm here to interrogate the girl who just ran in your house. It is really important. Will you please let me talk to her? Damn it. There are many other ways.* As soon as I turned around to leave the house, someone opened the door.

'I'm sorry. I'm looking for someone else,' I gushed and soon regretted it.

The one who opened the door was Infinity, the beautiful girl in my memories. My mouth went dry.

'I'm sorry. Can I come in?' I asked. She nodded and was a bit confused.

I entered and made myself comfortable on one of the couches. I looked around her house. It was full of photos. One of the photos had both of our families together. Infinity got a glass of water for me.

'Thanks.' I smiled.

After gulping down the whole glass, I let out a ragged shaky breath. There was a heavy silence between us. I didn't know where to start.

'So . . . who are you?' she asked and tried to be polite.

'It's me. Airik Patronus, your best friend,' I replied. She dropped the tray she was holding. I think I should've confessed it politely.

'Mom! Dad! Ariel!' she yelled. *Ariel? Who is she?* Everyone came out running. It included the girl who saw Fein. She was terrified when she saw me. She must be Ariel.

'It's Airik!' She jumped with excitement. They frowned at me. The frown was replaced with smile.

'You look really different.' Infinity eyed me from head to toe. I tried my heart not to blush.

345

'You still blush,' she teased me.

'Where are your parents?' Uncle Denel asked.

'They . . . died,' I admitted. He remained emotionless as if he already knew, but the females were shocked.

'Then how did you come in Duvollin?' he asked.

'Have you heard of the anegz in Selemara?' I asked.

'Of course we have, silly. I've been here longer than you.' She made me feel stupid again.

'Well, um, I'm its new protector,' I said hesitantly. Everyone had their eyes wide in shock except for Uncle Denel. He smiled as if he knew this was about to happen. Just then, Anedrin, Phileda, Palort, and Jason boomed into the house.

'Do you have any idea of how worried sick we have been?' Jason asked anxiously.

'Who are they, Airik?' Infinity asked.

Jason didn't let me introduce. 'Hi, I'm Jason, Airik's friend. This is Palort and Phileda. They both are twins and are the children of the chief executor of Selemara. This is Anedrin, the ruler of Selemara. And you must be Infinity,' Jason finished, leaving everyone's surprised. I pinched him.

'Ouch!' he yelled and faked a whimper.

'What are you doing, Airik? You are not supposed to hurt people,' Infinity scolded me just like old times. Jason smirked.

'Infinity, we are not kids anymore,' I reminded her.

'Exactly! Why do you need to behave like a kid then?' She turned her attention towards the rest of my friends. 'Please have a seat.' She gestured them towards the chairs and couches. My attention turned towards Ariel.

'Who is the beautiful little girl in there?' I tried not to be intimidating for her. Everyone here except the little girl knows how cool-headed I am.

'My sister, Ariel. She is 10.' Ariel felt a little comfortable and left the curtain's support to hide her. She still eyed me apprehensively.

'Airik,' Uncle Denel's firm voice commanded me. I turned around to see him and Aunt Scarlett with a straight face.

'I think we need to talk.' I followed them in a large room. They closed the door noiselessly behind them.

'I'm sorry to hear about your parents.' He motioned me to sit on the bed.

'There were many things Delphinium wanted to tell you.' He moved towards a cupboard and returned. He handed me a locket.

'This belonged to your father. I'm pretty sure he never told you about Duvollin.' The locket had my mom's photo. She looked so beautiful, so serene, so lively.

'He was just waiting for the correct time. He knew he would die soon, but I didn't know it would be this fast.' Even Mr Gandhi said the same thing to me.

'Wait a minute. How can someone sense their own deaths? It is technically not possible,' I reasoned.

'You don't know anything about your dad's past. He left me the job to complete it.' He ran his fingers through my dark black thick hair in a fatherly manner.

'Your dad and I were born in Duvollin.' The first revelation itself was indigestible for me. I felt numerous knots form in my stomach.

He continued, 'You see, we both were really good friends since we were kids. We served for Calsenai for very long. This is what our ancestors did and expected us to do the same. Everything was fine in our lives.' He sighed.

'One day, we were returning from Bunatil to Calsenai. We were attacked by some soldiers with litror venom. All of us got infected. When we reached Calsenai, King Calcaneal somehow came to know about us. He didn't want to waste his precious silver coins on us. And if he didn't get the antidote for us, we would've either grown really smart or way too mentally retarded or dead. He didn't bother to keep us alive. He ordered our public execution.' He sighed again. This story seemed really familiar.

'And then you and your another friend somehow managed to get out of Calsenai. You both ran until you realised that you were almost on the border of Allekior and Calsenai. Then a portal appeared out of nowhere, and then both of you were teleported in a small village in Himachal,' I completed his story. He blinked in surprise.

'How did you—oh, I get it, your mind games.' I didn't tell him about the identity thief who pretended to be Mr Gandhi.

'And you missed on the part where you are referring to my friend was your dad,' he said. My breathing hitched. The identity was none other than my dad in Mr Gandhi's disguise. I was this close to him, and I never realised. I cannot bear to listen the whole story, knowing that I could have saved my dad. I had a chance, but I missed it—again.

'I think we can keep the story for some other day. There are other things that need my attention first.' I stood and hurried out of the door. When I almost approached the room where everyone was seated, I could hear everyone laughing and having a good time together. I can't just terminate their happy moments of life with my silly reason. I forced a smile on my face.

'Did I miss something?' I asked casually.

'You missed all the fun, Airik. Infinity was telling us about you,' Ariel said.

'I liked the part where you fall off the willow tree while getting Infinity's teddy and fracture your arm, and then she stays by your side the whole night.' I didn't react over Jason's taunt. He jumped on his feet. Infinity and Jason together approached me. She grabbed my wrist and took me out of the house.

'What's wrong?' they both asked in hushed whispers.

'Nothing,' I replied and tried to keep my gaze away from connecting to theirs. Having true friends sometimes can be disastrous. I was literally squeezed between them. Someone needed to remind them I'm claustrophobic.

'You both are suffocating me,' I hissed. Both of them took a step behind at once. I took a deep breath.

'Are you sure you don't want to tell me?' Infinity crossed her arms.

'Whenever someone mentions the death of my parents, I just . . . get off my rails.' I almost mentioned the truth—almost.

'Why aren't you making eye contact?' detective Jason bombarded me with his interrogation.

'Because I don't feel like talking right now,' I said through clenched teeth.

'And why exactly you don't you feel like talking?' He was pushing me way too hard. It was enough.

'Ask me another question, Jason, I'll admit everything you feel for Phileda in front of Palort. Then you know it will be your head and his axe,' I threatened. Jason closed his mouth.

'You've changed a lot, Airik.' Infinity said as if she never wanted me to change; she wanted the old Airik Patronus back. Only if it was possible.

Connection

The whole day, Ariel kept my friends entertained by stories of Infinity's early childhood and the fights that happened between us when we were kids. Ariel slowly seemed to trust me and like me more than before. I was really close to get the truth out of her. I couldn't tell Anedrin about any of this. She might threaten Infinity to interrogate.

Infinity showed us the way around the house. There were four bedrooms: three were for Infinity, Ariel, and Mr and Aunt Scarlett; and the fourth one was for guests. It was seldom used. There was one dining hall, a living room, and a kitchen. Everything was made of wood. Jason and Infinity never left their gaze from me. I felt really awkward.

Soon, when it was close to nightfall, we all decided to spend our night in the house itself. We made ourselves comfortable in the luxurious room. There was a couch and two huge beds. Palort preferred to sleep alone, so he chose

their belronag. They looked around themselves and were bewildered to see nothing but concrete buildings.

'What is that?' Dad pointed towards the unrelenting constructions.

'I've been here for the first time. This place really stinks.' Uncle Denel covered his nose.

'That's not exactly called stinking. It's sullying of something. Smells like carbon dioxide . . . I guess,' Dad replied thoughtfully.

'Pollution in Duvollin?' Uncle Denel said as a matter of fact. He continued, 'Probably, it's Phoryus. They have the intention to suffocate every single person in their kingdom.' Uncle Denel scrunched his nose in repugnance.

'Who created the portal in first place?' Dad rubbed the back of his neck.

'We can think about it later on. First, we need to aid ourselves from the venom.' They walked farther and searched for someone to take help from.

'The houses in this area are very different.' Uncle Denel turned his neck in every direction to examine.

Dad didn't care about the houses. He was keen on finding someone. Soon, they hit the road.

'What's this?' Uncle Denel jumped when he saw the black road. Dad bent down. He touched and then smelt it.

'Seems like coal tar to me. Strange.' Dad knitted his eyebrows together in a deep thought.

He got up, and they together resumed their journey. After walking for a long time, they slumped on the ground beneath them with sweat all over.

'What do we do next?' Dad asked. Uncle Denel didn't reply.

'What will happen when the venom starts showing its effects?' he asked.

'We will figure a way out to keep the venom from fluctuating.' He closed his eyes as if thinking over the question his best friend just asked.

'Let's go.' Dad grabbed Uncle Denel's elbow and helped him to get up. They walked farther, and then they saw a group of kids playing soccer.

'Which sport is that?' both of them asked concurrently.

'Whatever it is, it seems pretty intriguing to me. The fashion this place follows too is different.' Dad grinned and folded his arms.

When the kids were done playing, they both walked towards them. When the kids spotted them, their eyes were wide with astonishment.

'Can you help us?' Dad asked.

'Are you from a theatre? I really like the costume of yours. Will you lend it to me someday?' a kid asked. My dad's eyes connected with the kids who asked this question.

'What is a theatre?' the Duvollinians questioned.

'The place where plays are enacted,' he explained to them as if they were small kids.

'We can see your theatre later on. Right now, we need help.' The kids stole a moment of murmurs among themselves and turned towards Dad.

'What kind of help do you need?' the kid asked timidly.

'We are new and hardly know anything about this place. It is quite different from Calsenai,' Uncle Denel kept on gushing about their position.

'There is venom that turns you into a superhuman? That sounds so cool!' A 7-year-old kid I assume spoke animatedly.

'Get your nerves in the right way, Aiden. All venom causes is harm, not superabilities.' Another boy eyed the Duvollinians suspiciously.

Aiden. The name seemed familiar to me. No, it was just my imagination. Every time I hear a name, I feel it is recognisable. Meanwhile, I could feel the boys getting uneasy around Dad and Uncle Denel. They were trying their best to hide it.

'I think we should get going, our parents must be waiting for us.' A mature kid said and slipped away.

'You were talking about some place called Calsenai. Where is it?' Aiden asked.

'You don't know where Calsenai is?' Dad furrowed his eyebrows. The kids seemed equally bewildered like the Duvollinians. Dad's eyes went wide with realisation.

'Other world,' Uncle Denel stated.

'We need more help than we thought,' Dad mumbled.

'It would have been better to be publicly executed.' Uncle Denel stomped his right foot.

'We have to go with the flow. We will figure out something,' Dad assured. They both moved away from the kids.

'Hey! Wait up.' The mature kid who sneaked away came back with a brunette lady with her hair flaring over her face. She gathered her dark-brown hair and managed it to assemble it in a ponytail. Mom. She was so young, probably around her early 20s, I could tell. Dad took a deep breath. Uncle Denel shook his head.

'Hi! I'm Christina.' Mom held out her hand enthusiastically. Dad frowned at her.

'I'm sorry,' she muttered and tugged the brown strands of hair behind her hair that was falling on her face.

'What are you sorry for, beautiful lady?' Dad asked. Uncle Denel huffed behind him. Mom blushed.

'I don't know,' she replied, totally dumbfounded.

'We need help, Christina. We really need your help,' Uncle Denel chimed in.

'No, we don't,' Dad snapped. I felt he wasn't trying to show how much vulnerable he was.

'Yes, we do.' They both were on the verge to fight. Mom cleared her throat.

'It will be my pleasure to help you, Mr—' She didn't know Dad's name.

'Delphinium. Just Delphinium.' He grinned with charm.

'All right, Delphinium and—' She didn't know Uncle Denel either.

'Denel,' he answered.

'I assume you don't have a place to stay,' Mom said in a businesslike tone. Now I know where I inherited these skills from.

They both shook their heads. 'In that case, I would like both of you to stay at my house until you both want to go back to the city where you came from,' she suggested.

'It's not necessary. We can find a place to live.' Uncle Denel tried to be reasonable enough.

'Don't listen to him. He doesn't know what's right and what's wrong for him. I am the one who normally makes decisions.' Wow. Dad changed his decisions really fast.

He continued, 'Thanks for your help, Christina. We have no other option than to come.' Dad had a goofy smile plastered on his face.

Mom smirked. Wait a minute. She smirked? *That is unusual. She normally doesn't smirk.* She surely had something going on in her intelligent head.

'Follow me,' she commanded.

'What's wrong with you?' Uncle Denel said in a hushed whisper. Still, anyone could make out he was annoyed.

'What have I done?' Dad spoke innocently.

'Don't act to be so naïve, Delphinium. You know very well what I mean.'

'Come on, man, I can say she will take pretty good care of us for a while. By staying with her, we will come to know more about this place. After that, we'll leave,' Dad explained his plan.

'I'm not stupid, Delphinium. I just . . . don't feel right about her. Something is going on in her head,' he admitted.

'You are being very insecure. If something is really not right about her, then we will figure it out when we stay with her,' Dad reassured.

'I can tell even you are planning something else.' Uncle Denel changed his tone on *something else*. Dad didn't say anything. He just let the impish grin spread over his face.

Revelation

I woke up early in the morning, trying to process the memory I saw last night. I wish I could be awake for a bit longer and see the consequences Dad and Uncle Denel were about to face along with my mom. I had yet another meeting to face with Anedrin arguing while the twins and Jason listening intently to it.

This family were kind enough to let us reside there for the next two days. Jason was busy trying to get Phileda's attention while Palort and Anedrin were nowhere to be found. Of course, they were planning their next move. Jason was talking about something serious.

To be precise, something casual that he manipulated to become serious? I have no idea why girls drool over him. Except for being sarcastic, funny, and adorable, I don't see any other suitable adjective to describe him. I grinned and made my way towards Ariel. I needed her to believe me, and

I hardly had time for that. I spotted her in the kitchen. She was struggling with making something.

'Good morning, Ariel,' I greeted her amicably.

'Good morning, Airik.' She smiled sweetly and got back with her work.

'Do you need help?' I offered her aid.

'To be honest, yes, I really do need help. You see, Infinity is turning 17 a month later. I don't know what to do for her upcoming birthday.' *Yes, 27 December is her birthday. How can I forget? My birthday is on 26 December.* Ariel washed her hands and gestured me to exit the house.

'Tell me something that would totally surprise her. I think she already has got her birthday present in the form of the long-lost friend Airik. Only if I would have been lucky enough to have a friend like you.' She batted her lashes dreamily. I laughed.

'I thought we were already friends,' I said hesitantly. I didn't know how she would take it.

'Really?' She looked up at me. She seemed like a younger version of Infinity: joyful, wonderful, smart, and talkative—the list seemed endless. But now, she had changed so much. Even she had problems with me changing. I had no right to go and question her. I kicked a pebble. *Everything in my life is so damn frustrating! I really need to talk to someone about this.*

'Is something wrong?' she asked timidly.

'I think we should be going back. Everyone might be getting worried sick.' She chuckled, and we made our way back to the house. I hurried towards the room where I think everyone was present. My prediction was right. All of them were waiting for me.

'Why did you think of coming back, Airik? We would've delayed the meeting for you,' Jason said. *Why does he need to be so damn sarcastic?*

'How sweet of you,' I spat.

'If you both are done with your little sardonic game, we should proceed with our meeting,' Anedrin walked in. We both sat on the chair.

'We aren't staying here for long. I hope you are aware of it,' Anedrin said.

'I know,' I said lamely.

'I hope you all know we will discuss the further plans to enter Allekior. I've cross-checked each and every postern soldier in there. Of course, they are not covering the whole boundary of Allekior, but this doesn't mean they don't know anything about the areas where their soldiers are not present to guard it,' she completed.

'I've been thinking about going through and bringing some soldiers, but it's not helping.' She continued, 'Stealth is the only option.'

'They must have tightened the security around Allekior after you tried to corrupt them. Even after managing everything cautiously, they might get hold of us,' Jason said.

'I'm not a fool. I've already replaced their memory with a new one,' Anedrin stated.

'You've already decided what has to be done. Then what are we here for?' I snapped.

'The meeting is done. Have fun in here until you have time.' Anedrin got up and left. Everyone turned in my direction.

'What have I done?' I grumbled.

'Clearly, she is annoyed with you,' Jason whispered.

'I've snapped at her many times. She didn't get infuriated then. There is something else disturbing her,' I replied thoughtfully.

'You should go and find out,' Phileda said. Jason agreed. Of course, he would.

'Why me?' I cried.

'Airik, you are so much like Fein. Even if she doesn't say anything, I can easily know everything about her. We have grown up together,' Phileda said.

'Then you probably know what will make her feel better.'

'You are the one who can anyhow make her feel better. Go and talk to her. You both are almost the same. You both seem like siblings,' she admitted. I sighed and walked out of the room in search of Anedrin. I found her sitting on the front porch of the house. I approached her and cleared my throat. She didn't pay heed to my presence.

'Hi.' *Genius, Airik. This is what you need to say after everything that happened?*

'I mean sorry,' I reframed my former sentence.

'Sorry for what?' she asked.

'I replied at you harshly. You must've felt bad about it.' I shrugged, not knowing what else to say.

'You really think I'll be mad at you for replying at me?' She shook her head and let out a long furry breath.

'No,' I answered swiftly. There was a heavy essence of silence hanging between us. None of us said anything.

'Is it something about Fein?' My subconscious was screaming at me to withdraw what I just said. It would complicate things.

'You know more about Fein, don't you?' she asked me to the point.

'What are you talking about?' I asked with puzzlement.

'I'm talking about my brother Fein's disappearance. You know more than you actually show.' She pinned me on the spot with her sorrowful stare. I felt sympathy towards her.

'Yes, I know a bit. I'll know more by tomorrow, and then all of us together will get your brother.' I squeezed her shoulders in a sign of reassurance.

'Why tomorrow? Why not today?' she questioned.

'I'll tell you everything once I come to know what I'm looking for. If I don't find it in here, then we'll choose some other option,' I spoke and abruptly walked away. *I'm running out of time. I somehow need to know more. I need Ariel to remember every detail she saw that day.* I wasn't concentrating hard until I bumped into Ariel.

'Ariel, can we talk?' I asked her. She briskly nodded. We walked out of the house. I was trying to frame everything I was about to ask her. She must not feel frightened. Before I could ask her anything, she spoke.

'I know the reason why you want to talk to me, Airik. That is the only memory I remember. The rest is blurry,' she spoke innocently.

'I would like to listen to everything you remember.'

'I was returning home after playing. I heard someone yelling for help. I saw him being dragged by a troop of soldiers. They all seemed to be from Allekior. They were trying their best to muffle his screams, but it didn't help. So they knocked him down unconscious. All I could hear after that was all about grabbing the opportunity when they had the biggest chance and then missing it because they want something more to happen,' she completed.

'Thanks for your help, Ariel.' I smiled. She sadly smiled back at me. We never spoke while returning back to the house.

Grabbing the opportunity when they had the biggest chance and then missing it because they want something more to happen. Had the something more already happened? I need to talk to Anedrin about it. I trotted towards the guest room. Only Anedrin was sitting in there.

'There is something really important I need to tell you, Anedrin,' I said in urgency. Her head snapped in my direction.

'Is it about Fein?' she asked tenderly.

'I want to know everything that happened after Fein's disappearance.'

'You just said that you need to tell me something.' She raised her eyebrows questioningly.

'If you are planning to annoy me like this, then I don't see any other option than to go back to my normal life in the orphanage and spend the rest of my life in there and leave the anegz unprotected,' I said in one breath.

'I'll answer your question and get done with it.' She stood up and closed the door.

'What happened after Fein left?' I asked again.

'Like I told you, there was a bloodbath all over. My father dead and my mother on a run. My relatives were constantly threatening me to go and get Fein even though hell barges my way. Then, Delver came and protected me from everyone who intended to inflict harm upon me. He tricked my relatives to leave the palace and proved me to be a caring guardian. I trusted him more than my life. With no one ruling Selemara, there were lots of attacks on its subjects. Delver was worried. He had to stop it somehow, but there was confusion all over Selemara. They didn't want Delver to command them, knowing there was no ruler above him to control. Then, Delver deliberately crowned me as the ruler of Selemara. There was no other option. He taught me everything necessary to be a good ruler. He guided me every time I needed him. With this, Selemara was happy again,' she finished.

'If you don't mind me asking, why did you ask this question?' I knew this query would be coming. There was no way I'll ever let her know the actual reason. She'll scare Ariel to death.

'I already gave you my word to get your brother back. For that, I need to research over everything related to him,' I answered. She seemed convinced.

'I appreciate how much you care for me, Airik.' Anedrin smiled. I returned the smile and patted her head in a brotherly manner and left the room. I straightaway walked out of the house and let the fresh air overcome my hormonal grumpy nerves.

Nothing serious had ever happened after Fein's disappearance. They hadn't yet grabbed their big chance. But now was the best opportunity to strike Selemara. With the ruler running around loose, people would surely try to kill her. *She is the one who needs protection, not me.*

The Brooch

Soon, it was time for dinner. I hadn't heard much from Infinity. I felt guilty about ignoring her even though we were so close to each other. Our birthdays were coming close, and we couldn't celebrate it together. I lapsed in the bed and groaned.

'Need help, Airik?' I heard Jason.

'Can't you just leave me alone with my thoughts?' I literally pleaded.

'That's what I had been doing back in the orphanage, Airik. You need to open up a bit and let your emotions flow out.' I sat up straight on my bed. Jason took a seat beside me, surely waiting for me to start spilling out. I was not going to make this easy for him.

'Is it about Infinity?' he asked. I simply nodded.

'I knew it!' Jason hissed.

'Come on now, spill out the details.'

'Her birthday is a month away from now. You see, we haven't talked much even after meeting after so many years. She wants me to be the same old Airik, and I want her to be the prior Infinity.' I sighed.

'All you want to do is talk?' he asked.

'I don't know.' This time, Jason groaned.

'Why are you so confusing? And how can you not know what you exactly want?' Jason yelled.

'Dude, you are exaggerating the situation. I just want to talk to her . . . in person.'

'Talk about what?' He dug for details.

'That is none of your business,' I snapped.

'Kids below 18 are not allowed to set up a business.' Jason laughed at his nonhumorous joke.

'Do I momentarily ask you about the talks Phileda and you share?' His laughing came to a halt. I hit the nail at the right point.

'I can tell you most of the things if you want to know,' he spoke sincerely.

'I don't have time for knowing about your love life. It's time for dinner, and I need to talk to her today. It's now or never.'

'Growing impatient. I like it.' He winked at me and left the room.

'Be on time for dinner,' he reminded.

I decided to talk to Palort about Anedrin's security. It would be really foolish of me if I didn't worry about her. Fortunately, Palort and I were the only one waiting for the dinner on the table. I cleared my throat.

'Hey, how are you doing?' I smacked his arm playfully.

'I'm . . . fine. What about you?' he asked. This conversation was getting very formal.

'I'm fine. I just need to talk to you about something,' I stated.

'Is it something serious?' He looked worried.

'I think Anedrin should go back to Selemara. It's not safe for her to roam around Duvollin without protection,' I whispered. Palort remained quiet, and I assume he was thinking over what I just said.

'Your statements hold value. I'll do something for her protection,' he assured me.

Soon, everyone arrived. We all finished our dinner with normal talks about business and economy of Calsenai and Selemara.

After cleaning our plates by ourselves, we thought of having a small family walk among the fields. Unfortunately, Uncle Denel and Aunt Scarlett were tired and decided to stay at home.

'What do you think about a walk in the forest?' Ariel asked.

'That would be great,' I said. Later, everyone regarded it and agreed.

We all walked in silence for a while. When we were quite near the forest, Ariel abruptly halted.

'I'm feeling very sleepy. I need to get back to my house. Can you drop me back, Anedrin? Please? I'm afraid of going alone in the dark.' She requested with her extremely innocent eyes shimmering against the moonlight. It would be difficult for anyone to resist such an appeal when a small girl was literally pleading for help.

'All right, I'm coming. Don't beg,' she said sternly. Palort and I exchanged looks.

'I think I too am coming with you, two,' he chimed in. Of course, he took his job seriously. And whenever it came to Anedrin, I'm pretty sure he'll do anything to keep her alive. Old protective brother.

'In that case, we should also go back and rest.' Infinity huffed.

'But I do want to roam around here, Infinity. I want to see the beautiful places in this place that you know of,' Phileda confessed.

Infinity took a bit longer than necessary to decide. 'Okay.' She came up with a decision at last. When Ariel, Anedrin, and Palort were not in view, I began my touring with the rest.

'There is a very beautiful meadow in here. Would you like to visit?' Infinity asked.

'Of course!' Phileda chirped. The two girls went busy with their talk about Bunatil's current king, who was very young. He had just crossed 18 and was crowned as king a month before I came in Duvollin. Infinity had met him in person. She described him to be a very gentle, handsome, smart, intelligent, and calm person. I internally felt jealousy stab over my heart. Infinity never used these adjectives to describe me. According to her, I was stubborn, silly, and dormant.

'Fuming, aren't you?' Jason asked.

'What are you talking about?' I kept my gaze low. I didn't want him to see me, at least not until I calmed myself. Jason chuckled.

'Come on, Airik, I understand. The girl you have liked since you know how long is appreciating someone you've never heard of. Even I don't like the way Phileda is spilling out over him,' Jason gushed. I smiled.

'I don't like her in that way, Jason. She is just my friend,' I addressed calmly. I don't have intentions of fighting with Jason in front of Infinity.

Liar, my subconscious said. *Get a grip on yourself, Airik,* I scolded myself.

'Fighting with your inner self?' Jason asked.

'That's none of your business,' I implored. Jason chuckled in response.

'Here we are,' Infinity said.

I couldn't breathe. The sight had taken my breath away. All I could see in front of me was a sheet of beautiful, sweet-smelling lavenders spread out on the horizon.

'Wow!' Jason exclaimed, taking me out of my trance.

Phileda broke into a run among the meadow. 'Are you guys planning to stand there all night?' Phileda asked us. Jason rushed behind Phileda. They found a spot among the meadow and began talking right there. They weren't going to come until we asked them to. So it was just me and Infinity.

'They look good together,' she stated.

'Yeah, they do. So how have you been these years?' I asked.

'Everything was a mess when we came here, but I got accustomed to this place eventually. Then, Ariel came in my life. She filled the space of a sibling I always longed for. But still, I missed you.' She tugged a strand of hair that was spilling free from her messy bun behind her ear. She missed me. I tried hard not to smile, but it just broke free. We walked farther and sat among the lavenders under the moonlight.

'If you don't mind me asking, were you still in Himachal after . . . after what happened?' She seemed hesitant to ask this question.

'No. I was taken to California's orphanage.'

'When did this happen?'

'I was 6.' Infinity had a horrified look over her face.

'They were very friendly. I never thought anything bad would ever happen to them.' Her angelic voice cracked in the end.

'Mom always said that death always came uninvited. It was a bitter truth of life. Whenever your time comes, death comes to get you and usher you in a new life. We have to accept it whether it is peacefully or forcefully. Only if I could live a bit longer with them. I lost my family, and now a destiny has been marked upon me.' I sighed.

'Don't you dare ever say you don't have a family, Airik. You have us,' she whispered and rested her head against my shoulders. As cliché as it sounds, I felt sparks. I rested my arms on her shoulders as she listened to my faint heartbeat.

'Tell me something about your friends,' Infinity demanded all of a sudden.

'I'll start with Jason. I met him in the orphanage. We both were room-mates for almost nine years until I came in Duvollin. He is there with me whenever I need him, and he gives me space whenever I need it. He is a serial dater. And most importantly, he is one of the Pimarvs,' I completed about Jason. Phileda was the next one on my list.

'You don't have to tell me about Phileda. We have grown to be good friends.' *I guess I'm not the only one with mind games.*

'Then next is Anedrin. She is full of skill, guts, and bravery. She remains reserved to herself. She is very close to the twins and their father, Delver. She relies and trusts him the most. And she loves to taunt me.' Infinity laughed gingerly. It sounded quite musical. I was dying to hear her beautiful laughter.

'Palort is the strongest and the most hardworking boy I've ever met. He is kind of a protective brother towards Phileda as well as Anedrin. He is very serious with the tasks that are provided to him. And I owe him a lot, for he has saved my life.' I discovered that I didn't know much about Palort even though he was the one I had been depending on after coming to Duvollin.

'Enough talking about me. Why don't we talk about you?' She jolted her head away from my shoulder. I was a little disappointed when she changed her position.

'Me?' she asked in puzzlement. She continued, 'You already know me. What can we talk about?'

'Do you know something about Fein?' I asked to the point. Her eyes widened for a fraction of a second, or maybe I was just imagining. First of all, why did the question roll off my tongue as if I always wanted to ask?

'I know it sounds crazy, but a few years ago, I met a boy. He looked so much like you. I actually thought it was you.' She laughed.

'He told me his name was Fein. I didn't believe at first, but then, I had to. He had given me a brooch and then ran away. The meeting was brief. I don't know anything more about him,' she admitted.

'Can you show me the brooch?' I asked.

'Well, sure,' she implied.

We motioned Jason and Phileda to come back. They seemed busy with the talk they were having, but unfortunately, they had to stop. Something really important had come up. And I somehow needed to find Fein.

My Impending Existence

Jason and Phileda were clearly annoyed for leaving the beautiful meadow. Someone needs to tell them that happiness doesn't last for long and also that they shouldn't be addicted to attractions.

'How was it?' Jason asked.

'What?'

'Conversation with Infinity,' he pointed out.

'It was . . . sentimental,' I implied sarcastically to shut him up. And it really did lock his mouth.

We walked the rest of the way in utter silence. Phileda and Jason fleetingly looked back and forth between Infinity and me. At last, we reached the house.

'Follow me,' Infinity gestured. I walked behind her. Soon, we entered her bedroom. She walked towards a bookshelf. She got a small box with her. She unlocked it. The brooch was safely kept in it, and I had to say it was very beautiful. It was carved in the shape of a dragonfly.

'Can I have it?' I asked Infinity.

'Of course.' She handed me the beautiful brooch. *There has to be some significance for this beautiful thing between my fingers.*

'You can take it if you want to,' Infinity said. 'That is what he told me, 'For the one who is a lot like me and familiar to you. He will figure it out.' I didn't know what it meant.' She sighed.

The words she said caught my attention. 'Do you mind if I peek in the memory?' She just nodded. I closed my eyes and focused.

The darkness was replaced by a crowded market. Infinity was around 12 in this memory. I could see her bargaining with a shopkeeper for a toy for Ariel. The shopkeeper at last got fed up with Infinity's arguments and gave away the toy.

Something among the crowd caught her eye. She walked past the crowd towards a black-haired boy. She tapped his soldiers. He turned around.

'Yes? How may I help you, young lady?' Fein spoke gently.

'Airik?' Infinity asked. He looked around himself to make sure she was talking to him.

'I'm certainly not the one you are talking about,' he stated politely.

'You are Airik. You should be him.' She was forcing him to be like me.

'There are certainly many people around this world who look a lot like each other,' Fein snapped at last.

'I'm sorry. You cannot be Airik. He'll never talk to me like that,' she said the last statement with her voice hardly audible. But Fein clearly heard it.

'Can I know your Airik's surname?' he asked.

'Patronus,' she spoke solemnly. Fein's brows burrowed in deep thought. He fished something out of his pocket. It was the dragonfly-like brooch.

'It is for the one who is a lot like me and familiar to you. He will figure it out.' He handed her the brooch forcefully and ran away.

I came back in the present and blinked several times. 'It is for the one who is a lot like me and familiar to you. He will figure it out.' He clearly meant me.

'Your revelation means a lot to me, Infinity.' I squeezed her hand. She just laughed and shooed me away.

'Don't ever say that. I'm always here for you,' she said.

Fein's statement rang in my brain like knick-knacks. What if he didn't mean me but someone else? *It is supposed to be me. Anedrin has already said I am a lot like Fein. But in which way? I need to talk to her.* I walked towards the guest room.

'Hey, Anedrin!' I waved at her to come over. She stood up and came.

'What are the qualities that are a lot similar in Fein and me?' I asked. 'If you think I'm just passing your time, then you are very wrong,' I clarified myself before she had a chance to taunt me.

'You both are bookworms, stubborn, impolite, shy, sassy, smart, intelligent, and handsome, and not to forget girl neglecters . . . until you have your brain set on the same girl for eternity,' she completed in a breath.

'Now, why did you ask?' The question was supposed to come. I would've felt disappointed if it didn't. I tenderly took the brooch out of the box.

'Are you familiar with this?' I asked, holding out the brooch to her.

She examined it from every angle. 'I don't know,' she replied. This wasn't the answer I was expecting. She handed me the brooch and went back in the room.

Now it was clear that Fein believed I was the one who could figure out the beautiful object in my hand. But what was there to reckon it out? I needed some space and time to think.

I sat on the front porch of the house. I closely examined the brooch in my hands. There was a coating of platinum over it, or so I assume. It was the smoothest thing I ever touched. I flipped it and examined its wings. Something caught my eye. It was a very small bulge, almost negligible, but it did mean a lot to me.

The rest of the coating done on it was very smooth. *Then what is this protuberance doing over here?* I inspected it very closely. The lump was formed for a reason. It was just very perfect to be accidental. Then again, it could just be my imagination. But still, the whole brooch was smoother than ice. *How can I just neglect it?*

I firmly pressed the perfectly formed accident. The brooch fell apart in two pieces. There was a small piece of paper neatly folded and tucked in it. I picked it up and opened it. It said:

Your Impending Existence . . .

When you will look around for answers,

The world will twirl like dancers.

All you need to do is focus.

Someone will deceive you as a beautiful crocus.

Remain aware of the dangers.

It is truly applicable for strangers.

Be as swift as a dragonfly,

And don't forget to be sly.

Don't ever try to be brave.

It is an injudicious move of someone naïve.

'What about Allekior? They want you dead. If your memory is not in a state of clarity, let me tell you, there was a prophecy about you taking a wrong step,' he reminded.

'Do I look like I've taken a wrong step right now?' I was annoyed.

'I didn't mean that. What's that in your hand?' He pointed towards the broken brooch and paper in my hand.

'Do you know about Hector in Trojan war?' I asked. I completely forgot about my situation.

'The one who killed Patrocles?' he asked.

'I think I did mention Trojan war.' I folded my arms across my chest.

'What about Hector?' he asked.

'Tell me a grave mistake he committed.'

'To be precise, there's not just one but many mistakes to begin with.' He lay back in his bed and clutched his pillow against his chest. I too slopped down on the bed after an exhausting day.

'The biggest mistake according to me is that he was against the war, but still, he participated in it,' Jason said after a few minutes.

'You sit quietly for so long, and then this is what you come up with.' I turned towards him.

'Think over what I just said, witty boy. Relate it to practical life. You are not able to do anything knowing that you can turn the whole situation upside down with some effort. Doesn't that sound bad?' he reasoned. And I found myself agreeing to him.

'Goodnight, Airik. I really need to sleep.' He yawned and fluttered his eyes close.

I read the paper again. *The first two lines are already happening with me. The next two lines were, well, no one has deceived me yet, whether it be in the disguise of someone close to me.* Just then, a thought struck me. *What if someone in here is not actually what they are trying to be? It can be anyone who's around me, or maybe I'm being extremely thoughtful. But still, I need to be extra careful with the work I'm doing.*

After reading the paper over three times, I understood some of the points it wanted to make clear with me. But the last two lines were creepy. I didn't exactly understand what it was trying to indicate.

Whatever Jason said made sense. *But why will I commit a mistake similar to Hector? This doesn't make any sense. I should consult Rimtzal after I get Fein and my parents back. He'll surely help me out, or maybe I'll figure it out myself in the course of time.*

The First Meet

I couldn't sleep. I kept on tossing in bed. When I was pretty sure sleeping wasn't an option, I thought about the next stride I would take. Thinking about the brooch was not on my mind either. Only if I had a science-fiction novel by my side. I snorted.

I wish Mom and Dad were here, telling me more about Duvollin, Elyrians, and, of course, them. Why didn't I think about this before? I sat in the bed in a quick move and concentrated on Uncle Denel's memory. I halted where I last left the memory.

'This is my house.' Mom shuffled her purse and at last found the key. She unbolted the door and motioned them to come in. She turned the lights on, and the room was in a total mess. Clothes scattered all over and books piled up in a weird sequence.

'I am going to kill Scarlett,' my mom mumbled under her breath.

'Who is Scarlett?' Uncle Denel asked.

'My friend. We live together,' Mom cooed.

'Please make yourselves comfortable.' She glared at the room and tried to make space for the guests. She hurried towards the kitchen and came back with two glasses of water.

'Tell me something about the place you used to live in,' Mom tried to make a conversation.

'Well, all I can say is people and their attire are very different from Calsenai,' Uncle Denel said without a second thought.

Mom furrowed her eyebrows. 'Can you spare me more details on Calsenai?'

'He is just . . . joking. There is nothing as Calsenai,' Dad interrupted Uncle Denel before he made a stupid move.

'Well then, where are you from?' Mom asked.

'Well, we . . . um . . .' Dad was lost for words.

'I'm back, Chrissie!' Someone burst through the doors. It was Aunt Scarlett. She spotted the Duvollinians and glared at them.

'Clean the room, Scarlett,' Mom said coldly.

'That can wait.' She gracefully walked towards her room and closed it behind her. Uncle Denel's eyes followed her everywhere she went. At last, Aunt Scarlett exited her room and made her way towards mom.

'Hi. I'm Scarlett,' she squealed.

'Stop it,' Mom hissed. Aunt Scarlett frowned at Mom and quietly sneaked out of the house.

'So . . . where were we?' Mom cleared her throat.

'You think we are lunatics, don't you?' Dad asked all of a sudden.

'Huh?' Mom gulped and scooted away from Dad, frantically looking everywhere, surely searching for a weapon.

'I don't understand what you mean, Delphinium.' Mom kept her voice calm. She found a vase lying beside her and gradually moved towards it and kept a strong grip on it.

'If I was in your place, young lady, I wouldn't have taken that vase,' Dad threatened.

'Stop it, Delphinium,' Uncle Denel said. 'You are scaring her,' he almost yelled.

'Who says I'm scared?' Mom implied in a shaky voice. Uncle Denel shook his head. Dad got up and sat beside Mom. He took her hand in his.

'I don't want to hurt you, Christina. Just be honest with me because I hate liars.' He squeezed Mom's hand a bit too bleakly. She yelped.

'You are hurting her. Get away from there,' Uncle Denel stated. Dad let go of Mom's hand and snorted.

'Tell me exactly what you want. I know you are up to something.' Dad returned to his menacing tone. Mom kept her gaze fixated on her hands.

'Answer me!' he yelled. Mom jolted in her sit.

'You are very intimidating,' Mom mumbled.

Dad smirked. 'I'm happy to know that. Now will you be kind enough to tell us about you and your intentions?'

'My name is Christina Diaz. I'm sorry. You already know that. I am half Indian. I left my hometown at the age of 17 to pursue my dreams, and then after working hard, I became a psychiatrist. Right now, I'm 24 and single. I live with Scarlett Walters, my best friend since the last eight years. And I love reading books,' Mom finished.

'You didn't tell us anything about your family,' Dad stated sternly.

'There is nothing much to talk about,' Mom said briskly.

'But I want to know,' Dad requested with the huskiest voice ever.

'But I don't like to talk about them.' Tears welled up in Mom's eyes. Dad's expression softened a bit, and he moved ahead to comfort Mom.

'Anything else you want to know?' She blinked back the tears.

'I'm sorry for his behaviour, Christina,' Uncle Denel apologised, and he glared at Dad. 'He sometimes tends to lose his senses.' Dad's head snapped in his direction.

Uncle Denel continued, 'It is not like what you think. The whole situation itself is difficult to explain. And even if we do tell you, you'll think we are mentally disabled.' He sighed.

'Then make me understand. I'll sure as hell try to help you guys out,' Mom squealed.

'First of all, tell us what you think about us, and be honest,' Dad warned.

'Well, if I begin with you . . .' She pointed at Dad. 'As I earlier said, you are intimidating, funny, smart, pompous, handsome, and a bit . . . different.' She gazed dreamily at Dad. Uncle Denel growled.

'Stop it, you two! Stop melting over each other right now!' he spat. Mom blinked several times to get in control of what happened earlier.

'We weren't melting. We were just . . .' Dad shyly bent his head and blushed. Now I know the reason I blush more often.

'Great,' Uncle Denel mumbled.

'I'll get to the point, Christina. Do you think we are mentally retarded?' Uncle Denel asked.

'Well, kind of.' It took quite long for her to answer.

'I'm glad you are being honest with us. Now will you be kind enough to tell us why?'

'You are talking about Calsenai, the place I'm not aware of. Plus, you wearing these . . . clothes. Anyone will get suspicious.' Dad sank back in his seat.

'Then why are you keeping us with you?' Dad asked.

'Because I want you to be with me,' she gushed. Dad smiled.

'No no no no. I didn't mean it that way. I just meant that you both seem really naïve. Anyone can take advantage of you in a bad way. When Garry told me about you guys, then I had set my mind to help you.' She sighed heavily.

'Who is Garry?' Dad furrowed his eyebrows. Was he jealous?

'One of the kids you were talking to in the morning,' Mom informed. Dad's expression melted, and he smiled again. I never believe in love at first sight until today.

'Thank Sressina,' Dad mumbled.

'Who is Sressina?' Mom asked with venom dripping in her voice.

'She is the goddess of dream, one of the Elyrians,' Dad said and then rolled his eyes as if saying, 'Yeah right, how would you know about them?'

'Enough talking about me. Tell me about you. I'm not the one to be interrogated. You are the ones who will be living in my house. First of all, tell me about the venom that makes you immortal, mad, or dead,' Mom said lamely. It was obvious she didn't believe them—yet.

'It is the litror venom, and it is very painful. You see, we have it running in our veins.'

'Now I know the reason you are acting like a maniac,' Mom muttered. Dad stifled a laugh. Mom blushed a little.

'Come on, you two, I don't understand what's going on. Are you both playing a blushing game? You know, making each other blush with your stupid comment or actions?' Uncle Denel intervened.

'Shut up,' Dad mouthed.

'What's that?' Mom pointed towards Dad's palms. There was a faint light glow.

'The effect is showing itself. I need salt.' Uncle Denel rushed towards Dad and held his palm. Mom was in shock.

'Get some salt! Now!' Uncle Denel yelled. Mom rushed towards kitchen and brought salt with her.

'What should I do?' Mom panicked.

'Give it to me.' Mom handed it to him. He took a handful of salt and rubbed it on Dad's palm. The glow gradually began to vanish.

'We anyhow need the antidote,' Dad said and moved towards the door with his friend following him behind.

'Wait!' Mom rushed towards them.

'You cannot leave. You need to understand this place. I really want to help you. I know I didn't believe at first, but whatever just happened right now banged my senses, and I'll try to understand you.' Dad and Uncle Denel looked at each other for a moment and then nodded.

'We think we can trust you. But if this whole thing doesn't stay confidential, then I'm sorry to say, Christina, I'll have to kill you,' Dad said threateningly. Mom gulped.

'I will not tell anyone. Besides, there is no one except Scarlett who can know about it.'

'Yeah right. That girl,' Uncle Denel beamed.

'I'll get normal clothes for you. Just wait for a few minutes.' Mom rushed out of the door.

Affectionate Souls

Soon, Mom returned with necessary garments required for her guests. They talked about their lives, and Dad told most of the things about Duvollin. Mom was fascinated, and it seemed as if she actually believed them.

A few days passed by, and Aunt Scarlett still didn't know anything about the secrecy and agreement between her dear friend and anonymous guests. Meanwhile, Dad and Uncle Denel were getting to know the place they were living in. They took huge interests in politics and the way the politicians made promises.

'I like this place. It's different.' Dad and Uncle Denel were having a small walk in the woods.

'I think we should get back to Duvollin. It has almost been a month, and the venom might start showing its effects in a few days,' Uncle Denel stated.

'We are using the dandelion, aloe, and castor oil plants, Denel. It will be almost impossible for it to change us. Stay calm.' Dad patted Uncle Denel's back and huffed.

'What if something goes wrong?'

'Nothing will go wrong. I will not let anything go wrong,' Dad said and kept his gaze steady on the ground.

'It's Christina, isn't it?' Dad didn't say anything.

'You need to stay away from her. We both know we cannot stay here forever. We have to return someday. I don't want her to shatter. She was really kind and helpful.' Dad's expression was changing drastically.

'You mean I'll hurt her?' Dad gritted his teeth in anger.

'I didn't mean that. When we will leave, she will get hurt.' He tried to knock some sense in him.

'Who says I'm leaving? I'll stay here for the rest of my life,' Dad argued.

'Do you have any idea of the wrath you are inviting upon yourself? Why would you? Practical Delphinium has turned into an admirer chap,' Uncle Denel mocked.

'I think we should get back.' Dad stormed off without another word.

'I hope you'll think over the conversation we just had,' he yelled behind Dad.

Dad was restless since the heated argument with his best friend. It was obvious that Mom and Dad were growing to have 'feelings' for each other even if they were trying to hide it.

Almost a year had elapsed, and there was no sign of the effects of the venom. Everything went normal between Uncle Denel and Dad. But still, it was awkward for Aunt Scarlett to live with them in such conditions. She didn't like them or hate them. Additionally, her suspicion was growing day by day. Meanwhile, Dad and Uncle Denel were thinking of living in Himachal. They were not yet ready to leave for Duvollin. Uncle Denel had taken up a job in the army after manipulating everyone while Dad had manipulated the hospitals into becoming a surgeon. Mom was surprised after she came home to know about their jobs.

It was Mom's birthday, sixteenth of January. Aunt Scarlett had planned a surprise for Mom. She had to take help from the Duvollinians to bring it into action.

'No!' Aunt Scarlett hollered.

'What happened?' Uncle Denel rushed towards her.

'We don't have a cake,' she groaned and stomped her foot. Uncle Denel laughed.

'You think it's funny?' She scoffed.

'You look adorable when you make that face,' he pointed out. When he realised what he just said, he dragged his fingers lazily through his copper hair.

'Thanks.' Aunt Scarlett tugged her hair behind her ear. 'Let's go before she comes.' She grabbed Uncle Denel's had and rushed out of the house.

She stopped out of the house, looked around her, and pulled Uncle Denel behind a willow tree.

'So . . . this is where we will get cakes for your best friend?' Uncle Denel looked around himself. Aunt Scarlett just rolled his eyes.

'Just shut up and wait here until Chrissie comes,' she whispered and went back on focusing on the road beside her house.

'I seriously don't understand the point of hiding behind this huge willow tree,' Uncle Denel bellowed.

'Why can't you understand a small thing?' She seemed pissed off. 'Look, Delphinium likes Chrissie, and I think it is the other way around too.'

'So what?'

'Do the math.'

'Where did math come in here from?'

'You are ridiculous.' She pouted.

'Your Chrissie is here.' He shoved his hands in his jean pocket. Aunt Scarlett looked over and spotted Mom hurrying from her car towards her house. 'Now can you be kind enough to take me back in the house?'

'No until something happens.' She had a wicked gleam in her eyes. Not so dangerous but dangerous enough for Uncle Denel to handle, I could tell.

'Follow me.' She tiptoed towards one of the windows.

'What are you up to, shorty?' he asked.

'I have a name, and I prefer to be called by it,' she snapped back.

'You are feisty,' he commented.

'Shut up,' she mouthed the word crystal clear. And Uncle Denel actually remained quiet not because Aunt Scarlett told him to but because something just happened in the house.

Dad was on his knee, his hand outstretched towards Mom with a ring resting in his hand. Mom's eyes were wide with shock.

'Christina Diaz, will you marry me?' Dad proposed to Mom. Aunt Scarlett squealed with excitement and hugged Uncle Denel. Mom's and Dad's heads snapped in their direction. They both ducked down.

'I heard someone. I'm damn sure about it,' Dad growled.

'Forget about it. It doesn't matter,' Mom soothed him. Uncle Denel and Aunt Scarlett slipped away from the window and moved towards the door.

'That was close,' Aunt Scarlett murmured. Uncle Denel just chuckled in return. They pushed the door and entered. Mom and Dad were still standing near the window.

'Did we disturb you?' Uncle Denel asked innocently. Aunt Scarlett elbowed him in the gut.

'Disturb, no, of course not. We were just . . . um . . .' Mom smiled slyly and blushed.

'Happy birthday, Chrissie!' Aunt Scarlett instantly engulfed Mom in a hug. She didn't want to see her friend stuck in some stupid, mocking question.

'Same to you. Sorry, I meant thank you.' Mom shifted nervously. Dad smirked.

'Is something wrong? You seem confused,' Uncle Denel teased. Aunt Scarlett was trying hard not to laugh.

'We can keep interrogation the aside?' Dad asked.

'You mean can we keep the interrogation aside? Now you are fumbling with words. I know there is something you both are keeping,' Uncle Denel implied grimly. He was a fabulous actor.

'We can talk about it later on,' Dad dismissed the conversation and walked towards the kitchen with Mom rushing behind him.

'That was quite pushy,' Aunt Scarlett walked over him and commented.

'He tells me everything, but now he is keeping things from me. I don't like it at all,' Uncle Denel confessed.

'It will happen to you too when you fall in love.' Aunt Scarlett gazed dreamily at the ceiling.

'Did you find the love of your life stuck in there?' He pointed towards the roof.

'You don't understand love at all, Denel.' She shook her head disappointedly.

'Girls are born with fantasizing about love,' he murmured and followed Mom and Dad towards the kitchen.

'You will understand when you fall for someone. I mean really fall for someone. Trust me, you will regret your words,' Aunt Scarlett almost yelled.

As Uncle Denel was about to enter the kitchen, he heard a glimpse of conversation between Mom and Dad.

'I'm sorry for the questions out there,' Dad apologised.

'Don't. It wasn't your fault,' Mom said in her melodious voice.

'So . . . will you marry me?' Dad asked.

'I don't know. Everything is just going hasty,' Mom answered honestly.

'But you already admitted you love me. What's wrong with getting married?' Uncle Denel's eyes widened with surprise. Dad wrapped his arms around Mom's petite waist.

'I just need time to think.' She leaned against his chest and took a huge breath.

'About what?'

'About my thoughts, options, future, career—everything.'

'Think about everything you want, Christina, not about the circumstances. Just tell me, what do you want?' There was silence between them for quite long.

'I want to be with you. I'll marry you,' Mom answered after pondering for a long time.

'Now I don't regret being away from Duvollin. I have a reason to live by my side. You are the best thing that ever happened to me, Christina Diaz, and I'm dying to make you Mrs Christina Patronus.'

'It's high time since you didn't tell me your actual surname,' Mom complained.

'What's the hurry? We have many years ahead of us.'

'Death cannot be anticipated,' Mom said solemnly. Dad sighed and made her face him.

'Whatever happened to your brother was just his fate, and I know we have a bright future ahead.'

'Future cannot be known.'

'And you cannot waste your present life worrying about the future.' Uncle Denel cleared his throat and entered the kitchen.

'Where have you two been? We have been waiting for you two for quite long.' Uncle Denel looked back and forth between Mom and Dad.

'Are you two all right?' he asked, knowing what happened.

'We will be back in a minute,' Mom replied in a raspy voice. Uncle Denel smirked and left the kitchen. He walked beside Aunt Scarlett.

'Christina agreed to marry Delphinium,' he informed.

'What?' she yelled. Mom and Dad came running from the kitchen.

'Is everything all right?' Mom looked concerned.

'You both have decided to get married?' she asked.

'We were about to tell you.'

'Oh my god! When are you getting married? I want to know everything—I really mean everything. Each and every detail.' She marched towards Mom, grabbed her hand, and rushed in her bedroom.

'So . . . do you mind to spare me the details?' Uncle Denel teased.

'What can I say except for the fact that we are getting married.' He laughed nervously.

'I'm really happy for you. You have picked the right one. I'm proud of you.' Uncle Denel hugged Dad.

'Why don't you get settled?' Dad asked all of a sudden.

'Settled? I have lots of time for that. I'm not going to hurry like you,' he stated.

'It's not called hurrying. It's called future planning, which you lack at.' Uncle Denel scowled at Dad, and then they both burst out laughing as if they were sharing a private joke. Just then, Mom and Aunt Scarlett exited the room giggling like teenage girls.

'Let's celebrate.' Aunt Scarlett pushed Mom towards Dad. He caught her in time. Uncle Denel walked towards Aunt Scarlett.

'They look so cute with each other. I swear this is one of the best couples I've ever seen,' Aunt Scarlett squealed.

'Don't you think this couple needs a nickname?' Uncle Denel chimed in.

'What about lovely doves?' Aunt Scarlett suggested.

'I was thinking about Chrisinium,' Uncle Denel said.

'Affectionate souls seem better,' Dad said.

'Sounds good to me.' Mom smiled.

Mom and Dad soon got married on 26 May. After a month of their marriage, that was 26 June, Mr and Aunt Scarlett got married. After exactly one year and seven months, Mom gave birth to a baby boy, who was surely me. Meanwhile, Aunt Scarlett too was pregnant with Infinity. She was born immediately on the next day of my birth.

'Have you thought a name for your boy?' Uncle Denel asked.

'I'm thinking about Airik,' Dad said.

403

'Seems perfect to me for your son.' He smiled. Just then, Mom and Aunt Scarlett exited their rooms with me and Infinity in their arms.

'I've named our son as Airik.' Dad seemed satisfied with everything he just said.

'Airik?' Mom seemed puzzled.

'Airik means the *eternal one* in Mertis.' Mom and Dad looked at me and smiled. Tears trickled down from Mom's eyes. I touched my mom's cheek with my chubby palms and tried to wipe away the tears, but my small arms were very weak. Everyone laughed except for me and Infinity.

'Airik, the eternal one,' my mom repeated.

Protector

The memory skipped to three years after. Mom and Aunt Scarlett were shopping while Infinity and I were at school. Uncle Denel and Dad were sitting on the front porch of the house and sipping a cup of coffee. 'I had a dream, Denel,' Dad whispered.

'A dream? What was it about?' Uncle Denel was alarmed.

'I couldn't understand what it meant. It was just . . . different . . . difficult to interpret.' Dad answered thoughtfully.

'What was it?' he asked.

'I just saw an older version of Airik, almost like 16. He was looking out for Christina and me in Duvollin,' Dad answered.

'Dreams carry meaning, especially yours.' Uncle Denel played with the vacant cup in his hands.

'What do you think that means?' Dad asked. He was much tensed about the dream that was for sure.

'Probably we will have to return to Calsenai,' Uncle Denel's voice trembled. It was obvious they didn't feel like returning to the place that wanted them dead.

'Are you sure it was Airik?' Uncle Denel asked.

'I know it was him. And I am sure it meant something.' Dad stood up and entered the house. Uncle Denel followed him. Dad refilled his cup.

'What if he is the protector of anegz?' Uncle Denel said tenderly.

'He can't be. He shouldn't be.' Dad shook his head as if being a protector was a big nightmare.

'The description fits Airik perfectly.' Dad was about to gulp the whole cup down, but he halted in his motion.

'What description?' Dad furrowed his eyebrows and got back to his menacing tone.

'Sorry I forgot to tell you. As you already know, I'm still in contact with Duvollin. There was a prophecy about the new protector.'

'That cannot be my son. I will not let him lead a miserable life of a protector.' He smacked the table and cursed under his breath.

'The description went something like this:'

The new one will rule with his terms,

He has the ability to take over thousands of firms.

His eyes are like beautiful emerald green,

His mere words will make you feel pure and clean.

He will be as pale as dead,

He has the ability to hold Duvollin on a single thread.

His hair is dark, thick, and black,

The only flaw in him is being slack.

If he has decided something to ensue,

Then he will do anything to hit the blue.

If you mess with him in any way,

He will make sure that you pay.

He cannot see the dear ones get hurt,

He is as striking as a cold dessert.

He will turn 17 to the day of doom,

His brain will be enough for the world to bloom.

'I think that's all,' Uncle Denel stated.

'Not everything matches my son's features and behaviours. Most importantly, he is not slack or as pale as someone dead.' Dad scowled.

'I just informed you. Now it's up to you the way you take it. And I do think it refers to Airik,' Uncle Denel said.

A few minutes later, Infinity and I returned from school.

'Daddy! I learnt how to make sandwiches!' Infinity exclaimed excitedly with her beautiful gleaming turquoise eyes.

'Wow! Did you save one for me?' Uncle Denel batted his lashes.

'No.' Uncle Denel's face dropped down and faked his feelings as being upset.

'I'll make a new one for all of us,' Infinity answered diplomatically and ran towards the kitchen with her long brown hair waving behind. I shook my head and moved towards my room.

'Airik,' Dad called me. He had a cold sensation in his eyes. I was sure of that.

'We need to talk,' Dad said as if I would understand there was about to begin a manly talk between Dad and me. First of all, I was still a kid, and I surely couldn't manage to be grim the whole time he would be talking.

'Yes, Dad.' I bowed my head down and walked towards him.

'What will you do when you are forced to do something you don't want to?' Dad asked.

I remained quiet for a very long time, surely thinking for an answer. 'First, I would consider the situation and see why I have to take the option, which I don't want to. And if I think it is valid, then I'll follow the choice even if I don't want to,' I relied in my compassionate voice.

'I'm proud of you, my son. May the Elyrians be with you.' He ruffled my black hair. He left my younger self confused. But I simply ignored the conversation I just had with my dad. Uncle Denel was still staring at me.

'You are smart.' It was all he commented.

Why is everyone acting weird lately? I asked to myself. Suddenly I stood there for a few minutes with my eyes wide, not blinking at all. Uncle Denel kept his gaze steady on me.

'Is everything okay, kid?' he asked. I blinked several times.

'What is anegz?' I asked. Uncle Denel choked on his cup.

'What did you hear?' Uncle Denel asked.

'I saw something. It was so real,' I answered.

'Tell me, son. Maybe I'll help you figure it out.' Uncle Denel knelt in front of me.

'I saw you and Dad talking about some kind protector for anegz.'

'You saw?' I simply nodded. An anxious expression crossed Uncle Denel's sharp features, but it was soon replaced with a fake smile.

'Do you see things like you saw today?' Uncle Denel asked.

'Well, yeah, kind of. Whenever I ask questions, I just see something that answers them,' I answered honestly.

'That's good.' He patted my shoulders and left the room. I rushed towards my room.

'Delphinium, I need to talk to you.' Uncle Denel leaned against the door frame. Dad didn't moved a single muscle. He was busy with his Kindle.

'It's about Airik,' Uncle Denel elaborated. Dad quickly ditched the Kindle and marched towards Uncle Denel.

'What happened?' He glanced anxiously around him.

'Your son is psychic,' Uncle Denel informed and left the support of the door frame.

'Who told you?' Dad asked in his threatening tone.

'He asked a question and answered it himself,' Uncle Denel answered.

'So? How does this prove he is psychic? Even we ask questions to ourselves sometimes and answer them.' Uncle Denel just stared at him with a look that said, 'Are you serious?'

'I didn't mean it that way. He asked why everyone was acting really weird. Then he stood fixated on the same spot for a few minutes without blinking. Then, all of a sudden, he asked about anegz.' Uncle Denel kept on blabbing about me for another few minutes, trying to convince Dad that I'm the one for anegz.

'Don't you think I'm speaking the truth?' Uncle Denel completed.

'I'll think about it,' Dad replied and shut the door on his face.

'People and their choices change,' Uncle Denel mumbled.

The Eternal One

'Uncle Denel! I saw another memory!' I yelled.

'You saw . . . what?' Uncle Denel rushed towards me.

'I saw people being engulfed by a blue light, and then they saw beautiful trees with purple mosses,' I answered.

'Beautiful trees with purple mosses?' he repeated.

'Thanks for sharing, kid.' He ruffled my hair. I ran away towards Infinity.

'Stop motivating my son to hallucinate,' Dad snapped.

'He saw a vision.'

'Did you make sure that it was just a vision?' Dad created air quotes for *vision*.

'I believe in Airik even if you don't. I have a feeling that Airik is the protector of anegz.'

'Can you just stop repeating that? My son cannot be the protector. I don't want him to be the one.' He clenched his jaw.

'You cannot stop something that is destined to happen.' Uncle Denel took a step towards Dad. Dad stared at him as if he will just rip Uncle Denel's head off.

'Talk about protectors and anegz again, Denel, I'll make sure to visit your grave every day. And if you want to, then don't relate Airik with this,' he threatened. He took a deep breath and stepped away.

'You don't understand. He saw a vision of people being teleported to a new world. You need to take this seriously.'

'Leave me alone for some time,' Dad said.

'Fine.' Uncle Denel grunted and walked away.

A few months later, the disappearing incidents began to take place. Infinity and I were 4 in this memory. I was able to see everything through dreams, and normally, I was daydreaming. Everyone was sitting under the willow tree and was discussing about the disappearing incidents.

'I'm going back,' Uncle Denel stated.

'You mean Calsenai?' Dad shifted in his chair. Uncle Denel nodded.

'They will kill you! How can you think of going in that hellhole?' Dad spat.

'I'll get the antidote first and then show myself to Duvollin. The king has changed.'

'So what? You shouldn't go there. Have you thought about Infinity? When they will come to know about her, they'll surely think that she has the venom in her veins, and what about her dreams?' Dad sighed.

'I know what's better for my daughter, and don't you say you care, Delphinium. I've seen your point of view regarding Airik's abilities, and you don't want him to develop it. You are afraid he'll leave you for anegz.' Dad had a hurt expression on his face. It seems that Uncle Denel's words stabbed his heart.

'They are still not sure of him being a protector,' Dad said in a small voice.

'Even if he is not a protector, you should try to promote his skills. Instead, you are supressing them.'

'Then what do you expect out of me?' He stood up briskly and clenched his palms into fists.

'I just don't want my son to be experimented as a lab rat!' He stormed off without another word.

Everyone stayed quiet for a moment. 'He is right,' Aunt Scarlett stated.

'This world is full of selfish people, and they will do anything to keep someone powerful with them,' Mom finished for her friend.

Uncle Denel heard the argument and felt guilty about indirectly calling Dad a bad father. He entered the house and saw my dad. He had his forehead buried in his warm hands.

'I know something is wrong, Delphinium,' Uncle Denel said.

'They suspect me to be different,' he said in a muffled voice.

'Who?'

'A guy at work. He has already met Airik before. He even stares at my son as if he'll devour him anytime.'

'It must be your imagination. But if you want, we get out of this place.' Uncle Denel gave a solution.

'How long will we keep on running away? We have a family, and we need to get settled down.'

'We can talk about this later on. You see, there are things that need to be taken care of. Airik had anticipated them a long time ago, and we aren't doing anything to stop it.'

'That's not the end, Denel. He saw another vision where Cristina and I were . . . dying.' Dad sighed heavily. Uncle Denel's hand dropped from Dad's shoulder. He sat beside him and hugged him tightly. They soon parted from the hug.

'Probably, Duvollin knows about us. I guess someone is sending troops to keep Duvollin a secret.'

'That is a stupid reason.' Dad scoffed.

'It seems reasonable enough to me,' Uncle Denel said as if he was in a deep thought.

'Now stop pretending. We need to do something to get out of this situation.'

'Don't get angry. I think we should get back to Calsenai,' Uncle Denel said gingerly.

'I don't want to leave this place. Calsenai must be mad at us, and after knowing about Airik's abilities, they will change their attitude towards me and take my son away from me.' Tears were threatening to fall from Dad's eyes.

'This is why you don't want to go back to Calsenai?' Dad nodded briskly.

'We need to do something before everything goes wrong. These incidents mean something.' Just then, both of them heard a scream. They both rushed down towards the voice where it came from. It was in my room. I was flinching in sleep. They both took my side and forced me to get up from my nightmare.

'Daddy!' I squealed and hugged him.

'What happened?' Dad ruffled my hair and tried to calm down.

'I saw her!' I almost yelled.

'Her?' Dad sounded puzzled.

'Yes, I saw her, and with her, there was another man with a black electrifying sword. I was chained, and they were trying to beat me,' I whined.

'It was just a dream, Airik. Everything is fine.' He shushed me. After a few minutes, I fell asleep against his chest.

'His dreams mean something,' Uncle Denel whispered. Dad snapped his glassy gaze at him.

'Don't glare at me, Delphinium. I'm speaking the truth. And truth normally is hard to digest.' He gulped.

'I need some time alone to think,' Dad said. Uncle Denel shook his head and walked away.

'I will not join you,' I mumbled in my sleep. Dad instantly sat by my side, waiting for me to say something more. Tears trickled down from the corner of my eyes.

'What should I do? I don't even know where Mom and Dad are,' I continued to ramble on about my feelings. Dad intently listened to them. All of a sudden, I screamed again.

'I'm right here, my boy.' Dad instantly draped his arm around my petite body.

'Tell me what happened.' He stroked my shoulders in a pattern.

'She wants me to join her, Dad. She will destroy everything. She is a very bad person.' I sniffed.

'I will not let anything happen to my prince.' He kissed my temple.

'What if she tries to do something bad?' I looked up at him.

'She won't. No one can hurt my powerful son. Now come on, show me your bulky muscles.'

I instantly got up and rolled up my sleeves in order to flaunt my muscles, which didn't exist. I patted my plain and pale bicep.

'Well, your muscles have grown since the last time I saw them!' Dad exclaimed excitedly.

'I've worked out a lot, Dad. It's not easy to make abs and everything.' I sighed.

'I think I'll have to take tips from my handsome son,' Dad commented, making me blush. He chuckled. I guess I had this blushing custom drilled in my mind. Dad laughed.

'I think you should get up and do something productive,' Dad said. I nodded and walked away.

'You don't have to hide, Denel,' Dad said. All of a sudden, Uncle Denel appeared out of nowhere.

'Why didn't you ask Airik about the girl, lady, or whoever she was in his dream?'

'I don't want him to be anxious every time just because he is dreaming about it and it might be true someday. It will just destroy his life entirely. He is special, but he needs to know the meaning of being normal.'

'Even Infinity talks with animals.'

'So . . . your daughter at last found her talent.'

'It's stronger than mine, though.' Uncle Denel scratched the back of his head.

'Stronger? What do you mean by stronger?' Dad asked.

'It's quite difficult to explain. You see, Airik dreams as well as daydreams. I just mean that your family is one of god of dream Sigirian's creations, so you have the ability of get to know the future through dreams sometimes, and they are normally not clear. But Airik's dreams are vivid. He knows exactly the reason when he thinks of the question. It is the same with Infinity. She talks with them, she can make them believe her, she can control them, and she can heal them with her single touch. But I can only control them and talk,' he tried to explain.

'I guess it is because of the venom. Probably, it enhances abilities too.'

'Then why aren't we developing our powers?'

'We are supressing the effect of the venom, remember?'

'Our life would've been much better without the venom.' Uncle Denel sighed.

'I don't think so. I wouldn't have ever met Christina if the incident wouldn't have taken place.' Dad plastered a smirk on his face.

'You have changed a lot since you met her.'

'Don't make me say something I'll later on regret.' Uncle Denel rolled his eyes. Dad and he talked a bit, and when each and every topic had been scrutinised by them, they decided to get back on their tasks.

'When were you planning to tell me?' Dad clenched his jaw. Uncle Denel and Dad were currently having a heated argument because Uncle Denel had decided to leave for Calsenai.

'I did tell you today.'

'How will you go back? That's not possible! How can you create a portal?'

'Leave that up to me.'

'I just . . . wanted to see all of you for the last time.' He gulped.

'Fine then. If you are so sure about your decision, then I'll . . . I'll . . .' he trailed off.

Uncle Denel and Dad experienced a manly hug. 'I'll miss my best friend,' Dad said in a raspy voice.

'So will I.'

'I respect your decision, Denel. Now go before I force you to stay here forever.'

'Airik needs to stay alive. Protect him,' Uncle Denel said before disappearing through the house with Aunt Scarlett and Infinity.

'Protection is needed for those who are weak. My son needs to stay alive for something needs to be done, and I will make sure it happens. Whether I'm alive or dead, I will make sure he lives through every journey forced upon him. He is Airik Sigirian, the eternal one,' my dad said.

Family

I woke up with a beautiful fragrance of rose hitting my nose. I woke up and saw Infinity sitting beside my bed.

'Good morning,' she greeted.

'G-good morning,' I stuttered and self-consciously grabbed the sheets on me.

'Do you need something?' I asked and looked around myself. There was no one around me. I guess everyone was up.

'It has been really late, so I got breakfast for you. Here.' She handed me a tray.

'Well . . . thanks. But you could've woken me up.'

'I didn't want to. You looked adorable in your sleep,' she said the last part below whisper. I blushed a little, and thankfully, she didn't notice. I got back to my normal colour.

'Did you say something?' I asked, secretly mocking her.

'Did you hear something?' she asked in reply.

'I think . . . I just did.' I smirked, and we both scooted closer to each other. My hand found their way towards her cheeks and caressed it adoringly. She blushed under my touch and leaned towards it. She closed her eyes, savouring in the feeling.

'I have been waiting for years for this moment,' I mumbled under my breath. On cue, our perfect moment was ruined.

'Are you awake yet?' Jason entered, and his eyes were fixed on the close space between us. He halted right in his tracks and eyed us suspiciously with a glint of playfulness in them.

'Are you two a thing?' he asked.

'No!' we both yelled at the same time. Jason seemed amused. Infinity got up and walked out of the room.

'So . . . did I disturb something?' he jeered.

'Just get out,' I mouthed.

'This is what happens when you fall for someone?' Jason asked.

'I think you know better. Now get out. I'm feeling sick.'

'Yeah right. You are lovesick.' I threw the sheets away from me and lunged at Jason, pinning him to the floor.

'Get everything drilled in your mind about whatever I'm about to say right now. First, I'm just sick of your pathetic teasing, not lovesick, and second, Infinity is just my friend,' I spelt every word crystal clear.

'You know the truth,' Jason teased.

'And that's what I'm saying right now.'

I got off him and helped him to stand up. 'You know better. Don't deny what you feel,' he said and left me alone in the room.

My thoughts were currently towards Uncle Denel's memory. I apparently came to know my real name is Airik Sigirian, not Patronus. So this means that my ancestors were the creation of god of dreams. But I still wasn't sure about the limit of my abilities. After having a shower and finishing my breakfast, I headed out of the room only to see a small get-together in the dining hall where I wasn't invited.

'It's time when Airik decided to join us,' Uncle Denel told me to come and join them. I sat between Jason and Phileda.

'What are we discussing about?' I asked and propped my elbows on the table.

'Nothing much. As it is your last day with us, we were thinking that you need to meet your grandparents and cousins,' Uncle Denel informed.

'Paternal grandparents?' I asked. Uncle Denel nodded with sympathy at me. I couldn't digest the fact that had just been passed onto me. I have living relatives. I had so many questions running through my mind. *Do they know about me? And most importantly, will they accept me?*

'We should get going now.' He stood up.

'Have fun, bro.' Jason patted my shoulders. I smiled at him. It was too bad he didn't have a family, but he has us.

I followed Uncle Denel out of the house. 'Do you have the locket that I gave you?' he asked.

'Yes,' I answered. He sighed with relief, and we continued to walk.

'Tell me something about them,' I said.

'Have patience. You are about to meet them, but for now, I can only tell you that you have tons of cousins who are not at all practical. They are good pranksters, and that is why I don't like them the way I like you. Your aunts and uncles are reasonable enough to talk to. They are extremely friendly unlike their children and your grandparents. Well, it is hard to figure them out. They were happy until Delphinium was safe in Calsenai.' He gave a small summary about my family.

'Do they know I'm coming? Do they even know about me?' I asked.

'No, they don't know you are coming, and yes, they know a little bit about you.' We remained silent for the rest of the journey. I could see Calsenai clearly now. There were the same houses made of strong wood with the fragrance of . . . lavender?

'Why does this place have a scent of lavender?' I asked.

'Calsenai is the biggest exporter of lavender and rose. This is the place where lavender is packed for export,' he answered.

'That's cool,' I said.

'Can I ask you for a favour, Airik?' he asked. *Favour? What does he need from me?*

'Sure,' I said.

'When you meet your family, don't tell them who you are. Just don't let them know that you are the protector of anegz. You have to keep the fact hidden, and you can tell everything else. I know it sounds very awkward, but you need to keep your family safe. If they know about you, then probably Allekior will make their move against you, and I want you to stay alive.' I nodded. I can't afford to get my whole bloodline wiped out.

After a few minutes, we reached a big castle—well, not like the ones of royalty, but it was really big. The height was equivalent to a five-storey building. I still couldn't believe that this tall building was mainly made of wood.

'This is where your family lives,' he said.

'Wow.' That was all that came out of my mouth as I admired the building.

'I guess I have too many relatives,' I murmured.

'More than you can think of,' Uncle Denel added. He got hold of my quivering hand and led me towards the massive house. He banged the door. After a few seconds, a young boy, almost 18, opened the door. He looked back and forth between me and Uncle Denel and smirked. He was really handsome, I should say. He had green eyes like me, but his hair was auburn, and his skin was tanned, not pale like mine.

'Is he your nephew or something? I guess not. He is way too good-looking to be your relative,' he said. I tried to hold back my laugh with a cough.

'You can ask your questions later, Callistemon. At least, let us come in,' Uncle Denel said.

'Please come in.' He stepped aside and let us pass.

'Where are the rest of your family members?' Uncle Denel asked.

'Hey, Den!' someone hollered from behind. We both turned around to see a middle-aged man running towards us. He attacked Uncle Denel with a hug.

'You'll kill me someday because of your voice, Ranunculus.' Uncle Denel laughed.

'Let's go. I have something for you.' He pulled Uncle Denel with him. I turned towards Callistemon.

'Hi, I'm Airik,' I said.

'Callistemon,' he said and eyed me from head to toe.

'You don't look like you are from Calsenai. Your pale skin tells you are somewhere from Selemara. Come with me. You should meet my cousins. They are very welcoming.' He offered his hand. I took it. He led me out of the house, and we walked around the mansion. Soon we reached a group of kids. They were laughing and chatting among themselves.

'We have someone here,' he yelled at them. Their heads instantly turned in my direction. I'm not used to with so much of attention, so I just blushed.

'Aw! You look cute when you blush,' I heard a girly voice exclaim. I looked at the source of voice to see a girl about 20 with long auburn hair. She was so adorable in a sisterly way.

'Thanks.' I smiled at her.

'Hey, stop hitting on my sister,' someone said. Everyone laughed except for the girl. Someone needed to tell them I am their cousin. But talking with them without them knowing about me sounded like fun.

'I already have my mind set on someone though,' I murmured loud enough for them to hear.

'Probably, my sister got unlucky today, right Azalea?' Callistemon looked at the girl who commented at me. She just rolled her eyes.

'How are you connected to Denel?' Callistemon asked.

'He and my dad were really close friends,' I said.

'Were?' Callistemon tried to get the details out.

'My parents are no more,' I answered. They all seemed sorry for me.

'Why don't you tell me about your family?' I asked, trying to lighten up the mood.

'What do you want to know?' Azalea asked.

'Anything and everything,' I said playfully.

'The eldest in our family are our grandparents. They don't look like what they are. Then, they had three boys and three girls. Every kid they had was married, and I attended every one's marriage except for my mom and dad's and also Uncle Delphinium's. He was teleported to the other world, and there, he married someone and had a kid. I wish I could meet him again. He was my favourite uncle.' She sighed.

'Don't mind her, but she gets very emotional whenever she talks about Uncle Delphinium,' Callistemon said.

'It's really bad you can't meet him again.' I tried to hold back my tears.

'I will meet him again, and I will meet his son too,' she said with dignity.

'We have heard this many times, Azalea. We don't even know where they are! If they want to come, they will,' Callistemon said.

'Why are you so angry at him?'

'I'm not angry at him. I'm angry at the ex-ruler of Calsenai for the decision he made those years ago. He just screwed up everything.' He buried his face in his palms.

Thunders began raging across the sky. 'I guess the skies don't like us being out of our house,' Callistemon commented and sighed.

'Let's go before it rains.'

'Are you f—— kidding me? You don't enjoy rain?' I asked.

'What are you talking about? Enjoying rain? You seriously are very weird.' Azalea smirked.

'It's just rain, not something that will drain my life away from me,' I said casually. They gave me an 'Are you serious?' look.

'You better get in the shelter, Airik,' Callistemon said. I just sighed and followed them. As soon as we reached the house, rain started pouring down.

'If you've never heard about the rain in Calsenai, then this is how it is,' someone said.

This wasn't any normal sweet-smelling rain but something that was destroying everything that was coming in its way. Just then, water accidentally splashed on my wrist. The pain was just like a little shock to my whole body—nothing more.

'Wow, wh-what was that?' I stuttered.

'Why didn't you get yourself paralysed?' another boy around my age asked.

'What do you mean?'

'A drop of rainwater is enough for a normal human to get paralyzed. But you are still alive,' Azalea elaborated for the boy.

'Well . . . I . . .' *Now how do I explain that? Curse this rain and the one who caused this rain.* The rain began spilling through the windows in the house. I held it back with sorcery. Everyone gawked at me. I have a lot of explanation to do.

'Who are you?' Azalea's intentions were to yell, but it barely came out as a whisper.

'Airik Patronus,' I answered bluntly.

'Patronus? That sounds so . . . out of Duvollin.' Damn it! I spelt my surname too. They all have huge working brains.'

'I'm your uncle Delphinium's son, Airik . . . Sigirian.' My new surname didn't suit me. I was better off with Patronus. Azalea's face instantly lit up.

'Where is Uncle Delphinium?' she asked with excitement until realisation hit her with a ton of bricks. 'Wait, you told that your parents . . .' her voice trailed off.

'He actually . . . he is . . . no more.' I gulped the lump forming in my throat. Then something unexpected happened. Azalea slapped me hard on my cheek. It hurt badly, but I didn't say a word. She needed to take her anger off on someone.

'You just watched your parents die?' I met her gaze and saw tears running down her cheeks.

'Answer me!' she yelled.

'I was just 6 back then. I didn't know what to do,' I answered truthfully and rubbed my cheek.

'Don't give me those reasons. Now that your mom and dad are gone, you are searching for a family to live by, and that is it, isn't it, Airik?' I didn't know her, but this didn't mean her words didn't hurt me. The rest of my cousins were trying to calm her.

'You are absolutely right, I desire a family for my basic needs,' I said sarcastically and exited the house in the storming rain. I didn't give a damn about the weather. *Why should I care when my family hates me? But I need to be alive for protecting*

431

that stupid stone. I felt as if each drop was sucking my life away from me. Azalea was right, though. I actually just stood there and watched them die. There was no one who could change that. I was somehow responsible for the death of my own parents. How frustrating can my life be? The rain instantly halted. Seems like Elyrians had mercy on me. I headed right towards the meadow where Infinity took us yesterday. I soon reached the meadow. The sight reminded me of my mom. I felt myself going back to my mom.

'Get up, sweetie, it is already eight in the morning,' Mom cooed. I was barely 2 in this memory. I pretended not to listen to her.

'I'm warning you for the last time,' Mom stated sternly. I didn't move a muscle.

'Fine then.' She tickled my sides, and I got up laughing.

'No, Mommy!' I said between my laughs.

'Listen to me before I do something bad,' she warned. I slightly bowed my head and nodded.

'I hope you are aware that we are going out.' Mom made me stand up. I smiled brightly at her. 'So I want you get ready without any tantrums,' she completed and moved towards my wardrobe.

'No!' I yelled and jumped off the bed. I ran towards my mom as fast as my small and chubby legs could carry me.

'I will do everything myself,' I lisped. Mom pretended to think.

'Hmm, I'm waiting for you in the living room.' She pecked my cheeks and left my room. I searched through my wardrobe for something sensible to wear. I took a shower and changed into my 'sensible' clothes. As I was rushing down the stairs towards the living room, I heard Mom and Dad whisper—yelling—at each other.

'How can you leave him alone to get ready? He is just a kid,' Dad stated.

'Who says he is alone? I have hidden cameras in his room to watch over him. Why don't you see it, Delphinium? He is different from other kids. I need to understand the way he reacts to certain situations. At the age of 2 years and 2 months, he deciphers everything a normal child can't. Airik is special.'

'Why are you treating your son as an experiment? Even if he is special, he needs to believe he is not. I don't want him to turn into an egotistical bastard.' I cringed at the word Dad used. They both were silent for a while. I knew they caught me.

'Do you care to come out, son?' Dad called out after a while. I shyly walked towards them.

'It is not good to eavesdrop on someone's conversation, son,' Dad stated sternly.

'I'm sorry. I'll make sure this never happens again,' I murmured. Dad ruffled my damp hair.

'Don't do anything out of fear but motivation and understanding.' I nodded and kept my gaze steady on the floor. He cupped my chin and forced me to look at him.

'And look in the eyes of the person you are talking to. When you look away, it is considered that you have done something wrong.' I gazed deep into his green eyes.

'You might just figure out everything about the person if you look at him or her this way,' Dad joked. I gave a tight smile because my dad was right. I did figure out something in his eyes, and that was concern and anxiety. It was pretty obvious he was concerned about his family's well-being—but anxiety? What was it about? I just ignored the question popping in my head.

'Come on, sweetie, I've prepared breakfast for you. We don't want it to get cold, right?' Mom coaxed. I nodded my head rapidly and followed my mom in the kitchen, leaving Dad behind. Mom made me sit on the chair and placed my breakfast in front of me. I quickly munched over the bowl of cereal Mom gave me. After finishing my bowl, I tried to get off the chair but failed in the attempt miserably.

'Mommy!' I yelled.

'I'm done.' I pointed at the bowl. Mom clapped her hands.

'I'm not a kid.' I rolled my eyes. Mom seemed amused with my behaviour but soon let it go and picked me up.

'My son seems to grow very fast,' she commented. I pretended to play with her silky hair. She carried me out of the house towards a familiar shop.

'Ally's Flowers,' I read the shop's name.

'We are visiting Aunt Ally!' Mom set me down on the ground, but I clutched my mom's finger. I didn't know who Aunt Ally was. I walked in with her only to be greeted by the sweet-smelling flowers.

'Wow!' I exclaimed after taking a good look around myself.

This place had every kind of flower in here. I let go of my mother's slender fingers and walked through until I bumped into someone.

'Whoa! Slow down, honey. You might just hurt yourself.' I flashed my million-dollar adorable smile at her.

'Aw! You are so cute.' She lifted me in her arms.

'Hey, Ally!' Mom came running towards us.

'Long time no see,' she said.

'I was busy with everything,' Mom reasoned.

'By the way, where is your son? You promised me you'll get him.' She pouted.

'The cutie in your arms is my son, Airik.' She looked between Mom and me.

'You are a lucky one.' She handed me to my mom.

'I can see that your son will grow into a handsome man someday,' she commented. I buried my head in the crook of my mother's neck shyly. She rubbed my back soothingly.

'He doesn't take compliments well,' Mom explained.

there, trying hard not to glare at me. Uncle Denel spotted me and instantly stood up and marched towards me.

'Where were you? Do you have any idea how worried we have been?' he scolded.

'And why did you leave the house during rain? Do you have any idea how dangerous it is? One drop is enough to kill someone, and you are completely drenched in that . . . liquid. You are lucky for being AB negative and left-handed.' The corner of my lips tugged a little as he rambled on about. He cared a lot for me. I should never pull out a stunt like this again.

'I'm sorry. I'll make sure this never happens again,' I apologised after he completed his instructions.

'Anyways, I present you to your family, the Sigirians.' Soon each and every Sigirian present in the room squashed me in a hug. I felt a need to tell them that I'm claustrophobic, but I didn't mind dying this way. Everyone started commenting in muffled voices.

'We missed you.'

'You are very pale.'

'You smell good.'

'Are you intelligent like Denel described you to be?'

'I guess not. He just had a small stroll in the freaking rain.'

'Shut up all of you. Maybe just like me, confident about what he does.'

'Don't you dare make him like you. I don't want my nephew to fantasise something that is impossible.' I stifled a laugh.

'Do you always stay this sombre? You are not speaking at all.'

'Well, he is not sombre. He'll speak if you let some air in this poor boy's lungs,' Uncle Denel stated. Everyone let go of me and grunted.

'You always have to ruin a beautiful moment, Denel, don't you?' the same man who stole Uncle Denel when we entered this house commented.

'I wouldn't have tried to ruin your beautiful moment if Airik wasn't claustrophobic.'

'It seems like he acquired lots of traits from Delphinium. He has the same eyes, same hair, and—do not forget—afraid in closed spaces or crowds,' someone said. I felt my cheeks colouring red again.

'Delphinium never blushed. Where did he inherit this from?'

'He never did until he met Christina,' Uncle Denel elaborated. Someone wolf whistled.

'What about his skin colour?'

'His mother. She was really pale,' Uncle Denel explained. There was a blanket of silence taken over the surroundings.

'Well, I don't know you guys really well, so do you mind introducing yourselves to me?' It came out as a statement rather than a question.

'Let me do the honours.' Callistemon stepped beside me.

'This is Grandfather Zion and Grandmother Serein.' Callistemon gestured towards an old couple. Grandfather Zion was in his late 60s. He looked like an older version of Dad, except that he had grey hair. Grandma Serein had grey eyes and the same sun-kissed skin tone and brown hair. She looked like she was somewhere near her late 50s.

'They look young according for their age. Grandfather Zion is 78, and Grandmother Serein is 72.' My eyes widened. *How can they be so damn young?* They both smiled at me lovingly.

'You just need to know that you have a very health-conscious family, and we don't intend to appear to be old.' Callistemon shrugged like it was nothing.

'Hush now, Callistemon. Don't joke with my handsome grandson. I'm 63, and you grandfather here is 71. And age is just a number. You need to be young from heart.' Grandmother Serein laughed elegantly. I like her already. Callistemon chuckled beside me.

'Moving ahead, this is your eldest uncle, my dad, Amaranthus, and this is my mom, Reagan. Azalea and I are real siblings and their only child. Azalea is 21, and I am 18.' I smiled at the couple. They looked really cute together. Uncle Amaranthus had the same hair like Dad's, but his eyes were like Grandma Serein's. He was around five ten, I assume. Aunt Reagan too had black wavy hair and brown eyes with the Indian tint to her appearance.

'After my dad, we have Aunt Rosemary and, of course, her handsome husband, Nermen.' Aunt Rosemary had the same hair, same eyes, and same skin tone like my dad's and a very beautiful smile that added to her beauty. Uncle Nermen was pale and had pure blonde hair. It seemed really awkward when the couple stood beside each other because Aunt Rosemary was very short and Uncle Nermen was unconditionally tall.

'And they both are Tulip and Jasmine, their daughters. They are 20. And they are twins.' I looked at the two identical-strawberry blonde girls. They had icy-blue eyes and pale skin like mine. They both giggled hysterically and waved. I waved back.

'Then comes our uncle Thistle. He is married to the beautiful aunt Halliz.' Callistemon smirked, and the couple instantly blushed. Everyone seemed to control the laughter trying to break free from them. Aunt Halliz intertwined her fingers with Uncle Thistle's.

'What's going on?' I asked.

'It's a very long story.'

'I don't mind. I have the whole day,' I indirectly insisted.

'Well, it started almost 20 years ago when Aunt Halliz moved in the southern part of Calsenai. She was our neighbour at that time. Uncle Thistle took an instant liking in her.' Everyone oohed and aahed, making Aunt Halliz blush darker.

'They gradually became good friends. Then our uncle Thistle decided to show the chivalrous side of him.' Everyone clapped, cheered, and hooted.

'So one day he decided to just go and make her agree to marry him. He had everything set up for her: flowers and a candlelight dinner with a beautiful background and music. Too bad, no one was allowed. Uncle Thistle kept everyone away because he didn't want to ruin the moment.' Everyone grunted together.

'But our dear uncle Denel had no idea about it. The place where Uncle Thistle had planned a sweet dinner was actually Uncle Denel's hanging-out spot. He soon reached the place and found it decorated. Uncle Thistle was practising the lines he was about to present. Uncle Denel walked towards him. He had his eyes closed, so he didn't realise that Uncle Denel was standing in front of him. So Uncle Denel seemed amused and just stood there. Then something really bad happened. Let's just say someone happened to be in the wrong place at the wrong time. Aunt Halliz arrived by the place and saw Uncle Thistle saying those phrases for Uncle Denel. She assumed it the wrong way.' I burst of laughing, so everyone joined in.

"You are the most beautiful human I've ever met. I would like to spend my whole life with you.' 'Everyone in the family quoted the lines Uncle Thistle said and laughed.

'She yelled at Uncle Thistle and took off running back to her house. He followed her and then used the same line Aunt Halliz heard. This caused her to bubble up in anger, and she slapped him. She kept on blabbing until . . . until . . . Uncle Thistle took her to the peak and hollered, 'I love you, Halliz.' 'Everyone oohed at this. They had a very cute love story. But I couldn't see how Uncle Denel was considered bisexual in this mess. It wasn't his fault.

Aunt Halliz also had the skin tone resembling my family's and black hair with brown highlights. Her eyes were pitch black. Uncle Thistle had the eyes and hair of Grandmother Serein.

'Anyways, they have just one daughter, Camellia, and she is 16.' A brunette smiled at me. I smiled back. What bothered me was that she was taller than me. Probably around five ten. She seemed like a perfect model to me.

'After Uncle Thistle, we have your dad. We know about Uncle Delphinium and Aunt Christina, but we don't know about you. Please enlighten us with telling us about yourself.' Callistemon smiled.

'I'm 16, I'll turn 17 in a month, and I have very good friends who are on a journey with me. I'll be leaving today at night for Allekior. I basically like chocolates, kids, and novels,' I said shortly. I can't tell them more about my life as it only included my abilities and anegz.

'Details were short, but we can dig on more when we have a whole life ahead of us.' Callistemon smiled broadly. He smiles a lot. I think he is my favourite cousin, though, there are three siblings and their kids I need to meet.

'We have Uncle Ranunculus married to Aunt Destiny.' I recognised Uncle Ranunculus from the one who pulled Uncle Denel to show him something. Aunt Destiny was an olive-skinned woman with jet-black hair and dark-brown eyes.

'Gladiolus and Edelweiss are their kids. He is 12, and she is 9.' He motioned towards the olive-skinned siblings.

'And now we have Aunt Lavender. You got that right. She has violet eyes. That's what people have named her after. She married Uncle Garon.' Aunt Lavender was pale and lean. Uncle Garon was rather short but taller than his wife with crop short black hair.

'They have a 3-year-old daughter, and she is pretty annoying at times. She—' Callistemon got cut off by a small girl hollering my name and running in my direction with her arms outstretched. I swiftly picked her up.

really obsessed with flowers. Everyone had a name related to flowers except for me and my grandparents.

I was currently having a small talk with my cousins and Aunt Anemone.

'I didn't exactly understand when you said you were travelling with your friends,' Azalea asked.

'Well, I met a group of travellers when I got teleported in here. They helped me to know this place, and since then, I have been travelling with them,' I fairly lied.

'How long have you been here?'

'Just a couple of days.' This was exact truth.

'How did you come here?'

'I don't know. I just saw a blue light, and it pulled me in.' This was absolutely true.

'Now you can live with us.'

'Well, I want to. But I've signed up to travel with them for a few days. After the tour, I'll come back to Calsenai and live here.'

'How did you meet Uncle Denel?'

'I just dashed into him luckily, and I remembered him. So he insisted that I stay in his house for at least one day.'

'It seems like you got lucky, brother. I've never heard of a combination of left-handedness and blood group of AB negative and, most importantly, a sorcerer. I swear you should be the one for anegz.' Azalea sighed.

'Hey, have you met the new protector of anegz?' Callistemon asked. I went rigid at this topic.

'No. Why?' I tried my best to be normal.

'I thought you travelled Selemara too. But people say he is also from the other world.' Callistemon seemed disappointed.

'Oh, that's great,' I gushed.

'People say he too is left-handed and is AB negative.' I gulped. *Please don't let them relate it to me.*

'Wow! That's a coincidence,' I faked happiness.

'Sure as hell it is,' someone muttered. I concentrated on each and everyone's minds present in here.

Poor boy didn't live with his family. I'll always be there by his side, no matter what happens.

He is so cool. I like his style. Only if I could get some tips.

Why is he so mysterious?

Why does he match so much with the description of the protector?

Who are the people he is travelling with?

How did he manage to live for so long alone?

'This reminds me of old times.' A tear slipped from her eye.

'I wish she was alive,' she murmured and stroked the photo.

'This is for you, Uncle Denel.' I handed him a forgotten dagger.

'I thought I lost it. Where did you find this?' he asked.

'When I was leaving for the orphanage, I took everything that reminded me of Himachal.'

He stood up and hugged me. He backed away after a few minutes. 'I just got carried away in the moment.' He ruffled my hair just like he used to when I was a kid. This felt right.

'I could tell you were a protector when I saw you growing. I am proud of you for you didn't let my belief drop down. Just make sure that you perform your job well.'

'This is my destiny, and I'll make sure I don't die without completing my job. I'll keep in mind that my parents gave up their life for me to live, and I won't let their sacrifice go for nothing,' I promised.

The couple smiled at me with dignity. 'You have our blessings. We pray that you never change like the other protectors did.'

'I'll give my best,' I assured them and exited their room.

The only one left was Infinity. I searched for her everywhere, but I couldn't find her. I exited the house and found her sitting on the front porch and gazing at the sky. I sat beside her.

'Can't sleep?' I asked.

'You are leaving tomorrow.' It came out as a matter of fact.

'Sadly, yes.' I sighed and turned my gaze towards my palms.

'Remember how we used to have sleepovers at each other's and talk for endless hours?' I smiled at that memory.

'How can I forget the time I had with the most beautiful girl in the world?' I smirked.

'Stop it now.' She blushed and hit the back of my head with her hand.

'I really mean it.' I turned on my serious tone.

'You don't look bad yourself,' she said friskily. We laughed a little.

'Can I ask you something?'

'Hmm?' she hummed without looking at me.

'How did you feel when you held Ariel for the first time?' she beamed.

'Ariel is the best sister, even though I have only one. But trust me, the day she came in my life, everything became better.' She kept on rambling on about Ariel, and I sat there and listened. She looked cute whenever she talked about something without taking a break.

'Airik, are you listening?' She waved her hands in front of my eyes.

'Huh?'

'I asked you who your favourite cousin is.' She pursed her lips.

'Callistemon,' I answered. After talking about certain topics, we fell quiet.

'It is so weird.'

'What is weird?'

'Moon. It is so beautiful because the sun helps it to shine. In reality, it is full of craters, but the ray of the sun makes its flaws gleam and appear it to be more beautiful. Not all of us have such people in our lives that make even the saddest moment of our life happy and memorable. I'm happy to say that your presence makes my life sparkle.' She hugged me. I hugged her back.

'You are wrong here. The moon shines only if it reflects the rays coming from the sun,' I reframed the phrase. She smiled at me. What she said next shocked me.

'I-I love you,' she said. I went rigid. *She loves me?* 'As a friend, silly.' She giggled.

I relaxed a little, but nonetheless, I was disappointed.

'How will I confess? Maybe not today, but someday I will.' I heard Infinity's thoughts that instantly brought a smile to my face. You might not be ready today, but I can wait for eternity for you.

The Hue Sisters

I felt myself flying through the cold cloud with wind splashing against my pale skin. 'Airik,' someone called me.

I flew towards the voice only to see Fein waiting for me. He stared at me expectantly and gave a tight smile. I landed on the ground in front of him.

'I don't have much time. You need to listen carefully.' He halted for me to say something, but I didn't.

'They are looking out for you. You have to stop searching for me and your family. It is absolutely true that your parents are alive, but they no longer will be if you walk around without any protection. Trust me, we all are absolutely fine. I'll make it short and simple for you to understand. The spirit of Pamretol is rising. She is doing something to Allekior. People are changing, and so will all of us . . . someday.' He sighed. Just then, a dragon came flying and screeching in our direction, taking him away from me.

I woke up next morning to leave Calsenai for Allekior. The dream was pretty weird, and it surely meant something. Anedrin had already specified that getting in Allekior won't be easy. Sorcery was required for every major step in Allekior. I just didn't understand the reason for why they were so keen on killing me. I didn't know them or they knew me. Why did the Elyrians choose me in the first place?

'Are you ready, Airik Patronus?' Palort asked. He had his axe in his hand again.

'To be honest, no. I'm very nervous,' I replied. He seemed amused with my answer.

'You are very different from the other protectors that came earlier. They all were so arrogant and overconfident. Everyone will be ready to die for the power you possess. But you simply deny what you are?'

'I would've been what you described the protectors to be if I lived in Duvollin. Who knows?' I shrugged. We exited the house.

'Be the way you are. Don't ever change.' By now, we were standing by our relites. Only we were in there—no one else.

'Why will I?' I leaned against my relite.

'I didn't mean it that way. I actually meant that when the protectors go crazy, when they talk different from what they are. They just . . . behave different.' He sighed and started pacing.

He meant that the way the spirit of Pamretol controls people. Rimtzal had earlier told that it was because of willpower. I had no idea of the strength of my willpower.

'Do you think I can control my emotions well?' I asked Palort. He furrowed his eyebrows in confusion.

'I think yes, you do. Why?'

'Just asking.' I shrugged off the question.

'You both are already here? I was searching for you everywhere,' Anedrin grumbled dramatically and jogged towards us.

'You never told us the way we will trespass in Allekior,' I nudged in.

'Whatever we are about to do right now is not trespassing. It is . . . uh . . . travelling without permission. That is it,' she hissed. I tried to hide the smile that was forming on my lips.

'Yeah right,' I muttered sarcastically. She glared at me before mounting on her relite.

'Where are those two?' I asked, referring to Phileda and Jason.

'I sent them to get some important stuff for journey.' She tested her relite and scrunched her face.

'I need to run a few errands. I find something different in here.' She ran her fingers through the relite and mounted on it. After a few minutes, she successfully took off with her relite. No one seemed to be coming. We both stood there and waited for them patiently.

'Why do we need so many weapons? I have my sword, Anedrin has her arrows, Jason has his shield, Phileda has her knives and daggers, and Palort has his axe. What else do we need?' I was particularly saying it to Anedrin.

'I can't risk telling all of you everything. Let's go. It's time to have some fun.' I shook my head and mounted on my relite. This girl will someday get all of us killed.

It was close to nightfall. We decided to set up our site under a huge tree. Anedrin told us to leave her alone for she had 'planning to do'. And everyone else had dozed off. I stood up and started walking. I didn't know where to go. I was just following the place where my legs took me. After a few minutes, I found an average-sized pond. I looked around myself, satisfied for the discovery I just made. I sat there for endless hours, enjoying the beautiful view of the moon trying to peek from the silver-illuminating heavy clouds. The green trees with colourful fruits and flowers showing themselves incompletely and trying to make the drowsy travellers insatiable. I felt my eyelids getting heavy, and I made myself cosy right there.

I woke up when I felt something tickling my ribs and some girlish giggling. I saw many girls surrounding me. I stood up and brushed my belronag. I turned my gaze towards the pond. I saw a group of girls submerged in the pond.

'I promise I won't hurt you,' I tried to reason with them. Their heads popped out at once, and I saw the most beautiful girls alive. They had all what we call a perfect beauty. They all looked identical blondes except for their eyes.

'Don't compose the potentials you can't retain,' someone murmured.

'No. You are getting me wrong. I seriously won't hurt you.' I smiled at them. They still had a straight face, so my smile drastically disappeared. Suddenly, they all erupted in laughter. It was so melodious and charismatic.

'Who are you to visit us, O, striking one?' I heard one of the sweetest voices asking me.

'I'm Airik,' I answered.

'The new protector of anegz?' she asked instantly.

'Yes. You still didn't tell me who you are.' I sat on the ground.

'I am Amber.'

'Jade.'

'Azure.'

'Carmine.'

'Orchid.'

'Sapphire.'

'Ruby.'

'Amethyst.'

All eight of them introduced themselves. They had the same colour of eyes as their name. 'Why don't you come out of the water?' I asked.

'So they are authentic.' ruby giggled.

'Who is authentic?' I asked, suddenly intrigued.

'The ones who say that you are from the other world.'

'Answer the question I earlier asked. Why don't you come out of the water?' I repeated my question.

'Because we live in the water. This is our life,' she stated sternly. Her beautiful smile was now replaced by an angry frown.

'I'm sorry if I have offended you. It was just a simple question.' I nervously dragged my fingers through my hair.

'We will always be there to guide you, and you always have to listen to us. Our job is to assist the protectors. Most of them never listened to us, and now they are with Airis,' Amethyst explained.

'Just remember that a blood clot is necessary to prevent a blood loss,' Azure said sadly.

'Airik! Where are you?' Anedrin's voice chimed in the atmosphere.

'Who are you?' I asked.

'We are the Hue Sisters.' They all smiled at me and disappeared in a mist, leaving back the colour of their names.

Different Aura

I ran back to the place we were camping. The Hue Sisters were different. I had a feeling from the time I met them. They said they were supposed to assist protectors. This meant that they were immortal. People probably know about the Hue Sisters. I soon found Anedrin struggling with the colourful mist around her.

'Why are you still awake?' I asked her. She narrowed her eyes at me.

'I should be asking you the same question, and also, why did you wander off somewhere?' she scolded me.

'I need to ask you something.' I tried to direct the discussion in another way.

'Don't you dare change the topic, protector.' She rested her palms on her hips angrily.

'I just . . . um . . . wanted to ask about the Hue Sisters.' I found a topic soon. Her hands dropped on her sides.

'You met them?' she asked with her voice barely reaching above a whisper.

'Then why do you think I'll be asking you that question?' I wiggled my eyebrows at her, resulting in a giggle.

She got in control after what seemed like minutes of misery. 'About the Hue Sisters, first, tell me about the conversation you had with them.' She folded her arms.

'Nothing much. They just told me that I need to listen to them and also that a blood clot is necessary for prevention of blood loss,' I sounded unsure myself.

'That is the only phrase they have been using since the protectors came into existence,' she groaned and stomped her foot.

'Tell me what they are,' I demanded.

'The Elyrians have set up the Hue Sisters to guide the protectors in the right path. They come only when they think it is truly necessary. They have the names of colour, as you have already observed, and they are extremely pretty. And you have seen that too. So I think there is nothing else to spare about them,' she spoke hesitantly.

'Can you tell me the whole truth, princess?' I literally begged.

'How did you know? Oh, I get it. Your mind games.' I rolled my eyes.

'I don't have to read your mind for that, kiddo,' I said playfully.

'Stop treating me like a baby,' she whined.

'You are acting like one right now,' I reminded.

'You can't expect me to act like a grown-up. I'm just 12.' She made her puppy-dog eyes.

'That doesn't work on me.' I winked.

'You are absolutely heartless,' she said sassily.

'Now get back on the topic and clear my query.' She went in her uncomfortable zone again.

'Fine, don't tell me if you don't want to, and don't worry, I won't peek in your head for the details. But you have to tell me soon.'

'But I don't trust you.' She turned away and started walking. Even though I don't know Anedrin well, her words still hurt. But it's good that she was honest and straightforward.

'You better do, princess.' I followed her. I could feel regret reflecting from her.

It was close to dusk, so we both decided to stay awake. I fixed my gaze on the purplish-black sky. I could feel Anedrin drilling holes at my head with her stare.

'Is there something on my face?' I asked without taking my eyes off the sky.

'Except for calmness, I don't see anything else,' she sweet-talked. I sighed and looked at her.

'Even if you coat bitter gourd with sugar, its bitterness doesn't disappear,' I reminded. She huffed and stared at the ground for a moment as if she was trying to form a sentence without adding sarcasm or rudeness to it.

'I'm sorry. I didn't mean what I said. Let's just say, I've had a very bad experience with the Hue Sisters.' She stared at her palms and refused to make an eye contact with me.

'It's all right. It happens.' I tried to make her guilt free with my words as if it would have helped. So I got up and walked towards her. I sat on my knees and patted her back soothingly. It was something my mother used to do whenever I used to get sad. Surprisingly, I heard her snoring. I picked her up and laid her in a comfortable position. I wish I had a sibling too. I already have Jason. I got up and stretched my frame. *Why is my life so confusing?* Just then, someone tapped my shoulder. I turned to see one of the Hue Sisters. Her name was Azure.

'You need help,' she stated as a matter of fact.

'Probably.' I shrugged.

'I have never seen a protector like you.' She giggled, and her long blonde hair cascaded from the bun her hair was tied into.

'Because I am the only protector who is officially not from Duvollin,' I said as if it was obvious.

'It's your life, Airik. We will be there to assist you. I know you've seen too much in your life. But you must know that the more pain you feel, the stronger you become. It's just that we don't have much time.' She sighed.

'I can't tell you anything else. Just remember that your destiny changes when you change, your fate changes when you change, but time is the only thing that changes you.' After saying so, she disappeared in the mist like her name.

We were really close to reaching Allekior. Just one major step and we would be in. The soldiers were patrolling around like watchdogs. There was no way we could get in without sorcery, and none of us were energetic enough to control their minds.

'Now what?' Phileda asked.

'We fly.' Anedrin smirked.

'Just wait for the bait,' she said poetically. I rolled my eyes and kept on the two soldiers with red belronag with dragons sign over it. A few minutes later, a lady came and gave them their meals.

'Now wait and watch.' She tiptoed towards them and climbed on a tree. She dropped something from a height that fell directly on their plates. She returned proudly with what she just did.

'Did you use some kind of sleeping pill?' I asked without taking my gaze off the soldiers. They had a very bad heating habit as if there was no tomorrow.

'Why do you ask so many questions when you can get your answers without rattling your brains?' She scoffed.

'I don't like to invade someone's personal space without their permission, not until really very necessary.' I glared at her.

'Whatever.' She flipped her brown hair.

The soldiers finished their meal, and as they were trying to stand up, they collapsed, signalling us that they were unconscious now. Anedrin balled in fists in the air and hollered her victory. We all walked towards the soldiers.

'Stop,' she ordered us all. I too stood still. If it wasn't her plan, I would have never listened to her.

'We are flying.' She sniggered.

'Flying with what? Sorcery? We can directly walk in there. We don't even have to fly.' I snorted.

'Half knowledge is a devil's workshop,' she mumbled and shook her head. Unfortunately for her, I heard it.

'Call me when you find a way.' I ignored her comment and mounted on my relite and started the engine. Instead of moving forward, it took off towards the sky. Its appearance changed. The hue was now thicker, and the wheels were taking the form of something that seemed like propellers.

'What is this?' I yelled. Anedrin laughed.

'This is how we will fly.'

'Why do we need to fly in the first place?' I yelled from above.

'Because they have a barrier that lasts for almost 40 feet,' she replied.

'So why did you knock those two down?' I asked.

'If they saw us, then something really bad would have happened.' She shook her head as if trying to get away from a bad thought or memory. The rest of them mounted on their relites and met the same height as mine.

'Why didn't we take another route?' It seemed like I was the only one who doubted Anedrin.

''Cause this was the most breachable place,' she answered annoyingly.

Why would anyone make a place so easy to break through? I wanted to ask this question badly, but Anedrin's mood seemed a little off today, so I just dismissed the thought and flew with my friends, enjoying the beautiful view from above. I could see the border of Pamretol by now. It was nothing but a dense forest with a black, blue, purple, golden, and silver aura mixing with one another. It was truly beautiful. I gazed at the rest of my friends, but they didn't seem to notice the beautiful forest in front of them.

Anubhuti Singh

'Why can't you see it?' I asked to them.

'See what?' Palort furrowed his eyebrows.

'The forest. Isn't it beautiful?' I admired the unique landscape.

'There is no forest in here, Airik Patronus. We can't even see it through the horizon.' He looked concerned. He was right. There was no forest with any aura, just small houses. Maybe I was just imagining, but seriously, this strong?

'Sorry,' I mumbled, loud enough for Palort to hear.

We landed behind a massive tree. Our relites retreated back to their original shape and size. The propellers turned back into wheels. Since Anedrin was the one who devised the whole plan, we followed her like lost puppies.

'I have a spy in here that works in Allekior's army. We will be staying with him. Let me tell you he is an amazing warrior and he is also a very close friend of mine and he would never betray me, so you folks better keep your suspicions to yourself,' she instructed to all of us.

'What if he is being controlled?' I asked.

'We can see that later on, protector,' she dismissed the conversation, and we followed her. I observed my surroundings, and to be honest, everything in Allekior was the same as Selemara and Calsenai, except that there was a dragon's sign everywhere I turned my gaze to. The people here also were very sceptical. They were just different from normal humans. I couldn't put a finger on it yet. I tried to read them, but every time I concentrated on anyone, all I could see was eternal darkness and just one thought in each and everyone's mind: God is just a figment to keep your hopes up—nothing more, nothing less. Fein had earlier warned me about the spirit controlling most of the people of Allekior. Maybe that was happening right now. Their gaze followed us everywhere we went but retreated when we were not in sight.

'We need to talk . . . like right now,' I announced. All of them stared at me as if I were crazy.

'This place doesn't seem right. Something is just off about this place. We need to get out of here as soon as possible,' I babbled.

'Endless babbling is better than a meaningful silence.' Anedrin smirked.

'None of you notice this, do you? Listen carefully. There is absolute silence: no birds chirping, no swishing of trees— nothing, just absolute silence. Plus, there is hardly anyone out in here. Don't you think that is really strange?' I tried to knock some sense in them.

'You are just being paranoid.' Jason rolled his eyes.

'That's what you all always think. Ever thought why the boundary in there was so weak?' I shook Palort for a dramatic effect.

'You seriously need to work on your orating skills, protector. Let's go.' Anedrin turned and marched towards the heap of plywood houses.

I sighed and followed them. I needed to do something before everything goes wrong. Frozen silence is the last step towards damage.

We reached a deadly silent and dark path with a few houses lying with huge distances between each other. This place sent shivers down my spine. The feeling I was getting regarding this place was utterly scary. Coming in this place was not a good idea at all.

'We are here,' Anedrin exclaimed and trotted in the house with permission. She obviously didn't need one. Being the ruler of Selemara was a very beneficial factor for her. I had a firm grip on my sword for any unexpected assaults.

'Relax.' I felt a hand squeeze my shoulder. It was Phileda.

'Anedrin always cross-checks everything before doing anything,' she reassured me. I sighed with relief. I just looked behind me for once, and then I saw a girl, maybe a year younger than me, looking creepily at me with her aquamarine eyes. She stood there emotionless. I smiled at her, but her expression wouldn't budge. My smile faltered. She cocked her head to one side and smirked at me.

'I'm looking forward to meet you. I've already made my move. You know what you need to do,' she stated in her beautiful melancholy voice and walked away with her black hair whispering against the wind.

Infesten Tower

After meeting that girl, I felt different. Something in me had totally changed. I felt powerful and full of energy. This was the first time when I didn't care about anyone. This also included my family. I felt normal and calm. This was something I never experienced in my entire life. But something didn't feel right about this feeling.

'Airik!' Anedrin yelled.

'What?' I snapped at her. She took a step behind, clearly intimidated from my sudden outburst.

'I just wanted to talk to you. Palort has something to tell us,' she mumbled softly. I felt guilt for yelling at her, but it was soon replaced with a feeling I was unaware of, a feeling that I hardly ever felt: negligence.

'What do you want to talk about?' It came out harsh. I didn't expect that. She scowled and continued, 'Just a discussion with the rest of us. Palort has something really important to say.' I followed her to a small room.

'Look, there is this place in Allekior. Something is just not right with it. You see this place over here?' He pointed at it. 'There are some activities going on in there that are totally illegal. The worst part is that it is coated with infesten, hence, its name Infesten Tower.' I had heard this term somewhere before. I'm sure about it.

'Infesten is a substance that resists sorcery. It in turn harms the sorcerers.' Now I remembered. It was the same thing when Airis got kidnapped.

'So what are we supposed to do?' I propped my elbow against the table.

'We think that is where someone really important is being held. I mean really very important,' he stressed out on his statement.

Maybe they have my parents. According to me, they are the most important people right now. Anedrin looked at me and nodded, confirming my assumptions.

'But there is absolutely nothing we can do about it, and why do we even care?' Phileda asked.

'I don't know. I just wanted all of you to know about it.' He shrugged and slumped on the wooden chair.

'We can totally understand. It's really late. I think we should sleep. Tomorrow is a very big day.' Everyone stood up and left. Now only Anedrin and I were remaining in the room.

'I'm pretty sure that they have your parents in there. We'll devise a plan and get them out.' She squeezed my shoulders. The shocking thing was I didn't feel excited or frightened about this expedition. All I could think was absolute power I could possess over humanity. But I still wanted my parents back.

'We'll go tomorrow. I already have a plan,' I said bluntly, clearly no emotion. I didn't give her time to react. I just left the room.

I woke up early in the morning before dusk and left for Infesten Tower as soon as possible. Everyone was still asleep. I took the map of Allekior from Palort's bag. Jason turned and mumbled something in his sleep, which I wasn't able to decipher. I exited the house and noiselessly closed the door behind me. The chilling air greeted me, and the darkness engulfed everything in its way. I right away teleported without any delay close to that tower. I unfortunately left my knives and sword back at the house.

Infesten Tower was almost equivalent to a four-storey building with a cylindrical structure. It emitted a very foul smell, which I presume was infesten. I tiptoed towards the entrance. It was widely open. It was pitch black. I couldn't see a damn thing. This must be the first floor then. I took a deep breath and entered my death trap. I looked above only to meet endless darkness. Meanwhile, my claustrophobic senses were kicking in after realising how narrow the passage was.

For my parents, I reminded myself. The hallway all of a sudden lit with candles. Something felt wrong with this place. Just then, something sloppy dripped on my belronag. I touched it. It was olive green with stickiness in its appearance. It seemed like a shampoo to me except that its smell was something like a burnt foul chicken. Overall, it was sickening. I turned my eyes above me.

My heartbeat picked up, and I felt a rush of adrenaline in me. I chose flight. I broke into a run. It was none other than a litror. And I am absolutely sure that whatever just fell on my clothing was its venom. Lucky for me, I was already diagnosed. I could hear it rattling and hissing behind me. I made a big blunder by looking behind me to distinguish the distance between us. Just then, I dashed into something really hard and fell down on the cold marble floor.

I turned my gaze towards my predator. It crouched and I knew it could pounce on me anytime. It already knew how scared I was. I backed up against the wall and analysed its each and every move. Its metallic four legs like a fragile white fabric wrapped up against something hard like iron. Its tail was wavering like a shiny contraption guarding itself. Its golden flecked eyes were eyes were fierce with determination to kill me. It snarled. I winced when its hot breath embraced my skin. Its large dull-yellow wings fluttered, sending frosty air towards me. The sandy fur hugging its body was contracting and reflexing momentarily. The tip of its ears was a beautiful shade of golden. This creature was very distracting. I should've got something for my protection. It darted its tongue out and licked its sharp and slender canines, lucidly teasing me. Its talons were warily scraping against the marble and making deep dents.

I gathered my courage and stood up. My knees were shaking badly. There was just a distance of two meters between us. I backed up against the wall and took a leap in the air. I kicked the lateral wall of the passage and landed right behind the litror. It growled at me in anger. I took off running with it trailing behind me. I spotted the stairs and climbed it. The creature had sharp talons, making harder for it to climb the iron stairs. It screeched and made very inappropriate sounds. I ignored it and climbed up the stairs. It was surprising how no one came in here.

As soon as I hit the second floor, I heard rattling of chains and someone being whipped and the painful shrieks of a boy. I mentally face palmed for the trouble I got myself into. I could feel the intensity of seriousness around me. I've heard that Infesten Tower is used to capture only those people who have committed a grave crime and they are tortured there until they die and the rest are just important people who are kept there to manipulate someone. It sounds really bad to me. Everyone deserves a second chance.

I shook my thoughts away. The only thing that troubled me was the way I'll be able to get my parents out without sorcery. *But I think I can use my skills. I don't have to use sorcery for that.* I concentrated on the cellars; and then I saw people, mostly men, whining in pain. *They are not on this floor, that's for sure.* I climbed up the third floor. There were hardly any cellars in here, only snoring people. I explored farther and at last found a sword in a small room. There were many uniforms in there. I picked one and changed into them. It had the same dragon's symbol. I climbed up the fourth floor. This was the place I needed to get through. This was the last floor. Plus, this place was eerily quiet.

'Hey! What are you doing here? It's not yet morning,' someone yelled behind me. I turned and face the man.

'Oh, I get it. You must be Screferd's son. Follow me,' he said. I just peeked in his head. I was a replacement for Screferd, a soldier in his late 30s, for today. He was injured badly.

'What did your father tell you about the job?'

'He was in too much pain, so he wasn't able to talk properly,' I reasoned. He seemed convinced.

'Come on then. I'll narrate you the whole story.' He leaned against the table and started, 'As you know, the new protector has arrived, and he thinks his parents are dead. But they are not.' He leered. I felt like stabbing him, but I had to listen to the whole story in order to get them out. I faked a shocked expression.

'How is it possible?' I asked.

'Your body dies but not your soul. They are eternal. And we have their souls. Have you heard of the technique called bremen?' he asked me. I shook my head.

'Sorcerers separate the body from soul. The body gets decayed, but we have the soul, and that is what we did to them. They never age. They remain as they were when bremen was performed. That's another story when we want them alive. We just have to reverse the process.' He smiled smugly.

'But why did you kidnap his parents?' I asked.

'Because he is powerful, more than anyone can imagine. He is different. To be precise, he has a good soul. And this is not what we look in a protector. We want a greedy soul in them—greedy for power. But he doesn't have it. And that is all that has turned the master down.'

'Master?' I asked with confusion. His eyes widened in realisation on how much he had given away.

'We can talk later. I'll get you to the work you need to do for them.' He quickly scurried away. I followed him. I took note of my surroundings. It was all with marble floor and flaunting paintings of the royal family. I tried to memorise each and every curve of the floor. He halted in front of a huge door.

'Don't look in the eyes of the woman and don't try to mess with the man,' he warned me. I gave him a questioning look.

'Just don't do it.' I was unsatisfied with his lack of details.

'Treat them like normal humans but keep an eye on them,' he explained while taking the lock off the door. The door opened to reveal my parents. They were cuddled together in their sleep. Just like this guy said, they were exactly like they were those years ago. It took a lot of willpower to keep the smile off my face.

'I'll wait for you in the office. Meet me after they have their breakfast.' I nodded at him and bowed my head down in respect. He left the room. I sighed and wiped off the sweat that was trickling from my temples. I walked towards their bed and sat at the end of it. *They just need to wake up and then, we will anyhow make it out of this place.* I tapped my feet impatiently against the floor. This made them stir in their sleep. I started pacing about the room, waiting for them to get up. I walked back towards the chair and sat there. I dozed off within a few minutes of waiting.

'Are you really Airik?' I squinted and gazed at my dad. I closed my eyes again. *Wait, Dad?* I opened them with a start, and then I saw my parents scrutinising me under their gaze.

I just sprang on my feet and held them in a bone-crushing embrace. I let go of them.

'We have to get out of here.' I got hold of their hands.

'Wait. Who are you?' Mom asked.

'Airik Sigirian.' I half-heartedly smiled at her.

'Why do you expect us to believe you?' my mom growled. I looked at Dad. It seems like he didn't tell her about our little meeting yet.

'Because I'm your son. Don't you see any similarities with the younger one and me? I could've reminded you if I wasn't so short of time. Let's go.' Just then, the door burst open.

'You lied to me!' the guy I met earlier hissed. There was another guy beside him, and he looked around my age. I assume he is Screferd's son. *This is it.*

'Let's go.' I motioned to my parents. I pushed that guy out of the door with my parents following me.

'Guards! There is an intruder in disguise!' the man yelled.

We climbed down the stairs, and when we were almost on the first floor, a troop of soldiers charged from behind us. The litror was still pacing around. Just then, an idea popped up in my mind.

'Stay close with me,' I told my parents. They just nodded. The creature spotted me and leapt towards me. I ran towards the troop of guards and blended in. Everyone was confused with my action until they saw the litror charging towards them.

I was busy trying to kill the rest of the soldiers. Three of us sneaked out of the tower.

I panted heavily and turned towards my parents. They were standing straight as if nothing had ever happened. 'Are you really my son?' Mom asked hesitantly. I just sighed and made them remember the memories we had together.

'My love for my family is like an unending journey,' I repeated the words my mom had once used. My parents hugged me and kept on apologising for not being with me when I needed them.

I teleported back to the house we were resting in. As soon as I opened the door, all my friends were sitting with their respective weapons in their hands. Rimtzal also was here.

'You went without me? Do you have any idea that you would've hurt yourself? To be precise, you almost got yourself killed. They have the most powerful litror in their possession, and you are acting as if nothing ever happened? I would've helped you out,' Anedrin yelled and kept on rambling.

'But I didn't do any of this. I'm totally fine,' I snapped back at her.

'So this is what I get after worrying for you,' she spat.

'I didn't tell you to worry for me, did I?' I barged into the house with my parents behind me.

'Stop it, you two. Nothing major has happened, so stop freaking out.' Jason stepped between us. Rimtzal was sitting and clearly enjoying the fight, but suddenly he spoke up.

'Don't waste your time fighting. We have to go back to Selemara. You are changing and we can't let you go there. Pack your stuff and come,' Rimtzal ordered in his grave tone.

'What do you mean by changing?' I asked and took a seat beside him.

'Don't you feel that you are very powerful to rule over the world?' he whispered so that only I was the one able to hear. He was right.

'Am I—' I couldn't complete the sentence.

'Trust me you are, and you better come back before you change completely.' His coal-black eyes were boring into mine, showing complete truth. I couldn't digest the fact that I was changing into a different person that I never was. We sat in utter silence until Mom spoke up.

'What is going on?' my mom asked.

'Mom, I don't have much time. I need to go. Till then, I think you should go back to Calsenai. Our family misses you.' I wish I could tell her how important going back is.

'I promise I'll come back in time.' My voice cracked in the end. I just met them, and now I had to part from them again.

'They should come with us,' Rimtzal said and stood up.

I flipped my gaze towards him. 'What do you mean?' I spelt each and every word crystal clear.

'I can see that bremen was performed on your parents, and second, if you leave them in Calsenai, these soldiers will look for them, and most importantly, what kind of explanation will they give to their family when they don't know the whole truth itself?' He raised his eyebrows questioningly.

'Are you the protector?' Dad asked. I just nodded.

'My son has grown.' His eyes watered. He walked up to me and ruffled my hair, just like the old times.

'Don't aspire to be like someone else because you have a beautiful skill that everyone doesn't own.' He winked and fought back the tears that were threatening to spill.

Aiden Skrenacle

As soon as we had a small 'discussion' with one another, all of us packed our bags and travelled back to Selemara. Since Rimtzal was with us, he insisted on teleporting. In no time, we reached our destination. Rimtzal constantly kept on stealing glances at me whereas my parents couldn't stop admiring me. My dad was proud of me for dealing with a litror alone without any weapons. I clutched my sword tightly and walked towards the palace.

The look on the every Selemarian's face was priceless. They sure as life wanted to know about Rimtzal all of a sudden gaining interest in the matters of the kingdom. It was strange how no one dared ask Rimtzal about his presence in here.

After taking a long shower in my room, I decided to show up in the library where Rimtzal would enlighten us the cause of his company, which was never seen after he left the job of a protector. I dressed in my black belronag and dragged my

484

fingers through my damp black hair. My cheeks were slightly red because of the cold water.

I took a deep breath and marched towards the library. No one had yet arrived. I took a look around the library, and my eyes soon landed on the bookshelf that said Glorious Legends of Duvollin. I walked towards it and ran my eyes through the titles. The one that caught my eyes was *The Protectors of all Time.*

I lifted it out of the shelf and placed it on the table. I sat on the chair and turned the pages on the book. The first few pages started with beginning of the story where the King Phinogar turned evil and destroyed most of the Duvollin, followed by a brief biography of every protector.

Most of them were quite interesting, which stated their skills and experiences with a brief introduction about their changing. My gaze halted on a familiar name: Aiden. *This name is so familiar.* I shook my head. Everything seemed familiar to me. I took a deep breath and read Aiden's biography.

AIDEN SKRENACLE

He is a patron of the goddess of emotions, Skrenacle. He has frizzy red hair and black eyes that add to his fair complexion. He stood at the frame of five six because the legend states that the protectors are normally short. He was born to Darioulus and Migis of Neadre.

Since a juvenile, he always intended to be a protector just like everyone desires to be. At the age of 15, he unearthed about sorcery, and leisurely, he was prepared so that he could guard Neadre. He turned out to be a remarkable person, but whenever someone came in his way of triumphing whatsoever, he would make it unquestionable that this never ensues once again, whether it be a reasonable way or the undue one. Being victorious is every way possible was his topmost desire. As soon as he turned twenty one, he was taken away to Selemara for protecting the stone.

He was said to be like other protectors but a little different. It is true that he was covetous and was affected by the forest of Pamretol, but it was in a distinctive way.

As soon as the prophecy about the new protector was heard, he was enraged at the new one for magnetising everyone's relevance. He left Duvollin very early and thus left his job.

He disguised as a small child and travelled to the other world and tried to get rid of him. But the regime of the other world held him back in there. He never returned. Everyone knows he cannot kill or harm the new protector because the prophecy states him to be different than the rest.

None of the Duvolliners have seen or even heard from Aiden for a long time. Many people denunciate the new protector for it while some of us deem that it was because of Aiden's envy, and for the rest of us, they don't reflect any deliberations about this affair.

His proficiency comprised in controlling emotions and manipulating people into considering his judgements.

I turned the page only to meet a blank page. I huffed and placed the book back in the rack. I knew Aiden. The biography itself stated that he wanted me dead. But I didn't remember him. I felt as if a major part of my memory was wiped away and I was left alone with certain recalls that held no meaning.

I groaned and clutched my head. Everything was fading, whether it be my memory, or the real me. *I can feel everything wearing off gradually. I know there will be nothing left, and I cannot stop from changing. I have my parents with me, but they are still far from me. I have changed, and so have my preferences. They did everything for me, even gave up their life only for me to stay alive. They were and always have been great parents, but I couldn't save them. They stayed locked up in that hell for 11 years, and I wasted my time in the orphanage. I have been a very bad son, and no one can change that.* I sighed and stood up.

'You are already here? I thought you were with your parents.' Rimtzal came in the library and noticed my distressed expression. He furrowed his eyebrows.

'Is something wrong?' he asked me with concern.

'I am good for nothing. I couldn't even protect my own parents. How can I protect the stone?' I clenched my jaw.

'Don't say so, Airik. You are still very small. Normal age for protectors is 21. But we got you here at the age of 16, and trust me, you are a lot better than the rest that came here.' He hugged me, and I felt a dearly warmth radiating from his body.

'Rimtzal, what happened to your family?' I asked. He loosened his grip on me. His coal-black eyes were unconditionally dark, and they held so much of anger and guilt. It's strange. He never showed emotion in front of anyone, but now he was overwhelmed.

'They were killed by Airis. She wanted me to join her just like other protectors have, but I wouldn't change. She asked me to join her, but I refused. So she targeted on everyone I loved. My parents had already abandoned me when I was a kid. Then I met her when I was your age. She was my reason to live. She supported me every time I took a decision. She was the only one I had, and she took her away from me.' He tried his best to cover up his emotions, but his eyes gave away his darkest secret.

'What are you guilty for?' I asked without a second thought.

'For not saving them in time. I could've brought her alive, but I failed.' He kept his shield of firmness on.

'At least, your parents are fairly alive. I have no one left, Airik—no one. Have you ever realised why I don't live in Selemara? It's because everything reminds me of my Rhina.' His expression softened a bit, and then it changed back to cold as soon as it changed to loving.

'I'm just waiting for the best time to strike back at her. I'll make her realise how wrong she has always been, and I'll make sure she doesn't die without guilt. Patience is all I have with me now. My wife was my last attachment. My last wish will be to kill her. The most important thing I have learnt from my life is that death is just a message to tell you that nothing stays with you forever even if it is the most beloved one in the entire world.' We sat there in silence, and this silence wasn't the awkward one. It was when endless babbling doesn't clarify anything, silence is the only excuse for the situation. It provides tranquillity, which I had never experienced with anyone.

This was the only time when I didn't care about anything. There was no changing, no anegz, no Airis, and just no one.

Except for me and my calm mind. I wish I could stay in this state forever, but everything in this world acts as a bait to make us work. Either it is about money or for someone you care and love, that is how things work.

'Life is a journey to make you a better person. It is not easy to change, but it is not tough either to improve into a more polite person,' Rimtzal said after a long time.

'Don't feel bad, but why don't you use this thought in your life?' I asked.

'I'm stuck, Airik. I'm stuck between my desires and my destination. My destination tells me to be cold-hearted and keep people away from me. I don't like the feeling when I lose someone close to me. So it's a lot better to have no one beside you. While my desire tells me to forgive Airis and every person who wished ill of me and my family, I just fail to understand what is more important: my desire or objective? As awkward as it sounds, I have a muddled thought about this.' I chuckled slightly. A man as old and experienced as him is confused.

'Which option do you think suits best for you? What will make you happy?' I smiled and flaunted my dimples more than ever.

'I want that spirit dead, and that is what will make me happy,' he answered awkwardly.

'Think and answer. Even if you kill Airis, will you ever be happy again? Sure, it is necessary for her to be dead, but will killing her help?' He remained silent for a long time.

'Killing her will only help the world, not me. The guilt will remain with me for eternity. It doesn't matter if I kill her.

489

Nothing will change except for the fact that I would've killed someone and thoroughly enjoyed it. I don't think I'll ever want that to happen.' He at last came up with an answer and flashed the broadest smile I'd ever seen.

'My mother always used to say smile even without a reason because sometimes people have a reason to smile for you,' he confessed and scratched the back of his head.

'Even after living for one century and half, you are still naïve.' I laughed.

'Being naïve is the only way to ignore the wicked world.' He said it again.

'Not everything is wicked. Each and everything in this world has its own consequences. It just depends on the way we use it,' I argued back.

'You haven't lived long, Airik. You have a lot of time in front of you. It's high time with me getting easy on you. I think I'll start with the ordeals about you changing.' He got up and slackened a bit.

'What do I need to do?' I stood up and followed him.

'Nothing much. Just follow everything I say.'

The Morphing

Right now, I was standing with only my black cotton trackpants on. I normally didn't pay heed to 'flaunt' my physical appearance. Rimtzal and I were in the castle's remotest basement. Jason, Palort, and Delver were yet to come. I was pacing around with nervousness.

'It's all right, Airik. The serum will illustrate what you feel. There is nothing you need to do except to control your hormones.' He smirked. I rolled my eyes. He knew how to lighten up the mood, a good factor to live a very long life. Just then, the three missing males entered, including my dad.

'I didn't know your biceps had grown stronger.' Jason wolf whistled.

'The last time you saw me shirtless was three years ago,' I reminded him.

'Well, that explains a lot.' He chuckled and walked towards me and gave me a hug. I returned it. *Something doesn't feel right. I'm just being paranoid,* I scolded myself. He let go of me and stood beside Palort.

'Let's start.' Rimtzal gave an apologetic smile. He gestured towards the bed. I took a deep breath and walked towards it.

'Lie down.' I did just as Rimtzal told me to. He took out iron chains and wrapped them securely against the bed's banister. I don't know why, but my breathing was quickening and my heart rate was picking up. I closed my eyes. *Calm down, Airik. It's nothing. Just a small test.* Something icy cold came in contact with my ankles. My gaze desperately shifted everywhere. Then I saw my dad. He smiled warningly at me, and I felt relieved.

'I don't think you can watch this, Delphinium. You should leave,' Rimtzal stated sternly. He ruffled my hair and left the basement. Rimtzal bent to my eye level, his black ones boring into my green orbs.

'You cannot trust anyone until you trust yourself.' He got up and took out the serum. It was in a small needle.

Relax, I'll just prick it. Everything will be fine. Rimtzal entered my brain and tried to get me cooled down.

As the needle was looming over me, something in me snapped, and I no longer wanted this to happen. 'Stop,' I whispered and struggled against the chains. But it was too late for them to hear. The needle had already touched the base of my neck, and now the serum was flowing in my veins. The dizziness took over me, and my eyes fluttered close. The last thing I heard was 'Negative.' Just one word was enough to destroy my existence.

I woke up with a dense forest surrounding me. I got up and brushed off my black cotton trackpants. The last thing I remember was drooping into unconsciousness. This had to be yet another dream. I felt someone digging holes at the back of my head. I turned around to see a familiar pair of aquamarine eyes.

'Missed me?' she stated arrogantly and twirled her index finger, and soon there was a gust of wind dancing around to form two chairs. She sat on one and folded her slender legs with a black gown cascading down her feet. Her hair was piled in a beautiful messy bun. If she didn't plot everything and caused so much harm to the ones I care about, I would've have surely admired her. I sat on the chair and concentrated on her head. She had a bored expression on her face.

'Doesn't matter how hard you try, sweetheart. You cannot read me.' She smirked and stood up from her chair, walking towards me. She trailed her index finger's nails across my jaw. That's when I squirmed and felt uncomfortable with the lack of clothing on me. If Jason was here, he would've thoroughly enjoyed it but not me. She is a monster. She kills people because she believes they are not worth living.

'I'm a patron of Delcie protector. I know the future. I can see the potential you have and what you can become if you join me. The Hue Sisters will eventually be on my side,' she tried to reason with me.

493

'You are wrong.' I stood up and faced her fierce eyes with determination. She scowled.

'Why don't you see it? They are trying to cage you, making you work for them. Rimtzal is their pet now but not you. You are a free bird, free to do anything you want to. Tell me, they do restrict you to some extent, don't they? The dos and don'ts, the boundaries of your life, and there is no option but to abide by them. They keep things away from you. They think that you are not worth knowing the secrets. They don't trust, Airik. Isn't that enough to stop working with those hypocrites?' Her voice was rising by degrees. She was right in some places, but everything they had done for me was for my own good. She was just trying to play with my mind.

'They care for me, that's why,' I replied. She let out her malicious yet beautiful laugh.

'You are so naïve. I must say I have a very loyal pet.' She headed back towards her chair, and something appeared in her hands. It was a bow.

'Do you know what this is?' she asked me as she ran the tip of her fingers over the bow with carvings of channels of water over it.

'How would you know? It was from Octavian, my best friend.' She smiled like a little girl.

'He was the only one who supported me besides Ikaria.' Her expression turned sour at her name.

'But everyone either abandoned me or broke my trust. They all had to die. Everyone who hurts me has to die but not Octavian and my parents. He did hurt me a little, but he changed. Maybe his and my parents' sacrifice was important to make me understand that attachment is what makes us weak as it is the emotion that derives every negative emotion.' She sighed.

'The protectors that I have encountered until now were weak and simply . . . pathetic. But you are different. You know why? 'Cause you have a lot in common with Melancus. That makes me want to kill you and at the same time come for your aid. He just does something weird to my heart.' She chuckled and shook her head. I gulped. *If she believes that I'm like Melancus, then there is nothing that can stop me from being killed by this bizarre girl.*

'But I'm not him. I'm Airik,' I defended myself from being assaulted by her in any way.

'I know. You have his eyes and a lot more other things. But you love her, don't you?' She got up from her chair and walked towards me. *Who is she talking about?*

'I don't understand,' I replied truthfully.

'I'm talking about the Calsenai girl,' she snarled.

'Whoa, wait. Why does everyone assume that I'm in love with her? She is a very good friend of mine, and that's it. Are you jealous?' I asked with slight amusement. She frowned.

'Why should I be jealous of a mere girl?' She faked a laugh. 'If you don't have feelings for her, then I don't think you'll care if she comes with me to Aegera, do you?' She raised her perfectly shaped eyebrows. I gulped. *I need to play cool.*

'What use could she make to you? Just like you said, she is a mere girl.' I smirked.

'Don't worry about that, but just keep one thing in mind. I want Melancus back. I know you will change, and no one can stop you. I offer you just one choice: join me, and if you don't, then die. I'll give you a day's time.' She disappeared. I was left alone with my confused thoughts.

I gasped. 'He is awake!' I heard a familiar feminine voice yell. I soon heard footsteps emerging. Everyone surrounded me. They bombarded me with questions.

'What happened?'

'Are you all right?'

'You were talking to yourself in your sleep. Were you dreaming something big?'

'You've been out for straight six hours.'

'Give the boy some space!' Rimtzal yelled. Everyone went quiet.

'She'll take her. Get her somewhere safe.' I panted.

'Who?' Rimtzal's eyes widened in alarm.

'Infinity,' I said and fell back into a deep dreamless sleep.

I tried to open my eyes, but I didn't have the energy to.

'The result was negative. What will happen?' I heard Jason ask.

'The same thing that has always happened. He'll venture off to Pamretol. Nothing can stop the protectors except for their willpower when they change.' He huffed.

'There is hope. Elyrians would stop it.'

'Gods are just figments to keep your hopes up.' I heard footsteps going away from me, and at last, the door closed. I felt the space beside me dip. Rough hands caressed my forehead.

'I know you are awake, Airik,' Rimtzal's raspy voice called out. I slowly opened my eyes.

'Is Infinity safe?' I croaked out.

'She is. Airis is just trying to scare you. Be in control. Don't flow out in emotions.' He stood up and exited the room. My eyes travelled through the room. I sighed as I was still in the basement. There were fruits beside me. I grabbed it and started munching on it. I yawned and stretched my body. After retaining my energy, I decided to leave the castle for a small walk. I just grabbed a black T-shirt, which stuck to my body along with my sword.

I sauntered out of the castle with just one thought in my mind. *The result was negative, so I will change. But what will I become?* I sighed. *Only I am the one who can stop me, but how? I'm pretty sure it's not easy. The way these Selemarians make it sound doesn't seem like it.* I sat under a shade of a tree. I took a lungful of chilling air and focused on the people around me.

My gaze halted on a group of kids playing. They were caretree. They enjoyed what they had now regardless their destiny, future, or even the anegz that they knew would someday be the cause of destruction just like it was in the past. Unlike me, I just overthink and complicate everything around me. I sighed. *No matter how much I reason, I will remain the same. It is my basic instinct.*

I smiled and let myself loose with the cool surroundings and the chirping of birds around me. I soon dozed off in the world of my imagination where there was just me and my thoughts and nothing else. It was something I used to do since I was a kid. My mom used to tell me that everyone should make sure that their words resemble the beauty of silence, which is impossible.

I flexed my muscles and let out a lazy yawn. I glanced at the evening purplish-blue sky with the reddish-orange sun, seeking to peek out of the sturdy grey clouds. I sat there for quite long as the beautiful sky was transforming into a navy-blue one. I stood up and brushed my pants lightly. Now there was no one in sight. They must be worrying about me now. I took my sword and decided to get back to the castle. Halfway through, there was something gnawing me from the inside. Selemara was shrilly quite, which never happened. I quickened my pace. Something was wrong. I heard heavy footsteps behind me. I began to run.

After a few seconds, I was tackled to the ground. The position was really awkward. My face was against the muddy ground, my hands were pinned behind me, and my legs were mushed. I struggled against the grip. I gradually stopped struggling, and after a few seconds, the hold on my wrists loosened a bit, and I took the advantage by flipping and getting him square at his jaw. I got up and took a fighting stance.

I eyed my assaulter with great attention. He was bulky and surely a few inches taller than me. He was covered from head to toe in grey clothing. Nothing was visible except for his hawk eyes. He never left my gaze. I felt as if he was reading my every thought and secret through his eyes. It was beyond unnerving. The way his eyes narrowed, I could tell he was faring a lopsided grin. He slowly took a dagger out of his waist girdle and twirled it, evidently mocking me. But I remained emotionless. There was no way I'll give him satisfaction with an unnecessary reaction. I took my out my sword out of its sheath. He took threatening steps towards me. I just stood there, patiently waiting for the time when he charges on me.

He furrowed his eyebrows as if trying to figure out a secret about me, and then he charged on me. He held his dagger high and aimed it towards me. I ducked in time as the dagger passed just my hair. I took the chance and closed the proximity between us. Now I was completely facing him. I held him by his throat as I had the wrong assumption of him being weaponless. He kicked right at my knee, and I fell to the ground. As soon as I regained my composure and took hold of my sword, the hawk-eyed man had already caged me in a repellent grip. I tickled his sides, and he soon let go of me with his sickening laugh echoing around me.

He cursed under his breath and charged at me with his dagger. I kicked his hand, causing the dagger to fall away from him. Without a second thought, I towed the sword through him. He had a shocked expression on his face as if he couldn't believe what just happened. He took a last glance at his wounded abdomen and collapsed on the ground. I tugged my sword out. I made my way back to the castle. I ran towards my room and locked it behind me. I made my way towards the inviting shower. It took a while for me to comprehend my condition.

There was a man who tried to kill me, but the reason didn't matter anymore. I just killed a man I didn't know. And the worst part was I liked it.

Guilt

I didn't share the incident with anyone. I could never bring myself to do it. I had never killed anyone before accidentally and enjoyed it. I was changing too fast, and no one seemed to notice it in my behaviour.

My training with Palort was done, so my job had already begun. I made my way to the old castle, the abode of anegz. I was currently outside the room where the anegz was. I was debating with myself if I was going in or not.

'Need help, Airik?' I heard a sweet voice call. I turned around to see the Hue Sisters giggling at me. They still had wetness welding to them.

'Why are you siblings so obsessed with water?' I asked.

'This is our habitat. This is how the Elyrians have made us. Water stands for calmness. Just like our job, we need to keep the protectors calm, and we are failing in our work.' Amethyst sighed. The rest of them gave her a death glare.

'Back to my problem.' I tried to avert their gazes from her, which thankfully they did. Amethyst mouthed thank you to me and sighed with relief.

'Just tell us what you feel,' they coaxed. I leaned against the door. *What do I feel? What would any individual feel when he just killed someone?* The first word that came into my mind was *horrible*.

'Don't think that way. Your life itself is a path of dangers. People nagging and pretending around you. Just focus on the stone that is your responsibility.' They surrounded me as if threatening in a secretive way. I couldn't help but glance at them suspiciously.

'You didn't kill him. You just saved yourself from being killed.' They wanted me to get out of remorse, which is just impossible. Killing was something else, and being amused by it is a whole lot different thing.

'We can hear your thoughts, Airik. There is connection between us. There is a reason behind every action, and there are reasons for us being paired up together.' They sighed. I felt a rush of anger in me.

'Seriously? If you would've thought about it before, then I think it would've been a lot better. If all of us are supposed to work together, then why are you guys keeping it all from me? I have my own reasons for keeping my secrets away because I'm a protector and I need to be safe! But still, you all find a way to know it all.' I laughed like a lunatic.

'Maybe you all should leave me alone right now.' I huffed in frustration.

'We understand. You need time to yourself and—' I didn't let them complete. I stormed off towards the anegz. I know it was quite rude, but something had gotten into me. I was no more the person I was. Being calm, cool, and collected was quite far from my features now. I practically dragged my feet towards the room. There was already a chair beside anegz. I sat and closed my eyes and tried to remember the message Fein had given me through the brooch. I did most of the things he told me I shouldn't have ever done, and now I felt regret.

A few hours had passed by, and I was pretty much getting bored by sitting beside the anegz. I could practically rule the world with the power I possess, and now, I was just sitting here with nothing but boredom. I could do everything I always desired if it wasn't for the fatuous anegz. *Why is this even a big deal? The spirit has quite a few years to come out of her shield, and Elyrians have eternity to create back the shield. They practically forced me into this. I'm not asking for it.* Slowly, I felt myself slumbering down bit by bit with my thoughts taunting me about my fate.

'Airik, get me out.' A husky voice pulled me out of my deep sleep. I forced my eyes open and searched around for the voice. Maybe I had imagined it all.

'Airik, get me out.' I heard the voice pleading again. It was imploring, yet it had a certain elegance to it that compelled me to pay attention and do as it said.

'Who are you?' I got up from the chair and roamed around the room with tender steps.

'You know me,' he said barely above a whisper.

'Where are you?' I asked.

'I'm right here, in the middle of the room.' My gaze drifted until I realised that the only thing in the room was anegz.

I walked towards it and halted right before the beautiful uneven-shaped stone. 'King Phinogar?' I asked.

'Yes, it's me.' I had an urge to touch it again just like I did when I came here for the first time. Anegz held me spellbound, and there was no turning back. Just then, the Selemarians along with Jason burst through the door.

'No! Don't touch it!' Rimtzal yelled. I touched it, and I felt a sudden rush of energy in me. It was painful in the beginning, but gradually, I was addicted to the pain. It derived pleasure of power. Suddenly, it stopped, and I fell on the ground with anegz fuming as if it were angry because it was empty. My head was spinning, and I felt weak all of a sudden.

'What happened to him?' a voice asked. I recognised it as Jason's.

'This shouldn't have happened. King Phinogar has taken control of him. Airik helped him to escape anegz.' Rimtzal took a deep breath. 'And now, Airik can be considered as King Phinogar,' his voice cracked at the end. I felt as if I was paralysed. I could hear everything. My brain too was working, but my body wasn't. I couldn't get up even if I wanted to.

'What do we do now?' Anedrin asked. I could hear the concern and vulnerability in her voice.

'We have to get King Phinogar out of him. He is using Airik as a shell to restore his lost possession. Anegz overcomes him to do so, but Airik has a young soul. He is naïve and the most powerful human considering Duvollin. I always thought Airik would bring the end to the period of protectors, but my thought doesn't seem to match with the circumstances.' He sighed with frustration.

'What is his lost possession?' Jason asked.

'His power anegz didn't allow him to use, but his charm always works.'

'Then what do you think we should do? Kill him?' Palort's voice echoed in the chamber.

'We'll have to if he is a threat.' Rimtzal fretted in his emotionless voice. There was a blanket of heavy silence wrapped around. I heard footsteps towards me. Someone grabbed my arms and flipped me on my back. My eyes were closed. Even if I tried, I couldn't open them. By touch, I could feel it was Palort as his sharp ring grazed along with his rough style. His fingers travelled across my forehead and then my neck. It took me a moment to realise that he was checking my pulse.

'Vazura,' Palort exclaimed. I heard gasps across the room.

'What does that mean?' Jason asked.

'When a soul without a body claims a person, then he or she is like a slave to the soul. The soul remains with the human until the soul doesn't feel like moving out or the human has the capacity to get rid of the soul without harming anyone around them including themselves. That whole process is termed as vazura. It is almost like a parasite trying to suck the life out, and in return, it gives pleasure. And King Phinogar has performed vazura on Airik,' Anedrin explained. The voices were slowly growing distant as I officially felt myself slipping into unconsciousness.

It was very dark around me. I was in another dream or so I felt. Everything seemed livid, just like it always was. But right now, there was just eternal darkness and numerous voices trying to get hold of me.

'Stop!' I yelled and covered my ears, trying to get rid of the voice. Everyone stopped all of a sudden. I exhaled a huge breath.

'People don't stop forever, dear,' a voice coaxed. I felt I knew it, but I couldn't remember. It definitely belonged to a male.

'Who are you?' I asked with a strong voice, but I knew I was tearing from inside.

'I am you, Airik Patronus. The only difference between us is that you restrain yourself and I do exactly what I want.' He let out a hysterical laugh. This didn't sound like me at all. I remained quiet.

'Don't you agree with my point? I mean look around yourself. No one trusts you. How can you trust them?' he taunted. He was right. They didn't trust me, but neither did I. Technically, that didn't count.

'Just leave me alone,' I hissed.

'That's exactly what I've been doing the past 16 years. You are incapable of making right decisions, and at last, your subconscious has to regret.' I didn't feel like speaking about anything. I know it's just a dream, but I couldn't stop thinking about the words I just heard. But no one is perfect, and this is what life is about.

'Maybe this is the end, Airik. End of both of us. Just let me take over. I'll make sure nothing wrong happens.' I didn't care to respond because something was changing in me. I could feel it. There was a sudden jolt travelling through my body.

'If not the straightway, then the gravelled path is the only option left,' he said in a mocking tone.

I blinked several times for myself to keep from slipping back to darkness. My eyes met with Anedrin's. Her eyes widened, and she immediately yelled, 'He is waking!' There was a rush of footsteps, and many people burst in at once. I forced myself to get up. Everyone was gawking at me.

'Take a picture. It lasts longer,' I grumbled and shifted towards the end of the bed. My feet soon came in contact with the cold marble tiles. I took feeble steps as if I'd been walking for the first time in a few days.

'What's wrong with me?' I asked more to myself.

'You've been out for 17 days.' Rimtzal informed. *Seventeen days?* I jerked my head up in shock. Rimtzal's eyes widened.

'What have you done to yourself? I can feel the negative aura coming from you,' Rimtzal scolded me. I scowled at him.

'No one talks to me like that,' I growled. Many gasps filled the room.

'Your eyes, Airik—they are red,' Anedrin breathed out. I blinked several times and gulped. This wasn't me. I was never so snappy and rude.

'Just leave me alone,' I muttered and walked out of the palace. No one tried to stop me. I chose my usual spot under the huge tree. Its shade made me feel relaxed. The former incidents came running back to me. The fact was I had King Phinogar in me and he was using me to gain back his power. The blending of my thoughts never stopped. I overthink about every topic possible concerning me, and that is exactly what makes it possible to happen. I closed my eyes and planned for a short nap. As soon as I made myself comfortable, there was someone to lapse it.

'Airik! Airik!' someone screeched. It had to be Anedrin. No one had an irritating and annoying voice except her. I sighed and got up. I turned around to face her. She wasn't scared. She was petrified. Her blue eyes were wide as if she just saw a ghost and sweat glistened on her skin. Her brown hair was sprawled all around her face, which made it look like a bird's nest.

'Now what?' I asked her. It came out quite rude. Her eyes dropped.

'I was just thinking when you'll come back. It's nearly night, and the dinner is ready. And everyone was worried about you after that incident,' she whispered with her head bowed down. I could tell she was lying. I felt bad for causing this. I placed my index finger below her chin and made her look up at me.

'Are you afraid of me?' I asked. She just nodded and averted her gaze. *I'm upsetting people away from me. What's wrong with me?*

'Look, you don't have to be scared. Whatever is happening to me is temporary. I'll fight it off soon,' I promised her. She just smiled at me like a kid receiving Christmas gifts.

'Now tell me, what is wrong?' I asked her. Her smile faltered a bit. She opened her mouth and closed it again as if debating whether to tell me or not.

'I'll come to know eventually. Better if you tell me now,' I reasoned and stuffed my hands in my pockets.

'Allekior and Selemara never get along. They are raging a war against us, and that's tomorrow. They claimed that someone tried to sneak in, and they think we placed our spies in there. We tried to reason with them, but they didn't listen.' Her lip quivered in the end. She looked with tear-filled eyes at me.

'I never came across such situations. I don't know how to handle it. What can I do? I'm still 12.' For once, she looked innocent.

'Everything will end up fine. All we need is a good plan,' I said in a low and convincing tone.

'The war starts tomorrow. We need a plan today,' she stated.

'I'll return to the castle shortly. Wait for me in there and get the ones important in the war,' I explained.

She nodded and left. She looked back at me last time and smiled genuinely, not the conceited look she normally had. A real smile. I felt happy for once in a long while.

I yawned and stretched my body up to the tension my limbs could take. The vibes this war was giving weren't good at all. I had a feeling that the war was more for a personal reason than the professional one. I made my way back to the castle, and as expected, all of them were seated in the library. I strolled in with a straight face and sat among them. Anedrin along with the twins, Delver, Rimtzal, Jason, and Maximus was seated in here. I sat on the only chair left between my best friend and the heir of Selemara. I cleared my throat, gaining everyone's attention.

'To begin with, how many soldiers do we have?' I asked.

'Almost 500, all of them well trained. Among which, 40 are archers and 60 are stealth hunters. The rest are swordsmen and combat fighters. We don't get new people to fight in the battle,' Maximus answered.

'In that case, the archers and stealth hunters must be stationed all around the battle. The rest of the 400 will be divided into eight troops, which will be led by each one of us. What kind of weapons do we have?' I shifted in my chair.

'If you are talking about the normal ones, we have a good amount of bows and arrows, spears, bristly hammers, daggers, axes, swords, and soul suckers,' he answered breathlessly.

'Soul—' Jason was about to ask what a soul sucker was, but Anedrin answered before he could complete the term, 'Soul suckers are weapons that leech souls out of any human and persuade them to do anything.' *These aren't enough. We need more. After all, we are against Allekior. Everything I've ever heard about Allekior is how ruthless they are.*

'We need more weapons of mass destruction . . . like grenades,' I suggested.

'What's a grenade?' Maximus asked. All of them except Jason and me had the same puzzled look over their faces.

'Never mind.' I sighed. At this pace, there was nothing we can do. We all sat silently. No one spoke a single word. In fact, the room was so serene that I could hear Anedrin's and Jason's breathing.

'So . . . I've heard that everyone in Duvollin has a special ability—' Jason tried to start a conversation, but I beat him to it. I just got an amazing idea.

'I want to know your special abilities,' I demanded all of a sudden. Rimtzal raised his eyebrows questioningly.

'I can persuade animals to do anything,' Maximus countered.

'I can change people's emotions or magnetise them or and then use them against someone else,' Anedrin retorted nonchalantly.

'I'm not bragging, but I have too much of manpower, and I can also carve weapons in the blink of an eye,' Delver said.

'The same goes with us,' the twins informed in unison. I should've predicted that after I first met with Palort.

'I can produce electricity and summon the clouds,' Rimtzal answered.

'And I can read and control minds and play with them until they don't know how to block me,' I completed with a sinister smirk.

'There is nothing special about our powers, Airik. Each and every Duvolliner has it. Allekior must have almost a thousand soldiers. And using them frequently can take a toll on our health,' Phileda said and leaned on the table.

'We need weapons of mass destruction. Since you don't have any, we will have to create our own,' I replied, and the room grew silent again. Meanwhile, I grabbed a piece of paper and absent-mindedly squiggled randomly in it. After the whole paper was filled, I examined my piece of artwork. Some figures looked like relites with thorns sticking out. I snorted at my juvenile behaviour and slapped the paper on the table. Anedrin flinched beside me and grabbed the paper. She gazed at it through every direction. All of a sudden, her face lit up like Jason's when I told him that our exams were delayed in eighth grade.

'Inform all the soldiers to get their relites, even the archers and stealth hunters. And I think we need to modify all the relites. I hereby end the meeting.' She smirked. I couldn't help but think what was on her mind.

'And don't you dare try to peak in my head, protector.' She rolled her eyes at me, even though I didn't utter a single word. *Typical. I just can't wait to see how tomorrow turns out to be.*

The night seemed to crawl by faster than imagined. I didn't get a proper sleep since that was my first official big battle ever. Jason was as clueless as me. Anedrin had an amazing idea for the relites to grow poisonous thorny substances so that people won't attack as mindlessly as they do. I walked down the royal corridors towards the training centre where everyone was supposed to come. The familiar smell of sweat and wood hit my nose. I took a deep breath and trudged in the arena. The soldiers were glumly sitting on their relites in eight troops. I walked in front of them and flashed them a tiny smile to assure them that nothing much would happen, but I wasn't too sure myself. I felt someone grip my shoulders from behind.

'We have been waiting for your arrival,' Anedrin whispered. She gestured at the sorrowful-looking soldiers and then looked back at me.

'They need your wise words, Airik. I've tried to get them out of their gloomy worlds. Maybe they need you,' she reasoned and faded back towards her relite.

'This is truly an uneventful morning for all of us,' I started.

'Then why don't you call off the war? We all know you have brains and powers,' someone from the soldiers grumbled.

I took a deep breath. 'If that was in my hand, I would've done that a long time ago. Since Allekior is craving for some blood, I think we have to give them a taste of their own medicine.' This still had no effect on them. They were blankly staring at me.

'All right, I'll get to the point. Why are you all so revolting?' I asked in frustration.

'We don't want to fight. Allekior has always enjoyed the spluttering of blood. Don't you want to make them pay for their bad deeds? The way they have treated us always drives us to the edge, but we can't fight the back? Are we such cowards? We have a very skilful army, but still, we are incapable of fighting a mere bloodthirsty army. There is no denying that Selemarians are a whole bunch of fatuous—' They didn't let me complete. All of them interrupted me by throwing random insults.

'You are just from other world. You know nothing about us!' That did hurt a lot.

'Is it? Then why are you denying fighting? If you aren't willing to serve your own kingdom, then I suppose you should leave now,' I yelled across the arena. They kept quiet.

'Let's go, Anedrin. You have breaded a bunch of crummy, deceitful, churlish imps.' I deliberately taunted them and walked out of the training centre. A few minutes later, I heard lots of passionate cheers behind me. I glanced behind to see the troop being led towards the battlefield. Their grim faces were now full of determination. I smiled and joined them, I hey noticed me and cheered.

'Let's show them the result of hurting the pride of the Selemarians!' I yelled to intensify their feelings for the war. I led my troop to the battlefield along the seven other troops and already-stationed archers and hunters.

After about half an hour, we reached a grimy land with tropical weather as the sun shone brightly above us even though it was still morning as if telling us to go back and save ourselves from getting killed. In front of us stood our enemy and the worst fears of our own soldiers. I could hear the soldiers droning and cowering back in fear. I glanced at Anedrin; she knew what she had to do. She closed her eyes, and suddenly the environment changed. It was more cheery. The whining of soldiers halted, and they had their cold faces back. I smiled at her, and she gladly returned it. I could tell that fatigue was taking over her, but she fought it back.

All of a sudden, I heard three gongs of a bell, and an impalpable screen appeared in front of her. A greasy black-haired man with beady eyes, serpentine nose, and long beard was grinning at us through the screen. His eyes wandered over each one of us until it landed on me. His grin faded a little but didn't diminish completely. He turned her critical gaze back to Anedrin.

'I must say, Empress Anedrin, your army is too enormous for us to handle. After all, we have almost a thousand soldiers as we all know how strong you are,' he mocked. There was a faint chortling in the background.

Anedrin took a deep breath as if trying hard not to kill him with her gaze. 'First of all, I hope you had a good sleep last night, Commander Dolkin.' I must say this girl knows professional tactics. 'You see, I've already told you my spies were never in Allekior. I assure you I'm being wholly honest. I would fancy negotiating and sorting out the issue before we get on a temperament-wrecking confrontation.' She chose her words wisely.

'You want me to believe your 10-year-old gaming—' Anedrin interrupted him.

'Twelve-year-old Commander, not 10,' she stated sternly.

'Whatever. I just want to say that the war has been decided by your own wrongdoings, and I don't think my superiors are reluctant to get a whiff of you,' he commented to get her on the edge. Anedrin seemed like she could kill him there and then if he was in front of him.

'Very well then, if that's what you want.' Anedrin huffed. She closed the screen through a small motion of her fingers before the pudgy commander could say something else to tick us off. The proliferate arrow propel were instantly set up, and the hunters and archers took their places in the air to get a good view of Allekior. The hunters climbed down and discussed in muffled whispers among themselves and walked off the Elyrians know where. Nonetheless, I trusted them.

'Let the battle begin!' someone yelled as the amplified version of his sentence echoed all around. I could hear hollers getting nearer as the time passed. When they came into view, the arrows from the proliferate arrow propel were showered towards them. We got most of them as I could hear horrific shrieks ringing in my ears and the bodies of those dark-skinned people fell limp on the ground. I turned towards my troop. 'Don't be daring, only cunning. Use more of your abilities,' I instructed them. They nodded in understanding. I took a deep breath and unleashed my lustrous sword and charged forwards on my relite. I flung my sword viciously at the unskilled soldiers.

Phileda was struggling as many soldiers pounced on her at once. I made my way towards them. I slit the throat of one of the soldiers, gaining all of their attention. They snarled in anger and left Phileda behind. They circled me and looked at me from head to toe. Ten of them, I mentally noted down.

They tried to intimidate me, but to their dismay, it didn't work. I placed my sword in front of me as a nature of self-defence I learnt from everyone. I could see a shadow emerging from behind in an attempt to attack me. I was agile enough to get out of the way and stick a leg out and trip him. I laughed as the soldier fell on the dirt and turned on his back to sit out the sand that entered his mouth. He glared at me and stood up on his feet again.

On cue, all of them attacked me at once from every direction. I ducked as a sickle came swirling towards me. It hit someone else instead of me. I smirked. One down nine to go. I took the sword from the recently deceased soldier and ran towards them. They mimicked me as we were ready to collide; two blades were instantly targeting me. Instead of gashing them with a sword, I jumped high and landed behind them. I snuck one of my swords through them, killing both of them at once. The rest seven of them were frantically trying to kill me as they flung their sword in every direction they could. Accidentally, they seized the swords from my hands.

They laughed as they realised I was weaponless, but this didn't make me vulnerable. I smirked, and their laughter instantly died. I ran towards them and jumped on the chest of the soldier who had my sword. I took this as a chance to snatch the sword from his hands, but unfortunately, I could take only one as the other weapon in my hand was a spear. The force caused me to flip back, and I landed gracefully on the ground. The spear was in my left hand. I lobbed it at them as it travelled through three of them who were completely dumbstruck to notice I had planned to attack them. The rest four of them were cowering back in fear.

'Who are you?' one of them asked.

'Airik Patronus, the protector of anegz,' I answered. They fled.

I turned towards Phileda. She smiled at me and nodded. I returned towards my relite. As I made my way through the soldiers, killing anyone who came in my way, I came face-to-face with the so-called commander of Allekior, Dolkin. He seemed to be deep in thought or should I say deep in being amused with the typical killings in front of him. I climbed off my relite and walked towards him.

'Hello, Dolkin,' I greeted him in my cold and distant tone. He turned towards me, and something flashed through his eyes. It went as quickly as it came. He composed himself and wore his infamous smirk, which I now grew to hate.

'You must be the new naïve protector of anegz.' He reached for his sword gradually as he spoke.

'Took long enough for you to understand.' I moved closer to him. I caught his hand before it could touch his sword. It was more like a death grip as he winced slightly. He tried to cover it up and failed miserably. I punched him in the face and held him up with his long black hair. I held him by his throat. His hands instantly found a way towards my palms as he tried his hard to free himself. I watched him as he withered in pain and agony.

'You know very well that you are enjoying watching me die. Tell me, were you like this before?' he choked out. I tightened my grip on him and clenched my jaw.

'I'll take that as a yes. Look at what you've become and compare to what you were. Don't you feel different . . . in a good way?' I released him, and he instantly collapsed on the ground and took a deep breath for his dear life. I hate him not only because he was disrespectful towards Anedrin but also because he was absolutely right. Every word he spoke was true. I couldn't help but deny. My subconscious knew well of what I agreed.

'Think about the massive opportunities the master offers you. You must join us.' He smiled at me. Before I could say something, Anedrin barged in the conversation. Dolkin turned his gaze towards her.

'Look who decided to join us. Have you taken up on that offer?' He faked enthusiasm. I clenched my fist and clutched his belronag.

'Airik, stop!' Anedrin yelled. She rushed towards me and made me leave him. She glared at me as if telling me to lay off as if he were her prey. She kneed him in the stomach, and he fell down. She sat on top of him and started punching him rashly.

'Your superiors want my whiff? Well, this is how my whiff is like. And I would love to show off my scent,' she said between punches. I encircled her waist and dragged her away from him.

'Leave me, Airik. I'm not in good mood now.' She flailed her arms around and ended up elbowing me at my nose. I closed my eyes as the shock travelled through my sensitive nerves to my brain. I felt stunned.

'What the hell?' I muttered and covered my nose. A few seconds later, I felt something wet rush down my fingers. I squinted my eyes only to see crimson blood. Soon, everyone came and controlled Anedrin. Delver treated my nose, and it pretty much appeared to be broken. But that didn't matter anymore. We won the battle. I could do a victory dance only if I didn't get my nose fractured by a 12-year-old girl. A few of our soldiers sacrificed themselves, and now we were reduced to a number of almost 300. We were still in the battlefield and treated one another's wounds. Just then, a hunter came panting towards us.

'Allekior tricked. More fighters. More powerful.' He panted and tried to convey his message between ragged breaths. I walked towards him and rubbed his back.

'Take deep breaths. Inhale and exhale. Just relax,' I instructed him. After a few seconds, he was able to get the bad news to us. He stated that Allekior was coming again, but now it was led by a cripin. I had no idea of what it was. Certainly, it must be one of the creations of Palatina to accompany her in Elyria. I could tell easily from the reactions that this creature was worse than everything I had ever faced in Duvollin. Their army was as huge as ours right now. Maximus stood up promptly and made his way towards the soldiers.

'Merge in!' he yelled. The soldiers stood up and stood in the previously formed troops. It was pretty surprising that no one from my troop was dead yet. Injured? Yes, but not dead. I couldn't help but feel proud of myself.

'It seems like your troop took your words seriously,' Anedrin commented. I just smiled. After barking a few orders at the troops, Maximus walked towards us.

'I've informed them of the current state. They are restoring their energies.' Maximus sighed and ran his fingers through his dirty-blonde hair.

Phileda let out a small whimper. 'Now what should we do?' She sniffed and tried to hold back her tears.

'We need a plan.' That was all I could say to make them feel better. Anedrin scoffed.

'You don't understand at all. We have lost lots of soldiers, and the rest of them alive are tired, and most of them are injured. Even a plan can't get us out of our misery. If we turn back, they'll come in Selemara and hunt us down, leading to the killing of innocent people. We are doomed,' Anedrin spoke and clutched her forehead in despair. Her brown curls rocked back and forth when she stood up.

'This is the time for us to use our abilities.' I stood up and turned towards Delver, Palort, and Phileda.

'I want the three of you to make nine-feet-long spears, and they are supposed to be made of silver—no other element. Am I clear?' I asked. They nodded briskly and set off to work. I walked towards Maximus. I tapped him on his shoulder.

'Cripin is an animal?' I asked.

He pondered of a moment. 'Yes. In a way, it is,' he answered.

'Can you control it?' I pleaded.

520

He sighed. 'I can but not for too long,' he answered truthfully. I smiled and made my way towards Rimtzal.

'Do you have enough energy to generate electricity?' I asked. He nodded.

'Do it when I tell you to.' He nodded again. At last, I found Anedrin.

'I know what I need to do with my ability,' she spoke before I could say anything. I smiled, satisfied with my planning. I just hope it works out. Everything seemed to be in place, except for my broken nose.

We have been waiting for a few minutes by now. The silver spears were dug securely in a proper depth. I summoned the sea water and made it invisible with sorcery. Everyone knew better not to step in that trap. As soon as the army was visible, Rimtzal let out an audible gasp.

'What's wrong?' I asked with concern.

'It's not a normal army, Airik. All of them were once . . . protectors,' he said quickly and heaved a sigh. He thought we didn't hear him, but we did as fear gripped our senses.

I cleared my throat. 'How is it even possible?' I asked.

'It's simple. All of them are reincarnated,' he stated as if it was very common.

'But that's illegal!' Jason yelled. We all turned to look at him. Did he just seriously say that?

'I thought Airik was the stupidest, but you proved me wrong,' Anedrin joked, and everyone laughed, except Rimtzal and me, of course. I gazed sternly at them. This caused them to turn grim as they glanced ahead at the emerging army. Rimtzal snickered.

'Nice going, Airik Patronus,' he said. This time, the palpable screen appeared in front of me. A young man, around his early 30s, was criticising me with his twinkling eyes.

'If it's not for the legendary boy, why would we come with 250 protectors?' he said in a smooth and monotonous voice. He turned his eyes towards Rimtzal.

'You haven't changed a bit from that solemn night, mate. I see the curse has acquired a virtuous variation on you,' he addressed him. I turned towards Rimtzal.

'What is he talking about?' I asked him.

'I presume that you didn't tell him,' the man joined in the conversation.

'Look, twinkle eyes, this is between all of us, and we don't want you in the midst of it,' I said collectedly.

'Twinkle eyes? I like the nickname, boy. Let's see if your battle skills are as good as your vivacious approach.' He snarled, and the screen disappeared. We heard a cry of battle, and then the battlefield was echoing with the hollers of reincarnated warriors. When they set their feet in our traps, I turned towards Rimtzal.

'Now!' I yelled. He summoned the clouds, and then, rain and lightning began to embrace our fears. Rimtzal deliberately hit the spears with thunders, and then everyone in the trap was getting electrocuted. Everyone cheered.

'Half of them are dead!' one of the archers exclaimed from high in the air. Our happiness was short-lived when each and every soldier on our side began to fall down in pain.

'What's going on?' I questioned over the sickening hisses of pain around me.

'You didn't think you are the only one with brains and abilities, did you?' Twinkle Eyes taunted me.

'I think I do.' I smirked and glanced at Anedrin. She grinned maliciously and closed her eyes. The soldiers thrashing over the ground in agony stood up. She released the pain towards our enemies. Now it was their chance to feel whatever our soldiers felt. Above the hollers of pain, I could hear a distant and unfamiliar screech making way towards us. I pretty sure it was a cripin.

'Maximus, you're on,' I said. He nodded and knitted his eyebrows. As soon as the cripin came into view, I was astounded.

Its yellow eyes had pinned me on the spot. The grovelling eight-feet-tall black body was contracting and flexing as it took deep breaths. It darted its cerise and wide tongue out and licked its black mouth. It walked towards me slowly as if trying to give me all the time I had before dying.

'Don't move. Remain as you are. Or else, it will attack. And also stay in control. It has the ability to hypnotise,' Palort warned. I nodded and remained motionless. It perched on my relite and looked deep in my eyes as if I were a puzzle he was trying to solve. I tried to get in his head and control it as Maximus was miserably failing to do so, but I couldn't. It was just empty. There was nothing to overwhelm him in any way.

That's when I realise that his eyes were changing colours. I could mask out just one emotion in his eyes behind the changing colours: hunger and the need to kill. His whiskers tickled against my cheeks as he tried to close the remaining gap between us. He licked my cheeks, and that's when I realise that he didn't have teeth. Instead, he had dried stout wood. He snorted resulting in smoke being emitted from his nostrils. Just as its smell hit me, I wanted to gag, but I couldn't. I was freaking out from the inside, but I couldn't show it.

It jumped back on the ground and left me alone. Its spiky tail wavered behind him as it disappeared back among the soldiers. It glanced at me one last time as if challenging me to follow him, which surprisingly I did. I ignored the cry of protests and followed him, and it was almost as if it had hypnotised me. The realisation punched the daylights out of me. I closed my eyes. I shouldn't be doing this. I halted before I could sign on my death warrant. But it was the worst choice ever. I was surrounded with evil-looking protectors. I gulped and tightly gripped my sword. One of then let out a shriek and dabbed the sword at my side. It moved, and it slightly missed me, resulting in a small cut. He didn't give me a chance to recover. He spitefully attacked me with both of his swords, and I was mildly blocking it. Just then, something took over me. I rolled over in a blur and knocked his swords out.

'Thought you kill me that easily?' I said in a huskier and much deeper voice that was never mine. He looked at me in horror.

'Your eyes are red,' he whispered. I smirked and closed my eyes. I raised my hands in the air and let myself fly. The weather was now windier as my black hair whipped against my forehead. I opened my eyes to see everyone looking fearfully at me.

Doesn't it feel good? To see that everyone looks upon you? Trust me, both of us can exercise this immense power over them. I agreed with the thought.

Let's show them who their superiors are here, the inner voice said. I laughed impishly and set my foot back on the ground.

'You.' I pointed at the protector who attacked me earlier. 'Die,' I completed. He dropped down on the ground before anyone could process the cause of his death. The crowd shrank back in fear. I locked my gaze with one of them. He too fell back dead.

'We have him!' Twinkle Eyes came out of the crowd towards me. He patted my shoulders. I glared at him, and he quickly withdrew his hand.

'You thought I was imprudent. You have no idea about me.' I caught him by his throat and choked him to death. Three protectors were already dead by my hands. Their core life energy was making me more powerful. I needed more. It was like a drug to me. Now I know why the 'good-hearted' king Phinogar could never stop. It makes sense why people can't quit smoking or drinking. It becomes a part of your life, a part of you.

No, Airik, we both are one. Phinogar connotes Airik, and Airik perfects Phinogar. Kill all the protectors. They deserve to die.

I smiled at the merry thought. *We are one*, I said to Phinogar. That's when everything broke loose, and I used my drug— no, our drug. The more people died, more I felt powerful. This was just the beginning of the new end for humans and the beginning of eternity for us.

'Who are you?' one of them asked. I smiled cheekily at them.

'I am King Phinogar,' I stated in my newfound voice. After finishing with the protectors, I moved towards the Selemarians.

Start with Empress Anedrin. Her young energy allures me.

I walked towards Anedrin, but someone stepped in front of me. It was Palort. 'You are not in your senses.' He placed his hands on my shoulders and shook me lightly. I hardly glared at him, but before I could add more to my power, Rimtzal pushed me off him. I stumbled and soon caught myself. I turned towards him.

'I know you are somewhere in there, Airik. This is not you,' Rimtzal said as he unclasped his bow. He shot me on my leg. I pulled it out, and then it healed instantly. I walked towards him.

'Don't let him get you. He is fetching you lies!' Rimtzal yelled.

'I'm not lying!' I let out a red streak of light towards him through my hands. It hit him in his chest, and he fell on the ground, coughing and sputtering out blood. I walked towards him, and I was ready to punch him.

'You think he will stay by your side forever, Airik?' Rimtzal questioned.

Don't listen to him. Just kill him.

No, let him say whatever needs to convey. After all, he doesn't have much time left, I retorted back.

'Trust me, he will kill you when his power will be restored. Didn't you hear what he said? Kill all the protectors. Don't forget that you are one of them.' He threw his weapons away. His words brought a certain change in me. Will Phinogar leave me?

No, stop thinking. I'll never do such things.

You didn't feel guilt in killing any of them. Heck, you didn't even felt remorse while you killed your wife and your parents. How can I be so sure that you'll never kill me? Phinogar didn't reply.

'This is what I'm talking about.' Rimtzal chortled. Even though he had a very little time left, he kept a positive attitude. I felt a jolt of electricity pass through me.

I have to control you, Phinogar stated in a threatening tone.

No, you are wrong. You can't. I won't let you.

I let out a blood-curling scream as I forced Phinogar out of me. *You deserve to be in hell.*

No! he yelled. I opened my eyes to see a very pale and sullen man trying to hold on to me for his dear life. Rimtzal noticed this and grabbed Phinogar

'I, being a patron of goddess Andria, hereby send you back in anegz,' Rimtzal yelled as Phinogar clawed at him, but he seemed unfazed. Anegz appeared in his hands, and he tried to force him back into the magical stone, but he wasn't strong enough after the blow he was hit by. I took a deep breath and grabbed Phinogar.

'No one deserves to be caged in forever,' I said. He beamed at me.

'You need an afterlife.' I smirked and forced him in the regime of Andria. The sky cleared, and it was clear evening again. Rimtzal smiled, and as he was about to crumple down on the ground, I held him.

'You need to see a healer.' I tried to call them, but Rimtzal pushed me down.

'I don't have much time left.' He unbuttoned the first few buttons of his belronag with great difficulty and snatched out a chain and forced it into my hands.

'I have many secrets. I want you to know them.' He took a deep breath.

'This chain isn't normal. It has a piece of paper that explains my whole life. I have lied about many things to you in the past including my unending youth. Every answer lies in this.' He cupped my hands that held the chain.

'Don't ever let your yearnings control you.' With that, he closed his eyes and was gone forever, leaving me behind with guilt and regret. Fein's words came rushing back, *When someone had to be sacrificed, remember it was you whom they overpeiced... but the question is, am I worthy of this value?*

The next day, we were giving the last goodbyes to everyone who was sacrificed in the battle. It is a ritual where the families of that individual leave a very important object with the sacrificed ones so that they can take it to Andrea's realm and 'feel' the presence of their loved ones.

Since there was no one for Rimtzal, the five of us were giving our last goodbyes to him. Anedrin spoke a few soothing words and left a toy beside his lifeless body. She lingered her lips on his forehead for a while as a tear rolled down. She wiped it furiously and left us with him.

The twins didn't say a word. Phileda left her knives, and Palort left his beloved axe beside him. Delver hugged him and handed him a beautiful bouquet of lilacs. At last, it was my turn.

I walked towards him and sat on my knees. I still had that chain in my hand. 'There is no use in making you remember me because I was the reason for your death.' I sighed. 'I don't have anything valuable to offer you. Still, I would like to give you this.' I placed the folded piece of paper between his fingers.

'It says that I'll avenge your death, reveal your secrets, and kill Airis. That's the least I can do.' I stood up and brushed my outfit. I backed away only to see a mist forming around him, which was as black as his eyes. I felt as if the mist was trying to overlap one another. Within a few seconds, the mist disappeared, and so did Rimtzal.

Epilogue
A New Beginning

The battle was depressing for all of us. Rimtzal was right. I did bring an end to the reign of protectors, but it was in the worst way possible. The real enemy still lives and craves for the spluttering of blood, especially mine.

Mom and Dad are planning to return to Calsenai, where they truly belong. Jason is now completely ready for the responsibility of a Pimarv, and the twins can't stop whining about how dearly they will miss him. I can see Jason too feels the same, especially towards me. Even though I remained cold and distant with Jason throughout our time in the orphanage, he always stood by my side to support me, just like a family would.

Before leaving for Calsenai, Dad and Mom approached me. She hugged me as if there was no tomorrow.

'Can't breathe,' I joked. She loosened her grip on me and stared at me as if memorising each and every feature about my face, even the emotions my eyes were holding.

'I have raised a very smart and handsome boy,' she whispered, stood on her tiptoes and pecked my forehead, and lingered her lips over there.

'You know I love you, sweetie. Don't get yourself killed in this wicked world. I have stayed without you for too long. I don't want to leave you ever again.' Tears started streaming down her rosy cheeks. I wiped away her tears from my thumb.

'My mom shouldn't cry. I'm here, and I'm not planning to leave you anytime soon,' I comforted her.

'I have no idea for how long your dad will keep me in Calsenai, so I want you to stick by certain rules.' She sniffed and focused her attention on me.

'It's very cold in Selemara, so you will always wear a jacket even if you are feeling warm. You will eat your breakfast, lunch, and dinner on time. And do not get into fight—I repeat, do not get into fights. Am I clear?' She placed her hands on her hips and narrowed her eyes at me. If she wasn't my mother, I would've pinched her cheeks by now. She appeared to be quite adorable.

'Come on, woman, give my boy some time. He is not an infant anymore. My son has grown up. He can take care of himself.' He chuckled and covered it with cough. Mom shot a death glare towards Dad. Now it was my chance to muffle my laughter.

'I will visit soon, sweetie. Take care,' she murmured. I pecked her cheeks as she left the chamber. At last, Dad nonchalantly walked towards me.

'I feel proud of you.' He ruffled my already-unkempt hair.

'You are leaving quite soon. You should've stayed.' I could feel tears pricking my eyes, and they were gone as soon as they came back.

'I'm always here for you.' He hugged me and patted my shoulder awkwardly.

'I'll always abide by your words, Dad. I just hate the fact that he is now dead,' I admitted feeling slightly skittish about the whole incident.

'Hate is just an understatement for the term called *fear*. If you hate something, then there is actually something that you are scared of. Just remember this, son. You will know how to use it against someone because when you inflict pain upon someone physically, it can heal within a few days, but if you play with emotions, it leaves a scar forever in your memory. A wound that has no possibility to heal. I don't know what future holds ahead, but just remember that it's your life and your decisions. I will just suggest to you. At last, what happens in your life solely depends on your actions. I think I should go. Christina must be waiting for me.' He took a deep breath and gulped slightly.

'I hope to see you again someday.' I smiled at him.

'So will I, son, and remember not to hurt my sentimental values I hold for you. I may have been with you only for the first 5 to 6 years of your life, but I still understand you better than yourself. If you need help, just ask. Don't hesitate.' He smirked as if he knew something that I didn't and walked away.

After Mom and Dad departed, it was time for Jason to go. I couldn't see him again. It's better not to meet him if my sudden outburst would surely ruin the moment.

'Couldn't say goodbye to your best buddy?' Jason came and hugged me.

'I can't believe that we are actually being separated. I mean you were the one who always annoyed me with your stupid jokes. Who will do that? And what about the dirty work you did for me?' I joked. He hit my arm playfully, and I let out a fake yelp and gasped dramatically.

'Sure thing, Airik. I'll see you around.' He smirked slightly.

'Wouldn't the girls of Selemara miss their dear Jasie?' I tried to lighten up the mood.

He chuckled. 'You shouldn't try to be funny, Airik, because you aren't. It doesn't suit you, just me,' he stated cockily. I pretended to be offended.

'Do you still have it?' Jason asked.

'What are you talking about?' I knitted my brows and asked in confusion.

'The peacock feather I gave you. Do you still have it?'

I unbuttoned a few buttons from the top of my belronag to unleash the beautiful feather Jason gave me. He smiled.

'Just don't forget what I told you while giving it to you. Other than that, I have invited someone.' He tried to supress his smile, but the corner of his lips twitched a little. What's wrong with this boy? I shook my head until my eyes landed on someone, to be specific, Infinity. My heart skipped a beat as I set my gaze on her. She walked towards me and hugged me as if her life depended on me.

'I missed you,' she stated with her muffled voice against the crook of my neck where her shallow breathing fanned against my pale skin tenderly. I snickered and wrapped my arms around her petite waist.

'Get a room, you two,' Jason said and left before I could come back with another snarky remark. She unwrapped her slender arms from my neck as I could see a tint of red over her face.

'Maybe we should marry each other since we are good friends. Jason agrees,' I teased mockingly.

'In your dreams.' She rolled her eyes.

'Do you want to make my dream come true?' I trifled. Now she was a beating red.

She hit the back of my head. 'Stop being something you aren't,' I groaned. I heard this remark for the second time.

535

'Why are you here?' I mentally cursed myself for sounding so rude.

'I mean why did you trouble yourself and travelled from Calsenai to Selemara?' I reframed my question. Her smile seemed to gradually fade away.

'I heard about the battle. I just wanted to see you again and make sure for myself that you are fine,' she admitted.

'I'm fine. Is that all you were here for?' I closed the distance between us.

'Since the anegz is gone, you don't have to protect it anymore. So are you . . . going back?' Her voice cracked in the end. I took her palms in my hands and caressed it to calm her down.

'The anegz is gone, but the elementary reason still exists. I'll die trying hard to diminish it.' She rested her head on my shoulders.

'You know I love you, right?' she spoke and heaved a sigh and blinked furiously as if trying to hold back the tears.

'What do you mean? Is everything all right?' I asked her. She removed her head from my shoulders and stared straight in my eyes.

'The life you are leading is dangerous. I don't want to lose you,' she murmured softly. I hugged her.

'Everything is fine, Infinity. Just have faith in me. I'll strive hard.'

As the day came to an end, I was summoned by Delver to his house. Phileda and Palort seemed very excited and nervous at the same time while Delver had a neutral expression on his face. Just like always.

'Present it, son,' he said in an unvaried voice. Palort nodded curtly and disappeared in another room. A few minutes later, he came in dragging a table. He pulled it in front of me and elbowed me in front of it.

'It's the perpetual sword. Go ahead and try.' He stood up from his chair and motioned towards the jewelled sword. My palms were getting sweaty. I have heard about this sword before. If my soul is not pure, there is no way these people would accept me. I knelt in front of it and detained the velvety sheath under my touch. I lifted it. So far, nothing went wrong. I took a deep breath and revealed the beautiful, fiery blade. It shone fiercely, blinding everyone but me. Its pommel and guard were humming and steering electricity as if it were just reincarnated to life, but it didn't affect me in any way. The light gradually dimmed to mediocrity, and then it was diminished completely.

'Is this the sword's way of rejecting me?' I muttered more to myself.

'It actually happened,' Phileda said and gripped my shoulders. I turned my gaze towards her.

'The rejection?' I asked.

She laughed heartily. 'No, silly, you brought the perpetual sword back to life. You are its owner now. It's accepted you,' she stated excitedly and shook me lightly.

I felt pure bliss. Nothing can be compared to my happiness right now. I needed to tell Anedrin. She hasn't yet talked to me after the battle. Things have changed between us. I stalked my way towards the library where I often find the brunette little girl sitting in a chair and her head stuck up in a book.

'What are you here for?' Anedrin scoffed at me.

'The perpetual sword accepted me,' I confessed and beamed.

'That doesn't change the fact that you killed Rimtzal,' she spoke sadly, and her expression softened a bit as she closed the book she was reading. I caught the glimpse of its title: *The Protectors of All Time.*

I stood there uncomfortably fiddling with my hands. I am sure she was reading about Rimtzal. It was certainly her way to cope with sadness. She deliberately bumped her shoulders with mine and glared at me as she walked past.

Anyone could tell that she was infuriated at me for the death of Rimtzal, the one who was the sole reason for the goodness that destroyed the sheer evil in me. The hate towards me from people was understandable. I know I'm not the actual reason for his death, but sometimes I can't help but blame myself for it. What if I didn't touch the stone and let King Phinogar control me? What if I didn't leave the castle like I did? What if I wasn't the protector at all and lead a normal life? Reality is always there to get you out of your regrets and caprices. I know these what-ifs don't hold any substance because past never changes. Only the future does. While I am completely relying on my past to make myself feel better, I still feel there is something more that's going to happen, deadlier than just the battle that King Phinogar had caused twice in his extraordinary life. And we will always be ready to stand against it no matter how angry we are at one another. After all, one can get out of distress but not his doubts. I still have to figure out a lot, but the thing is that I don't know what surprises my future holds for me. I'll just have to wait and watch.

My thoughts soon drifted to King Phinogar. It was easy for him to control me. And it was way easier for Airis to brainwash him. This situation is just a game, a game of chess where I am the pawn and Airis is the queen. She knows that she has control over each and every issue going on. I can move forward only until I am able to, and then I am being halted until someone comes and gets me out of the game. She moves freely about the board and eyes everyone carefully until mercilessly ripping their life away from them. She needs me only to play around with my emotions, so she anyhow keeps me in the game. The more I think about it, the more I realise that I am a clueless wanderer, trailing into oblivion like the former protectors did. Airis just made a path in front of us, and all of us blindly walked on them.

She has a rare ability, an ability to execute our fates. We protectors have always been the oblivious blokes being played around by a girl with a fake façade. Even after living for eternity, she is as confused as me, but the only thing is that she doesn't let go anything without a fight even if it's her fate. She is not the one to go with the flow but the one to change the flow according to her, and that is exactly what makes her different from us.

539

It is funny how in the place where I used to live, females were considered as weak and fragile beings while in Duvollin, the scenario is something else: the most feared one is a girl, no more than 16, and people don't even know about her.

I chuckled inwardly as I thought about her. A very beautiful and innocent face but a very strong personality and stubborn attitude. She knows what she is doing unlike us who just drift away to where our destiny takes us.

I held the chain Rimtzal gave me. Am I ready to reveal his secrets yet? Something tells me that this chain has more than the secret life of a former protector, something that would change our lead, something that would change me for the better.

CPSIA information can be obtained
at www.ICGtesting.com
Printed in the USA
FFOW03n1642110218
45027018-45381FF